SECRETS

SECRETS

Michelle Harrison

Little, Brown and Company
New York Boston

Text copyright © 2011 by Michelle Harrison
Interior illustrations by Kelly Louise Judd

Little, Brown and Company

Hachette Book Group
237 Park Avenue, New York, NY 10017
Visit our website at www.lb-kids.com

Little, Brown and Company is a division of Hachette Book Group, Inc.
The Little, Brown name and logo are trademarks of Hachette Book Group, Inc.

The publisher is not responsible for websites (or their content) that are not owned by the publisher.

First U.S. Edition: June 2012
Originally published in Great Britain by Simon and Schuster UK Ltd., February 2011

Library of Congress Cataloging-in-Publication Data

Harrison, Michelle, 1979–
   13 secrets / Michelle Harrison ; [interior illustrations by Kelly Louise Judd].—1st U.S. ed.
      p. cm.—(The 13 treasures trilogy)
   Summary: Now living at Elvesden Manor under her real name of Rowan, Red attempts to put her past behind her, while fairy messengers try to convince her to participate once more in the changeling trade and she is haunted by dreams of an old enemy who is determined to exact his revenge.
   ISBN 978-0-316-18563-9
   [1. Fairies—Fiction. 2. Changelings—Fiction.] I. Judd, Kelly Louise, ill. II. Title.
   III. Title: Thirteen secrets.
   PZ7.H256133Aap 2012
   [Fic]—dc23   2011033368

10 9 8 7 6 5 4 3 2 1

Book design by Alison Impey

RRD-C

Printed in the United States of America

For Carlene
and Teddy

1

Rowan Fox hovered by the school gate, scanning the yard as pupils spilled out, jostling in their eagerness to begin the summer holiday. There was no sign of Fabian's fair head in the crowd, and so, impatiently, she headed over to the shop opposite the gate. Jingling some loose change left over from her lunch money, she went in and bought two bars of chocolate. When she came out most of the crowd had gone, and the melody of someone playing a guitar had begun nearby.

Fabian was still nowhere to be seen. She wondered if he had walked to the bus stop without her for some reason. Tucking one of the chocolate bars into her bag, she held on to the other and began to walk. Then she saw the girl—the player of the guitar.

She sat cross-legged in the doorway of an empty

shop two down from the sweet shop, leaning back against the door as her fingers swept over the guitar strings. Her straggly white-blond hair was in need of a wash. Next to her, a tattered knapsack rested on a grubby sleeping bag.

As Rowan drew near she paused by the girl's open guitar case, lying on the pavement. It contained pitifully few coins. Reaching into her pocket, she pulled out her last few pennies and added them to the meager pile. Then, looking down at the chocolate bar in her hand, she threw that in too, and continued on her way.

"Thanks," the girl called.

Rowan turned back. The girl had stopped playing and was staring at her. "I was starting to think I was invisible. You're the first person to give me anything all afternoon."

Rowan's eyes moved to the coins already in the case.

"Mine," the girl said. "I just put them there to . . . well, never mind."

Rowan came over and put her schoolbag on the ground. "You put the coins in to make it look like you weren't being ignored," she finished.

"Right." The girl gave a little laugh and stood her guitar against the shop door. Reaching for the chocolate bar, she tore the wrapper off and took a huge bite, closing her eyes in pleasure.

"Not the friendliest of places, this," she said, between munches. "Don't think I'll stay."

"Probably best not to," Rowan answered, eyeing the girl sympathetically. It was difficult to put an age to her, but she looked older than Rowan—eighteen, perhaps. "You'd be better off somewhere bigger. Busier, with more people."

"You sound like you're talking from experience," the girl said. She licked chocolate from her thumb and trained her eyes on Rowan.

"That's because I am," Rowan muttered. "It's the reason I stopped—" She broke off and met the girl's eyes. "I was on the streets for over a year. I know what it's like."

"Really? What happened to you?"

"My parents died in a car crash, and me and my little brother were put into care. But my brother... he went missing. So I ran away to look for him."

"Did you find him?" the girl asked.

Rowan hesitated before answering carefully. "I never got him back, no."

"So what did you do?"

Rowan shrugged. "I was lucky. Met some people who... cared. I live with them now."

"Lucky," the girl echoed. She eyed Rowan's neat school uniform with envy. "It certainly looks like you're doing all right now."

"What are *you* doing here, anyway?" said Rowan. "Tickey End isn't the place to be if you want to stay unnoticed. I mean, people will act like they don't see you, but they don't miss a thing around here."

"I'll be gone before the day's out," the girl

answered quietly. "I wasn't planning on staying long." She leaned forward and lowered her voice. "Just long enough to deliver a message, after finding the right person."

"Message? To who?"

"To you, Red."

Rowan's breath caught in her throat. "What did you just say?"

"Red. That's what you used to call yourself, isn't it?"

Rowan dragged her schoolbag closer to her feet. "Who are you? What do you mean you have a message? From *who*?"

"From the Coven."

Rowan stood up. "Leave me alone."

"Wait!"

She turned back. "Who sent you?"

"Sparrow," the girl said in a low voice.

"Why didn't he come to give me the message himself if he knew where to find me?"

"He said you wouldn't listen if it was him. That I'd have a better chance of...getting your attention, making you listen—"

"He was wrong."

"Just hear me out. All he wanted was for you to listen."

"What's in it for you?"

The girl flushed.

"Of course. You're not homeless at all, are you? You're one of them."

She nodded. "He was certain you'd stop to talk to me, and he was right. But even then I had to be sure... it wasn't until you mentioned your brother..."

"Just give me the message."

"There's a meeting coming up, on the thirteenth."

"I know," Rowan answered. "There's always a meeting on the thirteenth."

"They want you there this time. No excuses."

Rowan nodded, eyes downcast.

"He said they need to let you know where it is, but to do that you have to let them in. That's it. That's the message." The girl stared down at the chocolate wrapper in her hands.

"And if I don't go?"

The girl opened her mouth to answer, but then looked past her. Rowan turned. Fabian approached, his face twisted into a scowl. He stopped next to her, loosening his tie and muttering under his breath.

"Where have you been?" Rowan asked him.

"Detention," he said sourly.

"For what?"

Fabian nudged a pebble with his toe. "Fighting."

"*Fighting?* With who?"

Before Fabian could reply, Rowan noticed that the girl was packing up her things. She stood up, slung her guitar case over one shoulder and her sleeping bag and knapsack over the other, and nodded good-bye.

"See you, Red," she said quietly, then moved off.

"Fighting with some of the boys in my class," Fabian said distractedly, staring after the girl. His scowl softened to a frown. "Who was that?"

"No one," said Rowan. "Just a beggar. I gave her some spare change."

Fabian's frown deepened. "You don't know her?"

"No."

"Well, she knew you," Fabian said suspiciously. "She called you Red. No one calls you that anymore, not since you've been living with us."

Rowan watched the girl's figure getting smaller until she vanished around a corner into one of the many crooked side streets of Tickey End.

"I spoke to her once or twice when I was on the streets," she lied, mentally reminding herself never to underestimate Fabian's powers of observation. "It was ages ago. I don't even remember her name—I'm surprised she remembered mine."

"Oh," said Fabian, rubbing at his cheek. "Funny how she ended up here, of all places."

"Coincidence," said Rowan, keen to change the subject. They began to walk. "So what was the fight about?" She checked him for cuts and bruises. "You must have got the upper hand—there's not a mark on you."

"It got split up as soon as it started," Fabian said. "And it started the same reason it always does—they were saying things, rotten things, about Amos. They said . . . they said they're going up to the churchyard to mess up his grave. One of them said he'd write things on the headstone. I lost my temper and walloped him."

"I don't blame you for losing your temper," said Rowan. "But they won't really do anything, Fabian. If they were thinking of it, then you'd be the last person they'd admit it to. They're just saying it to hurt you."

"Well, it worked. Why can't they just leave him alone? Even now that he's gone they won't let him rest!"

Rowan sighed. "You've got to ignore them. The more you keep rising to the bait, the more they'll keep on at you."

"That's easy for you to say," Fabian said hotly. "*You* don't have to put up with the whispers and the pointing. How would you like it if people thought *your* grandfather murdered someone?"

Rowan went silent as she pondered the dark history of Elvesden Manor, the old house she and Fabian both lived in. During Fabian's grandfather's term as the groundskeeper, a local girl named Morwenna Bloom had vanished in the nearby woods. Unfortunately, Fabian's grandfather had been the last person to be seen with her, prompting accusations that he had been involved in the disappearance. The rumors had followed him throughout his life, and now, it seemed, beyond his death two months ago as well.

"Of course I wouldn't like it," Rowan said eventually. "But I could bear it if I knew it wasn't true. And you know it isn't, Fabian. Everyone who really

matters knows Amos was innocent. Remember that."
She reached into her schoolbag. "Here. I bought you
some chocolate. It's a bit soft now."

"Thanks." Fabian cheered up a little as he took
it, and began eating messily as they walked through
the town square toward the bus stop.

"Anyway," Rowan continued. "I *do* know what
it's like to be whispered about and pointed at. I'm the
new girl, aren't I? And everyone knows I live at
Elvesden Manor now too. So, like you, I'm guilty
by association."

"I suppose," Fabian said, through chocolate-
coated teeth. "So how do you react to it all?"

"I don't say anything," Rowan replied. "I imagine their faces if they were to be told the truth. If we
actually came out with it—that Morwenna Bloom
willingly vanished into the fairy realm. Just think of
what they'd say."

"They'd think we're even crazier than they do
already," said Fabian, cramming the last of the melting chocolate into his mouth, but his expression was
lighter as they boarded the bus.

Rowan led the way to the back and sat down as
the bus lurched away, rattling through the streets of
Tickey End and on down the country lanes of Essex.
Fifteen minutes later they stepped off the bus and
began walking, passing acres of land that, in places,
was still boggy and damaged from the terrible flooding of the past winter and spring.

Soon they passed under the watchful gaze of two

ferocious stone gargoyles, which were mounted on their own pillars on either side of a great set of iron gates. Beyond the gates, across a graveled forecourt, stood the imposing ivy-wreathed mansion called Elvesden Manor. As they crunched through the gravel to the front door, Rowan stared up at the house.

"I still can't believe I actually live here."

"You say that every time we come up the path," said Fabian.

"That's because I think it every time."

She inhaled deeply as they went through the front door. The hallway was dark and musty-smelling—the kind of smell that would never leave a place, no matter how well it was cleaned. Moving toward the back of the house, they passed the huge old staircase where, on the first landing, a grandfather clock stood mutely, its hands frozen in place. From inside it, Rowan heard the telltale scuffles of its inhabitants and, further up the stairs, the monotone of a vacuum cleaner filtered down.

In the kitchen a shrill screech greeted them.

"Young whippersnapper! Off with his head!"

Rowan winced at the piercing sound, while Fabian glared at the speaker: a gray parrot with gleaming yellow eyes perched in a tall silver cage.

"Good afternoon to you too, General Carver," Fabian muttered sarcastically.

The bird narrowed its eyes, then started as the back door opened and Fabian's father, Warwick, stepped in.

"All finished for the holidays now, then?" he said, closing the door and filling the kettle at the sink. After leaving it to boil, he took off his long overcoat and hung it on the back door. The iron knife tucked into the belt of the coat thunked softly as it hit the wood.

Fabian grinned and nodded. "No more school for six whole weeks!"

"Well, don't start bickering with each other when you get bored."

Fabian snorted. "We won't get bored. And anyway, even if we did, you could take us on patrol with you in the woods—that's never boring!"

Warwick raised an eyebrow at the suggestion. He opened his mouth to answer but was interrupted as a thin, white-haired woman in her mid-sixties entered the kitchen, followed by a slightly younger woman, who was stouter and short of breath.

"I tell you, Florence," the stout woman wheezed. "That girl has problems, up there"—she tapped a finger to her head—"you know. I dread to think what kind of state her room's in. Youngsters shouldn't be allowed keys to their own doors, it's just not—" She broke off as she caught sight of Rowan and scratched at her mop of untidy brown hair.

"You know why I lock my door," Rowan said quietly.

"We've discussed this, Nell," said Florence briskly, but as she looked at Rowan her gray eyes were kind.

"As long as the room is kept tidy, then Rowan may keep it locked if she wishes."

"All the same," Nell continued. "I haven't been able to get into it to clean it for weeks now. It must be a bleedin' mess!"

"How many more times?" Rowan said in exasperation. "It's clean! And if you hadn't kept *moving* things I wouldn't need to lock the door! Don't you understand? Things need to be kept the way they are...the way I leave them...for a reason!"

"Well, if you insist," Nell said huffily.

"I do," Rowan retorted. "And if Florence doesn't mind then I don't see why you should—it's *her* house." She turned her back on the silent kitchen and left, running up the stairs. No one followed, not even Fabian. She was glad. She paused outside a door on the left, her breath coming in angry hisses, and pulled an old key out of her bag. Fitting it into the lock, she opened the door and went in, throwing her bag into the corner. Then she sat down at the dressing table and stared into the mirror.

Her reflection stared back: slanted green eyes in a pointed, pale face dotted with freckles. Her hair had been jaw-length when she first came to live at the manor. Now, five months later, a smooth sweep of auburn reached nearly to her shoulders. She picked at a strand.

Red. That's what they used to call you, isn't it?

"Red," she whispered to herself, looking around the room. She hadn't lied when she told Nell it was clean. The room was immaculate; nothing out of place. After such a long time of sleeping out on the streets, of belonging nowhere, having her own warm, safe room was something she would not take for granted in a hurry.

Safe.

Her eyes swept the room. It was a nice room, decorated just after she'd moved in. The walls were painted a vibrant crimson, making it appear warm and snug, and the worn furniture made it seem cozy, like she had been there for years. On the surface, apart from the tidiness, it was everything an ordinary fifteen-year-old girl's bedroom should be.

But Rowan was no ordinary fifteen-year-old girl. She got up from the dressing table and performed the same ritualistic checks that she performed every time she entered the room. Starting at the door, she knelt and rolled back the shabby rug to reveal the floorboards. A thin line of a white, grainy substance reached from one side of the door to the other.

Satisfied, she put the rug back in its place and checked the windowsill. Along the ledge, a matching line of white ran unbroken along its length. Pressing her finger to it, she lifted her hand and allowed a sprinkle of the granules to fall onto her tongue. The sharp bitterness confirmed it was salt.

Next she checked the grate, where, below the chimney opening, a wreath of dark green leaves and dried red-brown berries sat, sealing off another potential entrance to the room.

Finally, she crossed to the bed and slipped her fingers beneath the pillow. The coldness of the dagger there reassured her, and at last she allowed herself to relax.

The girl in Tickey End had worried her. Moving to the window, she stared out, beyond the walls of the garden and toward Hangman's Wood. But she did not see the trees, or the little brook that ran past the edge of the forest. Nor did she see the tiny church that stood in the distance. Instead, her mind's eye saw a cold, damp cellar beneath a stone cottage, where an iron manacle imprisoned a wrist with burned skin. Bitter words replayed in her head.

You'll regret this, girl.... I'll track you down and make you pay for this....

A sudden thud at the window made her gasp. Shaking herself from her thoughts, she peered through the glass, squinting in the afternoon sun. On the outside window ledge a small, winged creature scrabbled at the glass. It was about the size of a bird, and at a glance could be mistaken for one, for it wore garments of feathers and leaves. It was, however, a tiny man with sharp features and something square and white clamped between his teeth. She watched him, her face expressionless. The window had been left open a crack to ventilate the room. The gap was wide enough for the fairy to squeeze through, but even if he tried, she knew he would be unable to cross the salt barrier. It was a deterrent to fairies, just like all the other barriers she had set in place.

As the fey man stopped scrabbling, about to give up as he always did, Rowan relented and brushed away some of the salt, creating a small opening. The fairy blinked in surprise, then darted through the window, releasing the thing in his mouth, which fell to the floor.

"About time too!" he grumbled in a nasal voice. Then he took flight and was gone, leaving Rowan hurrying to sweep the salt back into an unbroken line again.

She knelt and collected the thing the fairy had dropped. It was a plain envelope with a single word printed on the front: RED. She stared at it, the name she had gone by for so long. The name she had tried to forget she'd ever had.

She was sick of pretending. Sick of hiding. Sliding her thumbnail under the lip of the envelope, she tore it open.

It was time to face her past.

2

Tanya arrived at Elvesden Manor a week later. As she followed Warwick over the threshold, a thrill of excitement to be back at her grandmother's old house rose up inside her.

"All right, Oberon. Stop pulling," she told the large brown Doberman straining at the end of his leash. His tail wagged erratically as she released the clip from his collar, then he shot through the house, claws clattering on the tiles.

"I'll take your things up to your room later," said Warwick, leaving Tanya's suitcase at the bottom of the stairs. "We're just in time for lunch."

Tanya followed him into the kitchen at the back of the house. There, her grandmother and Nell were heaping fat ham-and-cheese sandwiches, boiled eggs, and salad onto plates and transferring them to the table. Slices of fruit were piled up for dessert. Florence's face broke into a smile as she caught sight of Tanya, and after hastily brushing her hands on her apron she pulled Tanya into a warm hug, then stepped back to appraise her.

"Look at you," she said. "Brown as a berry—and freckled, as well!"

"Hello, dear," said Nell, beaming. "How was Devon?"

"Good," said Tanya, steering Oberon's long nose away from the tray of sandwiches. "We got back last night. Mum said I should wait another day and have a proper rest before coming here, but I wanted to come as soon as I could. It feels like forever since I last visited. Properly, I mean." There was an awkward silence. Tanya and her mother had last come to the manor only eight weeks ago, for Amos's funeral.

"Poppycock!" General Carver announced from his cage, his voice an exact imitation of Nell's. He clicked and began to preen his feathers.

"Sit down," said Florence, ignoring the parrot. "Fabian and Rowan should be along any moment."

"Where are they?" Tanya asked, reaching for a plate at the same moment that the lid to the tea caddy on the counter began to lift. She watched as the ill-tempered brownie who lived there squinted out, then reached forward with his walking stick. With a stab of the stick, he looted a piece of tomato before he vanished beneath the teabags once more.

"They're outside, helping Rose with the animals," said Florence, apparently not noticing the brownie's antics, though Tanya knew she must have seen and was turning a blind eye. Like Tanya, her grandmother was second-sighted, and they, along with Rowan, were the only members of the household with the ability to see fairies, though everyone else in the house knew of their existence. Until last year, Tanya had not known of Florence's gift, and the secret had prevented them from becoming close.

"You haven't seen the animals yet, have you?" Florence continued. "Rose has worked wonders with the old courtyard—you must go and see after lunch. Oh, that sounds like Rowan and Fabian coming in now."

"She's here!" Fabian could be heard exclaiming from the hallway in evident excitement. "Look, there's her suitcase!"

He burst into the kitchen, grinning wildly, accompanied by Rowan and a woman with the same long auburn hair. While Rowan and the woman, Rose, went to the sink, Fabian pulled a chair up next to Tanya and started to sit down. Tanya noticed a light brown feather stuck to his shirt.

"Just a moment, Fabian," Florence interrupted. "Your hands."

Fabian looked puzzled. "What about them?"

"You know what," said Florence. "You've been up to your elbows in chicken droppings all morning. *Wash* them."

"Bleedin' pest!" the General added, as though in

agreement. Nell chortled and took a slice of apple to the cage. Sliding it through the bars, she gave a little coo as the parrot took it in his scaly claws and nibbled at it.

"Oh, all right," said Fabian, getting up again and going to the sink. He nodded toward a dish of speckled hard-boiled eggs on the table. "Have one of those, Tanya. Collected them myself this morning!"

Tanya took an egg. Rowan sat down on the other side of her and began piling her plate with food.

"How was your holiday? Did you visit that old house you were telling me about?"

"What house?" Fabian piped up, sitting down again.

"Chambercombe Manor," Tanya answered. "It's similar to Elvesden Manor but not even half as big. My mum's wanted to go there ever since reading about it in a book of ghost stories—it's supposed to be haunted."

"I've heard about that," said Fabian. "That's the one where they knocked down a wall and discovered a secret room with a skeleton on the bed! And it's been haunted ever since!"

"There's a secret passage too," said Tanya. "One that pirates used to smuggle their goods from the beach. But it's completely caved in now."

"Huh," said Fabian. "I bet their secret tunnel wasn't a match for any of ours."

"Which none of you should even know about, let alone have been in," Warwick added gruffly. Tanya stole a look at him. He looked older, but better than he had the last time she had seen him. His eyes had been red-rimmed then, and his cheeks sunken. Warwick had been the one to find his father dead one morning when he had taken up Amos's breakfast. After years of a slow descent into madness, the old man's last few months had been eased after his memories of Morwenna were erased, until finally, he had slipped away peacefully in his sleep.

"Yes, but still," Fabian persisted. "One of ours leads into a *graveyard*. You can't get much creepier than that!"

"I'll say," Nell retorted, her plump shoulders wobbling in a shudder. "You grisly boy."

Fabian smirked as though the comment were a compliment while Tanya watched him and wondered whether "boy" was quite the right word for Fabian any longer. He had grown taller and broader over the past few months and was losing the gangly appearance she was familiar with. He was not so thin, nor so pale, and his cheeks were flushed with good health from spending time out of doors.

"How's school been?" Tanya asked Rowan, quietly. "It seems like you're settling in better now, from what you said on the phone."

Rowan took a bite from a sandwich and expertly smuggled the rest beneath the tablecloth to Oberon's ready jaws.

"It's all right," she said, "now that the attention has died down. It's always worse when you're the new person. The main thing is trying to catch up on the schooling I missed." She made a face. "Rose wants to pay a private tutor to give me extra lessons. So far I've managed to convince her I'm coping."

"And how are things with her?" Tanya continued, lowering her voice even further.

Rowan glanced over at Rose, who was chatting away to Florence, oblivious to the girls' conversation. "Strange," she said, chewing slowly. "We get along, but then we always did. Some days I completely forget, just for a moment, and it's like it always was. Rose is just my oddball of an aunt, nuts about animals. And then she'll look at me in a certain way, and I'll remember—" She broke off as the conversation around the rest of the table lulled. "Talk to you about it later," she muttered.

Tanya ate the rest of her lunch in silence. Rowan had grown up believing that Rose was her aunt, and had only recently discovered that Rose was in fact her mother. When her aunt and uncle, whom she'd believed were her parents, were killed in an accident, Rowan was placed in a children's home, along with her cousin, James, whom she had always thought was her brother.

While they were staying at the children's home, James was stolen by fairies, prompting Rowan to run away in search of him, using the name "Red" to remain unknown on the streets. Neither Tanya nor Fabian knew much of Rowan's past, but what they *did* know was that she'd been involved in switching back fairy changelings left in place of stolen human children. It had been her hope that one day she would make a trade that led to her getting James back.

Only by chance had Tanya discovered Rowan hiding out in the tunnels below Elvesden Manor. Since then, Tanya and Fabian had helped her in her search for James, but in finding him, the truth about Rowan's parentage had come out—and had revealed not only that Rose was her mother, but that her father was fey.

Now Rowan was rebuilding her life at Elvesden Manor...and building a new relationship with her mother.

❦

After lunch, Tanya helped her grandmother tidy up and chatted to her about school and her vacation. As they moved around the kitchen, the timid little hearth-fay skittered away from the table, where she had been keeping the teapot warm, to her favorite nook behind the coal bin, nudging it slightly.

Once she was finished cleaning, Tanya went out through the back and into the courtyard at the side of the house. Oberon followed close behind her, his nose bumping at her heels. Beyond the wild rose-bushes, an area had been cleared of weeds. A fence had been put up, and small hutches were placed around the edges within it. An old goat with only one horn was tethered to a fence post, and a chicken coop was at the back.

Inside the fence, Rose was bottle-feeding a calf. Tanya peered over the fence.

"What happened to it?" she asked softly, not wanting to disturb the young animal.

"Orphaned," Rose murmured. "Won't you come inside?"

Tanya went through the gate, careful to latch it after her. She left Oberon outside. He jumped up at the fence and watched her, his nose resting on his huge paws. Further back, Rowan was leaning over a pen containing a small, rust-colored fox with a heavily bandaged leg.

"What's the matter with its leg?" Tanya asked.

"Poacher's trap," Rowan answered. "Luckily nothing was broken, but he had a wound that was infected. Rose says it'll be healed in a week or so. We can't have much contact—we need to keep him wild for when he's released."

"What if he comes back for the chickens once he's better?" Tanya asked doubtfully, glancing over at the coop, where Fabian was scattering feed.

"He won't," said Rowan. "Rose found him in Knook while she was walking her dogs in the fields. We'll release him there. He won't find his way back—it's miles away."

Tanya nodded. "So what's the deal with this place, then? I mean, who pays for it all? And is Rose keeping her cottage in Knook?"

"Yes," said Rose quietly, from behind them. The calf trotted along after her like a lamb. "I'm keeping the cottage. The animal sanctuary is off to a good start. I already have offers of sponsorship to pay for any medical treatment they need, and Florence and Nell have come up with some fund-raising ideas for the upkeep of the facilities here." She smiled at Tanya, her green eyes crinkling. "It was kind of your grandmother and Warwick to offer to let me use the land for this. My cottage is so tiny, and there are so many animals that need helping."

Tanya shrugged. "Well, so much of the house and the land isn't used for anything. I think it makes sense. It's a good place for animals. Will you be bringing your dogs here? And Rowan mentioned that you've got geese too."

Rose shook her head. "No. The dogs are settled, and they have plenty of space. It's the larger animals I was struggling with. And the geese, good grief, no! They'd terrorize the rest of the animals— better that they stay where they are, in the cottage garden."

"Thank goodness for that," Rowan muttered.

"You know...you can always come to the cottage," Rose said quickly, her words directed at Rowan. "To visit, or even stay over. It's perfectly safe...and protected."

"I know," Rowan said, looking uncomfortable. "I'll think about it."

Rose forced a smile. "I'll see you tomorrow,

then." She left the enclosure. Minutes later Warwick's Land Rover rumbled through the gates as he drove her home.

"Give her a chance," Tanya said, watching as Rowan fastened the fox's hutch. "She's trying, you know."

Rowan shrugged. "I know. So am I." She left the pen and looked up as Fabian finally came away from the chickens to join them. "It was never going to be easy, was it?"

"I suppose not," Tanya conceded.

※

The afternoon gave way to evening. After walking Oberon by the brook bordering Hangman's Wood, Tanya went to her room to unpack. As she took her toiletry bag into the bathroom that she shared with Rowan, a gurgling from the sink caught her attention. Peering into the murky plughole, she saw two bulbous eyes gleaming back at her. In the autumn, a drain-dweller had taken up residence there. It was a slimy, amphibian-like creature with a fondness for all things shiny, much like a magpie.

It had not been the first of its kind, however. Another drain-dweller had once lived in the bathroom, and it had taken a liking to an old silver charm bracelet given to Tanya by her grandmother. Tanya had learned that the charms symbolized the thirteen treasures of the fairy courts. She had also learned that her ancestor and the first lady of the manor, Elizabeth Elvesden, had been a fairy changeling. The subsequent bloodline running through the family ever since was the reason for Tanya's second sight.

Rowan came in through the adjoining door opposite the one that led in from Tanya's room.

"Oh, sorry," she began. "I didn't realize you were in here."

"It's all right," Tanya answered. "I'm just unpacking. But on second thought, I'll leave my toothbrush in my toiletry bag—I don't want that slimy draindweller crawling all over it."

"Good decision," Rowan remarked. "Make sure you don't leave any jewelry lying around, either—it's an even bigger thief than the first one, according to Warwick. He's had to unblock the pipes three times since the winter to get back all the stuff it's stolen."

"I'll remember," said Tanya, watching as the gleaming eyes narrowed. Evidently the creature knew it was being spoken about, for it belched in her direction and then squelched further into the pipes and out of sight, leaving the smell of rotten eggs in its wake.

Rowan went back into her own room, leaving Tanya alone with the unpleasant scent of the draindweller. She left her toiletry bag zipped up and placed it on the back of the sink, then went back into her room.

It had been redecorated since her last visit. The

peeling wallpaper had been stripped and replaced with a fresh coat of cream paint, and the cracked glass in the dressing table mirror had been renewed. It was warmer, more welcoming. A new painting above the fireplace had replaced the one of Echo and Narcissus that she had taken down a year ago following a cruel trick the fairies had played: making her repeat the last words of other people's sentences. She pushed the memory from her mind. Things were different now.

She didn't have much to unpack, and soon everything was put away. She left the room, walked along the landing to the bedroom next door, and knocked.

"Come in," Rowan called.

Tanya went in. Rowan was sitting at her dressing table, and Fabian was hunched on her bed, reading. He pushed his glasses back up his nose as she entered.

"Oh, it's you," Rowan said in surprise. "You could have just come in through the bathroom."

Tanya sat down next to Fabian. He closed the book, a tome on folklore, and set it to one side.

"So what do you think?" he asked, his eyes sparkling.

"About what?" Tanya replied.

"The animal sanctuary."

"It's great," Tanya replied. "I think it'll be good for the manor if people know what's being done here. Maybe it'll go some way toward helping people to forget all the bad stuff that happened here...with Amos and Morwenna and everything."

Fabian nodded. "I helped Warwick build the fence, you know. And I painted the chicken coop."

Tanya nodded, only half-listening. Her eyes were drawn to the various charms and deterrents that were placed around Rowan's room. Salt; dried rowanberries and leaves; an iron horseshoe on the wall above her bed. Fabian had told her about them on the phone, but Tanya hadn't been able to visualize it. Even now, seeing it with her own eyes, she couldn't believe it. Nor could she get used to the new Rowan, with her neat hair and clothes and her quiet manner. Was this really the fearless girl who had trekked around the countryside with only a knife and a meager bag of belongings just a few months ago? It seemed impossible.

Tanya went to the window, looking past the unbroken trail of salt to the sprawling forest beyond the garden. Her mind swam with possible words, some way of broaching the subject gently. But before she settled on something she was comfortable voicing, Fabian interrupted.

"We haven't seen much of Mad Morag recently. I wonder if the compass she gave you is still working?"

"I don't know," said Tanya, thinking of the old gypsy woman who had helped them in the past. "I haven't even looked at it yet."

"We saw her in Tickey End in the spring, didn't we?" Fabian said, looking over at Rowan, but she was staring into space, gnawing her lower lip.

"Didn't we, Red?" Fabian persisted.

Rowan's head snapped up. "Don't call me that anymore!"

"Sorry," Fabian muttered, looking baffled and more than a little hurt. "I didn't mean to. It's just... an old habit. It just came out."

Rowan's fierce expression softened. "No, I'm sorry. I shouldn't have snapped."

"Anyway," Fabian continued uncomfortably, "we saw her in town. I spoke to her for a few minutes. I was hoping she'd let me have some more of that tonic to see fairies, but she said it wasn't to be used lightly." He sighed. "Warwick's being really stingy with his too. Says I've got no business messing with it."

"He's right," said Rowan shortly. "Here's me trying to keep them out"—she gestured around the room—"and you're positively looking to encourage them in!"

Fabian's face began to flush. "I'm not encouraging them. I just want to be able to *see* them." He flicked the book open and hunched over it again, muttering to himself. "I'll find my own way to see them. Plenty of ideas in here."

Rowan made a noise of exasperation, and Tanya decided to take the plunge.

"Why are you being so cautious?" she asked. "Do you even need all these charms to keep the fairies out? I mean... now that we know about your name...."

Rowan didn't look at her. "It's not a case of

whether I need it. I *want* it. And yes, being named after the rowan tree protects me from harmful magic, but what if that's not enough?" She lifted her feet up onto the chair and hugged her knees to herself.

"I don't understand," Tanya said. "How can it not be enough? You've faced the worst and won, surely? You defeated the fairies after they took James. They let you go! You're here, with us. You're safe!"

"Am I?" Rowan turned to face her. "Am I really? It's not easy to let go of the past. Not easy to start fresh, even when you want to, more than anything."

"But you already have," said Fabian, putting the book down again.

Rowan gave a short laugh. "Some things aren't easy to put behind you. I've done things, bad things. I can't help feeling that somehow, someday, they're going to catch up with me."

Tanya felt a chill at her words. "What things?"

But Rowan's face had changed, closed off. Whatever was on her mind was not about to be shared.

"Come on," Tanya said firmly. "Let's take all these deterrents down."

"We can help," Fabian said eagerly. He got up and reached for the horseshoe above the bed.

But Rowan shook her head. "No. Not yet."

Fabian lowered his hand, and then Tanya saw him lean closer to the calendar on the wall.

"You've circled the thirteenth," he commented, a forced brightness in his tone that told Tanya he was trying hard to change the subject and lighten the mood in the room. "That's today. What's the big event?"

His words seemed to have completely the opposite effect from what he had intended. Tanya glanced at Rowan and saw a look of panic and fury sweep across her face.

"Nothing! Mind your own business and stop poking around my stuff!"

"I wasn't exactly poking around," Fabian retorted. "I just saw it!"

The emotion left Rowan's face suddenly. It became unreadable.

"If you must know, I circled the date because I knew Tanya was coming today," she said smoothly. "I've been looking forward to it."

"Huh," said Fabian. "Then why didn't you just say so, instead of biting my head off?" He snatched his book and, looking decidedly grumpy, headed for the door. "I'm going back to my room."

"I think I'll go back to mine too," said Tanya. "I've still got some unpacking to do."

"All right," said Rowan, meeting her eyes. The look in them was challenging, as though she knew Tanya had lied about the unpacking.

Tanya shut the door behind her and stood in the hallway. She did not enjoy lying, but it was something she had grown accomplished at over the years. Consequently, she had also learned to recognize when she was being lied to.

So, standing in the cool, dark hallway with her back to the door, she trusted her own judgement enough to know that Rowan had just lied about the meaning of the date on the calendar.

She just didn't know why.

3

The cottage had been without an owner for several months. For a long time it had been a feared place, but news of its owner's death had spread, and the deserted woods surrounding it began to stir once more.

Inside, cold ash was all that remained in the grate of the fireplace. Jars and bottles cluttered the surfaces, their contents untouched, and around the edges of the cottage, cages stood empty, doors open. Animal skins of all kinds hung from the rafters, stiff and dried and no longer dripping. Below them the stone floor was dotted with old, dark stains, but the tangy scent of blood no longer filled the air.

Rowan stepped into the center of the cottage, her heart drumming a familiar beat of fear. She kicked aside the animal pelt on the floor, revealing the trapdoor beneath. Slowly, slowly, she descended the staircase into the cellar, not wanting to, but unable to fight the need to know what the cellar held.

The stench hit her a few steps down, sending her reeling. It was the smell of dead, rotten things. Covering her nose with her hand she urged herself to the bottom. Blindly stumbling in the darkness, she felt her feet hit something solid on the floor. A body. Suppressing a scream, she recoiled, allowing herself a moment of composure. Gradually, her eyes adjusted, and she was able to make out the dark shapes littering the cellar. Only one remained upright. As she edged toward it, her breathing quickened. It was slumped forward, one wrist encircled in an iron manacle. Greasy black hair fell over the face. There was no movement.

She moved closer. Things crunched under her boots, glinting in the light filtering down. Fragments of mirror, eggshell, and a curse that had gone horribly wrong. She remembered it all. She stopped in front of the motionless figure, trembling. Only then did she realize she had something clenched in her sweating hand. She looked down and found a key there.

Reaching forward, she jammed the key into the iron manacle and jiggled it around, trying to unlock it. Something was in there, some wedge of dirt perhaps, preventing it from turning.

The hand in the manacle sprang to life, grabbing her wrist. Rowan screamed, dropping the key as the head snapped up. Two black eyes burned in a waxen face, emanating hatred.

"I'm sorry..." she babbled in terror. "I'm sorry—"

The lips in the face parted, breaking a thin seal of crusted spittle. The face loomed as the hand pulled her nearer...nearer...and three words were spat into her face.

"YOU...LEFT...ME...!"

Rowan awoke, trembling and soaked in perspiration. The dream clung to her like a cobweb. It was the same dream she'd been having for months now. Everything about it felt so real: the memory of the hanging animal skins, the trapdoor, the cellar...the stench. She threw the covers back, sniffing at herself self-consciously. All she could smell was her own sweat. She shook herself, forcing it out of her mind. She would not think about it. Not now. She had other things to attend to, and drifting off to sleep hadn't been part of the plan.

She glanced worriedly at the clock but found that she had only dozed off for about ten minutes. It was late now, past eleven o'clock, and gradually the manor was going silent. Only Warwick was yet to go to bed, his heavy footsteps clumping through the house as he locked up for the night. Finally, she heard his boots on the stairs, then the sliver of light beneath her door vanished as Warwick turned off the light in the hallway. She heard his door close, and then silence.

She waited another twenty minutes to give him the chance to drop off to sleep. Silently, she drew back the covers and slid out of bed, fully clothed, and then padded silently to her bookshelf. From there she removed the slip of paper tucked into one of the books and cast her eyes over it again in the moonlight from the window. There was a map, roughly drawn in pencil, and a few lines of writing—a scrawled instruction. Committing both to memory, she crossed to the fireplace, took a box of matches from the mantelpiece, and lit one. In the darkness of the room the yellow light glowed brilliantly, the hiss of the flame loud. She held the piece of paper to it until it caught, then put it carefully in the empty grate. By the time she had collected her fox-skin coat from the wardrobe and slipped her knife into her belt, the paper had curled and blackened and fallen away to ash.

With a final glance around the room, Rowan crept to the door and opened it, stooping to collect her boots on the way out. In the hallway she paused for a split second outside Tanya's room, half-wishing she could knock. Swallowing down her regret, she continued onward, down the stairs and toward the front door. All was well until she reached the little table upon which the telephone stood. Something warm and soft moved beneath her right foot. An angry yowl pierced the silence.

Spitfire shot out from under the table and fled to

the grandfather clock, stopping to lick his matted tail where it had been stepped on. His single eye glowed through the darkness in a demon glare.

Rowan remained still, alert for signs that anyone had awoken. There were none. Edging down the hallway, she took her key from the hook and quietly opened the front door. Stepping outside, she pulled the door to and inserted her key to hold the latch back until the door was closed. On the porch she slipped her boots on and laced them. Then, standing up, she drew the fox-skin coat around her shoulders and fastened the clasp. The transformation, as always, was instant. Every hair follicle twitched, as though red-brown fur really was growing all over her. The night loomed large as she shrank into it, yet all her senses magnified and became pin-sharp.

Then she was off, over the courtyard and through the gates into the lanes beyond Elvesden Manor. The dream had been pushed into the furthest corners of her mind.

<hr />

Tanya's eyes snapped open at the sound of Spitfire's yowl. She lay quiet for a moment as sleep pulled at her, wondering if perhaps Oberon had dared to get too close to the crotchety old cat, but this seemed unlikely. She was almost asleep again when a draught unexpectedly whistled past her ears. It was enough to wake her fully, sending her eyes to the windowsill, where she expected to see Gredin, Raven, and the Mizhog. But there were no fairies.

She sat up. Somewhere in the house, a door had opened. She slid out of bed and crossed to the bathroom. Faint gurgles and gargles could be heard coming from the drain-dweller in the plughole. She ignored them and quietly entered Rowan's room, sniffing at a smoky scent. Something had been burning. Approaching the bed, Tanya reached out.

"Rowan," she whispered. "Are you awake? I think there's someone in the house!"

Her hand sank into the empty bedclothes. Where was Rowan?

She hurried back to her room, throwing on jeans, a sweater, socks, and sneakers. Then she left her room and tiptoed across the landing to Fabian's door. From Nell's room, next to Fabian's, loud snores were making the floor practically vibrate. Tanya twisted the doorknob and slipped into Fabian's room, closing the door behind her.

The lamp was on, but Fabian was fast asleep, still wearing his glasses. His right cheek rested against some loose pages. He had evidently fallen asleep while reading them. Tanya leaned closer, wrinkling her nose at the gusts of stale, dragon-like breath coming from Fabian's wide-open mouth.

She reached out and poked him. "Fabian! Wake up."

His eyes flickered open momentarily, then shut

again. "Drain-dwellers took it," he mumbled, and started to turn over.

"*Fabian!*" She pulled back the covers. Fabian huddled up like a squirrel at the sudden lack of warmth. Tanya prodded him again.

"Rowan's gone!" she whispered fiercely. "Get up, quickly!"

Fabian shot up in bed, a page stuck to his cheek.

"Gone where? What?" He straightened his glasses and peeled the piece of paper away from his face.

"I don't know!" Tanya hissed, throwing a rumpled shirt and trousers at him from off the floor. "That's the point. Get dressed; we're going after her. Nice pajamas, by the way."

Fabian blinked sleepily and peered down at himself. A brightly colored solar system was printed on the dark blue fabric.

She turned to face the door to allow him to get changed, but he appeared beside her so quickly that she realized he'd simply pulled his clothes on over his pajamas.

"Let's go."

They crept downstairs, walking a short distance apart to minimize creaks. When they reached the clock, Spitfire slunk out of their way as they passed.

Fabian grabbed some socks from a pile of laundry in the hallway. "Darn it, Nell," he muttered to himself. "These socks aren't properly dry." He pulled them on anyway, grimacing, and they backed away from the stairs toward the kitchen. There, Tanya quickly put a leash on Oberon.

"Did you even see which way she went?" asked Fabian. "Front or back?"

Tanya shook her head. "I didn't see anything. But I think we should go the front way. If Rowan's been so intent on keeping fairies away, then it doesn't make sense for her to head toward the woods that are full of them."

"Good thinking," said Fabian. "Now, where's my other shoe?"

Oberon stepped behind Tanya as Fabian huffily pulled his missing shoe, lightly nibbled, from Oberon's basket. Fabian glared at the dog and tugged the shoe on with as much dignity as he could muster.

"You were right. Rowan's key is missing," he whispered as they opened the front door. He took his own front door key from his pocket.

Outside, there was no crunching across the gravel. This time they stuck to the path through the forecourt.

"We're going to have to run," said Tanya, once they were safely through the gates. Broken moonlight played on the dirt road through the gaps in the trees. "She's got at least five minutes on us. She could be anywhere."

"Head for the bus stop," said Fabian. "All the main routes out go from there."

They began to run, wordlessly, side by side, with Oberon slightly ahead. Five minutes later they neared the junction.

"Slow down," Fabian said, his chest heaving for breath. "If she's close by, she could hear us running."

They continued forward, though with Oberon's heavy panting a quiet approach seemed unlikely. Tanya stared in both directions, searching the lanes. They were quiet even during the day. At night, they were deserted.

"We're too late," she said in dismay, seeing nothing. "We've lost her."

"Don't give up yet," said Fabian. "She would only have gone this way"—he nodded to the left—"or that way, toward Tickey End. Let's just pick one and take a chance. We can't be that far behind."

Tanya turned from side to side. She was desperate to know where Rowan was—what was going on. "You decide," she said finally. "I feel like whichever way I choose will be the wrong one."

Fabian raked a hand through his bushy hair.

"Tickey End," he said at last, as a look of recognition lit up his face. "I've just remembered something. Last week after school I saw her speaking to a homeless girl on the street. She acted like she didn't know her, but I heard the girl call her 'Red.' I didn't think of it until just now, but that's when she started acting cagey. It's something to do with that girl, I'm sure of it." He started to walk. "Come on."

Tanya made to follow, but a sudden jerk on her arm made her stop. Oberon was resisting, staring in the opposite direction with his nose twitching and his ears pricked up, alert.

"Wait," she said.

"What's up with him?" Fabian said impatiently.

"He doesn't want to go that way," said Tanya. "He's pulling to go the other way. He's scented something—it must be Rowan!"

They followed Oberon along the narrow lane, walking as quickly as they could while still remaining quiet. Less than a minute later, they followed the road over the crest of a hill. Before them, the lane spread out. There was no sign of Rowan's boyish figure anywhere. Yet the road was not quite empty, for a small animal was skirting along the shoulder. They both saw it at once.

"Of course," Fabian breathed. "That's her. She's wearing the fox-skin coat!"

"It could just be a fox," said Tanya.

Fabian shook his head. "Look at the way it's moving. It's sticking to the edges but it's bold as brass. Real foxes are more alert for predators, I'm sure of it." His nostrils flared indignantly. "What's she playing at? I say we just catch her up and confront her!"

"Don't be nuts," said Tanya. "She wouldn't tell us a thing if we did that. The only way we'll find out what she's up to is by following her. If she'd wanted us to know what was going on she would have told us, wouldn't she? Instead she's chosen to sneak out in the middle of the night without saying a word." Her throat tightened. "I thought she trusted us."

"So did I," said Fabian, bitterly. "Just shows that we don't really know her at all."

They set off, keeping at a safe distance from the fox-form up ahead. Thin wisps of cloud scudded across the moon overhead, and the stars winked at them.

"Keep to the edge of the road," Fabian whispered. "Walking on the grass is quieter, and it means we can hide in the hedges if she turns around."

They continued through the darkness, taking the lead from the fox. Once or twice the vixen slipped out of view, causing a flurry of panicked whispers between them, before one of them caught sight of her once more and the trail picked up again.

"Does she even know where she's going?" Fabian whispered.

They had been walking for nearly thirty minutes and, despite the coolness of the night, Tanya's cheeks burned with heat. Now that her senses had adapted to being outside in the night, she was picking up strains of whispering fey creatures and a few rustles from the trees surrounding them. Their presence was not going unnoticed.

"Maybe she doesn't have a particular place in mind," she replied. "For all we know, she's running away."

"Why would she run away?" Fabian spluttered. "She always says how much she likes it at Elvesden Manor. And, anyway, she hasn't taken any of her stuff. It looks like all she's got is the coat on her back."

"I know," Tanya said patiently. "But she's used to coping with having nothing."

"That still doesn't explain *why*."

"Something's rattled her," said Tanya. "That's the only explanation. She's scared anyway, it's obvious from the way she keeps her room full of protection against fairies. I think it's something to do with that girl in Tickey End. Are you sure you didn't hear what they were talking about?"

"No," said Fabian. "The girl was already leaving when I turned up."

They continued in silence. Above them, trees towered over the road and met in the middle, and Tanya recognized it as the route her mother took whenever she drove to the manor. Through gaps in the hedges they saw a wide expanse of fields and farmland. After another forty minutes they had twice more ducked into the bushes at the side of the road as Rowan paused to navigate the lanes, and Fabian complained that he had torn his shirt.

"Why is it we always end up doing this?" he muttered, pulling brambles from his thick nest of hair. "Skulking about after dark. I thought our skulking days were over—"

"Shh!" said Tanya. "She's stopped."

They backed into the hedge, watching as the fox sniffed the air, then vanished into the foliage.

"Where did she go?" Fabian whispered.

They waited, wondering if Rowan would emerge. There was no sign of her.

"She must have seen us," Fabian said. "She's waiting for us, I bet."

"Or maybe she's taken a shortcut," said Tanya. "We're surrounded by fields, she could have gone into one. Let's just head to where we last saw her. If she *has* seen us then we may as well confront her."

They eased out of the hedge once more and headed onward. Tanya kept her eyes fixed on the spot where she thought Rowan had vanished. When they reached it, they poked about for a bit before determining that there was no break in the hedge at that point. Tanya wandered on a little further, watching Oberon for any telltale signs that they were on the right track. He snuffled at the grass and shuffled forward, pulling her closer to some bushes several meters from where Fabian stood.

Up ahead there was a fork in the road, with a weathered signpost informing travelers that Tickey End was twelve miles away, in the direction they had just come from. Tanya viewed it, calculating that she and Fabian must have walked at least three miles from the bus stop.

Then she saw that Oberon had stopped by a gap in the shrubbery and was looking up at her expectantly.

"Fabian," Tanya whispered. "This way."

They both pressed into the gap. A short distance across the field, a tumbledown building squatted forlornly. The brickwork was crumbling and part of the roof was missing. A few meters from the ruin stood an old feeding trough and a cluster of trees.

"It must have been used by one of the farms," Fabian whispered.

"Doesn't look like it's used for anything much now," Tanya whispered back. "Do you think that's where Rowan's gone? Why would she go in there?"

"Only one way to find out." Fabian stepped into the scrubby field and began padding toward the building. He motioned for Tanya to head toward the trees with Oberon. She crept past the shabby building and took cover behind the trough, crouching with Oberon at her side. The trees whispered softly above her, their leaves making a canopy over her head, stopping her from feeling too exposed. From her position she saw Fabian moving silently around the building. The scent of rust from the old trough filled her nostrils.

She saw Fabian stiffen, his back to her. Moments later he crept back and eased himself down next to her.

"What did you see?" she asked in a low voice. "Was she in there?"

Fabian nodded.

"Well, what's she doing?"

"Just sitting there on the floor, facing the door. She's taken the coat off and has it draped over herself. From the look on her face, I'm pretty sure she's waiting for something, or..." He hesitated.

"What?" asked Tanya.

Fabian's eyes were wide. "I think she's meeting someone."

4

Rowan huddled against the wall of the stone building. The chill of the damp brickwork at her back was giving her the creeps, stirring up memories of the cold, damp cellar once more. She kept her eyes trained upward, watching the moon through the broken roof, and pushed thoughts of the cellar from her mind.

Once or twice she tensed as rustles came from outside. It was not one of *them*, not yet. It must be some nighttime creature, a fox or badger perhaps. She would know when *they* arrived. She shivered, breaking her stillness to blow into her hands.

The minutes dragged by, and she grew colder. She got up and began to pace, looking at her watch. Any minute now, they'd start arriving. A noise made her freeze. A footstep, outside.

The door creaked open, barely staying on its hinges, and a man stepped inside. Though the night had stolen his coloring, washing his features in shades of blue and gray, Rowan knew his face well. Dirty blond hair skimmed his shoulders, kept long to conceal pointed fey ears. His eyes were mismatched: one hazel, one green. She heard him draw breath to speak as the door swung shut.

"Well, well," he said in a low drawl. "Red—you've come back to us."

"Tino," she replied evenly. "Where are the others?"

Tino came closer. "They'll be along. Not much point in us getting started until they arrive. I'm sure they'll want to hear what you've got to say for yourself just as much as I do."

Rowan blinked at the barbed words but said nothing. She concentrated on holding his gaze. To look away would be a sign of weakness, but it was taking everything she had not to. She'd forgotten how intense his stare was, how scrutinized he made her feel. She'd felt that way ever since the very first time she'd met him.

Rowan remembered the smell of fresh mint in the caravan, steaming from the glass of liquid that Tino had passed her. She hadn't touched—and wouldn't touch—a drop of it.

"It all depends on how involved you want to get," he'd told her, his fingers tracing the rim of his glass.

"I'm already involved," she had replied, clutching her own glass tightly. "I'll do whatever it takes to get my brother back."

He knew he had her after that. His swarthy face had broken into a smile, and he had reached for her hand, shaking it. Sealing the words to a promise.

"There are thirteen of us working against them," said Tino. "We call ourselves the Coven."

"You're a coven?" Rowan asked uneasily. "Like . . . like witches?"

Tino shook his head, his mismatched eyes never leaving hers.

"No, not witches. The word 'coven' is older than that. It means 'gathering.'"

"So why are there thirteen of you? Don't witches' covens have thirteen members?"

Tino leaned forward. "Forget witches. Can you think of no other significance for that number?"

"The thirteen treasures of the fairy court?"

"Exactly."

"I don't see the connection."

"What happened with the thirteen treasures was the cause of the changeling trade in the first place," Tino said patiently. "The split into the Seelie and Unseelie Courts was the beginning of it all. There were thirteen members of the original fairy court. And so the Coven has thirteen members, to counteract them. Like the Seelie and Unseelie, we're divided.

Some of us are human, some of us are fey. Each member swears an oath—an oath to serve the Coven to the best of their ability, and to keep it from discovery at all cost.

"It's a dangerous job," Tino continued softly. "People come and go. We're always on the lookout for new...recruits. Those recruits need to be invisible. Nameless. People who are tough and hardy. People who have known loss." He leaned forward. "People with nothing left to lose. People like *you*."

"What do you mean about people 'coming and going'?" Rowan asked.

"The Coven is hundreds of years old," Tino replied simply. "And no one lives forever. When old members retire, new ones are recruited."

"And if people change their minds?" she asked. "What then?"

Tino's finger paused momentarily in its track around the rim of his glass before starting again, slightly more slowly. "People don't generally change their minds," he said softly.

❦❦

Rowan was jolted from the memory as the next member arrived. A stocky boy of about her age slid through the door, his sandy hair obscuring his face. He shook it back out of his eyes and stared at her. She waited for the easy smile she knew—the smile with the distinctive chipped tooth—but it did not come.

"Sparrow?" she said hesitantly.

The boy responded with a curt nod and moved closer. Still he did not speak, but now that he was nearer she could smell him, all unwashed clothes and body—the smell of the streets. It was the first time she'd noticed that smell, and with a shock, it hit her: the last time she had seen Sparrow, she had smelled exactly the same as him. Placing his back to Rowan, Sparrow faced Tino.

"Do we know if all the others can make it?"

"Most have confirmed." A muscle started to twitch in Tino's cheek. "A couple have gone . . . quiet."

"Who—" Sparrow began, but fell silent as two more figures slipped into the building: a petite, sharp-faced girl whom Rowan recognized as the beggar she had met in Tickey End, and a skinny teenage boy with a shock of messy black hair. The girl's eyes were everywhere—on the faces of the others, their surroundings, taking everything in. Rowan scowled at her.

The boy's gaze was slower, craftier, but Rowan knew who he was and knew he missed nothing. He set down the slim black case he was carrying, stuck his hands in his pockets, and casually leaned against the wall.

"So who is she?" Rowan asked Tino, nodding toward the girl. "Apart from a convincing actress, that is."

"She's called Suki," said Tino. "She's been with us for almost a year. She's Cassandra's replacement."

"And she can speak for herself," Suki retorted in a voice that was as sharp as her features.

Rowan studied her, for the first time wondering who her own predecessor had been. Tino had never volunteered the information.

"We lost contact with Cassandra last summer, in July," Tino said quietly, and this time Suki did not object to his speaking. "We don't know whether she'd had enough or whether something...happened to her. No one heard from her, or about her. I started to look out for a replacement. It was around that time that I remembered Suki."

"You already knew Suki?" Rowan asked. "How?"

"I was taken when I was five," Suki said, taking over from Tino. "I never thought I'd be coming home...but then Tino found me. He brought me back to my mother."

Tino nodded. "Suki was recovered by the Coven. Even then, we could see she was special. We could see why she'd been taken. Her gift was so strong—"

He stopped as Suki held up her hand for silence. Her head was tilted to one side, causing her short, white-blond hair to skim her cheek.

"What is it?" Tino asked softly.

Suki's head straightened, and her eyes narrowed. "Seems one of us has been careless tonight."

"What do you mean?" Sparrow asked.

Suki's eyes shifted across all of them in turn. "If I'm not mistaken, we were all told to come alone."

Tino's head snapped up. "That's right. What's the problem?"

"We've been followed."

❧❦❧

Still crouching behind the trough, Tanya began to shiver. The night was none too warm, and the new arrivals were unnerving her.

"Who are these people?" Fabian whispered.

"Only one way to find out," Tanya replied. "We need to get closer and try to hear what they're talking about."

"Or we could just go in and demand to know what's going on."

"I don't think that's a good idea. We don't know who they are or what they want with her—they could be dangerous."

"Shh," said Fabian. "Look, over there. There are two more people coming through the field, just about to go in. Look how soundlessly they move."

"How many is that?" Tanya wondered out loud, once the figures had crept out of sight. They heard the slight scuff of the door opening and closing.

"There're seven of them in there now, including Rowan," Fabian said. "How many more will come?"

The door scraped again and three figures came into view at the side.

"They're leaving!" Fabian hissed.

"We're going to have to follow them," said Tanya,

❦ 53 ❦

beginning to edge out from behind the trough. She stopped when she saw that the figures were walking. "They're coming this way!"

"Get down and keep quiet," said Fabian. "We'll follow once they've passed."

Tanya hunched down behind the filthy trough, pressing her back against it and pulling Oberon toward her. The first they heard of the approaching strangers was the hissing of their breath in the night air and the whispering of their voices.

"...Not far away," said a girl's unfamiliar voice. "Nearby...I can sense it."

Tanya turned to Fabian. His pale eyes were wide. The strangers were too close now, the trough the only thing separating them from Tanya and Fabian. When it was heaved from behind them, both fell back onto the soft ground with a shout, and Oberon ran for the trees, his leash trailing behind him.

Rough hands hauled Tanya up by the shoulder, forcing her to turn around. A hulk of a man held her effortlessly, unaffected by her struggles. Beside her, another man, similar in size to her captor, held Fabian tightly. Tanya's knees buckled as she saw a huge sword at his side. Both of the men were fey.

A slight girl with white-blond hair stood a little way back.

"They're only kids, Suki," the man holding Tanya told her. His voice sounded unusual, and when Tanya looked up she saw that he was missing some of his front teeth. "What are we going to do with them?"

"I don't care if they're just kids," Suki answered abruptly. "They were spying on us and we need to know why." She jerked her head toward Fabian. "I recognize him—he was with Red when I delivered the message—but it doesn't explain why he's here now. Samson, bring them both in. Victor, you go and get the mutt. In a moment or two, it'll recover its courage, so watch yourself."

Victor obediently handed Fabian to Samson, who proceeded to drag both captives toward the stone building.

"Who are you?" Fabian said to the girl, but he was shaken silent.

Twisting in Samson's grip, Tanya saw Victor heading toward the trees, where, sure enough, Oberon had emerged, snarling.

"Don't you touch my dog!" she yelled just as Samson's hand shifted from her shoulder to her mouth, cutting her voice off. She managed to catch a glimpse of Oberon bolting toward Victor before Samson steered her in the opposite direction. They stumbled over the uneven field until they reached the door of the barn.

"I've got them," Samson announced.

⟐

The door swung open, pushed from within, and Tanya and Fabian were herded through, with Suki close behind. Inside, Tanya saw four others: a man, two boys...and Rowan. She stared at them, plainly horrified.

The door closed behind them as Victor came in last, holding a snapping, growling Oberon at arm's length on his leash. He handed him to Tanya.

"Calm the dog down."

"Why should I?" Tanya demanded.

She caught Rowan's subtle nod and grudgingly took the leash, crouching to put her arms around Oberon. He stopped growling immediately and pressed himself into her, quivering.

Samson guffawed. "After all that—his bark's worse than his bite!"

The man with the mismatched eyes next to Rowan stepped closer, not joining in with the laughter.

"Who are you? Why were you out there?"

Tanya hesitated. She had no idea what to tell him. Whatever she said could endanger them all— including Rowan.

"They're with Red," Suki said, folding her arms.

"They're my friends, Tino," said Rowan. "They must have followed me. We can trust them. Just let them go." She faced Tanya and Fabian and spoke urgently. "You don't want to get involved in this. Don't ask me to explain. Go home."

"I don't think so," said Tino. "They're not going anywhere until we find out what they're doing here."

"And we're not going anywhere until we find out what you want with Red!" said Fabian through clenched teeth.

Tanya glanced at Rowan. Her lack of reaction to being called by her old alias told Tanya that these people knew her as "Red," and she guessed that Fabian's use of it had been intentional. Given that the group members were making no effort to conceal their names, she quickly concluded that all of them were using aliases and decided that, for now, it was safer not to use Rowan's real name.

Tino's eyes slid over them in assessment.

"At least we agree on one thing." He turned toward Rowan. "What have you told them?"

"Nothing," she replied curtly. "I know the rules."

"Seems you're not too good at keeping them, though," Suki put in.

Rowan bristled but continued to direct her words at Tino. "I've done my best. But it's not exactly easy when you send messengers in broad daylight—*noticeable* messengers. You were asking for trouble."

"You mean Suki in Tickey End?" Tino asked.

"Of course I mean her. She stuck out like a sore thumb."

"Red's telling the truth," Fabian said quietly. "I was there. It rattled her. We knew something wasn't right, so we followed her tonight. She never told us a thing."

"So what *do* they know about you, Red?" Tino asked. "Because one thing's obvious." He tilted his head in Tanya's direction.

Rowan nodded. "She has the second sight."

"But the boy...?"

"No. But he knows. He's used something before, a tonic to allow him to see fairies temporarily."

"Do they know about your brother?"

A look of pain crossed Rowan's face but she kept her voice neutral.

"They know everything except my link to you. I kept my word."

Tino nodded slowly. "And what of your brother?" he asked. "Have you given up on finding him? Or are you so cozy in your nice new home that you've forgotten about him?"

The scruffy blond boy shook his head. "Give her a break." He spoke with a strong Northern accent.

Rowan shot him a grateful look. "It's not like that. I...I found him."

There was a shift in the barn at this information, and a few low murmurs from everyone except Tino. He hadn't moved, hadn't reacted.

"I got into the fairy realm," Rowan continued, and Tanya could see her struggling to keep her composure. "I went to the courts and bargained for his return. They set me a task."

"What kind of task?" Tino asked.

"There was a bracelet. A charm bracelet, based on the thirteen treasures. They split the charms up and hid them in our world. I had to find them all." She gestured to Tanya and Fabian. "With their help, I did. But the whole thing was a setup. I found out that James isn't really my brother...he's my cousin. The woman I grew up believing to be my aunt is really my mother. And James didn't even recognize me. He was happy where he was, with a fey family who had lost their own son, who loved him. James was a replacement. So...I left him there." She paused as Tino's lips pressed into a disapproving line, yet he remained silent. "Afterward, I was given a chance... a chance of a new life off the streets, with a family that understood me. A family that had already helped. So I grabbed it. That's why I didn't answer your messages, and why I've avoided you."

"So what's changed?" Tino asked. "Why did you suddenly decide to come tonight?"

"Because I owe it to you—and to myself—to tell the truth. I don't want to be part of this anymore. I want...I want *out*."

Whispers and gasps rippled around the stone building. Again, Tino did not react.

"I heard something about a girl who'd humiliated the Unseelie leader a few months back," he murmured. "Not a widely known story, but one that was doing the rounds nonetheless, and gathering momentum. Only ever spoken about in trusted company, of course. And when I heard it, well, I wondered..." He smiled. "It was you, wasn't it? You stirred up quite a storm, so to speak. The worst winter on record, according to the mortal news reports, for six decades. Snow, hail, and floods all the way up until the Seelie Court resumed power in May."

"I heard that story," said Victor. "That was *her*?"

"She obviously drew attention to herself," said a

new voice from the other side of the building. The boy with untidy black hair rose to his feet. So far, he'd sat silently in the corner and not said a word. He wore trousers of burgundy and black, patterned with horizontal stripes. They were too short for him, giving the impression that he'd had a growth spurt and shot up unexpectedly. He looked older than the scruffy boy and Rowan; probably about sixteen or seventeen. He had a sly manner that Tanya immediately disliked.

"You think the winter king will have forgotten her?" the boy continued. "If she wants to leave, then let her. It's more dangerous to keep her in. For all we know she could have led them straight to us."

"I agree with Crooks," Suki said. "We should let her go—find someone to replace her."

Tino shook his head, frowning. "That's not how it works. We all take risks, and we all pose a threat. Any one of us could end up in a situation that compromises our safety. We don't abandon each other. We stick together."

"Crooks and Suki are probably right," Rowan protested. "I've already crossed the courts once—"

"You'd love it to be that simple, wouldn't you?" Tino retorted, his eyes flashing. "Sorry, but it's not going to be. Your search may have ended, Red, but there are others that are ongoing."

"The changelings," Tanya whispered, finally getting it. "These are her contacts—the people who make the switches."

Fabian gulped.

"I know that," hissed Rowan. "I did my bit, remember? Risked my neck for months on end, just like we all did. I knew those children were nothing to do with me, yet still I helped. Took on a few of the jobs no one else wanted too, if I remember right!"

"Exactly," Tino snapped. "And ask yourself why that is." He stopped suddenly, as if keeping himself in check. An awkward silence filled the building.

Suki was the one to break it. "So why is it, exactly?"

Rowan and Tino glared at each other, neither saying a word. But Tanya had a sudden inkling of what had been coming next, and why Tino had cut off what he was about to say.

It was because Rowan was the best. Out of them all, she was—or had been—the best at what she did. But even though Tino didn't want to say it in front of the others, it was clear they already knew it. As Tanya glanced from one face to the next, she saw the recognition of Rowan's talent there in all of them, whether through jealousy, resentment, admiration, or acceptance. Whatever the others felt, Tino didn't want to let Rowan go.

And he wasn't going to release her without a fight.

5

There were two new arrivals following Rowan and Tino's heated exchange. They were an elderly, red-faced man, oddly named Nosebag, and a wiry black woman with a shaved head and a thin, twisted leg. She moved slowly, and with the aid of a stick. Apart from her face, every inch of flesh on show was heavily tattooed. It soon became apparent that she was mute, for she communicated in simple gestures, and any questions directed her way were phrased to require a nod, shrug, or shake of the head by way of answer.

"Who's she?" Fabian asked, nodding toward the woman.

"We call her Fix," said Rowan. "She had polio as a child, in case you're wondering."

The small building felt crowded now, with eleven people jammed inside it. Yet still Tino waited.

Evidently, more were expected. The night was ticking away, and soon the group broke into small huddles.

Rowan stood protectively by Tanya and Fabian. They were joined by Sparrow. Suki and Crooks stood on the far side, making no attempt to hide that their conversation was about Tanya and Fabian.

Tino, Nosebag, Victor, Samson, and Fix stood talking quietly together, their eyes occasionally straying to the two intruders.

"Do you think they're going to let us go?" Tanya asked. "What are they going to do with us?"

"I don't know," Rowan muttered. "You've caused a lot of trouble by coming here tonight. You shouldn't have followed me."

"And you should have told us what was going on," Fabian retorted. "Then we wouldn't have needed to follow you."

"It would have helped if you'd stayed out of it," said Rowan. "The less you know, the better for everyone." She looked at Sparrow. "Who are we waiting for now? I just want to get this over with."

"Let's see," said Sparrow, glancing about. "Dawn's still not here. Neither are Peg, Merchant, or Cobbler. I think Tino's getting worried."

Tino's eyes were fixed on the door and his foot was tapping a little jig. "We'll give them another ten minutes," he said. "Then we'll have to start without them. Something must have cropped up for the four of them to miss this."

"And we still need to decide what to do with *them*," said Suki, nodding to Tanya and Fabian.

Tanya felt her stomach twist into knots. She wished Sparrow would leave them and stand with one of the other groups so she and Fabian could talk to Rowan properly, but she guessed he had been given some unspoken instruction to remain in earshot of them.

"Red," she whispered. "What do you think they're going to do with us? And how...how did that girl, Suki, know we were outside? I heard her say something as they came over to our hiding place. She said, 'I sense it.'"

"And something else," Fabian put in. "She knew Oberon was about to attack, just before he did. How did she know that?"

Rowan glanced at Sparrow worriedly before answering.

"She just...Suki knows things. Before they happen."

"You mean she's psychic?" Tanya asked.

"Yes."

"So she knows when children have been stolen and replaced by fairies?" Tanya asked. "Is that it?"

"Sometimes," said Rowan shortly. "Among other things. Stop asking questions."

"You didn't answer our question about what they're going to do with us," Fabian persisted.

Rowan looked at Sparrow again. "You've probably got a better idea than I do—you've been... involved for longer."

Sparrow nodded, his hair flopping over his face.

"He'll let them go. But maybe not tonight—"

"*What?* I can't go back without them!" Rowan hissed. "He's got to let them go."

"He will," Sparrow repeated. "But he's not going to risk them talking about what—and who—they've seen tonight, now is he?"

"What's he talking about, Red?" Fabian asked fearfully. "We won't say anything to anyone, you know that! Tell them we can keep a secret!"

"It's not as simple as that," said Sparrow. "You might not *mean* to tell no one else what you've seen, like. But if the wrong person was to find you...knew you'd been with us..." He left the sentence hanging.

"If someone...*made* us talk, you mean," said Tanya in a small voice.

"Exactly," said Sparrow. "What you don't know can't hurt you."

"But we don't know anything, not really," said Fabian.

"What you do know is too much," Sparrow replied. "And it can't be risked. My guess is that Tino'll see to it that you can't remember nothing."

"He'll wipe our memories?" Tanya asked.

"Just the memory of us, I meant," Sparrow said quickly.

"He's not doing anything with my memories," said Fabian. "I'll fight anyone who tries!"

"Calm down," said Rowan. "I'll talk to him. Just give me a minute. I need to figure out what I can say that'll persuade him to let you go." She raised her hands to her temples. "And to let *me* go."

"Then you've got a job on your hands," said Sparrow. He lowered his voice. "I can understand, though, even if they can't. Most of us, well, we ain't got nothing to go back to, or to change for. But you— you've been given a second chance." He gave a slow, sad smile, revealing his chipped tooth and the dimple in his cheek. "I was angry with you at first. I felt like you'd deserted us. But now, I don't blame you for wanting to take that chance."

Tanya rubbed her hands together, trying to warm them. The night had grown colder, and now her breath was clouding the air. Through the gap in the roof she saw bright stars peppering the sky. The heat from the long walk had left her limbs. Now they just felt sore and achy, and she knew Fabian must feel the same.

Nosebag shuffled over, eyeing her sympatheti- cally. "Cold, are ye?" he said.

Tanya nodded. The old man reached into the pockets of his overcoat and removed a cloth bag tied with string. Shaking it open, he offered it to her. "Just the thing for it," he said.

Tanya looked at Rowan for reassurance.

"It's all right," she said. "You can trust Nosebag."

Tanya reached into the bag and her fingers found something small and rough. She pulled it out. "What is it?"

Nosebag chuckled and offered the bag to Fabian. "Get it down ye—it'll put some fire in ye belly!"

"It's ginger," Fabian whispered as Nosebag walked away. "Raw ginger. You need to peel off the skin, and then you can eat it."

The smell of the ginger was warming in itself, but when Tanya nibbled a piece her eyes watered. Fire was certainly a good description. In a minute or so a blazing, delicious heat spread from her mouth to her tummy, and her mouth tingled with the spicy flavor.

"Here," said Rowan, throwing the fox-skin coat around Tanya's shoulders. "You get under it as well, Fabian, if you're cold."

Fabian obliged, huddling close to Tanya beneath the fox fur and coughing a little from the strength of the ginger.

"That's an unusual coat," said Suki, her eyes narrowed. The other Coven members turned to look.

"What *is* that thing?" Sparrow said in disgust. "It's hideous—the poor foxes." He reached out and gingerly touched one of the fox ears above Tanya's face. Looking past him she saw that the coat had drawn curious glances from a few of the others too.

"I know," Rowan answered. "You're right, it is gruesome. But I—"

"Then why wear it?" Suki said cattily.

Tino came closer, his eyes lingering on the coat with interest.

"Because . . . it's not just a coat," said Rowan.

Tino's eyes glinted. "Show us."

Rowan held out her hand without enthusiasm,

and Tanya and Fabian slid out of the coat and passed it to her. With a practiced touch, she flicked it around her shoulders and hooked the clasp.

There was a unanimous intake of breath as the transformation took place. Rowan pranced about, weaving around people's legs, her fox senses heightened once more. Oberon gave a little whine as she approached, then, catching her scent, he relaxed and allowed his tail to thump.

Tino's mouth was still open as Rowan threw the coat off and resumed her true form again. She made to pass it back to Tanya and Fabian, but Tino reached for it.

"Where did you get this?" he asked, running his hands over the fur. "This level of glamour—it's not easy to come by."

"There was a cottage...in the fairy realm," Rowan said. "It belonged to a woman known as the Hedge-witch. When I went into the fairy realm to look for James, she captured me. Threw me in her cellar and kept me prisoner. I didn't know what she wanted from me at first...but there were two others being held prisoner too. One of them...well, he told me she was a glamour-maker. Not only that, but that she sold dark magic, and curses too."

She paused and swallowed. She had not wanted to dredge this up, even though she'd known it was inevitable. The entire group was silent, waiting for her to continue.

"Go on," said Suki.

"She was an old woman when she first got me into the cottage. But then she pulled something out of her hair—another strand of hair that she'd tied into her own, looped with trinkets and charms. As soon as she took it out, she changed into someone else. The old woman was one of her captives—she'd been using her as a disguise. That's how she fooled her victims.

"She changed her disguises regularly. I don't know why—maybe they only lasted for a short time, or maybe she just did it to throw off anyone or anything that suspected her. That's what she wanted me for. Her new disguise. She was going to make a glamour...pretend to be me, so she could fool people."

"So the coat was one of her creations?" Tino asked.

Rowan nodded. "There were animal skins everywhere. Hanging from the rafters. Some were dry. Others were still...fresh. Dripping with blood. The whole place smelled of death. There were animals in cages all around the cottage. Before I escaped I set them free."

"So how did you escape?" Crooks asked with interest, if not concern.

"She took some of my hair and a few drops of blood and started to chant. She was working some kind of spell. But what she didn't know, what she couldn't have known, is that she couldn't harm me with her magic. No one can."

Suki cocked a perfectly plucked eyebrow. "That's a bold statement, isn't it?"

"It's the truth," Rowan said simply. "The reason I can't be harmed by evil magic is because my name protects me. My name is Rowan." She paused for a moment, scanning their faces. Tino's smile was calculating. Suki scowled and averted her gaze. Apart from Sparrow, who had known her real name after seeing a missing persons picture in a newspaper when they first met, she had never told any of the Coven her real name, and she did not know their true names either. It was safer that way. And judging from the reactions in the room, Sparrow had kept her secret.

"When the Hedgewitch tried to use her magic to harm me, it backfired," Rowan continued. "She'd started to look like me...but the change killed her, right in front of my eyes. I didn't know it was my name protecting me then, didn't know what had made it happen. But the witch made it clear that she thought I'd poisoned her somehow. After that, we ransacked the cottage and got back our belongings. That's when I saw the coat. I didn't realize what it did until I tried it on—it was the only one there that was enchanted. We knew then that she must have made it for someone, someone coming to collect it. We left pretty quickly after that and made our way to the courts."

"*We?*" Tino asked. "You and the two other prisoners?"

Rowan's eyes dropped to the ground. "No. I only left with one of the other prisoners." She nodded at Fabian. "His father."

"What happened to the other one?" said Samson.

Rowan cleared her throat. "We—" She stopped and corrected herself. "I left him there. In the cellar."

"You didn't help him?" Suki asked incredulously. "Why not?"

"I found out that he was there the night my bro— the night James was taken. He watched it happen and did nothing. I wanted to punish him. So I made sure he couldn't leave," Rowan said. Her face started to tingle with heat. She couldn't work out whether it was shame or anger. Maybe it was both. "I found the key that would free him. I threw it away. For all I know, he's still there."

The stunned silence that followed was broken by a low whistle from Samson.

"That's cold," he said. "You're cold, Red."

"She's *brilliant*," Tino said, laughing harshly.

"I'm not proud of what I did," Rowan muttered, unable to meet anyone's eyes now. "If I could go back and change it—"

"You'd do the exact same thing," Tino cut in. "You had your chance against one of the very people who'd wronged you, and you took it. You had your revenge. How many of us can say the same?" He grinned triumphantly. "There's no shame in it. This is another victory for the Coven and a lesson to those in the changeling trade that for every child they take, they'll pay the price. You see, this is *exactly* why we need you, Rowan. Why I can't let you go. Your ruthlessness is one of our biggest assets. And that coat—it's going to be one of our most valuable tools of the trade—"

"You're not listening to me," said Rowan. "I'm *not* proud of how I behaved. I *would* change it if I had a second chance." She gave a bitter laugh. "I feel guilty for what I did every single day. But I have to live with it."

Tino shrugged. "What's done is done. Think about this. You're stronger now. More powerful than we could ever have known! Think, just *think,* how much more you could do for us now that you've no emotional ties clouding your judgment or weighing on you. How much more effective you could be—"

"My *emotional ties* are what drove me to do the things I did!" Rowan spat, her anger surfacing at last. "Without them I'd never have got involved! Finding James was all that mattered, the only thing that kept me going. And when I did find him nothing turned out the way I thought it would."

"But you can still help others," Tino insisted. "There's no reason why you should stop now."

"There's every reason why I should stop! Haven't you heard what I've been trying to tell you? I don't want to live like that anymore. I'm... I'm happy."

"Just go," said Suki, sounding bored. "You can leave the coat, though." Her eyes lingered on it greedily.

"No, I can't," said Rowan. "Because it only works for me. So I'm keeping it."

"How *convenient*," Suki said. "You won't mind if I put that to the test?"

"Be my guest." Rowan took the coat from Tino and threw it at Suki.

She caught it, scowling, and tugged it around her shoulders. When she hooked the clasp, nothing happened.

"I don't understand," she muttered, looking inside the coat. "There must be something else, something that makes it work."

"The coat was made to fuse itself to the first person who wore it," said Rowan. "That person was me. So for anyone else who puts it on, it doesn't work." She held out her hand. "So I'll have it back now."

Sulkily, Suki took off the coat and returned it.

Tino rubbed a hand over his unshaven face. "I'll make a deal with you."

Rowan shook her head. "No. No more deals. I'm finished with all this. I'll never talk of you to anyone, you have my word. But for me, this is over."

"There's still the matter of your friends," Tino began, but he was interrupted by the door scraping open again.

Two people bolted inside, a man and a woman.

"What kept you?" said Tino, his mood clearly having taken a turn for the worse since Rowan's outburst. "You're almost an hour late."

"Something's happened," said the man. He was in his late twenties, with dark looks and a stubborn set to his jaw.

"What?" said Tino. "Where are the others? Aren't they with you?"

"No. Peg and I just came from the Burrow. We'd arranged to meet Dawn and Cobbler, then come here together."

Tanya ran through the names in her head. From what she could work out, this man must be the one they'd called Merchant. Peg, the woman, was very old, though still sprightly. She stood to the side, a clawlike hand clutching an old blanket in place around her, and her wrinkled mouth was pursing and puckering like it had a life of its own. She spotted Tanya and Fabian huddled next to Rowan and emitted a strange squawk.

"Who's them?" she demanded, pointing with her other hand. As she spoke, Tanya saw there was only a single tooth in her mouth, perched above her lower lip like a peg on a gummy washing line. "Who are they? New 'uns?"

"I'll explain in a minute, Peg," Tino said. "I just need to hear what's happened to the others." He turned back to Merchant. "Carry on."

"When we arrived at Dawn's, it was empty. There was no sign of Dawn or Cobbler anywhere. We didn't think anything was out of the ordinary at first, we just thought there had been a mix-up, and maybe we were meant to meet them at Cobbler's place. But as we left, Peg noticed that the curtains were open. It was early afternoon." He paused. "We all know Dawn never has her curtains open during the day."

"Why not?" Tanya whispered to Rowan.

"Dawn has a rare medical condition," Rowan whispered back. "She can't go out in the sunlight. It makes her ill, and exposure to it could kill her."

"At that point we still weren't too worried," Merchant continued. "It could have been that she was somewhere else and would be returning after dark. So we went to Cobbler's. We thought she'd be with him."

"And they weren't there?" Tino interjected.

A crease had appeared in Merchant's forehead, and a strand of his dark hair was stuck to his skin with sweat. "No." His voice was tense. "There was no sign of either of them, but...but the place was a mess. Furniture was broken, mirrors and crocks smashed up. I wondered if someone had broken in, looking for something. I checked his caravan out back. It was clean, ready to be used again, and everything was in place. That's when I started to think whoever had been there was looking for Cobbler. So I began looking closer for clues...and I found...I found..."

"Blood," Peg finished, in her clacking, toothless voice. Her hand trembled and she tucked it inside her blanket.

Merchant nodded, his dark skin ashen. "On the

doorframe on the way out, there was the tiniest smear of blood. Whatever's happened to them, they've come to harm. I don't know whether someone's holding them, or whether they're even still alive...but I think..." He hesitated. "What if someone knows about the thirteen secrets and is hunting us?"

6

Uneasy whispers broke out among the Coven, only halting when Tino raised his hand for silence.

"Just calm down," he said. "We've no reason to panic. For all we know there's a perfectly good explanation—Cobbler or Dawn could have had some kind of accident and gone for help. Even if someone did come for them, how do we know the blood belonged to Cobbler or Dawn?" he continued. "It could easily have been the intruder's."

"All the same, I don't like it," Samson said. "Something's off."

Tino began to pace. "I'll go back to Dawn's tonight, and to the Burrow tomorrow. See if I can find anything, or if they've turned up. Suki, I'll need you with me. You might be able to pick something up. Victor, you'd better come too." He paused suddenly and looked at Suki. "You've sensed nothing about them so far, nothing amiss?"

Suki shook her head, and a slash of her pale fringe fell forward over her eyes.

"No, nothing."

"Good. That's promising, at least. The rest of you continue as normal, but stay in touch, and keep an eye out for anything—or anyone—suspicious." He stopped pacing and clasped his hands together. "Now. There's nothing else we can do for them tonight. So let's get down to business.

"First up. This one's pretty straightforward— we've found a child who went missing two weeks ago. The changeling left in its place is not a fairy child, but an ancient fairy nearing the end of its days. It wants to be looked after. For this reason, the changeling is still with the family, so as not to raise their suspicions, although the mother noticed right away how ugly the baby had suddenly become. A fey woman found the human child abandoned in some woods. Luckily, she suspected it was a switch and the news got through to us. She's been caring for the child while we were tracking the family down."

"The fairy left the child to die?" said Nosebag, shaking his tufty head sadly. "What are we going to do with the wicked old cretin?"

"If I had my way I'd return the favor and leave him out in the woods to take his chances, like he left the child," Tino replied. "But it's not to be. The fairy woman fostering the child has agreed to nurse the changeling until it passes, which is more than it deserves. Like I said, this should be fairly simple—a two-person job. Crooks, I'm going to need you to gain entry into the family's house. It shouldn't be difficult for you. I want you, Fix, to prepare a sleeping draught to give to the changeling so that it won't create a disturbance during the switch. One of you will need to bring the human child to the house." He handed Crooks a scrap of paper. "Here's the address. You don't need me to explain any more—you two can work out the logistics of your plan together. Now, unless either of you has any updates, you can leave."

Hurried good-byes were exchanged, then Crooks and Fix left the barn.

"The second case tonight is trickier," Tino continued. "Suki met with a second-sighted boy who believes his mother has been switched for a changeling."

Fabian prodded Rowan in the back. "His *mother*? I thought only children were taken!"

"Quiet," said Tino coldly, before Rowan could answer. "I'm talking. Now, as we know, adult changelings are far less common than children and babies. And because we're dealing with an adult fairy, things are more complex and often a lot more dangerous. That's why we can't afford to get this wrong. We only get one chance, because if we mess it up, we could endanger this boy and the rest of his family. The boy noticed a change in his mother's behavior a few weeks ago but put it down to the fact that she'd been ill. But things have been getting stranger, and the woman has been acting increasingly out of character." He nodded to Suki.

"The time I had with him was brief, but I've organized another meeting with him to get more information," she said. "From what he's told me already it sounds genuine, and the boy's guardian—a goblin, from the description—hasn't been seen since the changeling came into the household. I didn't say it to the boy, but chances are, the guardian is dead."

"Has he done the iron test?" Peg asked.

"Touching a person with something iron," Rowan murmured to Tanya. "If they're fey, it'll burn, and they won't be able to hide their reaction."

"No," said Suki. "I didn't tell him to do anything like that. If she is a changeling and she knows he's on to her it could accelerate the situation. We need to be sure and we need to know what she wants. I've told him to keep monitoring her behavior and to act as normally as he can."

"How old is the boy?" Samson asked.

"Eleven," Suki answered. "But it's not just the boy who could be at risk. There's his father, who seems oblivious, and the boy's two-year-old sister."

"How are they at risk?" Tanya blurted out, forgetting herself. She cringed as Tino stared at her, but to her surprise, Suki responded.

"We don't know that they are yet. But in cases of adult changelings, they've usually developed a fixation with someone in the family. If the changeling is a grieving mother, they can latch on to a child bearing some resemblance to the one they've lost, disposing of the real mother to get to it. Sometimes it's an obsession with the person they're impersonating; if they're talented in some way, or beautiful. Until we know more we can't decide how to act." She sighed, her sharp features softening. "And this boy is scared. He's frightened out of his mind, which makes me think he's sure about what he's seen. We need to find out more from him, although if he's right, this is going to be tough."

"That's where you come in," said Tino, turning his gaze on Rowan. "And with that coat..."

"Me? Wait a minute, I've just told you, I'm not—"

"Hear me out," said Tino. "I know what you've said, but listen. I still think, no matter what you say, that this is something you have an instinct for. Even after James—this is what you do. Now, if you'll take this one last job, and you still want out afterward, then I'll let you go without question."

"And if I don't take it?"

"Then you'll never know if it's what you really want," Tino answered softly. "And any ties you have with us are gone for good."

"That's sort of the point," said Rowan sarcastically, but her voice trembled at the same time.

"There's still time to think about it before you make your decision," Tino coaxed. "Like I said, Suki's arranged another meeting with the boy tomorrow. If you want to, you can be there."

Rowan closed her eyes. "There's a baby involved?"

Tanya's head shot up in amazement. "Rowan!" she whispered. "You're not seriously considering this? What's got into you?"

Rowan opened her eyes and focused on Tino. "I haven't agreed to anything," she said firmly. "But if I were to, then I'd have two conditions."

Tino cocked his head to one side. "Name them."

"One, if I decide to meet this boy I'm under no obligation to go through with it after hearing what he has to say. And two, if I get involved, you let my friends leave with me tonight without doing *anything* to them. I mean it. It's my fault they're here, and I'll take full responsibility if anything should happen to the Coven because of what they know." She glanced at Tanya and Fabian, then back to Tino. "And that's the measure of how much I trust them. I trust them with my life."

Tino studied the three of them in turn. Rowan stood her ground, but behind her she could feel Fabian trembling, and she didn't know whether it was from cold or fear.

"You know," Tino said finally, "I believe you. And if these two are to keep their memories of us, then I think that could be put to good use." A strange light had ignited behind his eyes, one that made Rowan's skin prickle.

"What are you talking about?"

"We can use them," said Tino. "This boy we spoke of is eleven." He trained his eyes on Fabian. "How old are you?"

"Thirteen," Fabian replied in a small voice.

"And you?" Tino looked to Tanya.

"Fourteen."

"Perfect. If necessary, they can get into the house under the pretense of being the boy's school friends. If the mother is an impostor, she won't know any different."

"No," said Rowan, livid. "Absolutely not. You could use me for that, or Sparrow—"

"Wouldn't work," said Tino. "One, you're both too old to pass for the same age as this boy. And two, you both know and have seen too much." He nodded to Tanya and Fabian. "These two look the part. They look *innocent*."

"You know I can't agree to it," said Rowan. "Look, just let them go and I'll come to your meeting. They don't need to be involved."

"But I want to be," said Tanya.

"So do I," Fabian added.

Rowan turned on them both. "Don't start. It's not going to happen."

"I think we deserve a say in what we do," said Tanya fiercely. "And if it means helping you, then I'm in." She glanced at Fabian. "We both are."

"Tino, a word outside?" Rowan said coldly.

Tino smiled and opened the door. "After you."

They stepped out into the night, leaving Tanya and Fabian alone with the remaining members of the Coven.

"What time is it?" Tanya whispered to Fabian, after a couple of minutes had elapsed.

Fabian looked at his watch. "Nearly half-past two. What do you think they're talking about out there?"

Tanya shrugged miserably. "Rowan's probably trying to convince him to let us walk out of this mess. She's right. We shouldn't have come. All along she was trying to do the right thing, and all we've done is made it harder for her to leave. We should have trusted her."

Rowan and Tino returned a few minutes later. "We're leaving," Rowan muttered, refusing to look at them. "Now."

Tino moved aside as they stepped out of the barn into the chilly night.

Without a backward glance, Rowan set off quickly, heading toward the gap in the hedge they'd come through.

"Slow down!" Tanya hissed, running to keep up. She cast a fearful glance back and saw Tino's outline, perfectly still, outside the barn door, watching them leave. A shudder went through her and she turned back around.

"What have you done, Rowan?" Fabian asked. "What have you agreed to?"

Rowan squeezed through the gap. Tanya and Fabian followed. On the other side, Rowan had put the fox-skin coat on and transformed by the time they and Oberon had come through.

"I've agreed to do what he wants," she said flatly. "I'm in."

At eight o'clock the following morning, after Florence had hollered herself hoarse, Tanya, Fabian, and Rowan each managed to crawl out of their beds and down the stairs to the kitchen for breakfast.

"I don't know what's got into you three this morning," she grumbled, setting plates and cups on the table. "You all appear to be half-asleep."

"That's because I am." Fabian rubbed his eyes, unsuccessfully trying to stifle yet another yawn. This in turn set Tanya off yawning, and then Rowan. After trying to resist, Nell also caught it, much to Fabian's amusement.

"And what were you doing, that all three of you had such little sleep?" Florence inquired, her gray eyes narrowed as she poured herself some tea.

"Reading," came the unanimous response, earning a disbelieving sniff from Florence.

Tanya watched through bleary eyes as Fabian picked up his spoon and began to bash at a boiled egg a little harder than was necessary. The hearthfay, who had been devotedly keeping it warm, unbeknownst to him, ducked out of the way with a squeak and fled. Tanya's eyes darted to Rowan. So far she had hardly said a word to anyone, and sat staring at her plate, chewing halfheartedly on a piece of toast.

Warwick came through to the kitchen with the morning's mail. After helping himself to the newspaper he tossed the rest into the middle of the old oak table, where it landed with a slap. He passed General Carver's cage, which was open to form a perch at the top, where the parrot sat, leaning out in earnest for a peck as Warwick went by. Unfortunately for the General, the frequency of the pecks meant that Warwick was well practiced in squeezing past unscathed.

"Tricketty," the General squawked. "Tricketty, tricketty..."

Fabian was the first to notice the blue leaflet tucked in among the drab brown and white envelopes on the table. He pulled it from the pile and studied it, then showed it to Tanya. Bold, decorative violet letters stretched in an arched banner at the top of the page, spelling out VALENTINO'S CIRCUS. She skimmed the rest of the page and looked at Rowan. Her lack of reaction told Tanya that the leaflet had been expected. The knowledge sent goose bumps skittering down

Tanya's arms and prompted a memory of something Rowan had told her before, when she had been hiding out in the secret tunnels below the manor.

There's a circus that'll be passing through, Rowan had said. *I have a contact who travels with them, a fey man....*

Tanya leaned forward for a closer look. To the left of the banner, drawn as though holding its edge, stood a man in a top hat and elegant coattails, his face obscured by the hat's shadow. Drawn behind him was a big top in vivid stripes of mauve and silver. In the darkness of the tent opening, a list of dates was printed, along with directions. It was simple, yet striking. In a heartbeat Tanya understood that *this* was the circus Rowan had spoken of. Its arrival—and that of the Coven—was no coincidence. The two were connected.

"Oh, yes," Nell commented, craning her neck to read. "I saw the circus folk arriving on Halfpenny Field yesterday, when I took the bus. I've never seen them there before. Usually they pitch further down on Bramley's cornfields, don't they?"

Warwick lowered his newspaper. "I heard they couldn't pitch there this year. Not after the fields were so badly flooded—they'd never get the caravans through. It's still pretty boggy down there." He glanced casually at Rowan, who avoided his eyes. "The Halfpenny Field is one of the only ones higher up that isn't still like a swamp."

"Can we go?" Rowan asked, scouring the leaflet. She seemed alert all of a sudden; the cobwebs of sleep had been brushed away. "It says the grand opening is this evening at seven o'clock. We could take the bus and still make it back before dark."

Warwick looked surprised. "I don't see why not." He looked at Florence, who gave a distracted nod as she opened one envelope after another.

"I haven't been to a circus since I was a little girl," said Nell, looking hopefully at Rowan.

"That's a shame," Rowan replied, seeming not to notice the hint. But when she looked up at Tanya and Fabian her unspoken message was clear: they needed to go alone. "We can go to buy tickets in Tickey End this afternoon," she said. "Then we can walk the rest of the way to Halfpenny Field. It's not far from the square."

Nell sat back in her seat huffily, and Tanya felt a small pang of guilt. Rowan was the first to excuse herself from the table, heading back to her room. A few minutes later, Tanya also got up, grabbing Oberon's leash from the back door and heading out toward the brook.

The fresh morning air and brisk walk woke her up, and as she started back to the manor, she wondered what the circus—and the rest of the evening—would have in store.

❦

That afternoon, Tanya, Rowan, and Fabian were seated in a little booth at the back of Rosie Beak's noisy tea shop in Tickey End. On the table in front of them was the leaflet that had come in the morning's mail and three tickets.

"I hope Tino's going to pay me back for these," Rowan grumbled, smoothing the tickets.

"We didn't have to go to the circus," said Fabian. "We could've just pretended."

"No, we couldn't," Rowan replied. "If Warwick suspects anything, the tickets provide us with an alibi. Besides, I don't want to hang around for ages doing nothing while we're waiting for the others."

"So who *are* the others?" Fabian asked. "And why does Tino want you all to meet at the circus?"

Rowan's face darkened. "You know I can't talk about them."

"Surely you can tell us a little?" Tanya said. "Like how you met them. And some of them aren't even human." She glanced about and lowered her voice. "They're fey. I don't understand why they'd be involved in this."

"A few of the Coven members, including Tino, are part of the circus," Rowan said, relenting. "I met Sparrow first."

"That's the scruffy boy?"

Rowan nodded. "He was on the streets, like me, and still is, by the look of things. He was the one who gave me the name Red, because of my hair. He introduced me to Tino. The rest of them, apart from Suki, were already involved. Most of us have been affected by the changeling trade in some way."

Fabian frowned. "Even the fey ones?"

"Yes. Even fey people don't take kindly to their children being switched—if the children are loved. Tino lost a niece, Peg lost a son, and Merchant, a sister. But the brothers, Victor and Samson, and Dawn were all changelings themselves—they all grew up in a human family that wasn't their own."

"Dawn's one of the missing ones?" Tanya asked, and again, Rowan nodded.

"What about the other boy...Crooks?" Fabian asked. "Is he human?"

"Yes. Everyone apart from those I just mentioned is human." She blinked suddenly. "Except me, being half of each."

"I didn't like him," said Tanya. "Crooks, I mean."

"Not many of us do," said Rowan. "He's a professional thief—or at least, he was. He comes from a family of locksmiths. He was recruited after breaking in somewhere and accidentally witnessing a switch. Once Cobbler realized how useful he could be, he convinced him to join us—for a wage." She wrinkled her nose. "But I don't trust him." She stopped speaking and looked around.

"Did we *really* have to come here? We're getting stared at. I'm sure she remembers me, the old battle-ax."

Tanya glanced surreptitiously toward the counter. Rosie Beak and one of her cronies were having a whispered conversation, their gray heads bobbing and nodding like excitable pigeons. Every now and then one of them turned to look in the direction of the table where the three sat in a way that was not at all subtle.

Last summer, when Rowan had been on the run, Rosie Beak had provided the *Tickey End Gazette* with an eyewitness description after glimpsing her in the town.

"So what if old Nosey Beak *does* remember you?" asked Fabian, biting into a scone. With his finger he caught a mixture of cream and strawberry jam oozing out of the other side and popped that into his mouth too. "We're not doing anything wrong. Just having a nice, civilized tea"—he lifted a white china cup to his lips and sipped theatrically—"and one that doesn't taste like a grouchy old brownie, for once."

"All the same," Rowan growled below the clinking and clattering of crockery. "I wish we were somewhere else." She cast an impatient look at the clock on the wall.

"We've still got over an hour before the show begins," said Tanya.

"I'd rather wait on the field, then," Rowan retorted. "And you two are only coming to the circus. You're not coming to the meeting afterward."

"Yes, we are," said Fabian easily. "Otherwise we'll go back and tell Florence and Rose and my dad what you're up to."

Rowan glared at him. "Telling tales? I didn't think that was your style."

Fabian shrugged. "It is when it suits me." He pointed to the leaflet. "Anyway, why doesn't it list the acts? I thought circuses advertised their best acts on the posters and leaflets. It must be rubbish."

"That's where you're wrong," said Rowan, relaxing slightly. "There are three reasons why Tino doesn't advertise the acts anywhere. First, in case one of the performers is ill or has to cancel. He doesn't want customers to come away disappointed. Second, he doesn't want to make it easy for competing circuses to know exactly what he's got. And third, he likes the element of surprise."

"Huh," said Fabian, unconvinced. "He's good at coming up with excuses, this Tino, isn't he?"

"Very," Rowan agreed. "He has to be. But I promise you, you'll be impressed."

"How long does it last?" Tanya asked. "They're not cruel to the animals, are they?"

Rowan shook her head. "The show never uses performing animals. Just people. The only animals with the circus are the horses pulling the carts and caravans, and the pets of the performers, and they're all well cared for. It lasts for about an hour and a half."

At this Fabian looked even less impressed. "Some show this is going to be," he muttered.

Rowan's smile broadened. "Just you wait."

The lanes leading to Halfpenny Field were shaded and cool, and ahead they could see other groups of people walking in the same direction. On the field itself, a carpet path had been laid just beyond the wooden gate, and through it the field was bustling with activity.

People were milling everywhere, weaving in and out and around brightly colored tents. At the center of them all was the huge mauve and silver tent that was on the leaflets. It curved in a circle, dwarfing everything around it, and a line of people snaked back from the opening, waiting for the moment they could go in.

Beautiful Romany caravans were stationed on the field's edges in a kaleidoscope of color and pattern, and on the steps of some of the vans, the circus folk could be seen sitting and watching the approaching crowd of circus goers.

"They look like Mad Morag's caravan," Fabian said in awe. "But there are so many of them!"

"Look at all the other tents," said Tanya, craning her neck to read the wooden boards positioned outside each one. "Over there—Fortune Telling...and there, Curiosity Cabinet, Portrait Drawing—are they open now? Can we go in?"

Rowan shook her head. "They open after the main performance. Tino's noticed that most people are more likely to spend their money on the smaller attractions when they're still feeling excited after the bigger show. You can have a look around then."

They joined the end of the line, slowly shuffling forward to the opening as the people in front were admitted inside. Soon it was their turn, and as they reached the front a woman in an exquisite, sequined costume took their tickets from them and pointed them to their seats. She gave a faint nod as she met Rowan's eyes.

"Who was she?" Fabian asked as they went in and clambered up the steps of the tiered seating.

"Ariadne," Rowan answered as they took their seats. "She's been part of the circus for years. But she's not one of...*them*." She took a quick look around, but everyone in the surrounding seats was too involved in getting comfortable and attending to elderly relatives or young children to be interested in their conversation. It was rowdy inside and growing warmer as more people entered. Soon, almost every seat in the vast tent was filled, and the great opening swung closed with a swish.

Enough time passed for people to start fidgeting, and it was then that Tanya's eyes began wandering over the crowd, exploring the many people who had come to see the show. Hazarding a guess, she estimated that there were close to a thousand people in the audience.

Her eyes skimmed over various families: a young child crying and being comforted by his father; a large woman and a small, skinny man arguing over whose seats were whose; a little old lady having a fit of sneezing into her handkerchief.

Then her gaze fell upon a young boy sitting close to the front. Next to him sat a man who was obviously his father, for they looked very alike. Both had the same snub noses and wavy brown hair with a distinctive cowlick at the front. On the father's lap a small girl of about two years old wriggled and squawked, her own toffee-colored hair an unruly tangle. She erupted into peals of giggles, collapsing on her father's lap as he tickled her.

The boy stared straight ahead into the arena, taking no notice of the little girl's antics. At first Tanya wondered if he was feeling left out, but something about his expression made her think again. Was he simply excited about the circus, focusing on the moment it would begin? No, she decided. He looked solemn. Worried. Like something was gnawing away at him. And then the thought hit her.

"Rowan," she murmured, nudging her elbow to the left. "Look over there. That boy."

"What boy?"

"Straight ahead, in the third row back sitting next to the steps."

Fabian leaned over from Tanya's right. "What about him?"

"It's him, I'm sure of it. The boy Suki arranged the meeting with. Look, he's with his dad and a little girl, it must be the father and sister."

"It could be anyone," said Rowan, studying the family. "He could just be sulking about something."

"No. Look at his face. He's scared."

Rowan chewed her lip as she continued to watch the boy. "Well, I guess we'll be finding out soon enough."

The lights dimmed then, and their view of the boy was gone. A flurry of excited whispers filled the audience, and then a spotlight flicked on in the center of the arena. There, groomed and handsome, stood Tino, dressed in all his ringmaster's finery. His tawny hair was pulled back from his face and he wore a suit of black, embellished with glittering silver thread.

"Ladies and gentlemen," he called, in a voice quite different from his usual drawl. "I welcome you, one and all! This will be a night to remember—a fantastical feast for the eyes! Prepare to be mystified, and to marvel at what you're about to see... for what we are about to show you is that magic *does* truly exist!"

"And that's the beauty of it," Rowan murmured. "Half of it *is* magic, and no one even knows. It's magic disguised as a clever illusion. It's perfect."

With that, Tino swept out of the arena. The show began.

Dancers in dazzling costumes shimmered into the spotlight, each one's moves synchronized with the rest. Colorful feather plumes in their hair swirled and glided in a mesmerizing way as they whipped and twirled. Too quickly, they were gone, and the spotlight moved up to highlight several trapeze artists swinging and soaring through the air. Tanya found herself gasping with the crowd each time one of the acrobats launched into a free fall before connecting safely and somersaulting into another graceful display.

Next a man with a huge, lethal-looking sword entered the arena. He threw the weapon above his head. The crowd watched as it sliced through the air and cut back down again. He caught it effortlessly. From their place in the audience Tanya could not see the markings on the sword, but the shape of it was familiar, and so was the swordsman.

"It's Victor, isn't it?" she whispered to Fabian.

Fabian nodded, his eyes never leaving the man. His mouth was open, and his face was full of admiration. Victor continued to whip his weapon around in a complicated display, throwing, slicing, catching. He looked like an ancient warrior sparring with an invisible enemy. All of a sudden, he stopped and faced the audience. His expression was daring and tinged with arrogance. Slowly, he lowered himself onto one knee, placing the other foot in front of him. His back was perfectly straight. Then he tilted his head back, lifted the sword...and opened his mouth wide.

"There's no way he's going to swallow that," said Fabian.

"Don't bet on it," said Rowan, a small smile curling the edges of her mouth.

Victor fed the blade into his mouth. It began to vanish, a couple of inches at a time.

"It's got to be a trick," said Fabian. "An illusion. It must be a retractable blade...."

But as the sword rapidly disappeared down Victor's gullet, even Fabian had to face facts. There was nowhere for a blade of that size to disappear to, except down Victor's throat, for the hilt of the sword was only a fraction of the length of the blade. Soon, only the hilt was visible. The audience was utterly silent.

In one smooth sweep of his arm Victor drew the sword out of his mouth and held it aloft triumphantly. The crowd erupted into applause. Victor barely paused before sheathing his sword and turning to the side of the tent. Two dancers wheeled in a large wooden board that was taller than Victor and as wide, along with a tray of gleaming silver objects.

"What are they?" Fabian whispered excitedly. "What's he doing now?"

"A volunteer?" Victor boomed. It was the first time he'd spoken since taking the limelight.

At once, more than half the hands in the audience shot up into the air. The two dancers left the center circle and began to prowl the seats, looking for a suitable volunteer. Feeling daring, Tanya put her hand up as well. So did Fabian.

"Knives," Rowan said calmly.

"*What?*"

"You asked what was in the tray. They're knives. For throwing."

Fabian took his hand down. Too late, Tanya realized that one of the dancers scouring the audience was standing next to her, smiling. It was Ariadne, who had taken their tickets. And Tanya's hand was still up in the air. Before she could protest, Ariadne swooped down on her, tugging her out of her seat and down the steps. Twisting around, Tanya saw Fabian grinning from ear to ear. Rowan looked solemn, but as Tanya was about to turn back to the front, she mouthed, *He always drops one.*

Bewildered, but with no time to give more thought to it, Tanya reached the center circle. Victor was standing by the tray, making a great display of polishing the knives. Each of them looked as sharp as a shard of glass and, in the spotlight, they glinted like a jagged row of shark's teeth. There was a ripple of laughter and whispering from the audience. As Tanya dragged her gaze away from the knives, she realized that all eyes were on her. She tried not to show her nervousness, but felt it in her knees, which had started to shake. Ariadne smiled and led her to the raised wooden board. Tanya stepped up onto the platform, unable to make out the audience now, for the bright light trained on her made it impossible to see.

With a flick of her wrist Ariadne produced a long, black silk scarf. It trailed through the air for the benefit of the crowd, then was placed over Tanya's eyes. She felt the dancer's nimble hands tying a firm knot at the back of her head, then she was guided back to lean against the wooden board. Gentle hands pulled her arms out on either side of her.

"Spread your fingers," Ariadne told her. "Now stand with your feet apart."

Tanya did as she was told.

"Just relax," the dancer said. "And don't move a muscle."

After that she was frozen in place. Because she was unable to see, all her focus was on her hearing. The crowd was restless. The knives clinked as Victor finished polishing them and threw them back onto the table one by one. Then there was another sound— the metallic scrape of a blade being sharpened. Tanya's legs felt weak beneath her. The crowd stopped their noise and silence reigned once more. She knew then that Victor was about to throw the first knife.

She felt the impact of it hitting the wood next to her right leg. The audience cheered. Tanya closed her eyes beneath the blindfold. The next blade hit on the other side, by her left hand. Three more blades came in regular, short intervals.

A pause followed where nothing came. She strained her ears and heard two sounds: footsteps moving about, and the hiss of metal through the air. It came to her suddenly that Victor was juggling with the knives.

A blade hit the next second, close to her shoulder. Barely a heartbeat later another one landed by her ankle.

A horrid clang was followed by a collective cry from the audience. Victor had dropped one of the knives. Tanya felt sick. Heat rose in her, flushing her skin. She felt sweat slick out of her pores and soak into the fabric of the blindfold. He had *dropped* one of the knives.

What have I done? she thought, squeezing her eyes shut even tighter. *I'm such an idiot. What if he misjudges as he throws one of the knives?* Then she remembered Rowan's strange words as she'd left her seat.

He always drops one.

It was a message. The knife had not been dropped by accident. Rowan had been letting her know that it was a deliberate error, to fool the audience into thinking that mistakes *could* be made.

Even so, her limbs ached with the desire to move, to run. But she was fixed in place out of fear as surely as if the daggers were pinning her in place. Then, as she thought she could endure no more, it ended with a spray of blades piercing the wood around her head one after the other.

The crowd went wild. Without warning, the blindfold was pulled from Tanya's face, and the spotlight finally left her to focus on Victor, his chest heaving with short bursts of breath. He bowed, over and over again, to the audience, many of whom were now standing up and clapping.

As Ariadne helped her step away from the board, Tanya looked back and saw the outline of her skinny figure drawn in knives. Relief flooded through her and she felt a slow grin spread across her face as she stared back into the audience, for as well as cheering for Victor, they were cheering for *her*. She spotted Fabian, whooping and clapping for all he was worth. Next to him even Rowan had broken her sullen stance to put her hands together in applause.

Then Tanya's eyes found the small boy she had spotted earlier. Unlike everyone around him, he was not clapping or cheering. He simply stared into the arena, looking but not really seeing. Yet he was not the only one motionless in the crowd. Two more figures sitting side by side further back caught Tanya's attention. Her smile froze on her lips as she recognized them—a dark-skinned young man wearing a green coat, and a beautiful, pale-faced woman in a black, feather-trimmed cloak.

Gredin and Raven stared back at her. Neither of them was smiling.

The show was every bit as good as Rowan remembered. After it ended in a blaze of color and rapturous applause, the audience filed out of the huge tent, chattering excitedly among themselves. Outside, the sky was stained indigo and orange, and fragments of conversations filled the evening air.

"The sword swallower, he was my favorite...."

"No, the strongman was better. How did he lift that—"

"—and the costumes! I've never seen such creations—"

"Can we come back tomorrow, Dad? *Please?*"

Rowan surveyed her surroundings. All around her, people swarmed like ants around the smaller tents and the food carts, where hot, golden corn on the cob, chestnuts, and cotton candy were being sold. The smell of it all was mouthwatering, and evoked memories of the times she had spent with the circus folk before, when she had still been looking for James. She wondered what he was doing now, at this very moment.

"You must know how he did it," Fabian was saying, looking at her earnestly.

"How who did what?" said Rowan absently. Tino's lithe figure was visible through the crowd, slinking like a black shadow away from the attractions and over to the caravans.

"How Crooks escaped from those chains," Fabian pressed. "There were more than ten padlocks on him, and it really did look like he swallowed that key...."

"He did swallow it," Rowan replied. Tino had vanished through the door of his caravan. She started to walk toward it.

"So how? How did he manage to get free after he was locked up good and proper?"

"I don't know, Fabian. They don't give away how they do things. But Crooks is an expert on keys and locks—he knows how they work, and how to get out of them."

"Well, it makes sense now, anyway," said Fabian. "I can see why some of the Coven members are part of the circus: Crooks with his keys, and Victor with his sword skills. It's the ideal cover for what they *really* do, and they get to practice all the time without coming under suspicion. It's brilliant!"

"You're right," said Tanya, her eyes narrowed. "And the fact that they travel the country gives them the perfect opportunity to search for missing children—and new recruits." She shook her head slightly, as if to clear it. "Anyway, I've got something to tell you both." She pulled them aside, out of the main flow of people, next to a dark little tent. "There were fairies in the audience, watching me."

"Which fairies?" asked Rowan.

"Raven and Gredin," said Tanya. "They were in their human forms, but it was definitely them." She looked over her shoulder, scanning the crowd fearfully. "They're still here somewhere. I just know it."

"Why didn't you say anything before?" asked Fabian.

"Because I couldn't very well start talking about fairies in there, could I?" Tanya said huffily. "People could have heard."

"Why do you think they're here?" asked Rowan.

Tanya shook her head. "I don't know. But whatever it is, it can't be good. They didn't look happy."

"Perhaps they didn't approve of knives being thrown at you," Fabian suggested. "Do you think Raven will tell Florence?"

Tanya looked stricken. "I hope not."

"I suppose it all depends on whether Raven thinks it's in Florence's best interests to know," said Rowan. "But I thought fairy guardians only protected their humans from magical harm, or things relating to the fairy realm."

"In that case, that can't be it," said Tanya.

"Then they must know about the meeting," Rowan said grimly.

"Correct," said a cold voice from inside the tent, startling them all. Dark fingers curled around the flap and threw it aside, then Gredin stepped out, followed closely by Raven.

"If you think for one moment that I'll allow you to get involved with these people, you're sorely mistaken," Gredin said, his yellow eyes fixed on Tanya. "It will only lead to trouble, and you're to have no part in it."

"You can't possibly know about them," Rowan said. "So how do you know they're trouble?" .

Gredin eyed her.

"You're right. I don't know about them. What they do or who they are. But whatever it is they do is so strongly protected by magic—powerful magic— that I know nothing good can come of it. Something shrouded in such secrecy should be avoided." He cast his eyes on Rowan. "And after you crossed the Unseelie King, you would be wise not to draw further attention to yourself."

"I know," said Rowan. "That's why I'm trying to put an end to it all, for good."

Yet even as she said it, she questioned herself. Was getting involved in one last job really the way to cut off the Coven once and for all? Would it be easier just to say no? But then, what would the Coven do to Tanya and Fabian in light of what they knew?

"Your choices are your own," said Raven. Her long black hair fell down her back, mingling with the feather trim on her velvet coat. The feathers had the oily, rainbow-like appearance of the crow family about them, and from the coat's folds a twitching, glistening brown snout protruded, attracting Rowan's attention. The rest of the creature's head followed, its large soulful eyes peering at them. Raven looked down and patted the Mizhog's head. It sneezed suddenly, then vanished back into the coat. Raven continued to speak. "As Florence's guardian, I know it would cause her suffering if harm should come to you. But I have no say in what you do."

"Or in what *I* do," said Fabian, shakily. It was only the second time he had ever seen the two fairies, and their unnerving effect on him was evident.

"Correct," Gredin said again, his eyes boring into Fabian. Then he turned away dismissively, back to Tanya. "As your guardian, I forbid you to take part in whatever it is you have planned for tonight. Go home, and we will speak no more about it."

"You forbid me?" Tanya said thunderously. "You *forbid* me?"

"Yes," said Gredin simply.

Tanya's hands clenched into fists at her sides. "You can't tell me what to do."

"I can, and I am," said Gredin. "And that is the end of it."

"Really?" Tanya shot back. "Because to me, it

seems there's never an end. Are you ever going to stop interfering in my life and telling me what I can and can't do?"

"It's my duty to protect you," said Gredin. "To protect your best—"

"My best interests, so you keep saying," Tanya said furiously. Rowan had never seen her in such a temper. She put her hand on Tanya's arm, for Gredin's face was also darkening. Tanya shook her hand off.

"What if I think it's in my best interests for you to just leave me alone?"

"Then you're wrong to think that."

"No, I'm not. Everything you've ever done has made me miserable and I've had just about enough of it. I never asked to be able to see fairies. I'd never have chosen the ability. And I never asked to get stuck with *you*!"

"The feeling," Gredin said icily, "is mutual. Do you think I chose to be your guardian of my own free will? That I do this out of some kind of love or caring for you? Do you think I *enjoy* having to watch you, day in, day out?"

"I..." Tanya faltered, her mouth agape. His admissions stung her. And for some reason, they frightened her.

"I didn't choose you any more than you chose me," Gredin continued. "But I was given the task of protecting you. I warn you now—if you defy me tonight, I'll punish you."

"Go ahead," said Tanya. "I've had fourteen years' worth of your punishments—I'm used to them by now."

"Tanya," Rowan said warningly—but Tanya ignored her.

Gredin shook his head. "If you think what you've experienced so far has been tough, believe me when I say I have punishments that will make the earlier ones seem positively pleasurable. If you willingly defy me, after I have warned you against it, I'll have no option but to use them."

"Like I said," Tanya answered. She unbuttoned her jacket and gestured to her T-shirt where, at the side, the label was visible. The T-shirt was inside out. "Go ahead. I'm older now, and wiser. If you want to punish me you'll have to get past the deterrents I use first."

Gredin stepped closer to her, his golden eyes flaring as he stared down into her face. She could smell the woodland on him—from his clothes, his hair, even his breath.

"Here's the thing with deterrents," he said softly. "Each one has its weakness. Turning your clothes inside out? Only a matter of time before someone pulls you up on it and you have to turn the garment the right way. Wearing red? Not possible all of the time. An iron nail in the pocket? Small, sharp, pointed things can easily work their way through clothing and get lost. I could go on, but I think you get my point. It takes a lot of concentration to employ deterrents all the time. In fact, it only takes a moment's distraction, and you can forget all about them." He paused and stepped back a little. "It's only a matter of time before you slip up. And then, I'll be waiting."

"Don't count on it," said Tanya.

"Come on, Gredin," said Raven. With her right hand she reached up and massaged her ear with long, thin fingers. Tanya watched and saw that her ears, and Gredin's, normally pointed at the tips, were rounded into a human-like shape. Both fairies were using glamours to disguise their fey appearance, something that caused them discomfort. "Let's go."

But Gredin wasn't quite finished. "Of course, there's one major flaw with using deterrents. Can you guess what it is?"

"I can hardly take the suspense," Tanya snapped.

Gredin smiled without warmth. "The flaw is that you're presuming any punishments will involve magic. Which, in fairness, I can't blame you for. I mean, up until now, magic has been the most convenient method of controlling you. But you've just proved to me that I may have to change those methods."

Tanya went cold as she digested Gredin's words. The thought that he would punish her without magical means had never occurred to her before.

"What kind of...punishments?" she said hoarsely, her bravado crumbling.

"Oh, you'd like an example?" Gredin said brightly. "Well, let's see. There's that odious hound you're so fond of. Suppose, for instance, he runs off and gets lost somewhere...."

"You wouldn't..." Tanya choked out as his words sank in. "You wouldn't harm Oberon...."

"I'll do whatever it takes to get the message across to you," said Gredin, his voice harsh. "The sooner you realize that, the easier both our lives will become."

"Why?" Tanya said, her voice cracking. "Why do you do this?"

"I thought I'd made that perfectly clear—"

"No, that's not what I meant." It was dark now, and around them the tents glowed with little lanterns lit up outside. In the moment before she spoke next she heard the drone of gnats buzzing around their heads and the sounds of laughter further away. "Why are you my guardian? Why do we have guardians, if neither of us wants it? And why...why do you hate me so much?"

Gredin gave her a long, hard look. " 'Hate' is a strong word," he said at last. "I don't hate you. I just hate what I have to do." He broke his gaze and shook his head, then turned to Raven. "Let's go."

Raven pulled her cloak tighter around her and followed Gredin as he stepped away.

"Wait," said Tanya.

Gredin paused, but did not turn round. "Yes?"

"Aren't you going to tell me why we...I mean, why second-sighted people have guardians?"

She saw Gredin's shoulders tense.

"Ask your grandmother," he said. As he and Raven moved away, merging with the throng of the crowd, Tanya was aware that Rowan and Fabian had come to stand on either side of her.

"Oh, I will," she whispered to the fairies' retreating backs. "I'll ask her, all right."

"What are you going to do?" Fabian said, his voice dismal. "If you come to the meeting, Gredin will know and he'll punish you."

"It's not worth it," Rowan said softly. "I'll go to see Tino alone. You two can wait for me in the smaller tents—there's plenty to keep you amused. I'll be as quick as I can."

"No," said Tanya.

"You heard what he said," Rowan argued, exasperated. "You can't come—"

"I know that," said Tanya. "I'm not prepared to risk something happening to Oberon. But there's nothing to stop Fabian from coming with you."

"What? I told you, I'm going alone. There's no need for you two to be there, or to be involved at all."

"There is," said Fabian, fiercely. "Tino's not going to let me and Tanya just walk away, knowing what we know, is he? He knows that if we're involved, then it incriminates us and means we're less likely to talk. But if you insist on going alone, he'll think of a way to get to us, to make sure we don't talk."

Rowan glared at the pair of them. "You should never have followed me. I knew what I was doing, and now you've messed everything up."

Fabian glared back. "You might be glad to have us by the time Tino's finished with you."

"Look, just let me go alone so I can—"

"So you can lie and keep us out of what's going on?" Tanya cut in. "Not a chance. From what Tino said last night, we're all involved now. If you don't let Fabian go with you, I'll tell everyone at the manor what you're involved in myself." She ignored Rowan's scowl and focused on Fabian. "Be sure to get all the details. Gredin might have forbidden me to go to the meeting, but he didn't forbid me from hearing about it." She jerked her head to the smaller tents. "I'll be in one of those."

She strode away from them, regret and anger pricking at her like spiteful pins. She could feel their eyes on her still as she approached the fortune-telling tent. Intending to duck inside to kill a few minutes, her bad temper deepened upon seeing that a long line had formed outside. With a sigh she continued past, but as she did, raised voices from inside stopped her.

"All I see is that the brooch never left your house." It was a young, female voice, and one that was familiar. "It's there still—it's being hidden."

"What are you suggesting?" The second voice was an older woman. She sounded flustered.

"That you need to look closer to home to find the thief," the younger girl said. "Now, if you'll excuse me, the psychic strain has left me feeling faint. I must go and lie down at once."

The whispering line hushed as the curtains were thrown back. With one hand pressed to her temple and the other fanning herself, Suki theatrically swept out of the tent. Tanya, along with everyone else, stared after her. *Suki* was the fortune teller!

She was dressed rather differently from the previous evening, in an elaborately jeweled green gown that trailed after her. Her short blond hair was tousled and adorned with a flower garland that tumbled down her back. Her feet, padding nimbly away, were dirty and bare. She looked eerie and slightly crazy.

"Just a minute, young lady!"

Tanya's head snapped back to the disgruntled, red-faced woman who emerged from the tent.

"You can't just leave it there. That brooch is my inheritance—" The woman stopped abruptly, realizing she now had an audience, and that she was its sole focus. Suki was gone. A few seconds of craning her neck and one undignified huff later, the woman stalked away. As the line resumed its whispering over the exchange, Tanya watched a thin, surly-looking man come over to the tent and turn the wooden sign around. FORTUNE TELLING CLOSED, it said. BACK LATER.

As the crowd finally dispersed, Tanya stared at the sign. Tonight she had seen a different side of Suki. Her psychic ability was not only being used in the Coven, but also as an act in the circus. And "act," Tanya thought, was a good way to describe it, for although Suki had certainly touched a nerve with an accurate reading for the woman, Tanya knew with conviction that Suki's claims of feeling faint had been a convenient excuse to get away to Tino's meeting.

Brooding, she wandered off to the Curiosity Cabinet and stepped inside, wondering what was happening in Tino's caravan. Before long, as she wandered among stuffed creatures, ancient runes, and Egyptian death masks, her own heated exchange with Gredin also played on her mind. Her thoughts shifted to exactly how and when she would be able to broach the subject of guardians with her grandmother—and whether Florence would be willing to provide the answers.

9

When Rowan and Fabian arrived at Tino's caravan, the door opened before they'd even finished knocking. Tino beckoned them inside and pointed them past racks of glittering costumes into the kitchenette, where there were a small table with a brightly colored mosaic top and a few chairs.

Tino joined them. He had changed what he was wearing, his performance clothes from the ring replaced by a loose tunic and dark brown trousers. His blond hair fell about his face, no longer tied back as it had been earlier.

"Where's the other girl?" he asked, with a cursory glance at Fabian.

Rowan pulled out a chair to sit down. There was a grunt and a scrabble of claws, and Tino's huge, shaggy wolfhound, which had been lying under the table, got up and flopped down on the mat by the door.

"The girl?" Tino repeated, after Rowan had sat down.

"There was a complication," she said, glancing at Fabian. His eyes were huge behind his glasses, and he looked as though he didn't know whether he was excited or afraid. "She's here with us, but she couldn't... come."

"Why not? I told you to bring her. Go and get her if she's here, and be quick about it. The others will be arriving any minute."

"I *can't*," Rowan repeated. "Her guardian turned up unexpectedly. He told her she wasn't to come and threatened to punish her if she disobeyed."

Tino's face darkened. "*What?* If he forbade her then he must know something about us! What have you told him? What does he know?"

"Nothing!" Rowan insisted. "I never told him anything, and neither did she. He doesn't know any details, or who's involved, I swear."

Tino pushed the heels of his hands into his eye sockets and groaned.

"This is a disaster. Already they've brought trouble upon us. You should have made sure you weren't being followed!"

"Just hold on," Rowan snapped. "You were the one who insisted they be here tonight! I wanted to leave them out of it."

Tino ignored the comment. "How do we know this guardian will keep quiet?"

"Because he doesn't know anything. And because he was there, in the fairy realm, helping me when I was looking for James. He led me to the courts."

"Let's hope you're right," Tino muttered. "Damn guardians are more hassle than they're worth, sometimes."

"But surely the human members of the Coven have guardians too?" Fabian asked timidly. "Do they know about the Coven? And do they try to stop it somehow?"

A scowl marred Tino's face. "Not all of the human members had guardians. Crooks didn't, obviously, as he's not second-sighted. Suki insists she never knew of having one. As for the rest, arrangements were made for them to be relieved of their duties, to a greater or lesser extent."

"What do you mean, 'relieved of their duties'?" Rowan asked, her tone sharp.

Tino shrugged. "Nothing sinister—just kept out of the way. The Coven used to incorporate the guardians in the past, but things got too messy. No guardian wants their human exposed to unnecessary risk. So any ties with guardians are quickly... *dismissed*."

"Dismissed how?" Rowan asked. "And how come I knew nothing of this?"

"You didn't need to know," Tino replied. "Your guardian was already dead, killed in the accident that killed your aunt and uncle. And I'm guessing you were so wrapped up in getting James back that you never gave a thought to whether the rest of the Coven had guardians, or indeed, what had happened to them." He waved his hand in the air. "I didn't need you distracted by unnecessary information. If you'd needed to know, then you would have. And if you'd wanted to know, you'd have asked—but you didn't. All you cared about was yourself, and finding your brother. And as for *how*—"

A light tapping on the door interrupted them. Tino got up to answer it. He came back with Suki, Sparrow, and a small boy. It was the same boy Tanya had pointed out in the audience. His forehead was creased and damp with worry, his light brown hair curling over and sticking to it.

"We haven't got long," said Sparrow, sitting next to Rowan. He was more disheveled than usual. As he scratched at his head with long, dirty fingernails, the smell of greasy hair hit Rowan's nose. He must have noticed her expression, for he gave an embarrassed smile and moved away a little. She felt mean then. Sparrow was her friend, and she was judging him for things that were out of his control.

Suki sat on Rowan's other side, still wearing her fortune-telling garb.

"What?" she demanded of Fabian, who was ogling her curiously. "Let's get on with it, shall we?"

Everyone turned to look at the boy seated between Suki and Tino. He cringed under their scrutiny, his eyes darting from side to side like those of a trapped animal.

"I can't stay long," he said in a voice that was little more than a whisper. "I left my dad in the Curiosity Cabinet. Said I was going to look for the toilets."

"You can tell him you got lost on the way back," said Suki in a honeyed voice Rowan had never heard her use before. "That'll buy you some more time. Now, Jack. Did you manage to get anything that belongs to your mother, like I asked you to?"

The boy called Jack nodded and reached into his pocket. From it he withdrew a small, round object and placed it on the table.

"It's her engagement ring," he said. "One of the stones came loose, and she's been meaning to get it fixed. I managed to sneak it out of her jewelry box last night."

"Perfect," said Suki, reaching for it.

"What's it for?" Rowan asked.

"I'm going to see if I can pick anything up, anything at all about where Jack's mother might be," said Suki. "Sometimes an object belonging to a person can help me."

"Can you sense anything now?" Jack asked, his dark eyes hopeful.

"It's best if I do it later on, alone," Suki answered, not meeting his eyes. "I can focus better. Can you leave it with me for tonight?"

Jack nodded, dismal.

"Good." Suki pocketed the ring. "Now tell these people what you told me before, about your mother."

Jack looked hesitantly around the table.

"It's all right," Suki coaxed. "We can help you."

Jack gulped. "She started acting...*funny* about two weeks ago. Her voice sounded different sometimes. Sort of...scratchy, and deeper. She said she wasn't feeling well, but she wouldn't go to the doctor. I never see her eat anything. She says she's lost her appetite. And she started forgetting to get me up in the mornings for school, so my teacher said I needed a note to explain why I kept coming in late. When she wrote it, she used her left hand...and that's when I knew something was really wrong, because she's right-handed. In fact, she's been using only her left hand, and holding her other hand in a weird way sometimes...when she thinks no one's looking. Like it's hurting her."

"Odd," Tino said. "Did you make any sign that you'd noticed?"

Jack shook his head. "No."

"What else?" Suki prompted.

"Scrounger—that's our cat—won't go near her anymore," said Jack, sounding close to tears. "Her fur goes on end whenever they're in the same room together."

"And since you told me what was happening, have you noticed anything else?" asked Suki. "Anything different from what you've told us already?"

Jack nodded, his eyes downcast. "I started looking out for other things, like you said. I've noticed that every couple of days she keeps locking herself in the bathroom first thing in the morning. So three days ago I crept outside the door and listened. I could hear a snipping sound, like scissors. When she came out, I went in and looked in the trash. It was full of her hair—but when I went downstairs her hair didn't look any shorter. This morning the same thing happened—her hair is growing fast. *Really* fast. But she's cutting it so nobody notices."

"How is she acting around the rest of the family?" asked Suki. "Have you noticed anything unusual?"

A tear rolled down Jack's nose and dripped onto the table. He wiped his face quickly and took a deep, gulping breath.

"Until you told me to look out for it, I hadn't noticed. But she seems more interested in Lucy, my little sister, than anyone else. She doesn't like anyone picking her up, or taking her anywhere. Tonight, my dad had an awful row with her. She didn't want Lucy to come."

"What made her change her mind?" asked Fabian. Jack looked at him in surprise. "We noticed you in the audience," Fabian explained quickly. "You looked worried, and we saw you were with your dad and a little girl—was that Lucy?"

Jack nodded. "She only let Lucy come after my dad got cross and asked her why she was being so possessive of her. She let him take her but after... after he'd left the room..."

"Yes?" said Tino.

"Dad went into the living room and started to put Lucy's shoes on. Mum . . . *she* . . . was in the kitchen. I was in the hallway and I heard this weird crunching noise. I looked through the gap in the door and she was standing by the sink, grinding her teeth. She had a glass in her hand. Her knuckles turned white because she was gripping the glass so tightly. It broke in her hand and cut her. Dad offered to sweep it up and put a bandage on, but she just screamed at him to go. So we left." Another tear slid down his face. "Now I'm scared to go home." He looked up at Tino. "Can you help? Can you get my *real* mum back?"

Tino's hands were pressed together over the lower part of his face. He regarded Jack over the top of them for a moment, then lowered them to speak. "I'm not going to lie to you. Whatever it is that's switched places with your mother is dangerous. And it sounds like your sister caught its attention, which is why it's moved in on your family. Whatever we do next has to be handled with extreme care, and you're going to have to be brave, and continue to act normally. Do you think you can do that?"

Jack paled slightly. "I think so. I take drama class. My teacher says I'm good."

Tino nodded. "Then there's no time to waste. We need to act as soon as possible to try and get this thing out of your household." He looked up at Suki. "You know where the boy lives and how to contact him?"

"Yes."

"Good. Take him back to his father. We'll start working on the plan tonight." He looked at Jack again. "Once it's finalized, Suki will be in touch. Until then, remember: act normally and be careful around her."

Suki rose from the table and motioned for Jack to follow. He got up, wiping his tearstained face, and then the two of them left Tino's caravan.

"What do you think?" Sparrow asked Tino, once the door had closed.

Tino got up and set a pan of water to boil on the stove. He picked some leaves off a green plant in a pot on his windowsill and threw them into the water.

"I think Suki's right," he said. "The boy's clear about what he saw, and the signs aren't good. It sounds like a genuine case, and a serious one. We must act tomorrow. It's a risk even sending him back there tonight."

"Why?" asked Fabian worriedly. "What could happen?"

"If the fairy is determined to have the child, the little girl, all to herself, there's no telling what she might be capable of," Tino said darkly. "In cases like these, if the fairy impostor cannot adapt into the family, which is looking less and less likely, the impostor will often leave, taking the family member they've been drawn to with them. That's the most likely scenario."

"So she could take Lucy away?" Fabian said.

"It's possible," said Sparrow. "But there are other outcomes that could be much, much worse."

"Like what?" Fabian asked.

"Ever heard of a woman named Bridget Cleary?" Sparrow said softly.

"No," said Fabian. "Should I have?"

"Depends on how much fairy lore you read," Sparrow answered. "Bridget Cleary was a woman who lived just over a hundred years ago. She'd been ill for a while, but her husband became convinced she was a fairy changeling. In them days, people didn't have to be second-sighted to believe in fairies. Many of the beliefs of the Middle Ages were still strong. Together with his brother, her husband came up with a plan to drive the changeling away, like. They burned her and beat her. Starved her." Sparrow's eyes were sad through his shaggy hair. "But they went too far. They killed her. Went to trial for it and even insisted to the court that she'd been a changeling."

"And was she?" Fabian whispered.

"No one knows for sure," Tino said. "But it's an example of how humans can react to a changeling, or someone they believe to be one." He poured some of the boiling infusion into a glass and gestured for the others to help themselves. Only Sparrow did. "Other possibilities are even worse."

"How can it get worse than that?" Fabian said incredulously.

Tino and Sparrow shared a look. Rowan sat up

straighter in her seat, sensing that whatever was about to be shared was something new to her.

"You remember that I told you that Suki was one of the stolen children I recovered?" Tino said. He took a mouthful of his drink, and for the first time since Rowan had known him, he looked uncomfortable.

"I remember," she said.

"When we found her, Suki was being well cared for. She was even happy. For the briefest moment, I actually hesitated. I considered leaving her there. But the rules are the rules, no exceptions," he said, almost as though to enforce the thought. "And I had to be quick. Whoever had taken Suki had left her in her cot, unwatched for just a few moments. It was all I had, and so I took her.

"After we brought her home, a few of us took turns to watch her house—and the culprit's—from afar for a few nights. Just in case a repeat attempt was made to snatch her, as sometimes happens. There were some strange comings and goings from the culprit's house, but a week passed and no one came, and the woman who we'd taken her back from in the fairy realm made no attempt to take her again, or any other child.

"We stopped watching, and in time forgot all about Suki. She was just another case, after all. Then in June last year, Peg heard of an incident in which a second-sighted teenage girl had been orphaned. When Peg mentioned the town it sounded familiar, but I didn't think much of it. But then she said the girl's name. And I knew.

"The case was big news, in both the fairy realm and the mortal world. Suki was the sole survivor in her household. Her mother and stepfather were dead, strangled in their beds. Suki witnessed the entire thing. She'd seen a fey woman commit the murders and managed to fight her off—"

"She tried to kill Suki too?" said Rowan.

"No," said Sparrow quietly. "She was trying to take Suki away with her. Somehow Suki managed to fend her off. She was covered in scratches and bites when they found her, and she didn't speak for a month afterward. Neighbors had seen someone running away before Suki was found but it was later put down to a robbery in the same street. The whole thing remains an unsolved murder case in the human world, and in the fairy realm too. There's no trace of the fey woman who took Suki all those years ago.

"Suki was placed in a foster home for two months, until she turned eighteen," said Tino. "By then I'd already contacted her, asking her to join us once she'd come of age, and she'd agreed. I'd never intended to ask her to be part of the Coven, not after all she'd been through—but I felt responsible for her. Then Cassandra went dark, and some of the things Suki was saying about revenge against the changeling trade, not to mention her obvious psychic ability . . . well, it was like it was meant to be. She became Cassandra's replacement."

"Poor Suki," Rowan murmured. She thought back to how harshly she had judged her when they first met, and she regretted it. Suki had been through things, terrible things, that Rowan did not even want to start imagining.

"What about 'poor Suki'?" a cool voice inquired.

Rowan jumped and twisted around in her seat. Suki stood behind them, having quietly let herself back into Tino's caravan unnoticed.

"I..." Rowan faltered, but then Tino cut in.

"I was telling them about you," he said gravely. "Not to gossip, but to give an example of what can happen in these circumstances."

Suki walked wordlessly to the stove and helped herself to a glass of the cooling drink Tino had brewed. She stood sipping at it with her back to them, and when she turned to look at them her face was impassive.

"We were about to start planning," Tino said. "Will you sit down?"

Suki nodded and sat in the seat Jack had vacated.

"Who's doing what, then?" she asked.

"Here's what I think," said Tino. "The fewer people involved in this, the better. First, we have to be familiar with the family's routine. Did the boy tell you what we need to know?"

Suki nodded.

"The family are new to the area," she said. "They own The Spiral Staircase, a pub in Tickey End. Jack's father is the landlord. His mother handles the bookkeeping and office work, and she cooks the lunch menu, though Jack's father has been doing it all since she was ill."

Tino laced his fingers together in an arch. "This could be problematic," he said. "A public place means more people. Carry on."

"They get a weekly delivery, which is tomorrow. Jack's father gets up at seven o'clock to see it in. Jack often helps him, so we're using this opportunity to get a message to him about the plan. While his father stows the barrels, Jack will be busy checking the crates against the order. As the van is being unloaded, I'll stick a note into an empty bottle and sneak it into one of the crates. Jack will intercept that bottle, read the message, and destroy it.

"His father will be busy until the bar staff turn up at midday for the lunchtime shift. He'll then break for something to eat and a nap, but after that he's working flat out pretty much until closing time at eleven o'clock."

"Good," said Tino. "That means he's unlikely to be a problem. But we need to be certain. Sparrow, you're responsible for keeping an eye on him. We'll put things into motion at about two thirty, once he's had his nap. If at any time he looks likely to go upstairs to his family after that, you distract him."

Sparrow looked unsure. "Could be tricky. I'm not old enough to go in a pub, so how am I supposed to—"

"Watch him from outside," Tino cut in, exasperated. "Find a place to observe him and do it. It'll be less obvious than a stranger sitting in his pub watching him all day, at any rate. That'll only make him suspicious. If you do need to walk in, the fact that you're underage is an immediate distraction in itself." He frowned suddenly, his eyes sweeping over the boy. "Get yourself tidied up too. Otherwise he'll think you're a vagrant and chuck you out before you've even set foot in the place."

"Fair point," said Sparrow, not taking offense. "What about Jack? Is it safest to get him out of there altogether?"

"For Jack, it would be," Tino answered. "But Jack's sister is the one who's most at risk. The more time that's passing, the more obsessed this creature is becoming with her. I don't want them left alone. That means Jack must stay close by as long as possible."

"But that's endangering him!" Rowan protested.

"I know," Tino said. "But it's the best way we can make sure his sister remains safe. Plus, we'll need him when it comes to getting the impostor out of the way, which I'll come to in a minute. If, at any time, he feels seriously threatened, we're going to arrange that he signals us to get him out of there. The signal is this: he has a distinctive money box in the shape of one of the old red telephone booths. He'll put it on his windowsill, where it'll be clearly visible from the street." He stopped and looked at Fabian. "That's where you come in."

"Me?" said Fabian.

"You're going to be outside watching too. Upon Jack's signal, you'll go into the pub and ask to see him. Make up an excuse, a good one, which will ensure he's called downstairs. When he comes out, you both get away from there and *stay* away."

He turned to Suki next. "You and Sparrow will visit Fix tonight and ask her for a solution that will dispel glamour. Jack is going to have to get the changeling to take it somehow, and it's crucial that he succeeds."

"But Jack says she won't eat anything," said Rowan.

"I know," said Tino. "Jack will have to try to get her to drink it, or, failing that, slip it into her bath water, or even throw it over her. Once it's done, Jack needs to get out of there. The changeling may realize he's on to her and he'll be in more danger than ever. If he feels he can't get away, he'll use the signal for us to get him out."

"How will we get the potion to him?" asked Fabian.

"It'll have to go in the same way as our plan," said Tino. "Via the crates at the time of delivery. Suki, you'll have to get both bottles in."

"What will happen then?" Rowan asked. She had never been involved in a case like this before, and suddenly she felt inadequate.

"Once the glamour is destroyed the changeling will have no option but to leave," said Tino. "And it's at that point that everything will hang on a thread."

Rowan felt dread in the pit of her stomach. She glanced at Fabian and saw that he was scared but trying his best to hide it. Suki and Sparrow were solemn, but did not look afraid.

"One of two things will happen," Tino continued. "With its cover blown, the changeling will attempt to leave, either alone or with the child. What we're hoping is for her to leave alone, because this means she's going to her source of glamour to re-create it and carry on the deception."

"The source of glamour?" asked Fabian, hoarsely.

"Jack's real mother," said Rowan.

Tino nodded. "If the changeling was cautious, or merely wanted to observe or get information from the human it's impersonating, it's likely Jack's mother is being held somewhere. The moment she leaves Lucy alone, then Red, you get in there and bring her safely out. Meanwhile, Suki will follow the changeling in the hope that it'll lead us to the real mother."

Fabian nodded, taking it in. "And if the changeling leaves and takes Lucy with it?"

There was an uneasy silence around the table.

"Then it means that the changeling has no other source of glamour," Tino said grimly. "And that Jack's real mother is already dead."

10

With the exception of the fortune-telling, Tanya had visited every attraction the circus had to offer by the time Rowan and Fabian found her. Since the sun had gone down, there was a definite nip in the air, and the three of them were among the last few stragglers making their way back to their cars or walking the road to the bus stop.

They hurried along the lane to catch the last bus of the evening, Rowan and Fabian filling Tanya in on the events of the meeting as they went and for the duration of the bus journey. She listened without interruption. From their stop at Holly Bush Hill they walked the final ten minutes to the manor. The countryside was pitch-black, lit only by the stars and a thin scythe of a moon.

Not one of them gave a thought to the time until

they reached the gates of Elvesden Manor. Warwick's Land Rover rumbled toward them, the headlights snapping on, startling them. Warwick cut the engine and jumped out, slamming the door.

"It's late," he growled. "I was coming to look for you all."

"Why?" asked Fabian. "We told you where we were going."

"And you said you'd be home before dark," Warwick retorted. "The sun went down an hour ago. Everyone's still up, waiting and wondering where you've got to."

"I don't get what the problem is," said Rowan. "Why do you need to know the exact time I'll be in? Is there something we should be worried about?"

Warwick clambered back into the Land Rover and lowered the window.

"You're the one with the bedroom crammed full of fairy deterrents," he answered.

Rowan averted her eyes. "That's just because... because I like to make sure," she said.

Warwick's stony expression softened a little. "I can understand that. But the thing is, *I* like to make sure as well. So in future, if you tell us something, then stick to it. Now, go on. Inside with you."

Rowan nodded, her head bowed. Warwick wound up the window and took the Land Rover around the side of the house to park.

They slunk inside. Tanya led the way to the kitchen, where Oberon bounded toward her. He jumped up and knocked the air from her lungs, causing her to emit an undignified *oof!*

Her grandmother, Nell, and Rose were seated at the table drinking mugs of warm, milky coffee.

"What are you still doing here?" Rowan asked Rose in surprise. "I thought you'd have gone by now."

Rose got up. "Warwick offered to take me, but I wanted to stay until I knew you were all safely home," she said. "He's going to drive me back to Knook first thing in the morning."

"We lost track of time," said Rowan guiltily, but Tanya detected a hint of annoyance in her voice too.

"Young whippersnapper," the General squawked. "Off with their heads!"

Nell sniffed haughtily in agreement. She got up and put her mug in the sink, then trotted over to the birdcage and threw a sheet over it for the night.

"Good night," she said pointedly, wheeling the cage out of the kitchen and into the sitting room. The slap of her flip-flops against the quarry stone floor magnified the awkward silence in the kitchen. Rowan and Fabian each mumbled their good nights and skulked upstairs to bed.

Tanya lingered at the back door while Oberon sniffed around the back garden. She hoped to question her grandmother about Gredin's strange admission but, annoyingly, Rose was still hanging around. When Warwick came into the kitchen from outside, prompting another pan of milk to be set on the stove, Tanya gave up. She called Oberon indoors, then muttered good night and headed off up the stairs.

She lay in bed, the light off, but too much was going through her mind for her to be able to sleep. In addition to Gredin's threats and comments about guardians, Jack's mother and Suki's tragic past both fought for space in her head. To top it all off, she'd discovered a chain of gnat bites dotted all the way up one of her shins as she undressed for bed, and they now itched horribly.

Tanya got out of bed and snapped the light on, scratching. Already her leg was swollen with ugly red lumps. Throwing on her bathrobe, she padded bare-foot downstairs. The lamp on the telephone table lit the hallway. Someone was still up, and she hoped it was her grandmother so that they might discuss Gredin.

Voices carried from the kitchen: Warwick and Rose. As she went to push the door open, something about the manner in which they were speaking made Tanya hesitate.

Warwick's voice was low. "I don't know. She's lived by her instincts for so long…maybe we should let her trust them."

"But is it really instinct?" said Rose. "Or is she just so used to trouble that she's paranoid? I hate to see her like this."

"She didn't seem too concerned about staying out late tonight," said Warwick, thoughtfully. "If she lost track of time, it's a good sign. Maybe she's start-ing to relax, finally. She's had more upheaval in her life in the past couple of years than most people have in a lifetime. She needs time to adjust, time to start enjoying being young. I think Fabian and Tanya are good for her."

"But was she always this scared?" Rose whispered. Tanya strained to hear her. "You got to know her in the fairy realm. You said she was tough."

"She was," said Warwick, pausing. "But something happened while we were captured by that woman—the Hedgewitch. Rowan asked me never to tell you or Florence about this, but I think you need to hear it in order to understand. When we escaped, there was another prisoner in the dungeon, a fey man called Eldritch. We had the chance to free him, but we found out that he was involved in taking James away. Rowan flew into a rage. She had the key to his manacles, but told him she was leaving him there as punishment for what he did. Before we left, Eldritch threatened her. He said he was going to hunt her down and make her pay."

"My god," said Rose. "Do you think...I mean, is there any chance...?"

Tanya held her breath. Her bare feet curled with cramp from the cold floor, but she did not dare to move.

"I don't think there's any way he could have made it out," Warwick said grimly. "Not without help, and no one in their right mind would go to that cottage willingly. But just the memory of it is clearly haunting her. It's haunted me too."

"Why?"

"I'm as much to blame as she is. Probably more to blame, in fact. I could have got the key from her if I'd tried. If I'd really *wanted* to. But I knew if I challenged her she'd refuse to let me help her. And I needed to do that. So I let her decide whether to free him or not. She chose not to. Deep down, I think some part of me was glad, because I wanted him to suffer for what he'd done. Looking back, I see that he'd already suffered by being in that cellar for so long."

"We all make mistakes," said Rose softly. "If it weren't for my mistake, she would never have believed she had a brother to lose."

A long silence followed. Tanya waited for any sign that the conversation was set to continue, but there was none. She looked down at her leg, wondering if she should go back to bed and manage without anything to soothe it, but the bites wept and throbbed where she had scratched them so much.

She pushed the door open before the discussion resumed—and froze.

The silence in the kitchen was not merely due to a lull in conversation.

Warwick and Rose stood in front of the fireplace. His dark, work-roughened hands cupped her face. Hers were in his hair. They were kissing, and from what Tanya could tell, it wasn't for the first time.

"Oh!"

The noise escaped Tanya's lips in a hiccup of

surprise. She wasn't able to hold it in—hadn't even known it was coming.

Warwick and Rose broke apart, their faces etched with shock and guilt.

Tanya felt her own face flushing. She felt awkward and confused.

"I . . . I've got gnat bites," she said lamely. "I came down to get something. For the itching."

She could not decide who looked more horrified, Warwick or Rose.

"Vinegar," Rose whispered, her face suddenly even paler than usual. Tanya could see every freckle on her skin. "Vinegar will stop them from itching." She hurried to the cupboards and rummaged through them until she found the bottle. She moved toward Tanya, her hand outstretched. "You just need to dab it on. Here, do you want me to—"

"I can manage," Tanya said, the heat in her cheeks flustering her. She couldn't seem to gather her thoughts properly. The shock of what she had seen had caught her completely off guard.

"Of course." Rose gave her the bottle and stepped back, her hands clasped together.

Warwick hadn't moved. Tanya backed away, nearing the door. As she turned to go through it, he spoke.

"Tanya."

She met his eyes, barely. "Don't you think things are already complicated enough?" she asked him.

"You won't . . . say anything, will you?" His voice was pleading.

"Don't worry," she said hollowly, shaking her head. "I wouldn't know where to start."

She left them, shamefaced, in the kitchen and went back upstairs. In the bathroom she dabbed vinegar onto the bites and then stared at her reflection in the mirror for a long time.

"Another secret," she whispered. She was fed up with them. Secrets everywhere. And now this was a huge one that she had to keep from her two best friends.

When had everything become such a mess?

A belch from the drain-dweller in the plughole made her jump.

"And you can be quiet as well," she said crossly. She stuck the plug in the hole and left the bathroom, turning out the light behind her.

❧❀❧

In the room next to Tanya's, Rowan was also having problems sleeping. It took her a long time to fall into a doze, but then a *chit* of sound disturbed her. Her eyes opened.

Chit.

She sat up in bed, rubbing her eyes. The third time it happened she recognized the noise. She threw back the bedclothes and went to the window. Pulling the curtains back, she made sure her line of salt was still in place on the sill before unlatching the window and leaning out. The scent of the roses in the courtyard below hit her nose, heavy and oversweet. A second later a small piece of gravel bounced off her forehead.

"Ouch!"

"Red?"

"Sparrow?" she said hesitantly. "Is that you?"

One of the rose bushes rustled and numerous winces and muttered curses drifted up to her.

"What are you doing down there?" she whispered.

"Trying to wake you up," said Sparrow, finally disentangling himself from the bush. His figure was a silhouette in the dark gardens.

"You'll wake the whole house up if you don't keep it down," Rowan hissed. "What are you doing here?"

"I just wanted to make sure you'd got home safe, like."

She was immediately alert. "Why?"

"No reason. Anyway, I'll be off now—"

"Oh, no you don't!" she whispered fiercely. "Go around the back. I'll meet you at the kitchen door."

She pulled the window closed, crept to the door, and opened it. The hallway was in darkness and the house was silent. She slipped down the stairs and through the house to the kitchen, easily quieting Oberon—who scrambled to his feet and began thumping his tail—with a scratch behind the ears and a biscuit.

She unhooked the key from the nail behind the

door and turned it in the lock. Sparrow stood awkwardly on the back step, his face half hidden in the shadow of the house. She pulled him inside and locked the door, pointing him to the table.

"What's going on?"

"Told you," said Sparrow. "Just wanted to check you got home."

Rowan narrowed her eyes. "Since when do you check up on me? Since when does anyone check up on me? Something's happened, hasn't it?"

There was something different about him. Not only was he acting oddly, but he also looked different from the Sparrow she knew. His hair was shorter, neater. It showed his eyes more. Though it was dark— she hadn't turned on the light for fear of waking anyone—his skin looked brighter. Cleaner, in fact. A scent of lemony soap or shampoo wafted toward her.

A stab of fear pierced her as she realized she hadn't asked the vital question she should have.

"What are you?"

She saw him smile, his familiar chipped front tooth peeping at her.

He took her hand and pressed it over his heart. He let it stay there, just for a moment. Long enough to show her.

"You cut your hair," she said, relaxing.

"Yeah. Tino told me to neaten up, remember? Suki did it for me, just after you left."

Rowan frowned. For some reason, the thought of Suki cutting Sparrow's hair irritated her.

"You scrub up all right," she said eventually. "So are you going to tell me what's up, or not? And watch what you say. The walls have ears in this place, if you know what I mean." She pointed toward the tea caddy where the brownie lived. Though she could not be sure, she thought she saw the lid twitching and lifting slightly.

He nodded. "I wasn't going to say nothing, not until I saw you tomorrow," he said. "Didn't want to worry you, not tonight."

"I'm already worried. Any number of things could go wrong tomorrow—"

"It's not about tomorrow."

"What then?"

"It's about what happened tonight. After you'd gone." He lifted his hands to his face and placed them over it, leaving only his eyes visible. "Me and Suki went to see Fix, like Tino told us to." His voice was muffled a little from behind his hands, and she noticed his fingernails were short, and also clean.

"So you could get something from her to dispel the changeling's glamour tomorrow," said Rowan. "Did you get it?"

Sparrow shook his head and dropped his hands on the table. For a heartbeat it looked as though they were trembling.

"No. We got to her place but there was no answer when we knocked."

"What are we going to do?" she asked. "We *need* that potion, it's crucial to the plan. What if you went in the morning, first thing? Fix will probably be back from wherever she is tonight, and you can—"

"It weren't that she was out," he said. "That's what we thought at first. We knocked a few times, but everyone knows Fix don't really go out late at night. Not unless she has to. We was going to leave but then Suki remembered that she had a bunch of keys on her from the last job she'd done with Crooks. We decided to give it a go...we knew Fix wouldn't mind if we let ourselves in if there was a chance we could find something, a potion for what we needed. But when we got inside...she was there. She's... she's dead."

"*Dead?*" Rowan whispered. "Are you sure?"

He nodded. "We checked her pulse. But even before, we knew. The color of her face..." He blinked hard. "The place was full of potions, but without Fix, we'd no way of telling what they were."

"How...how did she die?"

Sparrow looked sick now. Rowan got up and filled a glass with some water. She set it before him and he gulped at it shakily.

"There was a bottle on the floor, near to her body," he said, wiping his hand across his mouth. "It must have been poison. One of her own. It was empty."

"I don't understand," Rowan said slowly. "If it was her own, then...are you saying that you think... you think she drank it on purpose?"

"That's just it. I don't know. Suki seems to think

that was what happened. I mean, we all knew Fix's life wasn't easy. She was in a lot of pain. But it could also have been an accident—the wrong ingredient in the wrong bottle. Everyone's capable of mistakes, but Fix was always so...responsible. And so careful."

"So if she didn't do it to herself, that means someone else did," said Rowan.

"I couldn't see no signs of a struggle," he said. "That's what's so odd."

"She must have let them in," said Rowan. The thought sickened her. "If someone killed her, she must have known them. Trusted them, even. Could they have slipped the poison in her food or drink?"

"Possibly," said Sparrow. "Some poisons are tasteless and have no smell, in which case she wouldn't have known until it was too late. The other possibility is that someone forced her to drink it."

"You mean, actually poured it down her throat?" Rowan asked him in horror.

Sparrow shrugged. "She wouldn't have been difficult to overpower, would she?"

Rowan swallowed. "Does Tino know about this?"

"Not yet, but he will soon. Suki's on her way back there now."

"Alone?"

He nodded, and Rowan's heartbeat quickened as she realized they were both thinking the same thing. "And what about Cobbler and Dawn?" she said weakly. "Any news on them?"

"Still nothing." He got up, uncomfortable. "I'd

better go and catch up with Suki. I told her we should really be sticking together but she insisted she'd be all right. We're both watching our backs now, at any rate. But I had to check that you were safe."

"Who's going to check on you?" she asked softly.

He gave a small, sad smile. "I can look after myself."

They went to the door, and Rowan opened it. She shivered as cool fingers of a breeze snaked around her ankles.

"What are we going to do about the potion?" she asked. "Are we still going ahead with the plan tomorrow?"

"We'll have to see what Tino says. For now, we have to assume it's going to happen."

"It's at two thirty that we're meeting, isn't it?" she asked.

"Yeah. Although Suki will be there way earlier, for the delivery."

"Unless we have some kind of potion it's going to fail though, isn't it?" she said desperately. "We have to think...is there anyone else who—"

And then it hit her.

"What?" said Sparrow, his blue eyes searching hers.

"I think I know someone who might be able to help. Leave it to me."

A glimmer of hope lit Sparrow's eyes. He nodded. "I'll see you tomorrow, then. Stay safe."

"You too," she whispered as he started to walk away. "Sparrow?"

"Yes?"

She hesitated. "What Merchant said the other night. Do you think it could be true, about someone knowing about us?"

Sparrow was quiet for a long moment. "Until we find out what's happened to Dawn and Cobbler, we can't be sure what's going on . . . but . . ." He broke off, biting his lip.

"But what?"

"I don't know. Just . . . something doesn't feel right. We don't know exactly what's happened to Fix or the other two. It could just be coincidence—"

"But you don't think so," she finished for him.

"No, I don't. I think something's going on and I got a bad feeling about this one, Red. A really bad feeling."

His words echoed in Rowan's head long after he had gone.

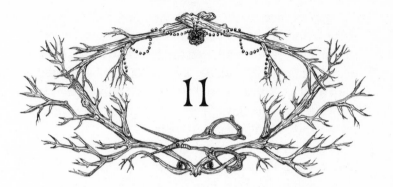

11

Tanya found herself unable to look Warwick and Rose in the eye at breakfast the next morning. She felt a grain of satisfaction at the mounting evidence that neither of them had slept well: Warwick gulped down mug after mug of strong coffee, while Rose's hair stood out from her head in an untamed auburn cloud.

Serves them right, Tanya thought tetchily. Her own sleep had come in fits and starts, and she rubbed at her gritty eyes in resentment.

Opposite her, Rowan watched the hearthfay flitting hopefully across Fabian's line of vision. Fabian, however, was oblivious as always to the fairy's demands for his attention and was muttering to himself as he wiped at egg yolk on his pajamas.

"You're a gloomy bunch this morning," said Nell, squinting around the table.

"How rude," the General agreed, nibbling a toast crust lodged between his scaly toes.

"We've got more animals arriving today," said Rose, evidently deciding to make an effort at conversation. "A litter of orphaned fox cubs and a hedgehog who had a lucky escape with a car." She looked hopefully at Rowan and Fabian, but skimmed over Tanya's eyes quickly. "Perhaps you'd like to give me a hand getting them settled in."

Fabian's head shot up, and he glanced at Tanya and Rowan. They all knew that they could not afford to get held up at the manor if they were going to help Jack at the Spiral Staircase.

"What time are they getting here?" Rowan asked, her voice calm. She did not look up from her breakfast, but despite her unruffled exterior, Tanya knew that her mind would be calculating exactly how to handle this.

"Warwick's going to collect the fox cubs after breakfast, and the hedgehog is being brought to us around midday."

Rowan glanced at Tanya and Fabian. "We can help, can't we?"

They both nodded their agreement, following her lead.

After breakfast, Tanya called to Oberon and took his leash off the back door. As she passed through the overgrown garden and went to the gate leading to the fields, she kept an eye out for Brunswick, the goblin who lived in the garden, but there was no sign of him. Heading toward the brook on the outskirts of the forest, she followed it along, watching Oberon as he snuffled in the long grass, his tail in the air.

She heard the thud of running feet on the ground behind her and turned. Rowan and Fabian had come to join her. She continued along toward the little church, waiting for them to get their breath back.

The scaffolding at the back of the church was still visible. Repairs to the crumbling building had been taking place for some months now, but the entire back wall had been reduced to rubble after they'd discovered the church was one of the locations for the missing charms in Rowan's quest to find James. They had been lucky to escape alive.

"Listen," said Rowan. "We've got a problem. Well, two problems, in fact."

"We've always got problems," said Fabian. "What now?"

Rowan flicked a strand of hair out of her eyes. "Last night, when everyone was in bed, Sparrow came to the house. He'd been to see Fix with Suki to get the potion we need for today. Fix was dead when they got there."

"Fix... she was the one with all the tattoos, and the walking stick, wasn't she?" Tanya asked, stunned. "What happened to her?"

"We don't know for sure," said Rowan. "But it looks like she was poisoned."

"Someone *killed* her?" Fabian blurted out.

"Again, we don't know," said Rowan. "She could

just as easily have taken the poison herself. But Sparrow doesn't believe that."

Tanya felt a cold dread engulf her. "You have to break ties with these people," she said. "After today, you have to stop seeing them. It's *dangerous*."

Rowan stared back at the house, her pointed features sharpened with worry. "I know."

"What's the other problem?" Fabian asked. He chewed his thumbnail nervously. "You said there were two."

"We don't have the potion to dispel the glamour," said Rowan. "Without it, I don't see how our plan can work, and from what Jack said last night I don't think we can wait much longer before doing anything."

The tale of Suki's past hung between them, almost tangible even though it was unspoken.

"Wait a minute," said Fabian. He pulled his brown leather book out of his pocket and thumbed through the pages. "There's something in here about getting changelings to leave...I wrote it down from that book of yours—"

"I don't think—" Rowan began with a snort, but Fabian continued.

"No, listen. Here it is: 'A changeling can be made to reveal its true nature by holding it above a hot poker, or throwing it on the fire. The fairy will fly up the chimney and send the real human back.'"

"That's a bit vicious, isn't it?" Tanya asked.

"Not to mention stupid, in this case," Rowan

said cuttingly. "This is a fully grown adult fairy we're dealing with, not an ancient one pretending to be a baby. The thing posing as Jack's mother isn't going to let anyone get near it, let alone grab hold of it and throw it on a fire."

"Then what about this," said Fabian obstinately. "'Another method is to take twenty-four halves of eggshells and go about brewing beer in them—'"

He broke off, pushing his glasses up his nose, and pondered. "I don't suppose we have enough time to find out how to brew beer, but we could try something else . . . brewing tea, perhaps.

"'When the changeling sees this it will announce its astonishment, saying: *The acorn comes before the oak, and the egg before the hen. But never before have I seen brewing done in eggshells!*'" He closed the book.

"Fabian, that story is as old as time," Rowan said. "I think the fairies have grown wise to it by now."

Fabian scowled. "Have you got another idea, then?"

"Yes. I think our best chance is to get a potion to dispel the glamour. Without Fix, there's only one other person I can think of who might be able to help us." She pointed toward Hangman's Wood.

"Morag," Tanya realized.

Rowan nodded. "She's our last hope, but it's a long shot. I'm guessing she would be able to provide what we need, but I don't know whether she'd need more time if she doesn't have one already prepared. Sometimes potions can take days or weeks to fuse properly. We've got only hours."

"I'll go," said Tanya. "She knows me, and I know the way to her caravan."

"But what about Gredin? If he finds out you're helping us—"

"I'm helping *you*," said Tanya. "I'm not directly involved, and going to see Morag doesn't put me in danger."

"All right," said Rowan. "As soon as you've seen her, come back to the house. We'll be outside with Rose. Once you're back, we'll leave to get to Tickey End before half past two. I'll think of some excuse to get us out of there on time."

"What if someone asks where Tanya is?" said Fabian.

"Just say I'm still walking Oberon," Tanya answered. "If I'm late then I'll say he ran off."

"You'd better go," said Rowan. "And whatever you do, don't let Warwick catch you in the woods, or he'll probably ground you, and that's the last thing we need today."

Tanya watched as Fabian and Rowan set off back to the house. While she had no intention of letting Warwick find out about her going into the woods, she alone knew that if he did, what she had seen last night provided her with more than enough to barter for his silence.

"Come on, Oberon," she called, walking back to where the stepping stones led across the brook. In a couple of places the water ran across her toes, wetting them through her sandals. Oberon splashed through to the other side, pausing halfway to lap at the water. Then, without a further glance back, she crossed the border of the forest into the dark shade of the ancient trees.

Mad Morag's caravan was hidden well, deep in the woods. However, if the way was known, it did not take too long to find, and Tanya had the advantage of having been there twice before.

What she *had* forgotten was how oppressive and disorienting the woods were, especially when she was alone. Every sound, every rustle of wildlife—both everyday and fey—was magnified tenfold. Chirps and whispers of fairies in their nests carried down to her, reminding her that she was an intruder here. She kept her head down, avoiding eye contact and anything that could be seen as aggressive or confrontational, and she kept Oberon close.

She had just reached the first catacomb when she realized that she had completely forgotten to protect herself. With a gasp, she pulled off her thin top and hurriedly turned it inside out, her hands shaking and tangling in the soft fabric. Tugging it back on, she looked around fearfully, feeling stupid and ashamed as she remembered Gredin's words.

It takes a lot of concentration to employ deterrents all the time. . . . Only takes a moment's distraction. . . . And then, I'll be waiting.

She leaned against the cool metal railings surrounding the catacomb, taking a moment to gather her wits and sense of direction. Through the railings, a cavernous hole yawned like a chasm. It was one of seven deneholes—mysterious caves which wound underground for miles. In the years before the railings had been put up, the deneholes had claimed many lives, earning them the name "catacombs," meaning "ancient burial chambers."

She went on her way, trying not to let her mind wander to the bottom of the catacomb and what it might hold. She came upon the second, smaller cavern soon after, finding it ominous, yet reassuring. It signaled that she was on the right path to the old gypsy woman's caravan.

Minutes later, just long enough for doubt to set in, she found it, tucked snugly away within a sheltered glade. Tanya made for the steps leading to the front door but stopped as a creaking sound caught her attention. She frowned and followed her ears to the far side of the caravan.

A pair of heavily veined feet, pale and twisted with age, popped into view, and then out again. They reappeared, then disappeared, reappeared and disappeared at regular intervals. Tanya peered around the side of the caravan.

Morag sat in a rocking chair, her eyes closed against the morning sun. A book of crossword puzzles rested facedown in her lap over a long raggedy dress. At her side, her smoke-gray cat snoozed in a sunny patch of grass, one eye an open slit on the lookout for predators. It leaped up after a curious sniff from Oberon, hissing and spitting.

Morag's eyes opened and she shielded them from the sun with a wrinkled hand.

"Sorry," said Tanya. "I didn't mean to startle you."

Morag chuckled. "Come, now, Grimalkin," she said to the fizzing cat. "That's no way to treat our guests, is it?" She stopped rocking and eased herself out of the wooden chair. Grimalkin stared balefully at Oberon and then stalked off into the bushes, tail in the air.

"Come in, then," said Morag, her knees clicking as she climbed the steps to the caravan.

Tanya followed her inside, breathing in the smoky scent of incense that filled the caravan.

"I'm sorry," she blurted out again. "I know that every time I come here it's to ask for your help, without ever giving anything back to you. I've been meaning to bring you a puzzle book to say thank you, but I've left it at my grandmother's house because I didn't even know I needed to come and see you until a few minutes ago and I—"

She cut off as Morag held up her hand for silence, beaming at the mention of the puzzle book.

"It doesn't matter," she said creakily, gesturing to the table near the kitchen window. "There's plenty of time for that. Sit down. Tell me what's bothering you."

Tanya sat down, scratching behind Oberon's ears as he rested his heavy head on her lap. Morag sat opposite.

"Someone's in trouble," Tanya began. "Not me this time, but someone who has my ability. He thinks his mother has been switched for a changeling, and we need something...some kind of potion, I suppose you'd call it, to destroy the glamour the fairy is using, so it will leave."

Morag nodded slowly, massaging her temple with her fingers.

"I see. And when would you need such a potion?"

Tanya swallowed, her voice sheepish when she spoke. "Today. *Now.*"

The old gypsy woman's birdlike eyes widened in surprise, and Tanya was reminded of how mesmerizing, and how very blue, they were.

"I know it's short notice," she hurried on. "And I understand if it's not possible. But I had to try. You're the only one who can help us."

Morag got up, shuffling to her wooden dresser. Locked inside the glass cabinet were numerous jars and glass bottles of strange and sinister-looking ingredients, and all with tiny labels tied to their stoppers. The old woman surveyed the contents thoughtfully, then peered at a small calendar hanging on the wall next to the dresser.

"What you ask for cannot be prepared in such a short time. A potion to dispel a glamour is complex and needs days to develop properly."

Tanya nodded, her disappointment too great for her to speak. Even though she had guessed it would be too late, she had hoped that Morag might have some solution up her patched and raggedy sleeves.

"But," the old woman continued, "there may be something I can do. It's not as powerful a spell, but it's simple to prepare and may be enough to reveal the real nature of whatever the changeling is."

"Anything," Tanya said, nodding vigorously. "I'll take anything, if you think it might work."

Morag tapped the little calendar on the wall. "It's largely down to luck, you see. The timing is just right for this spell, for the moon is on the wane."

"On the what?"

"Wane," Morag repeated. "The moon waxes and wanes; grows bigger and smaller. Any time you cast a spell, it will be more powerful if the cycle of the moon is on your side. Some spells cannot work without it. When you are trying to bring something into your life, then it helps if the moon is waxing. If you are trying to banish something, the moon must be on the wane.

"What I'm going to give you is a truth spell, to cast out any lies and secrecy. Did you know that the moon is also linked to secrets and deception?"

Tanya shook her head. "So . . . if the moon is waning, it will be easier to see through any deceptions?"

"Correct. It may not alter the changeling's appearance, but its true nature will rise to the surface if it comes into contact with this potion," Morag continued. "Here is what you need." From her dresser she took two empty bottles, one of clear glass and the other of dark green. She set them on the table in front of Tanya and went back to the cabinet, returning a moment later with a velvet bag, a scrap of red cloth, and a jar crammed with small, reddish-brown objects. Tanya leaned closer to the jar, trying to discern what its puckered contents were.

"*Amanita muscaria*," said Morag. "A type of mushroom. You know the ones—red with white spots—they're always shown in children's books, though I've no idea why."

"They don't look like mushrooms," Tanya said doubtfully.

"That's because they're dried," said Morag. "There aren't any fresh about at this time of year."

"They come out in the autumn," said Tanya, recalling the ring of red mushrooms that Warwick and Nell had been forced to dance a fairy dance in last October.

Morag nodded. "They're also poisonous, sometimes fatal, if eaten. So never touch them unless you can help it, and if it's unavoidable always wash your hands afterward. Now, in this spell, the amanita mushroom symbolizes deceit. Mushrooms are among the worst of nature's tricksters. If one kind is mistaken for another, it can have deadly consequences."

She opened the jar, reached in with a small wooden stick, pointed at one end, and hooked one of the mushrooms out. With her other hand she lifted the green glass bottle and pushed the mushroom inside it, poking it down through the neck until it fell to the bottom. She pushed a cork stopper into the top of the bottle and set it aside.

Next she reached into the velvet bag and drew out an object the size of her palm, passing it to Tanya. Tanya took it and found that it was a flat, gray pebble, rough and misshapen, and with a hole through it that was slightly off center.

"A wishing stone," said Tanya. "I've got one of these at home in London. I found it at the seaside when I was little. My mum told me that you can make wishes on stones with holes in them." She smiled faintly, remembering the wishes she had made: for the fairies to leave her alone, then later, for her parents not to go through with their divorce. Neither had come true.

"That's poppycock, as I'm sure you're aware," said Morag briskly. "These stones have about as much power to make wishes come true as a moldy old sock. What they *do* do is purify, and flush out untruths."

She paused, rubbing at her temple again with her fingers. Tanya watched her, noting a flicker of something cross her face. She seemed distracted.

"Are you all right?" she asked.

"Hm? Oh, yes. Just... I've forgotten something," said Morag, tapping her head with a spindly finger. "Yes, that's it." From another cupboard she pulled out a bag of something and shook it into her mortar. Coarse white granules came tumbling out, and she began pounding at them with her pestle.

"Salt," she explained when the grains were ground into fine powder. "Another means of purification." She scoured the caravan until her eyes rested on a brown paper bag. She tore a small piece from it and shook the salt into it, twisting the edges together to keep the salt contained.

"That's everything you need. I'll tell you what to do, but the rest is up to you."

"What if it goes wrong?" Tanya asked. "I've never cast a spell before. I don't know what I'm doing—"

"There's no reason it should fail," said Morag. "You have everything you need. The most important ingredient in any spell is your belief in it. But remember this: you alone must cast it. Your friend cannot have any direct contact with this spell."

"Which friend?" Tanya asked, puzzled. "Fabian?"

"Not the boy," said Morag. "Although now you mention it, it's probably best if he has no contact with it either. I know he believes, but he has a tendency toward a scientific mind, which muddles things. No, I mean the girl... the one you brought here. Red, is it?"

Tanya nodded. "Well, her real name is Rowan. Rowan Fox. She doesn't go by Red anymore."

"Ah," said Morag, nodding. "That's her. Rowan. I felt there was *something* about her. Now it makes sense."

"Why?"

"She should not come in contact with this spell.

Though she may not realize it, or intend to, there's a chance she could taint it, just by being who she is."

"How?" Tanya asked. "I know her name is a barrier to evil magic, but—"

"It's also a barrier to her *casting* magic," said Morag. "Rowan as a plant is very powerful. Powerful enough to stop other spells from being cast. And as you obviously know, that power can transfer to the power of a name."

"But she can cast a glamour," Tanya said, confused. "She has a coat that turns her into a fox."

"But you tell me that her surname is Fox," said Morag. "Which, again, lends her power. Had it been any other name, I think it would be quite different."

"I'll make sure I'm the only one who handles the spell," said Tanya, digesting this information.

"Very well," said Morag. "This is what you must do. It's very simple. Take the stone to the brook and hold it in the running water for a minute or two. The running water will charge it with energy. Afterward, wrap it in the red cloth. Next take the green glass bottle and fill it with water. Not just any old water from a tap, mind. Full of nasty impurities, that stuff. You need pure water, and for this, the stream won't do. It must be absolutely untouched."

"The well?" said Tanya, remembering the old stone well up by the church.

"Yes," said Morag. "Well water will do nicely. You then need to add the salt to the green bottle *after* the well water."

"After the well water, right."

"Unwrap the stone from the cloth and hold it over the clear bottle so that the hole is directly above the opening. Pour the liquid from the green bottle into the clear bottle *through the stone*, then cork the bottle. Finally, wrap the stone and the green bottle containing the mushroom in the cloth and bury it in blessed soil."

"Blessed soil? That's consecrated ground, isn't it?" Tanya asked. "I can bury it in the churchyard."

"The mixture is then ready," said Morag. "But it must be used within one day. After the sun goes down it will be worthless."

"I understand," said Tanya. She started to gather up the things on the table. Morag stayed unmoving, her eyes shut and her hand rubbing at her head again.

Tanya stopped what she was doing. "Are you sure you're all right? You look pale. Is there something I can get you?"

Morag opened her eyes. Even they seemed faded.

"I've got one of my headaches coming on," she said quietly. "I think something is trying to get through."

"You mean a vision? Do you want me to leave?"

Morag's clawlike hand shot out and grabbed Tanya's arm, her grip surprisingly strong. "No. Whatever I'm about to be shown has been trying to get through since you arrived today." She looked at Tanya, grimacing, and massaged her temple.

"Whatever it is, it's linked to *you*."

12

Upon Morag's instructions, Tanya collected a wooden bowl and three candles from the cupboard in the kitchen. She filled the bowl with water and set it in front of the old woman, who was now moaning softly, then pulled the drapes and lit the candles.

Morag whispered something to herself that Tanya did not quite catch—some kind of incantation. As she uttered the final words, she sat up straighter, her eyes clearing and the pain leaving her face.

The candlelight took on a murky blue glow, making Tanya think of freezing underwater caves. It was not difficult, for the temperature in the caravan had dropped drastically, forcing goose bumps to rear up along her arms. She spied Morag's shawl draped over her armchair by the window. She picked it up, hesitating. Morag sat motionless, staring into the wooden bowl, where shadowy images swirled in the water. Tanya was reluctant to disturb her. Apart from the curse-induced trance she had witnessed last October with Rowan, she had never seen Morag experience one of her visions, and it unnerved her.

Morag shivered, pushing the doubt from Tanya's mind. She edged closer and threw the shawl around the old woman's shoulders—then froze as she saw the image in the water.

The water showed a familiar face: Rowan's. Tanya heard herself gasp, but then Rowan's face was replaced with another that she recognized. It was that of the old man who had given her and Fabian the warming raw ginger when they had been cold in the barn the other night. *Nosebag*. The old man morphed into the homeless boy Rowan was friends with: Sparrow. His face vanished and was replaced by Tino's, followed by Suki, Crooks, Victor, Samson, toothless old Peg, and the dark-skinned Merchant.

Another face loomed into view; the tattooed woman, Fix. She lay slumped over a table. Her eyes were open and a fat fly crawled across her face. It flitted to her forearm, settling on another of her tattoos: an ornate dagger. Tanya choked back a cry, wanting to look away, yet finding she couldn't. Two more lifeless faces loomed into view. The first was a deathly white girl. Dark shapes flickered across her face like sunlight through leaves. The last was that of a man, slack-jawed, his hair matted with a dark, clotted substance.

Though Tanya did not recognize these last two faces, it brought no comfort, for she guessed that they must be the two missing Coven members: Dawn and Cobbler. And as Merchant had rightly guessed, it was now certain—through the vision Morag had summoned—that they had met with harm.

"*Thirteen secrets,*" Morag hissed, glassy-eyed. Her voice sent a tremor through Tanya. "*The thirteen secrets have been found out...*"

The water cleared. Tanya sank to the floor by Morag's side, trembling. Oberon nuzzled her, and she clutched at him for comfort. Without warning, Morag snapped out of her motionless daze, shivering. Slowly, Tanya got up and tugged the shawl, which had slipped down, back around the old woman's shoulders.

"Pull the curtains," Morag whispered, her voice dry.

Numbly, Tanya did as she was told, but even the late morning light flooding back into the caravan could not chase the dark images from Tanya's mind. Morag got up and hobbled into the kitchen, pouring the water into the sink and putting the candles on the side.

"You were not meant to see that," said Morag.

"But I thought you said—"

"The message is for you, yes," the old woman cut in. "For you to tell your friend, Rowan. But forgive me...you should not have had to see those poor souls."

"I know those people," said Tanya.

"You must tell Rowan what you saw," said Morag, her lips blue with cold. She rubbed at her arms, pulling the shawl tighter about herself. "And what you heard."

"The thirteen secrets have been found out," Tanya repeated, shuddering. "Did you see anything else, or sense anything about what these secrets might be?"

"I see only what I'm shown," said Morag. "But something tells me that message will be understood by your friend." She pushed the potion ingredients toward Tanya. "It's time for you to go now," she said, her voice distant.

"I know," said Tanya, reluctant. "But I don't like to leave you like this, so soon after a vision like that. I don't like the idea of you being out here all alone."

A half-smile turned up the corners of Morag's mouth, but it did not go up to her eyes. "That's kind of you. But don't you worry about me. I've been alone for most of my life. I've grown used to it."

Though there was nothing sentimental about Morag's manner, her words brought sharp and bitter tears rushing to Tanya's eyes. She turned her head away, blinking. "If you're sure," she muttered.

"Go on," said Morag. "You've got work to do." She got up, leading Tanya to the caravan door, and opened it.

Grimalkin lurked on the steps. He weaved past their ankles, ignoring Oberon, and went into the caravan. Before Tanya had even reached the bottom of the steps, however, he shot past her again, heading for the trees.

"What's wrong with him?" Tanya asked.

Morag gestured to the caravan. "Needs some time to clear the air after a vision like that. The atmosphere...he senses it, you see. He'll likely stay out for the rest of the day now."

Tanya stared after the cat. Even Morag's pet had abandoned her.

"You remember what to do?" Morag asked.

"Yes."

There was no more to say. Tanya set off, turning at the edge of the glade to see Morag watching her from the doorway. She did not look back again, knowing that Morag would be out of sight in a few more footsteps, and something within her clung to the image of the old gypsy woman. She imagined Morag watching over her to see her safely out of the woods.

By the time she had reached the smaller of the two catacombs she was past pretending. The vision of the fly crawling over Fix's face swam in front of her eyes. She started to run. Aside from Oberon, keeping pace beside her, she was now alone in the woods.

Almost as alone as Morag.

Crashing through bracken and undergrowth, she forgot the need to go quiet and unnoticed. Above her, fairies and birds chittered and squawked in the trees. When the edge of the forest finally came into view, she sprinted for it, somehow finding a last burst of energy that propelled her forward, lending her the speed to almost clear the brook in a single leap. She landed a few feet short of the other side, sending water spraying across the bank. Crawling out, she flopped onto the grass, heart pounding. She lay there gasping while Oberon drank from the stream, unperturbed.

She allowed her heart to slow before sitting up. Looking into the sky she saw that the sun was directly above her. It was almost noon. Hastening a glance at the house, she emptied her pockets and stared at the objects Morag had given her.

Focusing on them, she pushed the memory of the vision from her thoughts. Lifting the pebble, she took a firm hold of it and plunged her hand into the icy flow of the brook.

Whatever the thirteen secrets were, they would have to wait, for now.

13

Mrs. Beak's tiny tea shop heaved with customers. Good weather always brought the people of Tickey End out, and that afternoon was no exception. Every table in the place was taken, from the alcoves and nooks tucked inside to the little whitewashed benches and seats lined up on the outside terrace.

On one of these tables, beneath the red-and-white awning, sat Sparrow. A well-thumbed newspaper covered most of the table, in addition to an empty teapot, sandwich crusts, the dregs of an ice-cream sundae, cupcake wrappers, and three drained glasses with slices of lemon in them.

He stood up quickly when he saw them, knocking into the table. He grabbed a glass and stopped it from falling just in time. "Well?" he said.

"Relax," said Rowan. "We got something."

Sparrow sat, rubbing at his tummy. He looked uncomfortable.

"Been having yourself a little tea party, have you?" Rowan asked as she, Tanya, and Fabian took the empty seats at the table. She tucked a rucksack holding the fox-skin coat under her chair.

Sparrow hiccupped. "Never had much choice," he said in a low voice. "I been here since it opened, and it's pretty obvious that on days like this you're expected to empty your wallet if you're keeping other people off the table."

"And of all the places in Tickey End you managed to choose my *favorite*," Rowan said sarcastically. "The gossip hub of the town."

Sparrow shrugged and nodded across the street. "Like I said, not much choice. This is the best view of the Spiral Staircase, and the least obvious for me to keep watch from." He stopped speaking as fluffy-haired Rosie Beak came out and leaned over the table to collect the empties.

"Anything more for you, duck?" she asked Sparrow. Her voice was as sugary as the cakes in her window, but there was an underlying current to it such that they all knew she wanted them gone if the purse strings had been tightened.

Sparrow shook his head and suppressed a burp. He looked at Rowan helplessly, and she realized that if he ate or drank any more he was likely to burst, or be sick at the very least.

Rosie glanced around the table, her candyfloss

hair bobbing. "Oh, and now your little friends have joined you," she said pointedly. Her eyes lingered on Rowan. "Don't I know your face?"

"Of course," said Rowan, smiling angelically. "I was in here just last week, don't you remember?"

"Me too," said Fabian before Rosie could answer. "I gave you a ten-pound note and you tried to give me the change of a fiver. Does that ring a bell?" His deliberately loud voice attracted the attention of the people nearby. Rosie looked shocked, then decidedly annoyed.

"Can't say I remember, dear," she trilled, piling her tray with crocks and scuttling inside with a backward glare at Fabian.

"She didn't really shortchange you, did she?" Tanya asked.

Fabian grinned wickedly. "Nope. But it got rid of her, didn't it?"

"Don't count on it," said Rowan, grumpy now. "The old magpie will soon be back, trying to peck money out of us with that greedy *beak* of hers." She glanced through the door into the shop, past a red-faced Rosie, to the teapot clock on the wall. "We need to figure out how to get that potion to Jack—I think we need to stay here a bit longer, so we'd better order something."

Sparrow's eyes widened in alarm. "I can't fit nothing else in. But you lot have something, go on. Have what you like. Tino's paying."

Fabian dived on the menu. "Strawberries and

cream milkshake," he said. "And a piece of short-bread." Remembering his manners he quickly added, "Please."

"I'll have some lemonade," said Tanya, peering over Fabian's shoulder. "Thanks."

"Nothing for me," said Rowan. She felt nervous, and Tanya seemed unusually subdued, which wasn't helping. "Go inside and order, will you? I don't want to see that old busybody any more than I have to today."

Fabian and Tanya got up with a scraping of chairs and went inside.

"Where's Suki?" Rowan asked.

"Ain't seen her for a while," Sparrow replied. "She's scouting round the town, trying to sniff out any place the mother might be hidden. She's had no luck so far." He leaned back in his chair, fidgeting. "So what exactly did you get, and who gave it to you?"

"It's a truth spell," Rowan said, leaning close to keep their conversation private. The lemony scent of Sparrow's newly-washed hair swept over her again, and she found herself appraising him without really meaning to. He looked so very different. "Not as strong as something to do away with glamour, but all we could get at such short notice. There's an old gypsy woman living in the woods—I daresay Fix would have known of her. Anyway, she's helped Tanya out a few times. We can trust her."

"Good," said Sparrow. He looked relieved.

"Good." He turned to check that Tanya and Fabian were inside. "Did you tell them two? About Fix, like?"

"Yes," said Rowan. "I had to. They need to know exactly what they're involved in. Whatever that is. Have you told Tino?"

"Suki had already done it by the time I got back last night," said Sparrow. "Tino's getting word out to the rest. Said we all need to be vigilant, which I'd figured out by now, anyway."

"What did he think happened?" Rowan asked. "Does he think that...that someone else was responsible?"

"Too right he does." Emotion leaked into Sparrow's voice. "He knows as well as I do that Fix wouldn't have knowingly taken poison."

"Why does Suki believe the opposite, then?"

He shrugged. "She never knew Fix that well. She hadn't worked with her as often as the rest of us." He sighed and scratched at his head. Rowan watched. Sparrow was so used to his greasy scalp itching that the action had become a habit.

Tanya and Fabian came back to the table and sat down.

"Who's got the what's-it?" Sparrow asked.

"What what's-it?" said Fabian.

"The *potion*," Rowan said through gritted teeth, looking around warily. "Tanya's got it."

"It's in my pocket," said Tanya. "The bottle is pretty small."

"All right," said Sparrow. "Leave it there for now. We all need to think about how we're going to get that bottle to Jack."

"No need." Suki arrived at the table to catch the end of his sentence. She took a chair from a nearby table and pulled it over to them. "You managed to get something, then?"

Sparrow nodded. "I didn't think we would, but we had a stroke of luck." He quickly explained the nature of the spell to Suki, along with their source.

"You said you had an idea to get the bottle to Jack," Rowan prompted. "What is it?"

"Jack managed to get a message to me this morning just after I dropped off the instructions with the delivery. He put a note in a bottle and dropped it out through a window at the side—I just caught it before it smashed. He says he sometimes helps to collect glasses at the end of the lunchtime shift, around three o'clock. We wait until Jack comes outside to collect any glasses from the tables, then one of us can walk over and ask him for directions, giving him the bottle to pocket and take back upstairs. We then go ahead with the rest as planned."

"We've still got a while, then," said Rowan. "About half an hour."

They all turned to look at the Spiral Staircase. It was a crooked little pub, all white walls and dark beams, and the roof sloped forward into the street, giving it an unstable look. Like Mrs. Beak's, wooden tables were lined up outside, some with umbrellas, and a leafy archway to the side of the door led to a back garden with yet more tables.

"Where's the staircase, then?" asked Sparrow.

"Inside," Fabian answered. "It leads up to a gallery on the first floor that overlooks the stage when they have bands playing. Cast iron, it is."

"Shame it's in the public part of the place, and not used by the family," said Sparrow. "The changeling would never have got past the stairs, what with it being iron."

They watched the building in silence. Jack's father was clearly visible through the windows, drying glasses behind the bar.

"So this gypsy woman," said Suki. "She lives in Hangman's Wood? Whereabouts?"

"In a caravan," said Tanya. "It's near the brook, past two of the catacombs."

"We should speak to Tino," said Suki thoughtfully. "We might be able to use her in light of... of poor Fix." She stared at the table, her blond hair falling over her face.

"Did you get anything from Jack's mother's ring?" Rowan asked her.

Suki sighed and closed her eyes. "Not really. Only a feeling that she's somewhere close... but the more I try and force it, the further it slips from me."

"Do you think she's alive?"

"I'm not sure."

The conversation broke up. Across the street, the noise levels rose at the Spiral Staircase, and the laughter grew more raucous. Sparrow's eyes were trained on Jack's father, and Fabian fidgeted and adjusted his glasses repeatedly, watching the upstairs part of the pub for any glimpse of Jack at the windows. Once or twice there were shadowy movements beyond, but nothing clear. All the windows were thrown open to entice a breeze through.

Finally, the clock in Mrs. Beak's chimed daintily, announcing that it was now three o'clock.

"It's time," said Sparrow, not taking his eyes off Jack's father. "Everybody needs to be prepared. Until the changeling reacts to the spell we won't know how to respond. It all depends on whether she leaves with or without Jack's sister."

"And whether Jack is successful in the first place," Fabian muttered.

Moments later Jack appeared at the door, carrying a large plastic crate.

"There he is," said Rowan, tensing. "Who's going to deliver the spell?"

"I'll do it," said Tanya.

"No. You can't do anything that directly involves you, not after Gredin's threats. Give it to someone else."

"I'll do it," said Suki, holding out her hand.

Tanya pulled the tiny bottle from her pocket and handed it over.

Suki got up and left the table, crossing the street. The bottle was concealed in her palm as she casually approached Jack. He lingered at one of the tables, taking time to fill the crate with empty bottles and glasses and pausing to return the good-byes of the bar staff finishing their shift as they left. Tanya's sharp eyes caught sight of a label on Jack's top—it was inside out. Suki headed for the table, stopping only when close enough to touch him.

No one could hear what she said to him, but after some gesticulating and pointing down the street, Suki smiled at him and came back to the table.

"Done," she whispered, her smile gone, replaced by a furrowed brow. "All we can do now is wait."

Jack went back into the pub. Agonizing minutes passed, in which another member of staff turned up for the next shift. The clock in the tea shop chimed the quarter hour.

An upstairs window of the Spiral Staircase, the one furthest from them, slammed shut. The next window along the row closed seconds later. Then a third.

Rowan stiffened in her chair. "Who's doing that? Who's closing all the windows when it's still so warm?"

"Something's happening," Sparrow whispered, rising in his seat.

A figure appeared in the fourth window directly opposite them. A woman leaned out, her eyes cold and her hair wild. Her mouth moved quickly with unheard words as a thin arm reached out for the window. Her body twitched with small spasms, like she was in pain. With a clawlike grip on the window, she pulled it shut with a bang.

"It's her," said Suki. "The changeling mother."

Rowan felt the hairs on the back of her neck prickle. Whatever the changeling was, its façade was slipping. Jack must have succeeded.

"Where's Jack?" said Suki. She searched the windows. "He hasn't made the signal...but something seems wrong."

"Then maybe he *can't* signal," said Tanya. "Perhaps he can't get to the window."

"We've got to get him out," said Rowan. "*Now.* Fabian, are you ready? Can you do this?"

"I can do it," said Fabian. He got up, the milkshake moustache clinging to his upper lip making him seem young and vulnerable.

"No, you can't," said Rowan. "I can't let you go in there with that...that *thing.*"

"Stick to the plan," hissed Suki. "It's too late to change it now—everything's hanging in the balance!"

"I'll take care of Jack's father," said Sparrow. He stuffed a rolled-up twenty-pound note under Fabian's glass, then got up and sauntered across the street. Stooping, he collected one of the small plant pots by the door and hurled it at the nearest window. The pot missed the glass and bounced off the frame, fell, and smashed on the ground.

A customer at a nearby table stood up, outraged. Jack's father appeared at the door with a roar. Sparrow grinned obnoxiously and took off, fleeing down the winding cobblestones of Wishbone Walk.

Jack's father followed him, red-faced. *"Get back here, you little bleeder!"*

"That's him out of the way for a few minutes," said Suki. "The rest is down to us. Fabian, you go in and try to get Jack out. Remember, try *not* to go upstairs. Your aim is to get Jack called down. Rowan and I will wait around the back, near the alley."

They got up, Rowan collecting her knapsack from under the table. Only Tanya stayed seated, her hands clenched into fists on the tabletop. "Fabian, wait," she said as he started to move away. "Take these." She pushed a pair of tiny silver scissors at him. "I brought them, just in case. They're no good to me, sitting here. But they might come in useful to you. Remember, they'll cut through anything except for wood, metal, or stone."

Fabian took them, visibly nervous.

Then he, Rowan, and Suki walked to the Spiral Staircase. Tanya remained at the table, alone.

❦

The garden of the Spiral Staircase had more tables, spread out over grass and sheltered by trees and bushes. Only a couple of the tables were occupied. A back door led inside, propped open by an old iron. It provided a clear view into the pub.

Rowan and Suki sat at the table nearest the door. Fabian remained standing. To the left of the door an area of wooden fencing had been erected to stow the trash cans in. Either end was open—one for entry from the pub, and the other leading to the alley at the side, where the garbage collectors picked up the refuse. From the front, the trash cans were concealed from any customers in the garden.

Suki nodded to the trash cans. "You get in there and get that coat on," she told Rowan. "I'll wait here. Fabian, once she's in position, you go in. This is it."

Rowan stood, throwing the knapsack over her shoulder. She headed out of the garden toward the alley, then, once out of sight from the other tables, she doubled back into the trash area undetected. Quickly, she pulled the fox-skin coat from the bag and threw it around her shoulders, transforming as the catch was fastened. She took a moment to adjust to the peculiar shrinking sensation as she became fox-size, then took the knapsack in her jaws and dragged it out of sight behind one of the trash cans.

The stench of the rubbish pervaded her fox senses. Rotting food and waste reeked in the summer heat, and flies buzzed around her ears and tail as she made her way to the exit nearest the pub, poking her muzzle around the side to show Suki and Fabian she was in place. She took a quick snatch of air that wasn't fetid before shrinking back into her hiding place and trying not to breathe the rancid smell.

"Go," she heard Suki say.

The scent of fresh sweat, born of anxiety, reached her as Fabian passed her hiding place. Then he was through the door and out of sight.

Fabian blinked as his eyes adjusted to the gloomy light inside the Spiral Staircase. A little way in and to his right was a set of carpeted stairs leading up into the living area, and to his left a door was cracked open, revealing a small storeroom stacked with boxes of snacks and soft drinks. He waited at the foot of the stairs, but heard nothing from above.

Straight ahead was the bar area, and behind the counter a dark-headed girl adjusted the tuning on a crackling radio. The rest of the bar was empty, customers preferring to be outside in the sun. He could easily sneak up the stairs, but did not dare to, especially after Suki's warning. There was a risk he could be caught if he went up without permission.

He swallowed his nerves and approached the bar. The strong odor of stale beer hit him, leaving him queasy.

"Excuse me?" he said, his voice timid.

The barmaid looked up.

"I'm one of Jack's friends," Fabian said. "Is he coming out today?"

The girl shrugged, checking her reflection in the mirrored glass behind the counter. It seemed to please her. "He's upstairs, I think. Go on up and ask him—do you know where you're going?"

"Yes," Fabian lied. "I've been here before." He backed out of the bar, returning to the stairs. His forehead moistened with perspiration. He took two apprehensive steps up the carpeted stairway and drew a deep breath.

"Jack?" he called, in a surprisingly steady voice. "It's me, Fabian." He stopped, realizing his error. How many times had the power of names been discussed? Too many to think about, and now he had just blurted his out in the presence of something fey and potentially dangerous. "*Idiot!*" he cursed under his breath. There was no choice except to continue. "Are you still coming out?"

There was no reply. Something shifted upstairs; the sound of a footstep on a loose floorboard. Fabian took another slow step up. "Jack?" he called again. He craned his neck but could not see much further than the banister, except for a couple of doors in the hallway, both closed. With no natural light filtering through, it was dark. Fabian spied a light switch by his hand. His finger hovered over it as he tried to decide what to do. Any minute now Jack's father could return and complicate things.

Impulsively, Fabian flicked the switch, and the hallway flooded with light. He looked back up the stairs—and half-fell, half-leapt back to the bottom in fright, twisting his ankle.

The woman they'd seen at the window stood motionless at the top of the stairs, watching him. Her head was tilted to one side, alert, like a dog about to pounce on a rabbit. Her face was waxen, and her brown hair hung limply in greasy shanks on either side of her head.

Fabian fought the instinct to flee and forced himself to smile.

"Oh, you made me jump!" he said, giving a little laugh. "I was wondering if Jack's still coming out today? My mum's taking us for a picnic."

The tilted head slowly straightened.

"Jack cannot come out with you today." The woman's words were slow and controlled, as though she was fighting some deep-rooted urge. Adrenaline surged through Fabian. He shoved his hands in his pockets to hide them, for they were trembling uncontrollably.

"Oh, no," he said. "Did he forget to tell you?"

The woman's emotionless eyes bored into his, unblinking.

"He did not tell me about any . . . picnic. And now we are doing something else." She massaged her right wrist with her left hand.

"Typical Jack," Fabian said, forcing himself not to squirm or look away. "Never mind. I don't suppose you could send him down for a minute, could you? I just wanted to ask him something. It's about a school project."

"Jack cannot come down." The voice grew colder. "He is a little tied up."

Despite the fact that he was sweating heavily, the words sent a chill running over Fabian's flesh.

He is a little tied up.

It's the truth, he realized. *The truth spell means she can't lie... but she's managing to choose her words carefully to try to throw me off the scent.*

"Not to worry, then," he said, backing down the stairs. "I'll catch up with him soon."

On the last step he turned, skin crawling at the thought of the thing's eyes fixed on the back of his head. He carried on past the stairs, out of sight, and stopped short just before the back door.

He bent down, quickly pulling his shoelaces loose to buy time in case he was discovered by Jack's father or the barmaid. In his head he counted slowly to thirty, listening for any movement from the stairs. From the main bar he heard voices and low music from the radio. He forced himself to tune them out, his mind wrestling with what to do. Suki had warned him to avoid going upstairs. But he had failed to draw Jack away, leaving the boy and his little sister at the mercy of the changeling. For that, Fabian could not help feeling somehow responsible.

A slow, creeping footstep retreated on the landing above, and a tiny click sounded as the light was switched off again. Somewhere upstairs a door closed softly, and a young child began to cry. The plaintive noise set alarm bells clanging in his brain, making his decision for him.

Fabian finished counting and tied his shoelaces again. He stood up and wiped his hand across his face. Then he rounded the corner to the stairs, gripping the banister, and began to climb as quietly as he knew how.

14

The crying grew more pronounced as Fabian got to the top of the stairs. His eyes had adjusted to the dim light now, and he saw the outlines of doorways from daylight squeezing through the gaps in the frames. One door was open a tiny crack; he tried to get a sense of which room it might be, or whether anyone was in it, but neither saw nor heard anything. The wailing came from a door behind him, the furthest from the stairs. To reach it, he needed to pass the door that was ajar.

He crept along the hallway, the carpeted floor absorbing the sound of his footsteps. He passed two closed doors. The third was the one that was slightly open. He paused outside, pressing himself against the wall. His heart pumped like that of a frightened rabbit. A frantic whispering from inside the room made it to his ears. He strained to decipher any words, but could not.

Chancing a quick look through the gap, he assessed what he saw. Wooden units, a sink, and a black-and-white tiled floor. Liquid glistened on the smooth tiles. Nearby were fragments of glass. Something had been broken and spilled, and there was a horrid smell coming from the room, briny and metallic.

A loud bang from inside the kitchen made him bite his lip. The whispering became a mutter.

"I've tried to act like a good mother, haven't I? But it's not easy. *Never easy*. And what does a mother do? She makes dinner. But cooking isn't the thing. Cooking *spoils* it...."

A manic chuckle followed, and Fabian squeezed his eyes shut. Composing himself with great effort, he leaned around and this time looked through the other gap—the one in the hinge side of the door.

The changeling mother stood hunched over the work surface, its back to the door. Behind it the kitchen table was laid with four plates, and one of the settings was for a high chair.

The changeling's body shook with effort, but Fabian could not see what she was doing from where he was. Between the cries from Jack's sister in the back room, he thought he heard wet sounds, like something being cut. He contemplated creeping to the furthest door while the changeling was still occupied. But then it turned, cementing him to the spot.

In its right hand it clutched a large, dead fish. It was still raw and had been opened up, but it had not been cleaned properly, for its innards dangled in a wet, dark mass. The changeling mother slapped it down on one of the plates and stared at it. Speckles of red hit the white crockery.

"No good," she murmured. She lifted her hand, slimy with fish guts, and tugged at her hair. "Can't do it anymore... can't keep pretending. They'll know now. Only wanted *her*. I only want the girl."

Fabian retched, clamping his hand over his mouth and nostrils. Unable to watch any longer, he slid past the door and followed the crying noise, almost staggering in fear. He reached the door and turned the handle, silently begging it to open. It did. However, his next footstep yielded the very same creaking of the loose floorboard that he had heard earlier. Had the changeling heard it above the child's cries?

Panicking, he pushed the door open and entered the room. It was dim, for the curtains had been drawn, but he saw that it was a toy room. In a playpen over by the window, a toddler sat wailing, snot trailing from her nose. Jack sat on a chair in the opposite corner, a gag in his mouth and his eyes bulging in terror. At first Fabian could not see what bound him to the chair, but on approaching he recognized the glittering strands of weblike thread that encompassed Jack. There were crisscross cuts over the boy's hands where he had struggled against it. Fabian had seen it before a year ago in Hangman's

Wood on the night Tanya had almost vanished into the fairy realm.

Hurriedly, he yanked the gag away from Jack's mouth, holding his finger to his lips to indicate that they should keep quiet.

"She's in the kitchen," he whispered. "I couldn't get you to come down so I decided to come up." He glanced at the child. "And she's not leaving. I think we need to take your sister with us and get out of here. We can't wait for Rowan to come up—we just need to escape, all three of us."

Jack shook his head. "I can't get free—I don't know what this stuff is but it's not coming off! Just leave me.... Take Lucy and go."

"Shh. It's spidertwine," said Fabian. He pulled Tanya's scissors from his pocket and started to cut at the thread, which fell away at their touch. "It can't be broken by human hands, because it's magical." He held up the scissors. "But so are these. How did she tie you up? I thought you were protected."

Jack's face was pained. "I was. My dad noticed my shirt was inside out just after I'd got the potion and made me turn it the right way. I meant to turn it back again when I got upstairs but I was so focused on what to do with the potion that I forgot."

Jack brushed at the last of the disintegrating strands and stood up, rushing to the playpen. "I put the spell in a glass and made out it was a drink," he said, lifting Lucy out. The little girl clung to him, her crying easing to a whimper. "Then I dropped it on the floor for her to walk in. That's when she went crazy and tied me up. She said if I didn't let her she'd take Lucy…"

Fabian nodded and hushed him. "Is there any other way out apart from going past the stairs?" he asked. "Do any of the rooms below have bay windows that we could climb out onto?"

Jack's eyes darted over Fabian's face. "I don't… no. There's nothing. The only way is past the kitchen—"

The floorboard outside the room creaked, cutting him off. Fabian felt ill with dread as the door opened wider.

The changeling mother stepped into the room. Her mouth twisted into a snarl at the sight of Fabian and the freed Jack. From his position on the stairs minutes ago, Fabian had not had the advantage—or disadvantage—of seeing her fully. Now that he did, his eyes were drawn to her feet. They were bare, wet, and bloody from walking through the spilled truth spell and broken glass. They were feet that did not look human.

She took a limping step toward them, her maddened eyes sliding over Jack.

"How did you get free? That's not possible…."

Jack cringed away from her, holding Lucy out of reach. The child began crying again at the sight of the changeling mother. Fabian stood between them, brandishing the scissors as though they were a sword. The changeling eyed them, a spark of something in her eyes that Fabian could not read.

"Anything is possible when you've got the right tools," he said, using all his energy to summon an air of confidence he did not feel. "And unfortunately for you, you're beaten." He had a sudden, desperate idea. "These scissors will cut through almost anything. I *imagine* that includes skin and bone, but we'll all find out for sure if you take one more step toward us." With his free hand, he reached into his pocket, forcing his mouth into what he hoped was a smug smile. "And if you think the truth spell was bad, you don't even want to know what's coming next."

The changeling's chin dipped. She viewed him through hooded eyes. Fabian held his ground, his hand still in his pocket. He was certain she had seen through his bluff and was about to spring at him....

But to his amazement, she turned and fled, her footsteps beating a drum on her descent of the stairs.

❦❦

The changeling whipped past Rowan and Suki, momentarily stunning them both. Her lank hair trailed after her as she ran, barefoot and uncaring, through the beer garden and vanished into the alleyway.

Recovering herself, Suki sprinted after her. Rowan put her eyes up to the wooden slats of the trash area. Through a gap she saw that the few people in the garden were looking toward the alley, wondering what was going on. With their attention elsewhere, she darted from her hiding place and slipped through the door and up the stairs, unseen.

The smell of blood hit, like a punch to the gut, near to one of the rooms. She nosed through the door, terrified of what she was about to see. Why had she ever agreed to Fabian's involvement?

Because you had no choice, a little voice inside her said. Even now, she wondered if that were true.

Something wet and thick dripped from the kitchen tabletop. She skirted around the broken glass and wetness on the floor, coming closer to the table. Terror made the situation surreal. Pushing up, she lifted herself to balance on her hind legs, resting her forepaws on the table. The dead eyes of the mangled fish stared back at her. She slid back down, relieved, but for seconds only.

A noise drew her to the room furthest away: a muffled sob. She followed it, her fox ears twitching. The door was open, but not until she was through it did she see Fabian, Jack, and Lucy, frozen in position.

Fabian sank to his knees when he saw her. Rowan ran to him and he threw his arms around her, pressing his face into her rough fur.

"We thought you were *her*," he said shakily. "We thought she'd come back...."

"She's gone," said Rowan gruffly, her muzzle by Fabian's ear. His bushy hair brushed against her nose. "Now let me go, Fabian. I'm not a dog, you know."

"Right." Fabian dropped his arms, embarrassed. She gave him a quick affectionate nip.

"Now, follow me. I don't think she'll be coming back but we can't take the chance. We need Jack and Lucy away from here until we know where she is."

"She said she wanted the girl," Fabian mumbled, clambering to his feet. "She said she only came for the girl."

Rowan looked at Jack. Though Suki had undoubtedly told him about the fox-skin coat, he was watching her in astonishment. Lucy had burrowed her face into his neck, like a woodland creature hibernating.

"Thank goodness she didn't take her," said Rowan. She led the way out of the room, motioning for Fabian and Jack to follow. She considered removing the coat. It would not do to be seen as a fox inside a public building. Yet she dismissed it, for already another thought was brewing in her mind.

They crept downstairs, leaving the horrid, fishy scent behind them to gulp at the fresh air in the garden. Rowan scampered quickly to the trash area, speaking quietly to Fabian through the wooden slats.

"Take Jack and Lucy to the tea shop where Tanya is. Keep them there until I come back. You'll be safe there."

"Where are you going?" Fabian asked.

"I'm going after Suki. That thing has just shown how dangerous it is, and Suki could probably use the help."

"But—"

"Do as I say," she insisted. "There's not much time."

"Fine," Fabian said reluctantly. "We'll wait for you there. Just...be careful."

Rowan watched as they made their way through the leafy arch and left the garden. Once they were out of sight, she set off at a gallop into the deserted alleyway with only her fox senses to guide her.

The alley led straight on at first. Ivy dressed the fences and walls, litter caught in it like flies in a spider's web. Tall trees lined the gardens on the other sides of these walls, leaving the alley cold and dark, the perfect gathering place—or escape route—for anyone up to no good.

Soon the alley dead-ended into another running horizontally, offering two different directions. Rowan skittered to a halt, just managing to steer clear of a jagged shard of glass from a broken bottle. She nosed the air, trying to get an instinct for which way to go. The iron tang of blood and the smell of fish caught her nose. She saw a smear of something dark and wet on a fence post to the right. She took off, dodging trash, more broken glass, and stinging nettles.

The pathways grew tidier as she trailed away from the town and its shops and into the alleys behind the residential streets of Tickey End. Here the alleys bordered back gardens. In one of them she heard children playing, splashing in paddling pools and shrieking with laughter; in another she smelled the delicious waft of food being cooked on a barbecue.

She kept going, her claws clattering over the ground.

A piercing scream rang out up ahead, one that rose above the childish ones in the garden. This was a different scream, and she thought she recognized the voice.

"Suki," she murmured, racing toward it.

The alley ended unexpectedly and branched off again. She did not know which way to go, and she was afraid to call out for Suki in case the changeling was near. Rowan tried to scent the air but the barbecue was overriding things.

A slash of blond hair on the pathway to her far left caught her eye. She edged toward it, resisting the urge to run. It could be a trap.

Drawing closer, her caution vanished.

Suki lay sprawled on the dirty ground, eyes closed and one cheek pressed against the gravel. Her lower body was caught in an impossible tangle of ivy that could only be enchanted. Rowan nudged her face gingerly.

"Suki!" she whispered. "Suki, wake up!"

To her immense relief Suki stirred. Grit and dirt peppered her face and some of the gravel was embedded into her skin as she lifted her head.

"Wha—" she began. "My head feels like it's about to split in two. . . ."

"You're tangled up," Rowan whispered. "It's obviously the changeling's doing—you must have banged your head when you fell. Why weren't you protected?"

Suki groaned. "I don't know—I had an iron nail in my pocket but it must have fallen out as I ran. I nearly had her. . . ." She rested her cheek back on the ground. "She went . . . through there. . . ."

Rowan followed Suki's hand, streaked with blood, to where it pointed, through a broken gap in a fence opposite them.

"What's through there? Do you know?"

Suki shook her head, grimacing. "No. I was just about to follow when the ivy wound around me and pulled me back. She's probably gone by now."

"The trail might still lead to Jack's mother," said Rowan. "But I don't want to leave you like this—"

She was interrupted by a shout from the far end of the alley. Sparrow was hurtling toward them, holding his sides and fighting for breath.

"Suki!" he gasped, falling to his knees at her side. He turned to Rowan. "Is she all right?"

"I'll be fine," said Suki, trying to pull herself into a sitting position. Sparrow pulled a penknife from his back pocket and began to cut at the ivy.

"Where's Jack's father?" Rowan asked.

"Lost him," said Sparrow. "*Finally*. He can really run, but I think he's gone back to the pub now."

"Let's hope he doesn't go upstairs for a while, then," said Rowan. "Stay with Suki. I'm going after the changeling." She nodded to the gap in the fence. "Suki saw her go through there."

"I can go," Sparrow began.

"No. I've got the coat—she won't immediately know I'm a threat, and even when she does she can't use magic on me. I'm protected, remember?"

"All right," he conceded. "Watch yourself."

The broken wood surrounding the hole in the fence stuck out at jagged angles. Rowan jumped through it, but it was not a clean jump, and her paws gathered splinters from the wood as she brushed against it.

She landed in the large, overgrown garden of an old terraced house. It was prewar, for at the very back of it, past a neglected vegetable patch, squatted an old corrugated steel structure, dug into the ground with its roof curving out. It was an abandoned bomb shelter. She looked past it to the house. It was derelict. Some of the windows had been smashed and no one had bothered to board them up.

A ginger-colored cat wound its way out of the broken glass of a downstairs window, a squirming rat clamped between its jaws. The cat froze and then leapt to safety over the fence when it saw the fox. Rowan eyed the hole the cat had exited from, wondering if she could make it through into the house—but a whimpering sound stopped her.

She pricked up her ears. There it was again... coming from the bomb shelter. Skirting closer to it, she dipped her head to the open space between the rounded roof and the ground and peered past thick gray cobwebs to the inside.

Wooden crates and bundles of old sacking were strewn about. A terrible smell filled the air down there, and objects littered the stone floor. It was dark, and weeds had sprouted between the stones, making it impossible to see what the objects were, but on the other side Rowan saw a set of tiny steps. She set off down the side of the shelter, squeezing between it and next-door's fence, trampling weeds and sending a rat scurrying for shelter as she went.

The smell worsened as she descended the steps. At the foot of them, the small body of a goblin lay dead. This must be Jack's missing guardian, she realized. But she had not mistaken the whimpering, and now that she had reached the bottom, stepping over the goblin, she saw what she had missed from her viewpoint outside. A pale hand was visible from beneath a pile of sacking on a bed up against the wall. The objects she had seen from above crunched beneath her as she moved over them. She looked down, uneasy. Fragments of mirror; broken eggshells; strands of hair. She was uncomfortably familiar with the ingredients. Glamour had been worked here.

Cautiously, Rowan darted forward and pulled the sacking away with her teeth. Jack's mother lay beneath it, almost motionless, but certainly alive. Shaky little breaths were being emitted through her nostrils. Her mouth was tied with an oily-looking piece of rag. Her eyes widened at the sight of Rowan staring up at her. She shifted on the pile of cloth, maneuvering herself into a different position with one hand.

Her other hand was encircled by a manacle.

Rowan tensed, memories rushing back. She forced

herself to try to clear her head, but the broken items beneath her paws, and now the manacle, were too much....

Only then did it occur to her to wonder why the woman had not removed the gag from her mouth if just one of her hands was trapped. Rowan backed away, stumbling on something soft behind her: more sacking. And within it, something firm and just faintly warm.

She whipped around, tearing away the sacking with her teeth. There, a mirror image of the woman on the bed lay unconscious and most definitely incapacitated. She was bound with spidertwine. *This* was Jack's real mother.

Rowan turned, snarling, back to the changeling. It reached up with its free hand and pulled the gag away, smiling.

"I just came for the girl," it said. "Only wanted the girl...."

"You can't have her!" Rowan spat, trying to shield the woman behind her. She fumbled with the catch on her coat, but fear made her clumsy. "She's safe," she continued, stalling. "You'll never get near her again!"

The changeling's smile widened.

"That's where you're wrong," it said, reaching up into its hair. It pulled something out and threw it to the ground. It was a lock of Jack's mother's brown hair.

"Because she's exactly where I want her to be."

The changeling's hair grew thinner, dulling to ebony. Dark shadows below the eyes deepened, and the eyes themselves blackened. The features were changing, elongating, becoming masculine.

The voice was deeper next time around.

"She's right in front of me."

"*What?*" Rowan whispered, rooted to the spot.

The manacled hand rattled. Rowan screamed as the flesh and bone hand fell away, leaving a scarred stump to slip free of the iron casing.

The figure lunged at her, recognizable now as the face from her nightmares. Her next scream was shaped into a word, the name on her lips:

"*Eldritch!*"

15

Rowan hit the ground, the crushing weight of Eldritch's body forcing the air from her lungs. Pinned beneath him as he grappled to catch her, she was trapped inside the fox-skin coat with no time to take it off. The disadvantages far outweighed the advantages. Being fox-sized allowed for better chances of escape, it was true, but now she was in her enemy's grasp, and at a fraction of his size, she had little chance of fighting him off.

His weight shifted as he reached for something nearby. She sucked in a breath of air.

"Eldritch," she choked out. "I'm sorry. *Please*—"

"Quiet!" Scratchy material was pulled over her head, and a rough hand wrenched at her by the scruff of her neck, pushing her within the confines of the sack. "You think I've got time for your whining?

Please," he mimicked, twisting the neck of the sack closed.

Rowan tumbled to the bottom as he lifted it. Her claws scrabbled at the sides of the fabric, catching in it but too blunt to make a tear anywhere. A dizzying shake of the sack set her teeth rattling.

"Stop thrashing about!" he commanded, his voice cold. "Any more of that and I'll smash you against the wall and break a few bones. . . . It's your choice."

She stopped struggling at once. "What are you going to do with me? What are you going to do with Jack's mother?"

"Don't worry about her," he hissed. His mouth was close to the sacking, so close she could smell his breath. "My interest was never with them. They were just convenient. As for what I've got planned for you, well . . . you'll find out soon enough."

"How are you doing this?" she stuttered. "The glamour . . . when did you become so powerful?"

"I didn't *become* powerful," he said, his voice full of scorn. "I always had a talent for glamour. I traded with the Hedgewitch, remember? But when you last saw me, little fox, you thought I was weak. And I *was*. Rendered powerless—in every sense—by the iron I was trapped in. But while I was there, day in, day out, listening to the things the Hedgewitch did, well, I learned too. And believe me, there was no one better to learn from when it comes to glamour."

He set the sack down again, one foot on its neck keeping it closed as he knotted it.

Terror built inside her. She'd been in a sack like this before when she was captured by the Hedge-witch. Everything about it conjured memories—the rough weave of the fabric; the hard, cold stone floor below her; the lurching movements she couldn't control. Last time she had been held captive alongside a weakened fox. This time, she *was* the fox.

She sensed movement and pressed her head to the fabric. It was tough material but a thin weave, thin enough to see through. Eldritch was tugging off the stained clothes of Jack's mother and pulling on fresh ones from a wooden crate.

Precious seconds passed in which she tried to think. Would Sparrow still be nearby, or would he have taken Suki away from the alleyway by now? She pushed him from her thoughts. If she shouted for him there was no way she could guarantee he'd hear—and it would likely anger Eldritch into harming her more quickly than he intended to.

She contemplated taking off the coat, but the sack was too small. If she adapted into her human form the lack of space would completely restrict her movements. She had to stay as a fox.

She saw Eldritch struggling with the clothes, his speed in dressing thwarted by his stumpy wrist. The skin around it was red and tender-looking. She wondered what he had used to cut his hand off—and how long it had taken him to make the decision to do so after she had left him in the cellar.

Eldritch was nearly dressed, and time ebbed

away. She guessed now that he planned to leave and take her somewhere else. But where? And to do what?

Her claws had made no impact on the sack. The only weapon she had was her teeth, sharp little rows of needles. With as small a movement as she could manage, she started to chew on the fabric. It tasted sour and earthy, the texture of it squeaking against her teeth and scratching the soft tissue of her mouth. She gagged, but forced herself to carry on.

She had just succeeded in making a hole the size of a penny when the sack lifted up, jolting her out of position. Her tummy somersaulted with the sensation of the movement, reminding her of being on a fairground ride. She wriggled and strove to reach the hole again as the sack swung from side to side with Eldritch's footsteps. Her backside knocked painfully against the steps of the shelter as he half-carried, half-dragged her up them, and she heard herself yelp.

Abandoning the hole she began tearing anywhere she could lay her teeth. A small rip appeared in the loosely woven fabric. Through it she saw the overgrown garden as Eldritch carried her to the fence. The sack bumped against his legs as he walked, masking her own movements. Rowan worked at the tear, widening it as Eldritch clambered through the gap in the fence, pulling her through after him.

She heard a sickening crack, then his cry, and the sack hit the ground, jarring her again. Loud grunts, thumps, and the scrape of more than one pair of feet over gravel rang in her ears: Eldritch was being attacked.

Rowan tore savagely at the fabric, finally creating an opening large enough to squeeze her head through. Eldritch rolled on his back, dangerously near to her face, his assailant on top.

"Sparrow!" she gasped. She could not get any further out of the sack. Desperate, she retreated back into it and continued to bite and pull at it. Another section of it weakened and gave, and finally she scrambled through the opening.

Sparrow's element of surprise had bought him time, but seconds only. There was no doubt he was strong, but he was still a boy against a man, and now Eldritch took back control, strength lent to him by his madness. He flipped Sparrow over onto his back, his good hand clamped around the boy's throat, squeezing.

Rowan seized Eldritch's sleeve between her teeth, growling and tugging, but his grip was like iron. Sparrow's eyes watered, his skin flooding purple. His hands flailed, trying to push Eldritch's hand away from his throat. Eldritch's other elbow pinned Sparrow by the collarbone.

Suddenly Rowan knew what she had to do. Eldritch's weakness was her only chance. She released his sleeve and leaped over the two bodies to the other side. Then, with animal instinct, she sprang at Eldritch's stump of a wrist and sank her teeth into the puckered flesh where his hand had once been.

His scream was instantaneous. He thrashed his

arm, pulling away from Sparrow. Rowan held on as Sparrow coughed and spluttered, crawling to his hands and knees. Then the world spun, ending abruptly as she was slammed bodily into a nearby fence. The impact forced her to release Eldritch's bloody stump, but rain had softened the wooden fence and she hit the ground, gasping for breath but able to move. Nothing felt broken.

Sparrow had recovered sufficiently to square up to Eldritch once more, and now he had drawn his penknife. Eldritch clutched at his oozing wrist, biting down on his sleeve to prevent himself crying out. His skin was even waxier than Rowan remembered. His dark, red-rimmed eyes burned with hatred as he looked at her.

His mouth came away from his sleeve, a string of thick saliva linking to it.

"Run away, little fox," he said wetly. "Run far away and find somewhere to hide, because I found you once. I will again. . . ."

He glanced at Sparrow's drawn knife, staggered backward, then turned and loped off like an injured animal, vanishing into the labyrinth of alleys.

Rowan was too terrified and stunned to move straight away, but then she jerked to life, tugging the catch of the coat apart. Retching, she spat on the ground and wiped her mouth with the back of her hand.

"Sorry," she said to Sparrow. "I still had the taste of him in my mouth."

Finally she slipped free of the coat and stumbled toward Sparrow.

"He's gone," Sparrow said hoarsely, rubbing at his throat.

"How did you know?" she asked. "Where's Suki?"

"We were making our way back to the Spiral Staircase when I heard you shout his name," said Sparrow. "That's when I knew you were in trouble. I told Suki to keep going and doubled back. She should be there by now."

"He used magic on her," said Rowan, her voice shaking. "She wasn't protected. Let's get out of here—we need to get Jack's mother back to the Spiral Staircase somehow."

Sparrow's eyes widened. "You found her? Is she... alive?"

"Yes. She's through here," said Rowan, leading him back to the gap in the fence. They clambered through and she led the way to the bomb shelter. "This way. But she's unconscious...some kind of enchantment, I think."

Sparrow wrinkled his nose at the smell and shook his head at the sight of the dead goblin as they went down the steps to the unconscious woman. "Valerian," he said, kneeling to pick up a piece of shriveled root. "Probably used with something else to induce sleep. My bet is that he's kept her comatose the entire time. It'll wear off of its own accord but we need to get her back before it does."

Rowan closed her eyes in frustration. "How do

we do that? How on earth are we going to get her back into the building without being seen?"

"Simple," said Sparrow. "We just need to make sure the building's empty. We need to get everyone that's in it out of the way."

Rowan threw up her hands. "Again, *how*?"

"I've got an idea." He knelt and lifted Jack's mother into his arms. "Blimey," he said in disgust. "Lucky we found her when we did—she's a bag of bones. Come on, let's get out of here."

Between them, they managed to maneuver Jack's mother through the hole in the fence. They set off through the alleyways, heading back to the Spiral Staircase. Every so often Rowan glanced around, still dazed from the ordeal of seeing Eldritch again. The numbness of the shock she had felt was wearing off, and fear crept back into her.

"What if he comes back?" she whispered. "He's going to come after me again, I know it."

Sparrow stopped and faced her. They were surrounded by silence except for the trees lining the alley *shush-shushing* in the breeze.

"Yes," he said quietly. "I think that's pretty much guaranteed. But when he does, I'll be there." His blue eyes dropped. "We all will be. We won't let anything happen to you."

She nodded, a lump in her throat. "I...thanks."

Jack's mother stirred in Sparrow's arms, moaning softly.

"Move!" Sparrow hissed, his eyes full of alarm. "She's starting to wake up!"

Rowan broke into a run, leading the way. She heard Sparrow's breathing as he jogged behind her. Soon they were back at the rear garden of the pub, and loud voices came from within it.

"I can't risk being seen by Jack's father," Sparrow said, shaking his head. "You'll have to do it."

"Do what?"

"Find a fire alarm and set it off. It's the only way to get everyone out. Once the place has emptied we'll take her upstairs."

"All right." She slipped into the trash area, concealed from the alley, and stowed the coat in her knapsack, which she left hidden. Trying to look confident, she strode into the pub through the back door. Through the bar she saw Jack's father standing out front with a broom. He was red in the face and muttering to a customer.

She spied a fire alarm next to the small storeroom close to the stairs. A swift jab of her elbow smashed the thin glass, and an ugly, deafening bell rang out in a continuous drone. Quick as a cricket, she darted into the open storeroom and hid behind the door, listening.

"Out! Everyone out," a deep voice boomed. "This is not a drill. Everyone into Wishbone Walk at the front. Now, please!"

Through the hinges, Rowan saw Jack's father

stride past her hiding place. "Could anything else possibly go wrong today?" he muttered bad-temperedly to himself.

"More than you could have imagined," Rowan whispered, watching as he went into the garden and repeated the same orders there.

Within thirty seconds the building and its garden were empty, and mounting voices from the street in front reached her ears. This was their only chance.

She slid out of the storeroom and back into the garden, ducking her head into the alley.

"Sparrow?"

He emerged from behind a wild cluster of ivy, visibly straining to keep from dropping the woman in his arms.

"It's empty," she whispered. "Go, now!"

He vanished into the pub. Rowan dashed to the trash cans and grabbed the knapsack containing the coat, then waited in the alley. A minute passed with no sign of Sparrow. Sirens wailed in the distance.

"The fire brigade," she murmured. "Hurry up, Sparrow!"

He emerged, pulling his arm across his forehead in relief, and hurried to meet her. "I left her on her bed," he said. "But I don't think she's going to be out of it for much longer—she was starting to mutter by the time I put her down. The alarm bell definitely wasn't helping."

Together they exited the alley to the side of the pub, emerging in Wishbone Walk. The street was in chaos. A large crowd had gathered to watch the events unfold, and Jack's father was trying, unsuccessfully, to keep them back, while at the same time scanning the faces.

"Where's my family?" he said. "They should have come out...has anyone seen—"

He broke off. Jack was pushing toward him, Lucy in his arms. He pulled them to him, and anxious words were exchanged. Over his father's shoulder, Jack spied Rowan, his small face questioning and full of worry. She smiled and nodded, suddenly exhausted and grateful that for Jack and his family, at least, things were going to be all right.

Jack pointed suddenly. His father turned, then raced back toward the building where his dazed wife had appeared by the front entrance, rubbing her eyes. He tugged her away to their children, kissing her forehead as she hugged Jack and Lucy.

The sirens grew louder and flashing lights were visible as a fire engine rumbled down the tiny street, forcing the crowd back. Sparrow ducked his head and took Rowan's hand, pulling her toward Mrs. Beak's tea shop, now almost deserted except for one or two tables. Tanya, Fabian, and Suki were still seated, silent and stone-faced in their anxiety. Suki hooked a handful of ice from Tanya's empty glass, wrapped it in a napkin, and pressed it to her temple.

Tanya jumped up when she saw them.

"Time to go," said Sparrow, jerking his head for them to follow.

They scrambled out from under the awning and merged with the crowd of people on the street, heads down, until they reached the square. Sparrow led the way to the town hall, finally releasing Rowan's hand to collapse on the steps.

"We did it," he said, allowing himself a small smile. "Jack's family is safe." He rested his elbows on his knees and rubbed his face.

"I knew we could," said Fabian, his eyes shining behind his glasses.

"So it's over?" Tanya asked, gazing at Rowan. "Your last job. You don't have to get involved with all that anymore."

Rowan sat down next to Sparrow. Her knees felt weak, like they would not hold her up much longer. "No," she whispered. "It's not over."

"What do you mean?" said Suki sharply. "You brought Jack's mother back—you *saved* her."

"I meant it's not over for me. Not yet." From behind them, the sirens finally stopped wailing, leaving Tickey End eerily quiet. "We need to go somewhere and talk about what just happened." Rowan paused and swallowed dryly. "Because for me, I think it's only just begun."

16

Suki's caravan was one of the smallest, and was furthest from the performance area of the circus, a few doors down from Tino's. A deep sea-green, adorned with silver engravings and patterns, it stood surrounded by the circus community's tethered horses, accompanied by a pleasant munching noise as they grazed.

Suki opened the door and beckoned—then squealed and backed into Sparrow before anyone else was even through the door.

"What's the matter?" Sparrow barged past her into the living area. "Oh, it's Crooks." He turned to Suki in surprise. "Did you know he was going to be here?"

Tanya clambered up the steps, Fabian and Rowan close behind. Suki's face was clouded with anger when they got inside.

"No, I didn't." She grabbed a cushion from a nearby chair and hurled it across the caravan. Crooks was sprawled out on Suki's tiny bed, his boots resting on a patchwork blanket. The cushion caught him on the side of his face, but failed to remove the smirk from it.

"How many times have I told you *not* to keep letting yourself in?" she yelled, hands on her hips. "Just knock, like everyone else!"

Crooks gave a lazy shrug, a bunch of keys hooked around his finger. "You weren't here," he drawled, swinging the keys in a circle. "So I thought I'd come in and wait for you."

"Well, don't. You made me jump."

"Clearly." Crooks pushed past the velvet curtains on either side of the bed. He straightened his striped trousers and flicked his black hair back off his face. "I can see you've got guests, so I'll come back later."

"You might as well stay," said Sparrow, with a grudging glance at him.

"Fair enough." Crooks plopped back down on the bed, grinning.

Suki sighed and sat down next to him. "Close the door," she told Fabian, who was the last in. "You'll have to take a seat anywhere you can find one. I'm sorry it's so small; it's only designed for one person." She seemed lost all of a sudden. "It was Cassandra's before it was mine."

Sparrow perched on a wooden window seat close to the bed. Tanya, Fabian, and Rowan squeezed in and sat on a woolen rug on the floor. It was cozy in the caravan, and more homely than at Tino's, with intriguing items dotted around the place, a little like Mad Morag's. Yet there were no items that gave any indication of Suki's past beyond the circus—no family photographs or trinkets, nothing that was without function. Tanya wondered if she found reminders of her family too painful.

"So what's going on?" Crooks inquired.

No one answered at first. Eventually Sparrow broke the silence.

"That job we did today—there was a...something unexpected happened."

"The one with the changeling mother?" asked Crooks, still spinning his bunch of keys. "Did something go wrong?"

"Not exactly. We got rid of the changeling... found the real mother and brought her back, but..."

"It was all a ruse," Rowan put in. It was the first time she had spoken since Tickey End, and only after she had entered the caravan had she stopped looking over her shoulder. "The whole thing...it was devised to get me there. The person masquerading as the changeling used the family to get to *me*."

"*What?*" Tanya said, incredulous. "Who?"

"And why?" asked Fabian, looking equally shocked.

"Eldritch," Rowan whispered, fearing to say the name. "And the reason why is easy—he wants his revenge."

"Eldritch," Suki repeated. "The fey man you left in the cellar, is that right?"

Rowan nodded.

"Well, you can't really blame him," Crooks said. "I mean, you *did* leave him there, didn't you?"

"Yes, I know, but—"

"And you can't blame Rowan for reacting that way," Tanya snapped, glaring at the black-haired boy on the bed. "Eldritch was there when her brother—when James—was taken away! It's only natural that she would have wanted revenge."

"But he didn't deserve that," Rowan muttered.

"Maybe not," Tanya said. "But you acted in the heat of the moment—it wasn't out of spite."

"So if you left him there, how did he get out?" Crooks asked.

"His hand...the one that was manacled to the wall. It had been cut off—there was just a stump," Rowan said in a small voice.

Fabian let out a low whistle. "He did it himself?"

"It's possible," said Rowan. "But I can't think what he would have used—he had no weapons. The Hedgewitch would have taken them from him."

"So perhaps someone else helped him," said Tanya. "But who?"

"The coat," Rowan whispered. "It has to be."

"What about the coat?" said Fabian.

Rowan pulled the fox-skin coat from her bag. "This coat was made to order by the Hedgewitch. It was the only garment in the place that was ready—

someone was coming to collect it. But I'd already taken it. Whoever that person was would have been angry with me for taking it, and Eldritch wouldn't have held back in telling them. That would be reason enough for them to help him escape, leaving him free to come after me." She pulled her knees to her chest and began to rock. "I knew it. I knew he'd get out somehow and come after me...."

"So why now?" asked Crooks. "And why go to the trouble of involving Jack's family?"

"Because he knew he couldn't get to me directly," Rowan answered. "I've been protecting myself and surrounded by people. This is the only job I've done in months. With me using the coat it made things a lot easier for him—it's more difficult to abduct a person than it is a fox. To get to me he had to trick me into coming into contact with him. He must have been planning it all this time."

"But if that's true he must know about what you do," said Suki, her eyes wide. "That you were involved in all this... that it wasn't just James you were trying to find. And if he knows about you, then..."

"Chances are he knows about some of us... if not all of us," Sparrow finished.

"And with what's just happened to poor Fix, and Cobbler and Dawn still missing, I'd say we've got a problem. A serious problem."

"They're not... missing," Tanya said. Her chest felt tight with the pressure of the secrets she had been holding in all day. "They're dead."

"How can you possibly know that?" Crooks asked.

"Because I saw them. I mean...I didn't actually see them, but I went to Morag's—the gypsy woman's—today. While I was there, she had a vision. I was standing next to her, looking into the water where the vision appeared. I saw it exactly as she saw it." She glanced at Rowan and Fabian and saw their shock at this admission. "I'm sorry I didn't tell you. We already had too much going on, and I didn't want to panic anyone." She paused, looking from face to face, with the exception of Fabian's. "It showed you...all of you. Your faces, one by one. I recognized you all from the barn the other night. It showed Fix...dead. A fly was crawling over her. And it showed two more faces, faces I didn't recognize—but I knew then that it was Cobbler and Dawn and that they were—"

Sparrow's face had drained of color. The entire caravan was in silence, horrified by the revelation. "Go on," he whispered.

"She said something," said Tanya. "'The thirteen secrets have been found out.' That's what she said." She glanced at Rowan. "She said you'd know what it meant."

Rowan covered her face with her hands and started rocking again. Tanya saw Suki's hair swishing from side to side as she shook her head vigorously.

"No. That's not possible."

"'Course it's possible," Sparrow said, his voice husky. "And it makes perfect sense."

"No, it doesn't," Suki argued. "It makes sense for Eldritch to come after Rowan, but the rest of us? Why would he bother? We've done nothing to him!"

Sparrow rubbed his thumb slowly over his chipped tooth.

"True. But there are two things that would make sense. Firstly, given Rowan's past, if she knew she needed protection, who would she be most likely to turn to?"

"Us," said Crooks. His cockiness had dissolved, and one leg was bouncing up and down in a nervous dance. "She'd probably come to us."

"He could be making sure you've got no one left," said Sparrow. "No one to run to."

Fabian frowned. "But he tried to capture her just now. If he was trying to get rid of everyone else first, why would he have acted then?"

"Good point," said Sparrow. "And I agree. I don't think he's targeting us all. I think he found his way to the Coven and used it for information."

"You mean he used the others to get to me?" said Rowan. "Three people are dead...because of me."

"It's not your fault," said Sparrow. "I was there... I saw him, remember? He's crazy."

"I'd be crazy too, if someone left me in a cellar to die!" she retorted.

"He was there a lot longer than you," Sparrow said gently. "You don't know what sort of things he witnessed, or heard. He was probably half-mad when you arrived there."

"Right. And then I pushed him over the edge."

"We don't know for sure that it's Eldritch who's done all these things," said Fabian. "At the moment all we're certain of is that he's after Rowan. We've got no proof of the rest—that he's found out about whatever these thirteen secrets are that you lot are guarding."

Rowan, Sparrow, Suki, and Crooks shared nervous glances.

"So what *are* the thirteen secrets?" Tanya pressed. She knew she had gone too far now. This meeting, and her relaying of Morag's vision, had surely broken Gredin's rules about her being involved. Her heart quickened at the thought of Oberon. She hoped he was safe at the manor. "What exactly are you hiding that someone out there is willing to kill for?" She looked from face to face, but every one of them seemed to want to look anywhere except for at her. They were clearly not going to answer.

"Well, whatever they are, you'd better start thinking about whether they're worth risking your lives for," said Fabian, peeved at the exclusion.

Tanya averted her eyes in frustration. She noticed a small wooden bookshelf, where rows of books on the occult rested below a number of fortune-telling objects: a crystal ball, tarot cards, and a crystal-dowsing pendulum.

Tanya wondered if any of them genuinely helped Suki in her psychic endeavours, or if they were merely props.

"None of them," Suki said suddenly.

"I didn't say anything," Tanya responded, unnerved.

"You didn't have to. I can tell what you were thinking." Suki pulled the patchwork blanket around her. "I don't need any of them. They're just for show. Makes people feel they're getting their money's worth, somehow."

"So how do you do it, exactly?" Tanya asked.

Suki shrugged. "I'm not sure. I just get pictures and words in my head that I can't explain. I don't know where they come from. Sometimes I don't even know what they mean until later. I don't use a seeing bowl like your gypsy friend." She paused. "Why do you think she told you about the vision?"

"She said I'd triggered it by being there," Tanya answered. "I suppose it's because I'm connected to Rowan—and because I care about her."

"What about you, Suki?" Crooks asked. "Haven't you had any inklings about what's going on with all this? Any visions?"

Suki pulled at a piece of loose thread on the patchwork quilt. "No, no visions. But I've been having bad dreams lately. Strange dreams, where I'm lost in a storm. I can't see ahead."

"You said you felt something was blocking you when you were trying to find Jack's mother," said Sparrow. "And she was close by—*really* close."

Suki nodded. "That's the one thing that I do understand. She was hidden in an old bomb shelter—it had a steel roof. One thing I've noticed about my visions is that they don't see past or through iron. It... scrambles things, somehow."

"So you think she was put there on purpose?" asked Sparrow.

"Maybe. If someone *is* after us, and knows about us, then there's every chance they could know about my limitations. As for the rest, I don't understand it either. Sometimes, if I try to concentrate too hard on something it won't come to me. But this feels different. It's as though everything is blocked. Like my dreams are trying to tell me something."

"Maybe Morag can help us again," said Tanya.

"Worth a try," said Sparrow. "If she's had one vision, there could be more she could help us with." He hesitated. "Was there...anything you saw...in her vision that could help us find Cobbler and Dawn? Anything at all that you can remember?"

Tanya squirmed as she recalled the horrifying images of the dead faces. "It was fast. They were flashing by so quickly, and I...I wanted to look away. But there might have been something. With Dawn she looked pale. So pale. But it was bright, like she was in sunlight somewhere. Outside. With the other man, Cobbler, all I saw was his face. And blood in his hair. I'm sorry—I don't remember anything else."

"It's all right," said Sparrow. "It's a start." He glanced at Rowan and Suki. "We need to tell Tino about this. Suki, update him as soon as possible. And tomorrow, I say we go back to Cobbler's and Dawn's and have another look around. There must be something we're missing, something that will lead us to them."

"What about me?" asked Crooks.

"You come as well, if you like," said Sparrow, although he sounded less enthusiastic. "In the meantime, you two"—he nodded at Tanya and Fabian—"go to see this Magic Morag, and—"

"Mad Morag," Fabian corrected.

"Whatever. Just see if she's able to tell us any more about what's happening." Sparrow looked at his watch. "It'll soon be time for tonight's performance." He jumped up. "I'll leave you to prepare for it, and I'll be back in the morning. Be ready. We're leaving early." He gestured to Rowan. "Come on. I'll take you home."

"But you'll be alone when you come back," she said.

"Don't matter." Sparrow attempted a smile, but it looked unconvincing.

Crooks got up. "I'll come. Then Sparrow won't be alone on the way back."

"All right," said Sparrow, but Tanya noticed that he did not thank him.

They left Suki's caravan and set off. They saw Tino nearby, distributing masks and costumes, and then they heard Suki call out to him. Sparrow led the way, his head darting from side to side, taking everything in, but nothing seemed amiss. Gypsy children ran about, laughing and playing with each other and the many dogs of the circus folk. Meals were being prepared on outdoor fires, while circus folk sat on the steps of their wagons, chatting and sometimes singing songs.

In the lanes leading back to Tickey End, Rowan walked close to Sparrow, jumping at every sound and movement. Crooks took up an annoying whistle, earning him several scowls from Sparrow, all of which he ignored. Tanya tagged along beside Fabian, who looked deep in thought about something. Once or twice he took out the brown, leather-bound book he always carried and hurriedly scribbled notes in the back of it.

"What are you doing?" Tanya whispered, trying to look over his shoulder, but Fabian nudged her away and closed the book.

"I've just had a thought about something," he muttered. "I'll tell you later, when I've got a better idea."

Only when they were through the gates of Elvesden Manor did Rowan finally seem to relax. They paused in the shadow of one of the stone gargoyles on the pillars that stood on either side of the entrance. Crooks's jaw dropped as soon as the house came into view.

"*This* is where you live?" He gave a low whistle. "You landed on your feet all right. The folks here adopting you?"

"Fostering," said Rowan, staring toward the front door. "Oh, no."

Nell was on the porch, shielding her eyes against the glare of the afternoon sun to stare at them.

"We'd better go," said Sparrow.

"You mean you're not going to ask us in for tea and cake?" Crooks said in a ridiculous, posh voice.

"Shut up," said Rowan. "No, I'm not. Go on, go. I'll see you tomorrow. And be careful."

Sparrow and Crooks vanished into the lane beyond the manor. Tanya, Rowan, and Fabian approached the porch. Nell stood at the door like a sentry, wielding a mop and tapping one flip-flopped foot.

"I've just done the floors," she said. "And I'm not doing them again, so you can all go around to the back."

"Fine," Rowan muttered, turning and traipsing back down the steps. They passed the rose garden at the side of the house. Further on, Warwick leaned over one of the animal pens to speak to Rose. They both looked up and waved. Rowan and Fabian offered quick waves back, but did not stop to talk. Tanya stared straight ahead, making out she had not seen.

At the back door a small, chocolate brown dog hurled itself at her legs with excited, high-pitched yaps.

"What...?" Tanya stared down in confusion. It was a puppy with rolls of fat rippling over its back. Its paws and ears were huge and outsized, and its entire lower body shook as it madly wagged its tail. Tanya's heart plummeted as she saw the puppy's collar. It was so large that, as the dog jumped up at her, the collar slipped past its neck and went around the middle of its body. "Oh, no..." she whispered.

"Whose dog is this?" said Fabian, kneeling to pat the puppy. "And where's Oberon?"

The puppy yapped and lunged playfully for Fabian's earlobe. Fabian yelped and pried it away.

Tanya took the collar and slowly turned it in her hands. "This *is* Oberon."

Rowan pushed past her and knelt at the puppy's side. *"What?"*

Tanya looked at her, her eyes wide and angry. "Gredin. He said he'd punish me by getting to Oberon if I defied him, and that's exactly what he's done!"

Oberon lavished her with licks before turning his attention to Fabian and Rowan. After enduring a few licks, Fabian escaped and went to the fridge, noisily drinking milk straight from the bottle. "It could be worse," he said between gulps. "He makes a cute puppy, I think. Apart from the biting."

"That's not the point." Tanya gathered the puppy into her arms, then released him when he began to squirm. "Gredin's got no right to mess around with my dog! And Oberon was just about the naughtiest puppy you could imagine. My mum said she'd never get another puppy again after him."

"What are we going to do?" said Rowan. "You'll have to tell Gredin you're sorry. Maybe he'll change him back."

"I'd rather be turned into a puppy myself than apologize to *him*!"

"Young man! Would you please use a glass?" Nell had followed them around the back, evidently wanting to keep her mopped floor pristine. She frowned at Fabian, then tipped her bucketful of dirty water into the drain and came into the kitchen, shrieking as Oberon bounded over to her.

"Where did this dog come from?" She flapped her arms. "It's bad enough having one set of muddy paws to clean up after. Take it away, it'll snag my tights!"

Tanya pulled Oberon away. "It's the same dog, Nell. The fairies...they've turned him back into a puppy."

Nell shrank back from Oberon as though she thought he were contagious. Then her mouth dropped open as a small, trickling noise began. Tanya looked down, already knowing what she was going to see. Oberon stood in a widening yellow puddle, still wagging his tail.

"I'll get some newspaper in a minute," Tanya said lamely.

Nell tutted. She turned to Rowan. "Who were those two lads with you just now?"

"Friends of mine," Rowan answered shortly, leaving the kitchen and heading for the stairs. Nell, Tanya, and Fabian followed, and Oberon bounded after them.

"Friends?" said Nell. "I haven't seen them before."

"That's because they haven't been here before. They're part of the circus."

Nell gave a surprised little squeak. "It's a good thing Florence is out. I'm not sure she'd approve of you bringing vagabonds back here. That dark-headed boy looked especially shifty."

Rowan raced past the grandfather clock, not bothering to reply. Nell waited by the clock as Rowan cleared the top step, evidently expecting an answer. It came in the form of a loud bang as Rowan slammed her bedroom door.

"*Well!*" said Nell, indignantly. "Friends of hers. My left foot!" She waltzed past Tanya and Fabian at the bottom of the stairs, leaving them alone in the hallway. In the silence, a snide voice sounded from the depths of the grandfather clock.

"Her left foot!"

Mischievous, tittering laughter rang out, followed by low whispering, but Tanya had neither the time nor the energy to wonder what it meant.

Oberon was now tugging at her trouser leg, wanting to play. She tried to disentangle herself and glanced about the hall to make sure she and Fabian were still alone. "What were you thinking of earlier, on the way home?"

Fabian took off his glasses and rubbed them against his shirt. "I can't say yet, in case I'm wrong. I need more time to think."

"Fabian!" she exploded. "Don't be stupid, of

course you can say! I don't care if you're wrong, just tell me what's going on in that head of yours."

"But I don't like being wrong," Fabian began to object, then gave in. "Oh, all right. Just don't tell Rowan. I want to be sure before I confront her."

"Sure about *what*?"

Fabian put his glasses back on. "Where's that charm bracelet of yours?"

"In my room, under the floorboard," Tanya said in surprise. "Rowan gave it back to me after she lost James. It's been there ever since, wrapped up in my red scarf."

"Can you get it?"

She hesitated. "Do I have to?"

"What's the problem?"

"The problem is that every time I go near that bracelet, something bad happens. It's like it's cursed. Why do you even want it?"

"Forget it," said Fabian. "Never mind." He pulled out his book and flicked through the pages. "I've still got the notes I made on each of the charms when we were hunting for them last year—I can work from that. I just thought it might help if we had something visual to look at as well."

Tanya sighed. "If you really think it'll help, then I'll get it. Just don't blame me if things start to go wrong."

"Things are already going wrong," Fabian said darkly. "Get the bracelet and bring it to my room."

Tanya returned Oberon to the kitchen, first cleaning up the puddle, then laying newspaper down. Then she shut him in, despite his whines. Her head pounded as she tried to think of what she was going to tell her grandmother and how she was ever going to get Oberon back to normal. She pushed it from her mind. There was nothing she could do just yet.

Ten minutes later Tanya was at Fabian's door, the bracelet safely concealed in the red scarf. Fabian called her into his room, his head bent over his desk as he wrote in his notebook.

"Close the door," he said.

She did, and sat on his bed. "It's tidy in here," she said in surprise.

"I know," he said, disgusted. "It's Nell. She keeps on putting things away and muddling everything up. I can never find anything after she's been in."

"I've got the bracelet," she said, unwrapping a corner of the scarf. A glimmer of light bounced off one of the charms. "Why did you ask me to bring it?"

"Come here," said Fabian.

She got up and went to the desk. In Fabian's notebook, a column of names had been written in the margin of one of the pages.

"Rowan, Sparrow, Tino, Suki, Crooks, Samson..." Tanya read. "You listed all the people who came to the barn the other night."

"Plus the two who didn't come," said Fabian. "Cobbler and Dawn." He put a light pencil line through both their names, and Fix's too. "There are thirteen names on this list. Three of them are already dead."

"Wait a minute," said Tanya. "I don't understand your reasoning. How does this link to the thirteen treasures just because there are thirteen names?"

"It doesn't. But I've been noticing things—things about these people. Maybe you've noticed things too."

"Like what?"

"Like Suki, having visions and being able to sense things. Crooks, always carrying keys about with him, plus the fact that he seems to be able to break into just about anywhere."

"He's an escape artist in the circus," said Tanya with a frown. "And Suki is the fortune teller, but she's genuinely got the ability. . . ."

"Then there's Victor, with his sword-swallowing and knives," Fabian rushed on. "*Clearly* an expert on weapons—he has to be for his part in the show. And his brother, Samson, the circus strongman—you felt how powerful he was when he grabbed us outside the barn. Don't you see? Don't you get it?"

Tanya unwrapped the bracelet and set it down next to Fabian. "Yes," she whispered. "I think I do." She took the pencil from Fabian's hand and wrote down four words, one next to each of the names: Cup, Key, Sword, Mantle. Then she put the pencil down and picked up the bracelet, looking through the charms.

"Suki: the Cup of Divination," Fabian said

solemnly. "Crooks: the Key to open any door. Victor: the Sword of Victory, and Samson: the Mantle, a staff for strength. Now, I don't know about you, but to me that seems an awfully big coincidence."

"I don't think it's coincidence," said Tanya. She picked up the pencil again and held it next to Fix's name. Her eyes drifted over the bracelet. "I remember now. One of her tattoos—it was a dagger. She tapped the dagger charm. "The Dagger, dripping blood that can heal any wound. Fix made potions and remedies. She had the power to heal." She wrote "Dagger" down next to Fix's name.

"She also had the power to kill," said Fabian. "One of her own concoctions killed her. Write that down."

Tanya wrote down "poison" on the same line. Then, almost subconsciously, she wrote "Glamour—a mask of illusion" next to Tino's name.

"Just a guess," she muttered. "With all the costumes and masks."

Fabian nodded. "I was thinking the same."

Tanya raised the pencil and rested it next to Rowan's name, looking at Fabian questioningly.

"That's what we need to find out," said Fabian. "We don't know enough about Rowan or the rest of them—or what they do—to make a judgment. But I'm guessing that every one of them symbolizes one of the thirteen treasures in some way, which indicates that this group of theirs is much more strongly linked than they'd like anyone to know. No wonder Rowan wants out."

"Why do you say that?"

A muscle twitched in Fabian's cheek. "Because with something running this deep, you can bet they've made some pretty dangerous enemies."

Nell's voice could be heard all the way up the stairs the next morning. Rowan woke, dragged herself out of bed and dressed, then went downstairs to the kitchen. Florence sat at the table, calmly sipping a cup of tea while Nell stood barefoot in front of the fireplace; a mound of shoes was strewn across the hearthrug. Already they had been well chewed by Oberon, who was still very much a puppy.

"Every single one of them!" she fumed, brandishing a scuffed shoe. "Just look! Even me bleedin' flip-flops! Now what am I supposed to wear while I do the housework?"

"You can borrow a pair of my slippers," Florence said with a sigh. "We'll have to go into Tickey End and get new ones."

Rowan sat down and reached for a slice of toast. "What's the matter?"

"Left feet! Every one of them." Nell threw the shoe to the floor. It landed near Oberon's nose, and he sniffed it longingly. "You might as well have that one too," Nell told him. She stomped to the table and sat, sulking. "I've had it up to here with those fairies!"

The General cackled from his cage. "My left foot!" he croaked. "My left foot!"

"Quite," said Nell. "It seems protecting myself isn't enough if they can still meddle with other things to annoy me."

"Speaking of which, nobody has told us what exactly Tanya did to anger Gredin," said Florence, glancing at Oberon, who was now pouncing on a pile of newspaper he'd shredded earlier.

Rowan pretended not to hear. "You need to appease them, Nell," she said, slathering her toast with butter and jam. "They've been targeting you ever since you caught one of them in your mousetraps. They're not going to forgive you that easily."

Nell scowled. "What do you suggest?"

"Leave some food out for them," Rowan said with a shrug. She bit into her toast and looked away as Warwick came into the kitchen. He frowned at the pile of shoes and at the puppy, but said nothing, busying himself by fetching the boot polish and brushes from under the sink.

Tanya and Fabian came down a few minutes later.

"What the..." Fabian began. A slow grin spread across his face as he studied the mountain of shoes. "Your left foot!" he crowed.

Nell glowered at him.

"That's enough, Fabian," Florence warned. "Any more of that and you'll be helping Nell with the housework for a week."

Fabian stopped grinning immediately.

"And Tanya, whatever you've done to annoy Gredin, will you please sort it out? Oberon has piddled just about everywhere this morning, apart from the garden, and you can't take him back home like that."

Tanya glowered into her cereal. "I know."

After breakfast was eaten and cleared away, Rowan, Tanya, and Fabian huddled on the landing upstairs.

"Right. I'm meeting Sparrow and the others in five minutes," Rowan whispered. "I should be back early this afternoon. I just told Florence I'm meeting some friends from school to talk about homework, in case anyone else asks." She collected her bag from her room, stuffing a notepad, a textbook, and her pencil case in the top to obscure the fox-skin coat hidden beneath, and locked her door.

She slipped down the stairs, leaving Tanya and Fabian behind, and left through the front door. She sat on the porch and pulled on her walking boots, and was lacing them up as Warwick came out. She saw his eyes slide over her bag, clocking the pencil case in the top where she had purposely left it open.

"Off to the library?" he asked.

"Yeah."

"Haven't seen much of you, considering it's the school holidays. Rose has been hoping you'd spend more time with her."

She stood up, fastening her bag. "I will," she muttered. "I'll come and see her this afternoon."

He nodded and strode off in the direction of his den at the side of the house, leaving her alone in the forecourt. She passed through the gates, and after a quick glance around, opened the bag and ditched the books and her pencil case in a bush at the side of the dirt track.

"Nice dress," a voice remarked.

She turned to see Sparrow and Crooks emerge from behind a cluster of trees opposite the gates.

"You look like a proper lady," Crooks said, smirking.

Rowan stared at him and lifted the hem of the dark green fabric slightly to reveal the tip of the dagger strapped to her right thigh. "Looks can be deceiving," she said. "I thought we all knew that by now." She let the dress drop back into place and started to walk. "Where's Suki? I thought she was coming."

Sparrow fell into pace beside her. Crooks skulked behind them.

"She's still at the caravan," Sparrow said. "She had another one of them dreams last night, and she's convinced someone has put some kind of a jinx on her, to block her visions, like. When we got there she was turning the place upside down, searching it all over for spells or curses. We're going back there now—if she hasn't found nothing by the time we get there she says she'll come with us to Dawn's."

Within twenty-five minutes they were heading toward Suki's caravan. A handful of people had gathered outside. Suki and Tino were there, along with Samson and Victor. Sparrow broke into a run, closing the gap. Rowan started to run as well, leaving Crooks trailing behind.

"You found something?" she asked, arriving beside Tino. Wordlessly, he pointed. Suki's caravan had been pulled back a few meters to reveal the ground beneath it. Next to her she heard Sparrow's intake of breath.

A large circle had been gouged into the grass, patterns and odd symbols carved within it. At its center, fenced in by a host of burnt-out matches and candles, a pebble weighted a photograph of Suki to the ground. Hardened candle wax had been dripped over her face, obliterating it.

"I knew it," Suki whispered, white-faced. "I just knew it. Someone's worked magic against me. This is why my visions have stopped." She leaned forward, reaching for the photograph.

"Don't touch it!" Tino batted her hand away. "Don't touch anything! You don't know what kind of spell this is—it needs to be properly disassembled." He glanced around, seeing more groups of people approaching. "Samson, move the caravan back into place for now. And all of you keep quiet about this. We don't want the whole camp knowing—the last thing we need is to cause a panic."

Samson dragged the caravan back into place, hiding the sinister circle from view, despite Suki's protests.

"We can't leave it," she insisted. "We have to get rid of it, now!"

"We will," Tino replied. "But we need to find out how to go about it. Without Fix, that could take awhile. But for now, a simple purge spell should be performed. I can tell you how to do it, but you'll need to do it alone...."

Suki and Tino walked off in the direction of his caravan, leaving the rest of them behind.

"That settles it, then," said Crooks, his eyes tracing the tracks in the mud where the caravan had been dragged. "Looks like we're going to Dawn's without Suki."

⬥

Almost an hour had passed since Rowan had left Elvesden Manor. While Fabian cleaned out the chicken coop and collected the morning's eggs, Tanya hung around the kitchen waiting for him to finish. She had held off on walking Oberon until Fabian returned to accompany her so that they might use the opportunity to talk about the previous night's discovery and to think about how to tackle Gredin's punishment. She was so preoccupied that, for several minutes, she did not realize that she was alone with her grandmother.

"Something on your mind?" Florence asked, emerging from the pantry.

"No," she said quickly, before realizing that there *was*, in fact, something she had been meaning to discuss. "Actually, yes." She sat down, silencing Oberon's whines with a biscuit. "It's about Gredin."

Florence closed the pantry door. "Are you going to tell me what's happened?"

"Not exactly. It's about guardians...fairy guardians in general," Tanya continued. "I know that every child born with the second sight has one, but what I don't understand is *why*. Because they don't seem to enjoy it, or want to protect us." She stroked Oberon's head, then lifted him onto her lap. "Sometimes they even seem to resent it."

She averted her eyes guiltily. "I know that he only punishes me when I do something he doesn't want me to, and he says it's for my own good, but..."

"You don't have to tell me whatever it was." Her grandmother's gray eyes were suddenly wistful. "I was young once too, you know." She stared down at her hands, crinkled and faded like a years-old newspaper. "I remember what it was like." She shook her head faintly. "I wasn't much older than you when I found myself asking the same question of Raven. She didn't want to answer, but eventually I wheedled it out of her.

"As you know by now, Elizabeth Elvesden was a

changeling. Her fairy bloodline resulted in some of the family, including you and me, having the second sight. That lineage will stay in our family for many, many years to come before it weakens. Now, we know from Elizabeth's diaries that her mother believed she was switched when she was a child. Most changeling cases are similar. What we may never know is *who* was responsible for switching her, or why.

"But sometimes, those involved in the changeling trade *are* found out. And when they are they must face trial in the Seelie Court. Of course, some of those who are guilty are protected—employed even—by the Unseelie Court, and so they escape notice, and punishment. Those who are caught are handed a sentence." Florence paused and stared into Tanya's eyes.

Tanya's pulse quickened. "I think I can guess what's coming."

"That sentence is to serve the best interests of both the human and the fairy changeling. Depending on the circumstances, this could involve either switching them back or protecting them in their new environment. But the punishment doesn't stop there. If any children are born following a switch, leading to a bloodline like ours, the sentence is also handed out to the descendants of those found guilty."

"So...some fairy guardians were never actually involved in the changeling trade, but are paying for the actions of their ancestors?" Tanya asked. "That doesn't seem fair."

"No, it doesn't," Florence agreed. "But the view is taken by the Seelie Court that it's not fair for the descendants of the changeling, like you and me, to have the burden of the second sight through no fault of our own, either."

"Then what about someone like Rowan?" Tanya asked. "Someone who's half-fey, half-human? That's not the same as a changeling switch, is it?"

"No," her grandmother replied. "But in Rowan's case, it was still a matter of fairies meddling with humans. Rose was enchanted and deceived by a fairy. It amounts to the same thing."

"Is there a way we can release them, so they don't have to be our guardians anymore?" Tanya asked.

"There is a way," said Florence. "It's forgiveness and acceptance. If you can truly say that you accept your ability, and blame no one, then your guardian will no longer be bound to you out of duty. But in my experience, you'd be better to keep Gredin around for now. Just until you're a little older. . . . I'd wait until you make that decision."

"But why?" Tanya asked, frustrated. "Why wait if I'm certain now?"

"Are you certain? Are you really? I thought I was certain once, about something. That something was the plan to run away to the fairy realm with Morwenna Bloom. I was sure it was for the best. Now, when I look back, I'm so grateful I was talked out of it. And who do you think was the one to do it?"

"Raven," Tanya whispered.

Her grandmother nodded and smiled. "Don't be hasty. You could regret it one day." She reached forward and patted Tanya's hand, the gesture less awkward than usual. "Now, how about a nice cup of tea?"

"Thanks," said Tanya. She watched as the lid to the tea caddy lifted. Two tea bags were thrown out onto the counter before the lid slammed down.

Florence retrieved them without batting an eyelid and popped them into two cups. The back door opened and Fabian appeared, ruddy-cheeked and carrying a basket of large brown eggs.

"Actually, I'll leave the tea." Tanya caught Fabian's eye and gave him a meaningful look. "Thanks all the same, but I really need to take Oberon for his walk."

While Fabian washed his hands, Tanya ran to her room and ducked inside before Nell, who was trundling along the landing with her vacuum cleaner. She quickly grabbed the puzzle book she had bought for Morag, then, after a moment's consideration, the compass and scissors from under the loose floorboard.

"Better to be safe than sorry," she muttered. The smaller objects she tucked in her pockets. The book she hid under her top. She replaced the floorboard and threw the rug back in place just as Nell knocked on the door.

"All yours," Tanya said, squeezing past her to run downstairs. She took Oberon's leash from the back door. "Ready?" she asked Fabian.

They fought their way through the jungle of weeds in the garden.

"I'm going to see Morag," she said in a low voice, as they shut the gate after them. Oberon bounded off ahead, then stopped a little way off. "Are you coming with me?"

"Only if you've got the compass," Fabian said.

Tanya patted her pocket. "The scissors too. After yesterday I'm going to carry them with me all the time."

"But are you sure you want to go?" Fabian asked. "If Gredin finds out we've been asking Morag about the thirteen secrets, he could punish you again."

"I'm not going to *ask* about the thirteen secrets," said Tanya defiantly. "But if Morag tells me something more about them, then I can't stop her, can I? I'm going to ask if she can help me do something about Oberon, and I'm going to give her this book of puzzles."

Oberon barked at the sound of his name, then yawned and lay down, his head on his huge paws. By the time Tanya and Fabian drew level with him he was fast asleep.

"Oberon, come on," Tanya said. She nudged him with her toe, but he gave a tired, squeaky groan and didn't move.

"What's up with him?" Fabian asked.

Tanya knelt and picked the sleepy Oberon up. "Puppies always fall asleep at the worst times. I'm going to have to carry him until he wants to wake up."

By the time they arrived at the brook, Tanya's arms were already aching. They paused before the stepping stones.

"Are you protected?" she asked breathlessly.

"Socks are inside out," Fabian replied. "You?"

"Iron nail in my pocket. Let's go, then."

Before they were even halfway across the brook, Tanya staggered and was forced to put Oberon down. He woke up with a jerk as his rear hit the icy water and gave a startled bark. This time, it was a deep sound. Something was happening.

"He's too heavy!" she gasped. "He's growing again!"

And he was. Within moments, Oberon was full size once more and standing on the other side of the bank, shaking water droplets from his coat.

"Running water," said Tanya, grinning triumphantly at Fabian. "Of course! I completely forgot—crossing running water dispels magic!"

"Do you still want to go into the woods?" Fabian asked.

Tanya patted the puzzle book in her waistband. "Yes. We're not doing anything wrong by going to see Morag, at least as far as Gredin is concerned."

They set off. Within minutes the forest yawned above, the veil of branches above them a leafy lip, and the trunks impaling the ground like twisted wooden teeth.

❦❦

The stench hit like a choking, cloying wall the instant Crooks pried the door open. Rowan clamped her hand over her mouth and nose as it beat them back, away from the caravan and into the vast field that was its home.

"Let it air," said Sparrow, pulling Rowan back from the entrance.

They stepped away, silent with anxiety, and surveyed the rundown structure that had been Dawn's home. Unlike the traditional caravans used by circus folk, Dawn's home had been relatively modern and was far larger. It was an ugly beige, accumulating rust in places, but it was otherwise clean and well-kept.

Rowan breathed the scent of the surrounding fields. A bee buzzed near some clover by her foot, its drone almost matching that of a tiny tractor in the distance. The sun blazed above in a cloudless sky, but it filled her with dread rather than pleasure. Its heat, beating down on the old metal caravan, was no friend to whatever lay waiting for them, stinking and rotting.

"Stay here," said Sparrow.

She watched him step up and go inside, the neck of his T-shirt pulled up to cover his nose and mouth, and squirmed at her own cowardice. Crooks hung around by the door, making no effort to keep the disgust from his expression—or to go in.

Tap. Rowan looked up. A large, black bird peered down at her from the roof, its head cocked to one side. Then it straightened and bobbed, pecking. *Tap.*

"Raven?" she whispered.

The bird ignored her, continuing to peck stupidly at the roof. Another one joined it, and she averted her eyes dismissively. It was just a bird after all.

Sparrow leaned out of the door. "You can come in. That smell…I didn't find nothing, except the rubbish." He jerked his head over his shoulder to an open cupboard under the sink. A swarm of flies buzzed over an open trash bag.

Queasy, Rowan stepped inside. As Merchant had described, nothing seemed out of the ordinary. Everything was neat, with the exception of the stinking trash and a few crocks submerged in stale, greasy water in the sink. All the heavy, dark curtains were open. Her eyes lingered on one of the windows, the curtain tiebacks hanging limply.

"She kept the curtains closed in the daytime," she murmured. "And opened them at night, when the sun went down."

"What are you thinking?" Sparrow asked.

"Merchant said the curtains were open during the day when he came here. But if they haven't been touched since, then they're still as he saw them."

"So?" said Crooks, having finally entered the caravan.

"So, if they'd been opened by Dawn at night, she'd have used the tiebacks," said Rowan. "But they haven't been used. Whoever pulled them open did it quickly. I'm guessing they came here in the day when they were drawn, then pulled them back to render Dawn powerless in the sunlight…."

"Then what?" asked Crooks.

"I don't know."

"Well, wherever she is, she's not here," said

Sparrow. "And if what that gypsy woman saw was right, she's outside somewhere. We should start searching."

"Like we've a chance of finding her," Crooks said, his dark eyes scornful. "She could be anywhere."

"I don't think so," said Sparrow. "If someone killed Fix, they made no effort to hide her body."

Crooks leaned against the kitchen counter, sullen. "Maybe they didn't mean to kill her. They might have thought the poison was something else, a sleeping potion, perhaps."

"Well the vision suggested that all three of them are dead," said Sparrow. "One death might have been an accident, but three?"

The heat and the smell oozed over Rowan, making her skin crawl. Pushing past Crooks she stood in the doorway, gulping at the sweet meadow air. Above her the birds continued to peck at the roof.

Crooks swiped a hand across his forehead, brushing away a strand of hair, limp with humidity. In the pause where no one spoke, the clip of beaks on metal was extraordinarily sharp.

"What *is* that bloody noise?" he said, irritable.

"Birds," Rowan answered, staring out across the field. She wanted to get away, to be anywhere but there in Dawn's empty, forlorn home. "They're pecking at something on the roof."

She's outside somewhere.

A sick thought hit her, making her sway. Sparrow hurried to her side, holding her elbow. "What is it?"

he said urgently. "The heat getting to you? Come outside—"

"The roof," she protested weakly, allowing him to pull her out onto the grass. "The birds on the roof..."

She steadied herself on the side of the caravan and looked along its length. At the rear, a thin metal ladder attached to the side led up to the roof. She pulled away from Sparrow and stumbled toward it. Her foot was on the first rung when Sparrow pushed her aside. Her eyes searched his and found the same grim thought echoed in them.

"What are you doing?" Crooks called from the door, as Rowan tried to jostle Sparrow out of the way.

"Don't," Sparrow told her gruffly. "I'll go." Nimble as a monkey he took the ladder. She watched, feeling both guilty and horrified as he steeled himself with deep breaths before peering over the edge of the roof.

"Oh, *god*!" He slid back, his feet thunking against the rungs before he fell to the ground.

"Sparrow!" she cried, rushing to him.

He rolled onto his hands and knees, his body wracked by dry sobs. Crooks grabbed him roughly by the shoulder and shook him.

"What's up there? What did you see?"

"Get off him!" Rowan shoved Crooks away and fell to her knees beside Sparrow.

He turned to them with haunted eyes. "It's her... it's Dawn."

18

Despite the lack of sun in Hangman's Wood, Tanya's hair stuck to the back of her neck. The forest was damp and airless, keeping her movements sluggish as she traipsed over brush and undergrowth.

She heard a breathless Fabian stop walking behind her and turned. He peeled his thin shirt away from his skin and flapped it in a fruitless attempt to create some kind of breeze.

"Are we going the right way?"

Tanya pointed ahead. "Yes. There's the first catacomb."

They began walking again, reaching the clearing presently. As always, Fabian went right up to the railings, peering through to the denehole.

"Come on," Tanya called, impatient. "We don't have time to hang around." Her voice stirred things in the trees above; a few whisperings and flutterings floated down to her. She continued onward, her eyes on Oberon, ambling ahead. The whispering died down. The heat was making even the fairies lazy today.

Fabian drew level with her by the time they were near the second catacomb. The further they ventured into the woods, the less the heat seemed to have penetrated.

"Have you had any more thoughts about Rowan or any of the others?" he asked.

"You mean to do with the thirteen treasures? I've thought about it, but I haven't had any more ideas."

"We need to find out more about each of them and the role they play within the group," Fabian said thoughtfully. "But in a way that Rowan doesn't suspect what we're doing."

"That's going to be difficult," said Tanya, swatting at a cloud of gnats humming beneath a tree. "Rowan's sharp. She could easily see through it if we're too obvious."

"Then perhaps we should just ask her up-front," said Fabian. "Faced with what we've got so far, she might come clean."

"Perhaps," said Tanya. "But I don't think so."

"Do you think Mad Morag will be able to help us? If she was able to see any more, wouldn't she have seen it in the first vision?"

"I don't know," said Tanya. "I'm not sure how

her visions work. But at the very least I wanted to give her the puzzle book I bought to thank her for everything she's done for us so far. And I'm sure she'd appreciate it if you stopped calling her *Mad Morag*."

"Sorry. It's just...you know. Habit."

Glimpsing the familiar daffodil-yellow of the old gypsy caravan, Tanya headed toward it, the forest floor tamer where Morag maintained it. Fabian paused to admire first the herb garden, then the caravan itself, and she was reminded that this was only the second time he had seen it.

"Do you think she'll let me come in?" he whispered, clearly dying to look inside.

"If you're polite." Tanya weaved her way up the little path, climbed the steps, and knocked. The door opened a little at her touch, but there was no reply. The chirrups of birds and shuffles of woodland creatures filled the empty silence. She knocked again, pushing the door open a little further.

"Hello? Morag?"

Still there was no answer.

"She might be doing a spell," Fabian said uneasily. "Or she might be asleep."

"Then why would she leave the door open?" Tanya wondered.

"Well, she's probably not expecting any interruptions. It can't be like she gets many visitors," Fabian pointed out.

"I don't like it," said Tanya. "Something doesn't

feel right." She pushed the door open the whole way and stepped inside. "Go and look around the side—she was sitting out the back in her rocking chair when I came the other day."

The steps creaked as Fabian retreated down them. Tanya went further into the caravan, but it was empty—even the deep red velvet curtain at the back, normally closed, was open, revealing Morag's sleeping place. She looked for Grimalkin, half-expecting the yellow-eyed glare from some dark corner, but it never came. Everything was tidy, organized.

"Tanya!"

Fabian's shout, almost a scream, sent prickles of fear over her skin. She flew to the door, tripping down the steps, and scrambled around to the back of the caravan.

The sight before her sent her reeling: Morag slumped and motionless in her rocking chair, her skin ashen and her eyes closed. Fabian was at her side, frantically tugging at her shawl, which had been tightly and viciously wrapped around the old woman's neck.

"Tanya!" Fabian whispered, his voice a half-sob. "It's knotted too tight—I can't get it off! The scissors, quickly..."

"No," Tanya choked out, rushing to Morag's side. She pulled out the scissors and hacked at the shawl, tearing it apart.

"Hurry," Fabian begged. "She's not breathing..."

"No, no, no..." Her words rushed out in a meaningless jumble as her vision clouded. She worked the scissors, as hard and as fast as she could, and the mutilated shawl loosened and fell away.

Tanya grabbed the old woman's wrist, her fingers searching for a pulse.

"I can't feel anything!"

"She's still not breathing. Loosen her clothes!"

Tanya bent over Morag's body, tugging at her neckline. There was no movement. Tears of despair dripped from her face and fell onto the old woman's. "We were too late," she whispered, brushing the tears from Morag's face. She was still warm. "I'm so sorry...."

Fabian fell back against the caravan, his face a mask of shock. "Who did this?" he said. "Who would do this?"

Oberon began to whine, a pitiful noise that rang through the clearing. He pawed at Tanya, bowed over Morag's unresponsive form, but she could not bring herself to pull away.

A loud rustle sounded a few meters away. Something had shifted in the woods. Tanya straightened, scanning their surroundings. The forest blurred green through her tears.

"What was that?"

The next thing she knew, Oberon jumped up at her, but his huge paws landed in the center of Morag's chest, jolting the old woman's body. Tanya pushed him away, horrified—but Morag's eyes suddenly flew open. She drew in a huge gasp of air.

"She's alive!" Fabian yelled, springing forward.

The distinctive snap of a piece of wood beneath a footfall sounded nearby. Tanya jerked around to meet it. Fabian clutched at her arm with one hand. His other hand rested on Morag's shoulder. The old woman coughed and heaved, her eyes bloodshot.

Tanya stood in front of Morag. "Who's there?" she demanded, staring into the trees. At her side, Oberon stiffened, his hackles and his ears pricking up. A low, rumbling growl burst from his throat.

"It's them," Tanya whispered. "Whoever did this is still here. *Watching*."

Fabian froze. "What if they come back? We don't even know how many of them there are!"

"One," Morag wheezed. "Only...one."

Another crackle of branches set Oberon barking. Tanya felt her limbs start to shake with adrenaline. It was a weird sensation, for half of her was afraid, and the other half surged with anger. She stepped closer to the trees.

"You see us?" she shouted. "There are two of us, plus a dog. There's only one of you!"

"What are you *doing*?" Fabian hissed. "Trying to get us all killed?"

"I'm trying to save us," she murmured. "If we show fear they're more likely to attack."

An agonizing silence followed. Then a hooded figure shot out from a nearby cluster of trees and fled away from them, cutting through the woods.

What Tanya hadn't counted on was Oberon taking off after the figure.

"Oberon!" she yelled—but in a few bounds he had vanished into the forest. "No, come back!"

"Don't even think about running after him!" Fabian said fiercely. "If you get lost you could end up like Mad Morag—and there's no guarantee anyone will find you in time!"

"Less of the 'Mad,'" Morag said, still weak, but indignant.

"I'm sorry. I didn't mean it." Fabian held out his arm and helped the old woman out of the rocking chair. "Steady. Do you think you can walk?"

"I don't know." She swayed on her feet, clutching at Fabian, then collapsed back into the chair. "No. I feel too dizzy."

"What are we going to do?" Tanya was pacing now. "How are we going to get Morag away from here? And what if Oberon catches up with whoever attacked her? If he gets hold of them...they could...they could..."

Fabian shook his head, helpless. "I don't know. We *do* need to get away from here. It's not safe. But I don't see how we're going to move her."

"We need someone else.... What if your father's in the woods? We could shout for him! He found us once before."

"But he doesn't patrol the woods so much any more," said Fabian. "There's less of a threat since Morwenna Bloom...but we can try." He cupped his hands around his mouth. "Dad! DAD!"

Tanya joined him. "Warwick! Are you here? We need help! Warwick! *Anyone!* HELP US!"

There was no answer. They continued to shout, their voices weakening. Minutes passed.

"No one's coming," said Fabian finally.

Morag's teeth were chattering. She huddled into herself.

"She's in shock," Tanya said in sudden realization. "Go into the caravan and get a blanket off her bed. She needs to be kept warm. Bring some water too."

Fabian vanished inside, returning with a thick woolen blanket and a glass of water. They tucked the blanket around Morag's shoulders and held the glass for her to drink from.

"Now what?" said Fabian, raking a hand through his hair. "Where do we go from here?"

"Maybe Oberon will get help," Tanya whispered. "Maybe he'll go back to the manor and—"

"*Oberon?* Get help?" Fabian snorted.

Tanya glared at him. "What I meant was that if he goes back to the manor without us, someone will come looking—"

Something rustled in the undergrowth.

Tanya's heart leapt. "Oberon?"

A small and ruddy face appeared among the foliage.

"Brunswick!" she cried.

The goblin pushed his way out from his hiding place and ran toward them, his eyes widening as he saw Morag. His face and fingers were stained with the dark juice of some kind of berry, and drips had spilled down onto his hodgepodge suit of cast-off human clothing.

Fabian stood very still, staring at the goblin. Fey folk rarely showed themselves to those without the second sight, but Brunswick had appeared in front of Fabian last autumn and now knew and trusted him.

"You asked for help, so here I am," Brunswick said in his deep little voice. "I'll help in any way I can." He went to Tanya and slipped his sticky hand into hers. She knelt and threw her arms around him, grateful tears welling in her eyes.

"Thank you for coming, Brunswick," she whispered. "I'm so glad you're here." She pulled back, releasing him. "Someone attacked Morag just now. We have to get her out of the woods, but she can't walk by herself, and Fabian and I aren't strong enough to carry her. Whoever did it could still be in the woods—if one of us goes alone for help they might attack us too. Will you go back to the manor and bring Warwick here? You can go unseen, and more quickly than we can."

Brunswick nodded, backing away to the bushes. "Go inside and lock the door." He pointed to the caravan. "You'll be safer there, I'm sure."

The bushes rippled as he vanished into them.

"He's right," said Fabian. "Let's go inside and wait. Come on."

Between them, they assisted Morag out of the chair and up the steps to the caravan, locking the door behind them. Once inside they helped the old woman to her chair by the window and rearranged the blanket over her.

"At least she's stopped shivering," said Tanya. She took a seat at the table, tugging at a strand of her hair. "Poor Brunswick. He must have been frightened—he was talking in rhyme again. He only slips back into it when he's scared, or nervous." She got up, unable to relax, and stood by the window, looking out. "Whoever it was, they must have left after Oberon chased them off."

"Do you think he would have caught them?" Fabian asked.

"I don't know. I just...I just hope he comes back."

"Check the windows," Morag said hoarsely. "Make sure they're all locked and fastened."

"Don't worry," Tanya told her. "Help's on its way. We won't let anything happen to you." She nodded to Fabian to check the windows. "Did you get a glimpse of who attacked you?"

Morag's hands wandered to her throat and hovered there, shaking. She shook her head. "No. They came from behind. I only heard something at the last moment. I tried to turn, but it was too late. They had me—wouldn't let go. I couldn't breathe...I couldn't *breathe*. Everything went dark...and then you were there." Her eyes darted about the caravan, over her belongings. "Nothing has been disturbed, and nothing taken, unless they planned to rob me after... after I was dead."

"I don't think it was a robbery," said Fabian. "Most thieves will only attack when disturbed during a burglary. But this . . . it's like they came straight for you."

"Do you have any idea of who would want to harm you?" Tanya asked. "Any enemies?"

Morag managed a wry smile. "Plenty that would wish me ill. After all, superstition and fear go hand in hand. But none, I believe, would go to such lengths to make it happen."

For the first time since cutting Morag free, Tanya became aware of a sharp pain in her palm. She realized she was still clutching the tiny silver scissors. A small red dot bloomed on her skin where the point had pierced her. "If I hadn't had these, things could have ended very differently," she said quietly. She sheathed them and pushed them back into her pocket.

Morag closed her eyes. "What I saw was true, then."

"You saw that this would happen?" Fabian was aghast. "You saw that someone would do this? You must have some idea who—"

"No." Morag shook her head. "I saw that with those scissors, you would one day save my life. But I did not see how."

"Is that the reason you gave them to me?" Tanya asked. "You knew that all along?"

Morag opened her eyes. "I gave you the scissors because I saw you would need them, for you. But it was *after* I had given them to you that I had that vision. And I knew then, without any doubt, that my decision to give them to you was the right one." She squinted suddenly, peering closer. "What's that you've got there?"

Tanya looked down, remembering the book of puzzles. "Oh." She pushed it toward Morag. "I brought it for you. I hope it's not one you've already got."

Morag's eyes lit up. She settled back in the chair, pulling the blanket tighter around herself. "Read them out," she said. "There's a pencil on the dresser. It might help take our minds off things while we wait. And you, boy." She looked at Fabian. "Make something for us all to drink—some cocoa, I think."

Tanya fetched the pencil while Fabian set some milk to boil in a pan over the little stove. She drifted through the next three-quarters of an hour in a dream-like state. It seemed too surreal, drinking cocoa and filling in crossword puzzles in the home of a witch. If the circumstances had been different, she might have enjoyed it.

The knock, when it came, frightened Morag so much that she spilled the dregs of her cup all over her blanket.

"Fabian?" Warwick's voice rang out on the other side of the door. "Tanya? Open the door!"

Fabian rushed over—then hesitated, his hand on the key.

"Fabian!" Warwick bashed on the door again, hard.

Fabian gnawed at his thumbnail. "We're here."

"Let him in then!" Tanya exclaimed.

"How do we know it's really you?" Fabian said through the door. "How do we know it's not someone pretending to be you, like some sort of...glamour?"

"Stop being obnoxious and open the blasted door!"

Fabian turned the key. "It's him, all right."

Warwick burst into the caravan, Brunswick at his heels. "Morag." He knelt by her chair, examining her throat with thinly veiled fury. "If I find out who did this..." He lifted her gently into his arms and stood up again. "Get the door, Fabian," he commanded. "Tanya, lock it behind us and bring the key."

Outside, they gathered in a circle.

"Here's what we're going to do," Warwick instructed, his voice low. "Brunswick will lead the way back to the manor. Fabian and Tanya, you will walk behind Brunswick. I'll walk behind with Morag, where I can see you. If anything happens on the way, you fall back immediately with Morag, and *stay behind* me. No one talks until we're out of the woods. Got it?"

A succession of nods answered him. They set off through the woods, flinching at every noise; every squawk, every rustle, every thud of fallen tree fruit. Tanya brought out the compass and held it until it was slippery with sweat. The needle stayed fixed on the tiny "H" as they followed Brunswick, offering a small reassurance that they were on the right path.

The edge of the woods took forever to appear.

When it did, finally, Tanya wept silent tears as they crossed first the border, and then the brook. She wept as a release of the pent-up fear she had felt while in the woods, and she wept knowing that Oberon could still be lost somewhere in the depths of them.

Only when they reached the garden gate did her tears stop flowing. For there, on the back doorstep, sat Oberon. At the click of the gate he raced toward them, almost knocking her over, but Tanya did not care.

"There's something in his mouth," said Fabian as they crowded through the back door into the kitchen. "Look."

Gently, Tanya pried the thing from Oberon's jaws and held it up.

"It's a piece of material," she said. "It's quite thick—it feels fleecy. It's torn."

Warwick showed Morag to a seat in front of the fireplace and held out his hand for the scrap of fabric.

"I think it's safe to say that Oberon caught up with whoever he was chasing," he said grimly. "And this could hold a clue to who that was." He folded it up and pushed it into his trouser pocket. "But for now, I think you'd better start explaining exactly what just happened in the woods—and why you were there in the first place."

19

Sparrow dropped the telephone receiver back on its hook, his head bowed. On the other side of the door, Rowan and Crooks watched through the glass as he used his cuff to wipe away fingerprints from both the receiver and the keypad. With his hand still covered, he pushed the door open and came out of the telephone booth, his eyes cast downward.

"We better get away as quick as we can. That field, and everywhere around it, will be crawling with the police pretty soon."

"Should've called them when we were further away," said Crooks. "Not when we're still in the area."

Sparrow shook his head. "They'll probably trace the call. Better to do it closer to the scene than near to where we're settled."

"What did you tell them?" Rowan asked.

Sparrow kept his head down and started to walk. "Told them I was a traveler, and that I'd found some-one...that I'd found a body, while I was out walking my dog. Said I didn't want to give my name." He kicked out at a pebble. "Happens all the time."

"What are we going to do about Cobbler?" asked Crooks. "Should we go to his place and look for him?"

"No point," Sparrow said flatly. "We already know he's dead. No sense in us putting ourselves at another crime scene. No, the best thing we can do now is get everyone together until we've figured out what to do. If we're split up, we risk being picked off one by one." He checked the lane both ways before crossing the road, heading for a little path that cut through a wooded area. "This way. We should hit the village in the next twenty minutes."

They spoke very little on the journey back. Rowan felt jittery the whole way, her eyes darting over each passenger once they got on the bus. She thought she saw Eldritch at every turn—in every pale face, every head of dark hair.

Run away, little fox, his voice said in her mind. *I found you once. I will again.*

"Where are you going?" Sparrow asked once they had climbed off the bus.

Both he and Crooks had set off in the direction of Halfpenny Field, but Rowan remained standing in the road, a cloud of dust swirling around her from the departing bus.

"I'm going home. I'm not going back there."

Sparrow came toward her. "Just come with us for a few minutes—we need to tell Tino about Dawn."

"You don't need me there to do that."

"No, but I thought we'd decided to stick together." He reached for her arm. "Even if you go back to the house, there's no guarantee you'll be safe."

"I know that." She glanced at Crooks, then lowered her voice. "I'm going to leave, tonight."

"What? Why?"

"All this is happening because of me. It's *me* Eldritch wants, and he's going to cut down anyone in his path in order to get to me. If I'm at Elvesden Manor then that includes Tanya and Fabian and everyone else who's there. If I'm not around...if he knows I'm gone, then he'll stop coming after the rest of you. You'll be safe."

Sparrow's eyes searched her face. "You're not seeing the whole picture, Red. If he wants you that badly, he'll find you. He won't stop looking. And you'll be all on your own, with no one to help you."

"He won't find me. I can vanish. I can stay missing." She tilted her chin, defiant. "I know places where I can go. It's what I do, remember?"

Sparrow gazed at her. "All right. Then I'll come with you."

"No! Sparrow—"

He was no longer by her side, but striding toward Crooks.

"What's going on?" Crooks asked, suspicious.

"Nothing." Sparrow's tone was clipped. "Let's get back." He turned back to Rowan. "Just ten minutes, all right? That's all. Then we'll go to the house."

Helpless, she turned and stared into the deserted lanes leading to the manor, then at Sparrow's and Crooks's retreating backs. "Ten minutes," she muttered, setting off after them. "And that's it."

A large white van blocked the entrance to the field when they reached it. The engine was still running, and the driver's door was open. Rowan followed Crooks and Sparrow as they squeezed past the sides to find Samson at the rear in a heated conversation with the driver.

"I can't find Tino—haven't seen him all morning." Samson's arms were folded. He towered over the driver. "But I'm telling you, nothing's been ordered."

The driver pointed to his clipboard. "It has according to this. It doesn't have to be this Tino who signs for it, but it was ordered yesterday—you can check the details yourself. There it is, see?" He tapped the top sheet. "That's the reference: 'Curiosity.'"

"Something for the Cabinet?" Crooks asked, peering over the driver's shoulder to look at the clipboard.

"Apparently." Samson remained stone-faced. "Only Tino never mentioned anything about a delivery, and he's conveniently gone off somewhere."

"What do you mean?" asked Sparrow. Rowan heard the alarm in his voice. "Gone off where?"

Samson shrugged, but stood up a little straighter

and unfolded his arms. "No one's seen him since this morning."

"Look, I haven't got all day. Can someone just sign for this?" The driver glanced back at his van. "Anyone? It's all paid for."

"I don't like this," said Sparrow. He reached for the clipboard. "What is it? And who sent it?"

"Sender's details can be verified at the office." The driver handed him a card. "And whatever it is, it needs to be kept cold."

Sparrow squiggled in the signature box and returned the clipboard. "Cold?"

The driver took the clipboard and threw it onto the front seat.

"That's right." He stepped to the rear and pulled down the back of the van to create a level platform. A waft of cool air descended as it hit the humid outdoors, and wreaths of vapor curled into the air. Inside, the van was carefully stowed with bulky packages.

"Ice sculptures," the driver explained. "We do a big trade in them for parties, weddings mainly." He hopped up onto the platform and went toward a large wooden crate. It was almost as tall as he was and stood on a metal trolley. Releasing the brake, he lugged it onto the platform, then pressed a button on the side of the van. The platform lowered slowly to the ground, whirring and shuddering under its heavy load.

"What's inside?" Rowan asked. She stared into

the van, eyeing the other sculptures, but they were covered in plastic sheeting and bubble wrap.

"I haven't seen it." The driver wheeled the trolley off the platform. "It's not one of our designs—it's collection and delivery only. Where do you want it?"

"Over there." Sparrow gestured toward the Curiosity Cabinet.

"Here, let me," said Samson, taking the trolley from the driver. The crate rattled over the uneven ground, but he pulled it easily, guiding it inside the tent.

"There's no space for it," Sparrow muttered, glancing around the shadowy interior. "It's full. Just leave it here, by the door."

Rowan followed them inside, apprehension growing in her gut. She had never liked the Curiosity Cabinet, with its glass cases of shrunken heads and dried, shriveled creatures, stitched together into freakish creations. It gave her the creeps.

She averted her eyes and concentrated on the trolley. At the press of a lever, the two metal prongs holding the crate sighed to the ground. Samson withdrew the trolley and handed it back to the driver.

"Now what?" said Crooks.

Sparrow drew back the tent opening and watched as Samson accompanied the driver back to his van. Moments later it rumbled away, and Samson could be seen coming back. The inside of the tent fell into gloom momentarily as he brushed through the opening, his massive bulk filling the entrance to the tent.

"Do we open it?" asked Crooks.

Samson edged around the crate. "Can't see a way in—it's all nailed up. We'll have to force it." He glanced at Crooks. "What have you got in the way of tools?"

Crooks's sly gaze slid over the crate. "A crowbar should do it." He exited the tent.

"Why would Tino order something new for the cabinet now?" said Rowan.

"Tonight is the last show," Samson answered. "Maybe he wanted something special for the grand finale." He frowned. "But if it's ice, wouldn't it have melted by then?"

"The driver never said Tino ordered it," Sparrow interrupted. "All he said was that it was *for* Tino. When was the last time anyone saw him?"

"This morning, like I said," Samson replied. "Outside Suki's caravan, after she found the hex." His eyes flitted from Sparrow to Rowan. "Didn't you two and Crooks go back to Dawn's today?"

Sparrow opened his mouth to answer, but was saved by Crooks's return. Victor and Suki were with him.

"Here." He thrust the crowbar at Samson. "Are you sure we should do this? I mean, with Tino not being here..."

"That's exactly why I'm sure." Samson swung the crowbar at the crate, hooking a plank of wood and tugging it away easily. "Tino's gone and we're left with a strange delivery. Something's not right." More wood split under the crowbar. Victor joined him, using a small knife to pry the edges of the wood apart.

"Can you see what it is yet?" Rowan asked, standing back with Sparrow.

Another length of wood hit the ground. "No—it's covered in plastic."

"Whatever it is, it seems to be a solid cube," Victor muttered, slitting the plastic. "It's not sculpted."

Rowan nudged Sparrow for the card supplied by the driver. On the back were a few small pictures showing sculpted forms of a castle, and a pair of swans, and other objects encased in ice.

"It's something held in the ice, then," she called. "On the back here, there's a picture—a red rose at the center of an ice block."

Victor tugged a section of plastic away, letting it fall to the ground. He pressed his face closer to the ice. "It's something big...can't quite make it out—"

He broke off, staggering back. And with that, Rowan knew.

"Who..." she choked out. "Who is it? Tino...?"

The crowbar slipped from Samson's hand and landed with a thud on the grassy ground. "It can't be...." He brushed his hand over the ice. "Could be something else...a mannequin, perhaps. It *has* to be." Recovering himself, he picked up the crowbar and set to work again, his movements frantic this time. The wooden casing fell apart, no match for his strength, and he lifted the rest of the plastic off in one smooth motion.

"That's not a mannequin," Crooks whispered.

It was not Tino, either. The man inside the ice sat on a chair, staring out through his frozen window. His prison obscured his hard features a little; a hawkish nose and a jutting jaw appeared softer through the thick layers of ice. On his lap a silver goblet rested, his hand curved around the base. Around the center of the ice block, near the man's chest, frozen swirls of red leaked from a small tear in his clothing.

"Cobbler," Suki whispered, her hands flying to her mouth.

Rowan had no words. She simply stared at the frozen body, as unable to move as it was.

"Cover him...*it*...up!" Victor gasped.

Samson reached out with one hand, the plastic sheeting still clenched in the other. He lightly rested his fingers on the ice. After a few seconds he withdrew them and rubbed them together.

"It's not melting under my touch. It's enchanted somehow."

"What do we do?" Crooks hissed. "What are we going to *do* with him?"

"We've got two options," said Samson. "We cover him up or leave him uncovered. Either way, it needs to stay here for the time being until we work out what to do." He gestured to their surroundings. "Apart from us, no one here has even met Cobbler. No one will suspect this is a real person—they'll assume it's a fraud, like the other stuff in here."

Victor nodded slowly, casting his eyes around.

"Samson's right. Leave him uncovered—it'll draw more attention otherwise." His eyes glimmered with unshed tears before he averted them. "First Fix, now Cobbler..."

"And Dawn," Sparrow added, breaking his silence.

Victor spun to face him, aghast.

"No...." murmured Suki, shaking her head. "Not Dawn...."

"It's true," said Rowan. "We were at her caravan today. Not expecting to find her, but looking for something, *anything*...a clue. But she was there all along. Sparrow found her...she was on the roof."

"On the *roof*?" Samson moved closer.

"Tied to the rack," said Sparrow. "By her wrists and her ankles, which suggests she was alive when she was put there. She'd been there a while, I'm guessing since Merchant first found she was missing. The crows had been at her...."

"But she—if she was out there all that time...the sunlight would have..."

"The sunlight would have killed her," Rowan finished.

"Why?" Suki's voice was weak. "Why would someone do that to her?"

"Why would someone put Cobbler in a block of ice?" Victor shot back, his voice rising. "Why would someone poison Fix? Whoever wanted them dead—whoever is attacking us—is going to a lot of trouble in their methods. Think about it." He jabbed his finger at Cobbler's frozen resting place. "He was already dead, or dying, when he was put in that—the wound is visible!"

"Keep the noise down." Samson took a hasty glance outside the entrance. "This isn't the time or the place—"

"Then let's *make* a time and a place," Victor hissed, his hands clenching into fists. "And where the hell is Tino?"

"Exactly," said Samson. "If he's vanished, then it could mean he's next...."

"B-but," Crooks stammered. "Not here, not with everyone around—we're safe here, aren't we?"

"Right. So safe someone put a hex on me, right under our noses!" Suki snapped. "All I've been able to do is wash everything down with salt water, in case anything else of mine has been tampered with. But as for that thing—that symbol—under the caravan, we can't even find out what it means or how to get rid of it without Tino!"

Victor sheathed his knife and pushed the curtain aside. "Follow me."

"Where are we going?" asked Sparrow.

"To try and find Tino."

Rowan batted her way out of the tent, Sparrow at her side. "I thought you said people had been searching for him all day?"

"I said no one had *seen* him all day," Samson answered. "There's a difference."

They all followed as he weaved his way past the

performance area and through to the caravans. A few of the circus folk were about, and Suki was called away by one of the dancers. She went with a grudging glance at the group, the rest of whom carried on without her. When they arrived at Tino's, Samson pounded on the door.

"Tino? Open up if you're there." He knocked once more, and then turned to Crooks. "I'm not wasting any more time. Get it open."

Crooks pulled a bunch of keys from his pocket, taking a moment to look through them before selecting one. In seconds the door lay open. He stepped aside as Victor and Samson barged past him. "I'm not going in," he muttered.

Neither Rowan nor Sparrow said anything, but both of them remained outside. The heavy tread of the two brothers sounded through the caravan from one end to the other. Victor reappeared at the door. "He's not here, and there's no sign of him."

Tentatively, Rowan stepped up into the caravan. Sparrow and Crooks came after her, but stayed close to the door. "Is anything disturbed?"

Samson stood by the racks of costumes on the walls, looking up at the row of masks. "Doesn't look like it." He reached for a mask that had fallen off the wall onto the floor.

"What are you doing in here?"

At the sound of the voice behind her, Rowan whipped around. Simultaneously, Samson froze.

"Tino!"

Tino pushed past Crooks and Sparrow, his swarthy face darker than usual. "Who else did you expect? This was my caravan last time I checked!" He slammed his keys on the table, glaring at Crooks. "Clearly no need for those when you're around."

Crooks stuffed the guilty keys in his pocket. "Thought that's what you wanted me for."

"So why are you in here?" Tino demanded.

"We thought something had happened to you," said Samson, his beefy face reddening. Rowan wondered whether it was with embarrassment or temper. "No one's seen you all day. If you'd told us where you were going, we wouldn't have panicked."

"Panicked about what?"

"We found Dawn and Cobbler," Sparrow said.

"And?" Tino's hand, still on the table, gripped his keys more tightly.

Sparrow opened his mouth then closed it, slowly shaking his head.

Tino's knuckles turned white. A strangled gasp escaped his lips and he sank into a chair, raising his fist to his mouth.

Victor went to Tino's side and rested his hand on the fey man's shoulder. "It's not the worst of it," he said softly. "Cobbler...well, he's here. We're still trying to make sense of it."

"He's *here*? Where?"

"The Curiosity Cabinet. Someone arranged his body in a block of ice."

An animal roar burst from Tino. Rowan jumped

aside as he stood up and kicked the chair he had been sitting on across the caravan. It smashed against the kitchen units, leaving one of the legs dangling by a few splinters. Tino leaned over the table, gripping the sides. His head was down and his body rigid. "This whole thing...it's falling apart...."

He stood up straight, brushing his hair back off his face. "After finding the hex under Suki's caravan this morning I acted on impulse. I didn't tell anyone where I was going in case word got around that I was gone and another attack was made—"

"You think someone here was responsible?" Victor interjected.

"I think at the moment we shouldn't rule that out," Tino answered somberly. "Even if no one here is directly responsible, someone could have been compromised by being persuaded to grant strangers access to the camp, or even used in a glamour. We know that this Eldritch is after Rowan, but we've no evidence that he's responsible for the rest—"

"But if he knows about me then he probably knows about all of us," said Rowan. "And let's not forget that he was involved in the changeling trade— it would make sense for him to want us out of the way."

"Out of the way, yes," Tino agreed. "But there are simpler ways to do things if that's the intent." His voice hardened. "Whoever is targeting us is sending a message with each act. I didn't see it with Fix—the poison could just have been a convenient way to kill her. But then Suki's powers were blocked by a hex, and it made me start to wonder. Without knowing for sure what had happened to Cobbler and Dawn I couldn't assume anything further, so I said nothing. With Fix dead, the only person I could think of who might be able to help undo the hex was Peg. By then, I also realized that all of us are under threat. So I went to Merchant's, and then the two of us visited Peg and Nosebag, planning to bring them back here and wait it out."

"Is Merchant here now?" Crooks asked.

Tino nodded. "He's with Nosebag and Peg in one of the spare vans."

"Thank goodness they're safe," said Rowan.

Tino's gaze dropped. "They're here, although by the time we arrived it was already too late. Someone had got to them first."

"How was it too late?" Sparrow asked fretfully. "When you said Merchant was with them I thought you meant they were still alive!"

"They are alive," said Tino. "But whoever got to them knew exactly what they were doing. They didn't have to kill them to make their point. Either way, their job is done—Peg and Nosebag can't help us."

20

Oberon heralded Rowan's return with a volley of barks the moment her key slid into the front door. Tanya and Fabian rushed to the hallway to meet her, but found that she was not alone. Sparrow and Suki had accompanied her to the manor.

"You've been ages," Tanya whispered. "It's nearly four o'clock!"

"Sorry," Rowan muttered. She beckoned Suki and Sparrow through the door and closed it behind them. "Wipe your feet."

"No offense," said Fabian, "but why have you brought those two with you?"

Suki rewarded him with a cool stare. "No offense, but we wanted to make sure she got back here alive."

"Yes, but why have you come *in*?" Fabian persisted.

Rowan brushed past him. "They've come in

because I need to talk to everyone in the house, right now, and I want Sparrow and Suki with me. Depending on what happens after I've said what I have to say, I might not be staying."

"They're all in the kitchen," said Tanya, bewildered. She followed her down the hall. "What did you mean, you might not be staying? Rowan, wait, we need to talk!"

Rowan was already in the kitchen. She halted in the doorway and stood, tense, as her eyes scanned the room. "You were serious when you said *everyone* was here." Her voice shook slightly as Tanya arrived beside her. A moment later, Fabian, Suki, and Sparrow shuffled up behind them.

Rowan's eyes settled on Morag, seated at the table. Tanya saw her lips part as she took in the scratches and bruising around the old woman's neck.

"What's been going on?"

"Sit down," said Warwick, pointing to one of the few empty chairs.

She sat between Florence and Nell, facing Rose and Morag. The others lingered in the doorway.

"I didn't realize you'd brought guests," said Warwick, assessing Sparrow and Suki in one quick sweep. "Will they be staying long?"

"As long as it takes," Rowan replied, still staring at Morag. "And anything you have to say can be said in front of them. They know everything there is to know about me." She fidgeted in the seat. "More than anyone else here, in fact."

"Is that so?" said Warwick. "In that case, they'd better sit down as well."

As Sparrow and Suki entered the room, Oberon rose up from the hearth, his hackles raised. He growled, long and low, then went into a flurry of barks.

"What's got into him?" said Rowan. "Tanya, take him outside!"

Tanya went to Oberon and placed her hand on his collar. He stopped barking but continued to growl. "He doesn't like them," she said, frowning at Sparrow and Suki. "And he doesn't trust them."

"Well, *I* do," Rowan said stiffly. "So just take him out."

"No." Tanya shook her head, her eyes fixed on the two newcomers. "He's never been wrong before. He's staying."

Chairs scraped as Sparrow and Suki sat down, with wary eyes on Oberon.

"It might be me that's upsetting him," Suki said quietly. "I get afraid around dogs, at least until I know them a bit. My parents kept dogs when I was little. I was never scared at first—used to curl up with them in the shoe cupboard. Until one day... one of them just turned on me." She pulled up her sleeve and put her arm on the table. An ugly scar puckered the flesh on the inside of her elbow. She gave a nervous smile and tugged the sleeve down. "He's probably picking up on my fear."

"I'm sorry." Tanya got up and led Oberon to the

kitchen door, shooing him into the hallway. "I didn't realize." She sat back down to silence, half-expecting her grandmother to start bustling about making tea. But even Florence was subdued and still.

Warwick leaned across the table. "I'll get straight to the point. Someone tried to strangle Morag this morning. Tanya and Fabian were in the woods at the time and disturbed them—whoever it was ran off. They managed to get away but Oberon chased them and came back with this." He held up a scrap of dark material. "Until we know why, Morag's staying here with us. Now, I've tried to get the truth out of Fabian and Tanya about what they were up to in the forest, but all I'm getting is a poppycock story that Oberon ran off." He pushed the fabric into his pocket, and Fabian and Tanya shared an uncomfortable glance.

"POPPYCOCK!" the General shrilled from his perch. A bark from Oberon outside the kitchen door silenced him.

"I suspect they've been holding out until you got back," Warwick continued, a challenging look in his eye. "Something tells me you haven't been studying today. So where have you been? Because I know something's going on with you three, and none of you are leaving this table until I get the truth."

Rowan nodded. "I was coming to tell the truth, believe it or not." She motioned across the table. "This is Sparrow and Suki. I've been with Sparrow all day, and another boy, Crooks." She glanced at Nell. "The boy you saw me with before."

"The shifty-looking one?" Nell queried.

"Yes. All three of them, plus nine others, are part of a group I used to... that I've belonged to ever since I ran away."

"What kind of group?" Rose asked, but Warwick shook his head, and Rowan carried on talking.

"I met Sparrow first. I told some of you about him already. He was on the streets, like me, and he soon realized I had the second sight. After I told him what had happened to me he said he knew some people—people who might be able to help me get James back from the fairies. People who switched changeling children for those they were stolen for. At the time I had no idea of what I was getting into, only that I'd do whatever it took if there was a chance I'd see my... that I'd see James again.

"He took me to meet a fey man who works in a circus—the circus that's now over at Halfpenny Field. His name is Tino."

"What sort of a name is Tino?" said Nell. "And Sparrow? And Crooks, for that matter?"

"The sort of name that's a bit like Red," Rowan answered. "An alias." She turned her gaze back to Warwick. "I repeated my story to Tino, but later I found out that Sparrow had already given him a head start. He must have seen something in me that he wanted, *needed*, for this group of his." She cleared her throat and looked away.

"By then, I'd become good at most things I needed to be good at to survive on the streets. Lying, stealing, sneaking about. Staying unseen—invisible—to most, anyway. But the one thing I was especially good at was finding hideouts. I never liked sleeping in parks, or in shop doorways." She chanced a quick glance at Rose, shamefaced. "So I started to break into places. Empty shops, empty houses, even empty pubs.

"Tino was impressed. He said he wanted me in the group. Once I'd agreed I was in, he swore me to secrecy. I was to source hideouts for myself and other members, and in turn, I could learn from them. Because that was the thing about the group—each of us had something to offer. As time went on, I got more creative. I found that by listening, and even by researching places in libraries, I could learn things. Valuable things. It's how I learned about the tunnels under this house."

"So who are the others?" Florence asked. She looked at Suki and Sparrow. "And how did you two become involved in all this—what responsibilities do you have?"

"I first met Tino when I was five," Suki began.

"*Five?*" Florence exclaimed. "Good lord! Surely he didn't recruit you for this group of his then?"

"No, I..." Suki faltered, plainly struggling to speak of her past.

"Suki was one of Tino's jobs," said Rowan. "She'd been taken. She's gifted—like Morag. She sees things. Tino thinks it's why the fairies wanted her. He got her back from them. But..." she hesitated, looking to Suki for permission to recount the tale.

"It's all right," Suki said softly.

"A few months ago the fairy who took Suki found her again, and killed her family. Tino heard about it, remembered her, and recruited her because of her ability."

"I can use it to find out about children who've been taken, among other things," Suki mumbled, looking pale.

"And you?" Florence asked of Sparrow.

"I'd been on the streets awhile," he said, fiddling with the tablecloth. "Met Tino by chance, really. He knew I was second-sighted straight away, but he didn't ask me to be part of the Coven for another year or so."

Rose looked alarmed. "The Coven?"

"It's just one of the names for the group," Sparrow explained hastily. "Nothing to do with witchcraft. It's an old word for 'gathering.'"

Rose nodded, her green eyes flitting to her daughter's.

"I'd been doing a bit of work for him here and there, and he grew to trust me," Sparrow continued. "Said I was honest. He also told me I was brave, and good-hearted. That's when he told me about the Coven. He said that at times it was hard to keep sight of the good in the world, and that the Coven needed someone like me in it." He shrugged and gave a slow smile, his chipped tooth peeking out under his lip. "No one had ever told me I was good for anything before that."

"So, this Tino recruits people on their qualities and abilities," Warwick said, frowning. "Presumably that's his role in things? And—"

"Actually," Suki put in, "it isn't Tino's role to recruit, as such. That job was someone else's. Luckily he wasn't precious about it—Tino found all three of us by chance. It was Cobbler who looked out for new members, and he told everyone to keep an eye out."

Warwick's eyes narrowed. *"Was?"*

Suki bit her lip. "Three of the Coven members have been murdered. Three more of us have been attacked."

A stunned silence hung over the table. Rose was the one to break it, her face crumpling despite her efforts to remain composed. "That means whoever's doing this...they're going to come after you, Rowan. Aren't they?"

"Yes." Rowan let out a shaky breath. "They're going to come after all of us. And there's something else." She looked at Warwick. "Eldritch has escaped. He's tracked me down...like he said he would."

"Eldritch? That's not possible, Rowan." He glanced at Rose, and Tanya remembered the conversation she had walked in on. "Whatever you think you saw...the mind plays tricks...."

"I'm not making this up!" she said sharply. "Or imagining things. His hand had been cut off—that's how he got out." She glanced fretfully about her, as though she was afraid he would come bursting into the room at any time. "He nearly caught me—if it hadn't been for Sparrow, I wouldn't have escaped. It's only a matter of time before he finds me again."

The lines in Warwick's face deepened all of a sudden. "You saw him too?" he asked Sparrow hoarsely.

Sparrow nodded. "So did Suki."

"Then could he be the one that's targeting you all?"

"We don't know," said Sparrow. "It's possible— Rowan says he was part of the changeling trade. The fact that we work against it could be a motive for him to attack us."

"He was there the night James was stolen," Warwick remembered. "But he wasn't *actively* a part of it. He was adamant about that."

"He's our only lead so far," said Rowan. "It doesn't mean he's our only enemy."

"Or that he'd be the only one with a motive," said Fabian. "There are also these thirteen secrets— whatever they are—that you're hiding. And they must be pretty big if someone is hunting you down for them."

Morag reached a bony finger toward Sparrow, then Suki. "That's right. I saw you in my vision...."

"'The thirteen secrets have been found out,'" Tanya repeated. "I was there. I saw your faces in the water. And Red's . . . and all the others."

To her surprise, Sparrow shook his head. "You've got the wrong end of the stick," he said softly. "And that was the whole point. There are no thirteen secrets—not in the way you think, anyway. I mentioned earlier that the Coven is one of the names for the group." He paused, glancing at Suki and Rowan. "Well, the thirteen secrets is another. It's a newer name, one we've been using to protect the Coven. See, the Coven has been around for hundreds of years, doing what it does. Over time, that name's been compromised. 'The thirteen secrets' is a code between us. Because if anyone overhears it, they'll be led away from the fact that the 'secrets' are, in fact, people. *We* are the thirteen secrets."

"Which means that if someone is hunting us, it's not because of what we know," said Rowan. "It's because of what we *are*. Someone knows about the Coven and is trying to finish us—for good."

"How far does this thing, this *Coven*, go back?" Warwick asked. "You said hundreds of years—presumably that means there have been hundreds of members...no wonder word of it has leaked."

"There are only ever thirteen members at one time," said Suki. "As members retire, or die, they're replaced by new members and sworn to utmost secrecy. But the Coven is always thirteen."

"Why?" asked Rose. "Why that number?"

Fabian pulled his brown book out and rested it on the table. "I think I can answer that." He flipped the pages as every head in the room looked toward him. "Tanya and I started to figure it out," he said. "The Coven members each symbolize one of the thirteen treasures of the fairy courts." He tapped the page as Sparrow's mouth dropped open. "Suki is psychic—she's the Cup of Divination. The Dagger was Fix, who was a healer. Crooks is the Key—he can literally open any door, break into anywhere. Tino, we think, is Glamour—he makes costumes for the circus, but I'm betting he's a glamour-maker as well. Samson is abnormally strong—he's the Mantle. And Victor is an expert swordsman—he's the Sword, obviously." He closed the book, the slap of the pages loud in the quiet room. "That's as far as we got. But now, after what you've just said, I'm guessing Sparrow's bravery makes him the Heart, and..." he paused, his blue eyes focused on Rowan. "And your knack of finding hideouts, staying unseen, means you're the Halter—the ring of invisibility."

"He's right," Suki said, dumbfounded, but clearly impressed. "The Coven was founded soon after the divide of the Seelie and Unseelie Courts. Although there were instances of changeling children before then—usually when fey children were sick, or ancient fairies wanted caring for—after the fall out it became far worse. Children were being switched out of spite, used as weapons.

"A rebel group formed, made up of fairies and second-sighted humans who'd had their children switched. They started to work together to find the children, but found that as the group grew, it became harder to control. They began to argue, until one of them realized their situation was going the same way as what had happened with the thirteen treasures, leading to the division of the courts and the predicament it had put them into in the first place. They decided to define the roles within the group and link them to the thirteen treasures. Not only did this give a clear definition, and give each of them an identity, but it was felt that using the treasures as a basis balanced the negative effect of what had happened with them in the fairy world. They were using them to do good—and each of the roles, when put together, covered everything, all the skills they needed in order to be able to work together to the best effect.

"Some time was spent working out the members' strengths, and any who weren't selected to act as a treasure became a silent member—a watcher. The watchers were used as spies, and for a while it worked, but over the years it was phased out—too many spies were caught and interrogated. For years now, the Coven has consisted of only thirteen active members—it's safer that way."

Warwick exhaled slowly. "I've never even heard of this Coven, only a few rogue changeling dealers, and lone vigilantes getting changelings back."

"Up until now it's been a well-kept secret," said Sparrow.

"So why did you decide to tell us?" asked Fabian.

"Because the truth is out now anyway," said Rowan. "And with the way things are going, the Coven might not be around much longer. If something happens to me, then I wanted you all to know why."

"I think I need a cup of tea," said Florence, breaking her silence at last. She stood up and filled the kettle. The rattles and clatters of the cups were louder and more frequent than usual as she set about making drinks for everyone.

"So Cobbler recruited people," Tanya said finally. "Which treasure did he represent?"

"The Goblet of eternal life," Sparrow answered. "His duty was to keep the Coven going indefinitely." Pain crossed his face. "Perhaps that's why he was one of the first to die—the start of our downfall."

"Then there was Dawn," said Rowan. "She symbolised the Light."

"But I thought you said she was sensitive to sunlight?" said Fabian.

"She was," Sparrow answered. "Which was kind of ironic. But the part she really played was hope. See, Dawn was a changeling—she never found her way back. It's thought she was switched because of her condition, but by the time she found out what she was, she felt it was too late to go back to the fairy realm. Even though she couldn't live a normal life, she adapted." His voice cracked. "She was our reminder of what the Coven was really for—but at the same time a reminder that even if changelings never make it back, they can still survive. She counseled others in the same situation."

"We found Dawn this morning," said Rowan. "She'd been left in the sun to die. Her condition was what killed her, in the end."

Horrified whispers went around the table like a ripple.

"What about Cobbler?" Fabian asked. "Did you...did you find him, as well?"

"His body turned up in a block of ice," said Rowan, bitterly. "Whoever put him there even placed a goblet in his hand. The killer knew what he was—which treasure he symbolized."

A crease appeared in Fabian's forehead. "But the *ice* is symbolic, too. Fix wasn't preserved like that. Bodies in ice can last forever, potentially." His head snapped up. *"Eternally..."*

"And Fix was poisoned by one of her own potions," Tanya added, her hand flying to her mouth.

"All the murders have been carried out in a way that's relevant to the role of that particular member," said Suki. "We didn't see it at first...it was only this afternoon that we realized."

Warwick rubbed a hand over his stubbly chin. "That leaves three more people and three more treasures—the Cauldron, the Platter, and..."

"The *Book of Knowledge*," Fabian finished.

"Merchant is the Cauldron," said Rowan. "He doesn't restore the dead to life exactly—but he restores things to how they should be. He makes the actual trade-off with the changelings."

"What about the other two?"

"Nosebag is the Platter. He's an expert forager. He's trained us all on plants, roots, and berries in the wild that can be eaten if any of us happen to be stranded somewhere, or hiding out for a long time. He made sure we'd never go hungry."

"So that only leaves Peg, the old woman," said Tanya. "She has to be the Book."

"Yes," said Suki. "Peg is the oldest of the Coven members. Her knowledge is vital to us—not only does she have extensive information on the history of the Coven, but also the history of the fairy world and the human world and their relationship with each other."

"So she'd know of any grudges against the Coven," Warwick said thoughtfully. "Because that's what this is—a grudge. If someone simply wanted the Coven finished with, there are easier ways of doing it. But these acts—they're personal. Sadistic."

"We'd hoped that Peg would be able to help," said Sparrow. "But whatever knowledge she had has been destroyed. Her and Nosebag were the latest targets, just this morning. Peg's library had been wrecked, and her mind wiped. She can't even remember her own name. As for Nosebag, he's alive, but barely. He's ingested something toxic—Tino thinks it was mushrooms that had been switched for another kind that looks identical. They found him in time to give him an antidote, but he's weak." He scratched at his scalp. "Neither of them can help us now."

"You said there were three attacks," said Florence, returning to the table. Her thin face looked drawn, and her lips were tight. It was a look Tanya had grown used to over the years; a look she had not seen for many months, but now it was back. Her hands shook as she set steaming teacups in front of everyone.

"The third was on me," said Suki. "My awareness—my powers, have been blocked. I found a strange symbol carved into the ground under my caravan. Normally, Fix would be able to help with stuff like that, but with her gone, Tino thought Peg might...might..."

"And now Peg's gone too," Tanya murmured.

"I may be able to help," said Morag. Her voice was a dry leaf crackle, as bruised as the rumpled skin on her neck. "If we can identify the hex, I may be able to work something to lift it if we have the correct ingredients."

"That may have to wait, Morag," said Warwick. "Right now it's too dangerous for you to return home, until we know why someone tried to harm you. And I can't help feeling that after what we've heard, it's linked to all this."

"That's right," said Tanya. "Morag already saw something about the thirteen secrets in her vision. If the killer even *suspected* she was on to them, that would be reason for them to want her out of the way."

"But we were the only people who knew about Morag's vision," said Fabian, nudging Tanya. "And the only other people we told were the Coven. Someone must have overheard."

"Either that...or one of us has leaked information," Rowan said. "Which would make sense, because whoever is doing all these things knows about us. What we do, who we are, and where to find us."

"Surely not," Suki whispered. "Who would be so stupid?"

"Maybe it's nothing to do with stupidity," said Sparrow. "Any one of us could have been duped. It would only take an experienced glamour-maker to imitate one of us, tricking another into spilling everything."

"But that's what we're trained against!" Suki snapped. "We're trained against being fooled!"

"We're only human," said Sparrow. He winced as Rowan's face clouded. "I mean, well, half of us are. What I'm trying to say is that whether human or fey, none of us are perfect. Mistakes happen."

"The question is, what happens now?" said Warwick. "How are the surviving members of the group going to stay alive?"

"We've got two options," Rowan said. "Fight or flight. If we fight we could put an end to it...as well as pay back whoever did this to us. The problem with that is we're not even sure who or what we're fighting against. Or we can run. Take our chances, scatter and go quiet."

She stared around the table, her green eyes watery. They settled on Warwick. "There's a problem with that option too. Even if Eldritch isn't the one who's doing this, he still wants revenge against me. And after seeing him—seeing how mad he was—I wouldn't put it past him to come for you too." She bowed her head. "I know it was my fault. I'm the one who had the key, and who threw it away, but…I blamed him for being there and doing nothing when Snatcher took James. There's every chance he could feel the same way about you, for doing nothing when I left him in the cellar. So what I'm saying is that even if I leave and disappear, I'll have brought danger to you. If I go, you could still be attacked. Whichever way you look at it—I'm being tracked, and sooner or later the trail will lead to here."

"Then I say we fight," said Warwick. "The Coven has strength in numbers—splitting up is only going to make it easier for you all to get killed, one by one. If the trail leads here, then let it." He stood up and paced before the fireplace. "With a few well-placed clues we can bring the battle to us, and we can pre- pare for it. That's the best chance we've got. If Tino and the others accept, and if we're all together, we stand a chance. We'll turn this place into a fortress— and be ready for them when they come."

21

Rowan stood in the bathroom she shared with Tanya, a cold washcloth pressed to her face. On either side of her, the bedroom doors were locked. Her head pounded with a hot pressure, and lights flickered at the edges of her vision. She moved away from the sink and sat on the side of the bathtub, willing the headache to pass.

Aside from the gurgles and gargles of the drain-dweller in the plughole, the bathroom was quiet. She allowed the peacefulness to wash over her, fighting the sting of tears and the telltale ache in her throat.

She should never have come back; she knew that now. She should have gone ahead and done what she always did—what she did best—and disappeared.

Now it was too late.

A light knocking came from the other side of the

door to her room. She let the washcloth slide down her face a little, listening.

"Rowan?"

It was Rose.

"Are you all right? Can I come in?"

Rowan stayed quiet. From the bedroom she heard Sparrow's voice.

"I think she just wants a few minutes alone, like."

She heard Rose move away from the door. "Will you tell her..."

A pause as she hesitated.

"Tell her I'll be outside, with the animals, if she wants to talk."

Rowan waited for the click of the bedroom door. She got up and dropped the washcloth into the sink, then unlocked the bathroom door and went through it. The room was still bright with early evening sun. Sparrow knelt on her bed, looking out of the window. He turned as she sat next to him.

"So that's her, is it?" he said, his voice soft. "Your real mother? You look like her."

Rowan stared blankly at the bedroom door. "My real mother is dead."

"I used to have a mum once," he continued, ignoring the comment. He looked around. "And a room. There was mold in the top corner, by my bed—but I didn't mind."

"You've never told me why you ran away."

Sparrow sat down. "You've never asked."

"I'm asking now."

Sparrow stared into his lap. "Actually, I had two mums. Both very different."

"You mean, like a stepmother?" she asked.

"No. I mean like one person who turns into someone else completely when they get a drink inside them. I put up with it for years, then one day I just had enough." He rubbed his thumb over his chipped tooth. "The day this happened." He turned to her, a sad little smile on his lips.

"Not everyone gets a second chance, Red."

"Don't preach to me," she muttered, turning away. To her surprise, Sparrow reached for her hand awkwardly, and held it in both of his. She looked down. His skin was brown next to hers and, already, grime was building under his fingernails again. Strangely, she didn't mind.

"I'm not preaching." He squeezed her hand. "I just don't want you to throw this away."

"It doesn't matter now, anyway, does it?" she said, her voice thick with emotion. "Who knows what'll happen. I bet they wish they'd never taken me in."

"Don't be stupid."

"So now you think I'm stupid?" she said huffily.

"No. I don't think that." He turned to face her, and she was suddenly aware of how close he was. "Not at all." Slowly, very slowly, Sparrow leaned toward her and touched his lips to her cheek.

"What was that for?" she asked, stunned.

"In case I don't get a second chance." He leaned back and let go of her hand, not meeting her eyes.

"Suki and Warwick should have found Tino and the others by now."

"Don't change the subject—"

The room shook as a door slammed nearby. Rowan got up.

"Was that Tanya's door?" she wondered aloud.

"Tanya!" Florence's voice sounded from the hallway. "Don't walk away from me when I'm speaking to you!"

Rowan went to the door and opened it a crack. Through the gap she saw Florence hurrying up the stairs and walking toward her. She stopped outside the door next to Rowan's and rapped quickly.

"Leave me alone!" Tanya's voice was a muffled yell. Within the room next door, something else slammed. "I'm packing, *remember*?"

"Tanya." Florence rattled the handle. "I'm not having this conversation through a locked door. Open it, please."

"I don't *want* this conversation, in case you hadn't noticed. I think you've already said it all!"

"Unlock the door, or I will."

Rowan stepped out into the hall. Florence fumbled with a bunch of keys at her side, her thin lips pressed into a line.

"What's happened?" Rowan asked. "Why is Tanya packing?"

Florence looked up, glancing first at Rowan, then at Sparrow, who had come to the door as well. She opened her mouth to say something, but then Tanya's door flew open.

"I'm packing because my grandmother is making me." She stood there, wild-eyed, her empty suitcase clutched in one hand. "She's sending me back home to London."

"Because it's not safe for you here!" Florence's eyes were pleading. "What kind of grandmother would I be to let you stay in a house that's likely to be attacked?"

Tanya let the suitcase slip through her fingers to the floor. "How am I supposed to go home and act like nothing is happening? How can I go home, wondering what's going to happen to you all? Knowing that maybe I could have helped somehow?"

"The best thing you can do to help is to go somewhere safe, away from here," said Florence. "Where I won't have to worry about you."

Tanya shook her head. "Almost everyone I love and care about is in this house."

"But your parents aren't," said Florence. "And they love and care about you."

"I know, and I love them too, but..." Tanya's shoulders sagged. "It's not the same. I can't even talk to them about all this."

"It's for the best," Florence said quietly.

"What about Fabian?" Tanya asked.

"Fabian will have to stay here," said Florence. "If Eldritch wants revenge against Warwick, he could target Fabian. Warwick won't let Fabian out of his sight."

"And you?" said Tanya. "And Rose, and Nell?"

"Nell is leaving. She's packing up her things right now. Given all that's happened to her since she's been here, I'd imagine she's relieved to go. Rose is staying."

"Because of Rowan."

"Yes. And as for me, well. This is my house, and I'm not leaving it."

Tanya picked the suitcase up from the floor. "I suppose that settles it, then," she said stiffly.

"Yes," Florence replied. "I suppose it does."

Tanya stood in the doorway as Florence retreated downstairs.

"When are you leaving?" Rowan asked, once they were alone.

"Tomorrow, on the first train." Tanya made a face. "I tried to persuade her to let me stay until the afternoon, but Warwick says it's too risky. There are only two trains a day, and if the second one is canceled..."

"Can't your mum pick you up?"

Tanya shook her head. "She's in Scotland on some sort of work conference. She won't be back until tomorrow evening. And my dad's on vacation, so I can't go to his house." She leaned her head on the doorframe. "Everything's a mess—I can't even think of a reason to give for going back early. I was supposed to be staying the whole summer." She stepped back into her room. "I'd better finish pack-ing." She closed the door, leaving Rowan and Sparrow alone in the hall.

⚬⚬

Dinner was late that night, a subdued meal that no one seemed to enjoy. Rowan was surprised to find that she missed Nell and the General, for the house was much quieter since they had left a couple of hours earlier. Warwick returned alone just as the plates were being cleared.

"Did you speak to Tino and the others?" Sparrow asked, rising from his seat.

Warwick walked past the plate of cooling food Florence had set on the table, hung his coat on the back door, and then stood at the kitchen window, staring out.

"I spoke to them."

"And?" said Rowan.

"They're coming." Moving to the back door again, he took his iron knife out of his coat and slid it into his belt. "I suggest you all get some sleep. Tomorrow we've got our work cut out."

22

The first of the caravans arrived in the night. Tanya counted three of them through the garden gate the next morning, a medley of color and pattern dotted a short distance from the walls of the manor, between the house and the woods.

A spiral of smoke curled into the air from a small campfire. From where she was, she could make out Crooks's dark shock of hair and Suki's petite form against the tall bulk of Samson and Victor. Sparrow was also with them, despite having stayed overnight in one of the spare rooms at the manor. Every now and then one of them looked toward the house. She could not tell if they saw her, although Oberon skirted the outside of the garden walls in plain view, sniffing here and there and turning back to her with frequent encouraging looks as though to try and coax her beyond the gate.

"I can't, boy," she told him. "I'm not allowed to leave the garden." She whistled to him and turned, startled to see Warwick standing on the path behind her.

He looked toward the caravans. "Already been over this morning myself—Florence offered to have them here for breakfast, but they declined. Polite enough, but they're funny folk. Keep to themselves."

"When's Tino coming?" she asked.

"This morning," Warwick replied. "He said he needed to be there when the rest of the circus pack everything up, but as soon as that's done he'll be here with Merchant."

Tanya closed the gate as Oberon came back into the garden.

"Are you all packed?" Warwick asked.

She scowled. "Yes."

He nodded. "I'll meet you out front in an hour."

"Until then I might as well make myself useful," said Tanya.

Warwick grunted, scuffing the earth underfoot.

"Is that a yes?"

"Find Fabian and Rowan," he muttered. "You can help them, for now. And remind them that none of you are to leave the grounds of the house."

Tanya went indoors. She found Rowan and Fabian on the first floor, in Fabian's room.

"Are you leaving now?" Rowan asked, as Tanya entered. "We'll come downstairs to say good-bye properly."

"Not yet. Warwick says I should help you." Her eyes rested on two half-open black trash bags on the bed. "What are you doing?"

"Filling these with red fabric," said Fabian. "Florence says we need to search the whole house. It can be clothes, sheets, towels, curtains, anything. Collect it all." He closed one of his drawers and opened another, rifling through his things.

"I'll make a start on the second floor," said Rowan. "Most of the rooms are empty but there's that old cupboard full of junk. Tanya, you look in the other rooms on this floor."

A few minutes later, Warwick's voice echoed up through the hall. Tino had arrived. Tanya led the way downstairs, with Fabian and Rowan close behind.

Everyone had gathered. It was a bizarre assembly: the inhabitants of Elvesden Manor, the remaining Coven members, and Morag. The kitchen was full, with the back door open and a few people spilling out into the garden. People murmured among themselves, eyes darting around to assess each other.

"Where's Oberon?" Tanya asked her grandmother. "I can't see him."

"I had to shut him in the pantry," Florence answered. "He started growling again."

Tanya frowned.

"Good one." Fabian rolled his eyes. "There goes the food supply—but at least it'll keep him quiet for a while."

Florence's mouth dropped open and she rushed into the pantry. A minute later she emerged with a sneezing, white-nosed Oberon, straining against his collar. "Up to his neck in flour," she said tightly. "This dog of yours really will eat anything." She maneuvered him out of the kitchen, pulling him back as he lunged toward the newcomers.

"Listen up," Warwick called once she'd returned. The murmurs ceased. "We don't know each other, but we all know why we're here. A number of us are being hunted." He glanced at Morag. "And others are caught in the crossfire. So far, as individuals, we haven't fared well. But together we stand a chance of beating whoever, or whatever, is after us. At the moment we have only one lead—a fey man named Eldritch who has good reason to want revenge against Rowan, or Red, as you know her, and against myself.

"We also know that he had contacts involved in the changeling trade, which is a possible motive against the Coven, and that he has a strong command of using glamour for a prolonged amount of time."

Tanya felt Rowan shiver beside her.

"Whoever is doing this knows the movements of the Coven," said Tino. "By coming here we may have bought some time, but to lead the trail here we've had to leave clues. However, we've no idea how soon our location will filter through. It could well be that we have a spy within the circus, in which case I believe we may have a day or two to prepare, if we're lucky. And preparation is the key."

"If it's known that we're all together maybe the attacks will stop," said Rowan. "They've been attacking one by one, taking us by surprise. Perhaps they won't be so bold now."

Tino narrowed his eyes. "Or perhaps they'll relish the opportunity to try and slaughter us in one fell swoop."

"Some of us have already made a start gathering defense materials," said Warwick. "Once we know what we've got we can work on where to implement it. Rowan and Fabian, you two carry on collecting red fabric—anything you can find. We'll drape it in the windows to disguise the entrances to the house that aren't being defended. Any smaller items can either be worn or sewn together and made larger.

"Tanya, I want you to check the pantry and use any salt to seal up remaining windows and doors— again, not the ones that are being defended or used by the Coven. The fey members need to be able to cross those ones. Save a little, and then empty all of Nell's cleaning products away and fill the spray bottles with salt water. Once you've filled them, bring them to the kitchen.

"Rose, you collect anything made of iron—knives, pokers, horseshoes, nails—whatever you can find, and bring it back here. We'll amass all potential weapons here and decide who's using what.

"Finally, Florence—I want you to rally the fairies of the house. It's as much their home to protect as it is ours, and we need their loyalty now more than ever. All of them can help in some way, even if it's just keeping a lookout." He stopped speaking and looked to Tino.

"Victor and Samson will be overseeing the weapons, and will take the time to give some basic training to anyone who needs it," said Tino. "We need one room to be a safe room. If or when an attack comes, those who aren't either fighting or acting as lookouts will be in that room—and you'll be guarding it, Sparrow." He glanced at Florence. "It needs to be a room with an escape route, if possible."

"I think…the library," Florence said. She brushed an errant wisp of white hair away from her face. "There's a one-way escape passage—people can leave, but there's no way through into the house from it due to a fault of some kind with the door when it was built."

"I marked the way out with a ball of string when I was using the tunnels as a hideout," Rowan added. "It leads straight to the graveyard."

"Perfect," said Tino. "Crooks, I want you to organize a lockup. By that I mean a secure room to hold enemies in, if any are captured. Killing is only to be in self-defense or as a last resort—we don't need any more repercussions. Anyone held can later be taken to the courts."

"Or, at the very least, interrogated," Merchant put in darkly.

"Agreed," said Tino. "And again, we'll need the most suitable room."

A strange look crossed Florence's face. "I..." She stopped and caught Warwick's eye. "There is something. Not quite a room, but a...place, in the house, that we found once—accidentally—years ago."

Warwick nodded. "More of a space than a room—about the size of a cupboard."

"Do you mean a priest hole?" Fabian asked suspiciously. "I asked you once if this house ever had one, and you said no."

"It's not a priest hole, exactly," said Warwick. "The house isn't old enough for that. But it's something similar—whether it was intended to be a hiding place or something like a self-styled prison cell, we're not sure. Elvesden's wealth meant he was a man who feared for his safety, and it seems the idea of something like a priest hole appealed to him."

"We never told anyone about it because it's dangerous," said Florence. "Once you're in it, you can't get out without somebody else opening it from the other side. We always feared somebody getting stuck in it." She looked at Fabian and Tanya. "Playing hide-and-seek, perhaps. That's why we kept it a secret."

"Well, where is it?" Fabian demanded.

"It's in the old music room," Warwick said.

"The one you always keep locked?"

"Yes. And the fewer people who know exactly where it is, the better. If Crooks is to be in charge of it, then we'll show it to him, but no one else."

Fabian pursed his lips.

"What about me?" asked Suki.

"You stay in here with Morag," said Tino. "She's your only hope of lifting the hex on your abilities."

"Can you remember the symbols you found?" Morag asked her.

"Yes, I think so," said Suki, closing her eyes. "I'll try to draw it for you."

"Good," said Tino. "The rest of us—Warwick, Merchant, and myself, will discuss the next steps. Is everyone clear on what they need to do?"

There was a unified murmur of assent.

"Good," said Tino again. "Let's get to work."

⚜

Since Amos's death, none of the rooms on the second floor of the house were occupied, though the old man's belongings still remained as though he might return any moment. They sat waiting for the day that Warwick would be ready to face them. Upon emptying the cupboard of junk, Rowan found four red cushion covers, stained with age. She added them to her bag and piled everything else back in the cupboard, not quite as neatly as she had found it, and moved on.

The other rooms, or at least those that were

unlocked, were devoid of much furniture. She made a mental note of one room with tattered curtains of crimson velvet and then went to the alcove in which a wall tapestry concealed the hidden door to the servants' staircase. Again, her search of the rooms it led to proved fruitless, and so Rowan went in the other direction, up to the attic. Gaps in the roof allowed some light in to guide her. She emerged from the alcove thirty minutes later covered in dust and with little to show for it.

Through a small window overlooking the back of the house she caught sight of flashes of light bouncing off shards of silver below. Victor was throwing knives, one by one, at the horse chestnut tree. To the rear of the garden Merchant and Samson were parrying, each with a sword that must have belonged to Victor. Beyond the walls, Tino was locked in conversation with Warwick, who stood sharpening the blade of his iron dagger.

A slight scrabble sounded from the roof above the window, and she wondered if birds, or even rats, were nesting in the roof.

She shuddered and hauled her cargo of fabric to the top of the stairs, ready for distribution, and then descended the staircase. Down on the first floor she saw that Fabian was having better luck. His bag brimmed, and he had even started a new pile. She left him to it and continued downstairs. On the landing, Florence was speaking earnestly to the grandfather clock.

"...and if you see anything, or hear anything

suspicious, you're to make the clock chime loudly, very loudly. Is that clear?"

Rowan fought an insane urge to laugh as she imagined the scene from an outsider's point of view. Florence's solemn words to the clock would appear to be utter madness.

She squeezed past and jumped the last few stairs to the bottom. In the dining room, Morag and Suki were poring over some circular drawings.

"There was a picture of me here," Suki was saying, a pencil in her mouth. "And then the symbols were something like this...."

Rowan carried on past Tanya, who was carefully arranging salt on windowsills, until she glimpsed Sparrow in the library. She stopped in the doorway, her heart quickening.

"Looking for the secret passageway?" she asked.

He turned and shrugged, grinning. "I give up. Where is it?"

"Hang on," she said. "Back in a minute." She darted into the kitchen to collect another trash bag from the cupboard under the sink. Already the room was starting to resemble an armory. The huge oak table was clear of kitchenware and instead had begun to fill with other objects. Ironware, knives, and a skein of gossamer-like thread stood in the company of two large cages. On the other side of the cages, a vat of an ugly green liquid had been placed next to some smaller, empty bottles, and beyond that was Warwick's air rifle.

Rowan ripped a bag from the roll and left, heading back to the library. Sparrow was prodding in various nooks of the bookcases' intricate woodwork tracery.

"Here," said Rowan. "I'll show you." She placed her fingers into three tiny indents and turned the circular panel until it clicked. Slowly, the partition opened and stale air wafted over them.

Sparrow peered into the stone passageway. "I don't fancy the look of that."

"It's creepy," Rowan agreed. "If you go in, don't stay in there for more than a minute—the mechanism springs back and there's no way in from the other side."

"Think I'll stay put," Sparrow said. "How's the clothes hunt going?"

"Not as well as I'd hoped." She spied a bulky knapsack on the floor by the desk, next to a sleeping bag. "Is that yours?"

"Yeah. Don't think I've got anything red, but feel free to dig through it." He went over to the bag and unzipped the top, then upended it. A jumble of clothes fell out onto the floor. Sparrow stepped over the pile to return to the bookcase, craning his neck to view the musty stone staircase once more.

Rowan knelt and picked at the garments gingerly. Suddenly she felt uncomfortable about going through Sparrow's clothing. It was limp and stale-smelling. Some pieces were worse than others. She wished that he would come away from the secret passage to save her from the embarrassment of looking through his personal things.

She coughed lightly. "Sparrow, I don't think there's anything red in here, but I wondered if you'd like me to..." She hesitated, wary of offending him. "I mean, while you're here, I could wash some of it for you. Florence wouldn't mind." She began stuffing it back in the bag. "We could get it dry in no time."

"Did you say something?" Sparrow's voice was muffled from the tunnel. She turned and saw that curiosity had gotten the better of him. He'd gone right into it after all.

"I said, we could wash your clothes." She picked up another garment, sighing as her hand went straight through a scraggy hole in the back of it. "On second thought, half of it needs to be thrown away," she mumbled, dropping it to the floor when, as predicted, the partition clicked back into place, sealing Sparrow into the tunnel.

"What did I just tell you?" she called as Sparrow banged on the wall from the other side. "You're lucky I'm here to let you out."

Her hand froze as she reached for the indents. An image had flashed in her mind, coming from somewhere deep, somewhere unexpected. Slowly, she turned away from the bookcase to face the knapsack again. Her legs trembled as she crossed the floor to the last thing she had touched. She bent down. Picked it up.

The black hooded top was bobbled and worn, and it smelled of Sparrow and the streets. With one hand she held it as the other felt down the back and found the waistband. Her fingers went straight through the jagged tear in the material that was about the size of her hand.

Sparrow thumped the wall again. "Don't tell me it's stuck!"

She took a step back, staring at the tear. She suddenly felt hot and queasy, trying to blink away the image swimming in her mind, but it wouldn't leave her.

All she could see was the scrap of dark material Oberon had torn from the clothing of whomever he had chased in the woods. She had committed it to memory.

It was a perfect, horrible fit.

23

Another thud came from behind the bookcase.

"Red, are you still there? This isn't funny—I'm getting claustrophobic in here!"

Rowan continued to stand, clutching at the hooded top. *It couldn't be,* she reasoned. There had to be some kind of explanation. Sparrow couldn't be the one Oberon had chased, *couldn't* be the one who had tried to strangle Morag.

But the torn fabric in her hand suggested otherwise. Her fingers reached for the mechanism again, then withdrew once more. If Sparrow *was* guilty, and she released him from the tunnel, he could run. Yet if he stayed in the tunnel, he could still get away— she had spoken of the ball of string leading the way out in front of everyone. And not for the first time. She remembered how pleased she had been upon finding the way into the tunnels, how she had bragged to the other Coven members even then. Now she wished she had kept her mouth shut.

Behind the wall, Sparrow started to thump at it repeatedly. He clearly thought she'd gone. Without another thought, Rowan left the library, holding the top.

Warwick and Tino were outside. They looked up as she hurried over to them, still talking as she interrupted.

"Warwick, can you come inside? I found this." She held out the ripped top.

Warwick's eyes widened. He fumbled in his pocket and pulled out the scrap of material. It flapped in the breeze like a desperate bird trying to get away.

"It's a match." His mouth was set in a grim line. "Whose is it?"

Her lips didn't seem to want to form the right shapes. They were saved from doing so as Tino grabbed the top from her and held it to his nose.

"Sparrow," he whispered. "Where is he?"

"The library," she choked out. "But there must be an explanation."

Tino was already striding into the house. She ran after him, with Warwick following. In the kitchen they rushed past Crooks.

"What's happened?" he called.

None of them answered. Warwick overtook Tino, leading the way to the library.

"He's gone."

"No, he hasn't." Rowan pointed to the bookcase. "He's behind there, in the tunnel. He doesn't know I've found it."

Tino clapped his hand on her shoulder approvingly. "Well done."

"No, I didn't—"

"Is someone there?" Sparrow shouted from the other side. "I'm trapped in the tunnel! Get Red, she knows how to open it!"

Warwick stood in the doorway and nodded to Rowan. "Get him out of there. Let's see what he's got to say for himself."

As the partition opened, Sparrow stumbled out, blinking and gasping. His eyes focused on Rowan, hurt. "That your idea of a practical joke?"

She bit her lip. Tino moved to stand in the way of the partition, blocking the only other exit from the room.

"Want to tell us about this?" he asked coolly. He held up the top.

Sparrow eyed it blankly. "It's a top. Er, it's black...." He shrugged. "And it's mine. What you getting at?"

"It's also got a rip in the back," said Warwick. "And this is the missing part—the part Oberon came back with."

"After chasing the person who tried to strangle the gypsy woman," Rowan said.

"You can't be serious!" Sparrow's voice rose in disbelief. "I never tried to kill the old woman! I've never even been *near* her until today!"

"Then how do you explain it?" Tino growled.

"I don't know," Sparrow hissed. He held his hands up. "It's been so warm that I haven't even worn the thing in weeks—it's been festering in the bottom of my bag. Anyone could have taken it and used it, but I'm telling you, I haven't been near those woods! Why? Why would I do it?"

"Why would anyone want the gypsy woman dead?" Warwick said. "To cover their tracks. They would have known she was helping us and tried to silence her."

"Then it was someone else," Sparrow said angrily. "Someone must have gone through my stuff and taken it."

"Why would anyone want to put that on?" Tino sneered. "It reeks."

"Exactly." Sparrow's face flushed with humiliation but he held his ground. "If someone wanted to frame me, then using my clothes is an easy way to do it."

"Oberon went berserk when you entered the house," Rowan remembered.

"If I'd been the one to do it, do you really think I'd have brought that top anywhere near this house? That I'd even still have it? Whoever was wearing it knew the dog had taken a chunk out of it—they'd have got rid of it first chance they had!"

"He's right," said Rowan. Relief washed over her.

"He knew I was about to look through his things and he didn't even react—he was more interested in investigating the tunnel. That's how he ended up shut in there."

Sparrow stared back at her. "And how convenient for you that I did," he said. "Made it all the easier, didn't it?"

His quiet defeat hurt Rowan more than anything.

"Sparrow," she said weakly. "What would you have done?"

"Spoken to you. At least *asked* you, before running off and telling tales."

"If it had been anyone else, I would have. But with you, I couldn't think straight...."

"Maybe he's just being clever," Tino continued, shifting as the partition finally swung back into place. "After all, he's been taught by the best."

Sparrow shook his head. "What's that supposed to mean?"

"If you were the one who attacked Morag, you knew the dog would have gone for you even if the top had been destroyed," Tino answered. "It was your scent he was reacting to. That alone could have raised suspicion. But keeping the top and claiming someone else used it is altogether more plausible." His mismatched eyes swept over Sparrow from head to toe. "That's what I'd do. And that's why I don't believe you."

"Tino..." Sparrow began. "You can't think that of me. How long have you known me...?"

"Are you sure about this?" Warwick asked, evidently uncomfortable. "I mean, you know him better than anyone—it's your decision, but—"

"I'm not sure of anything at the moment. And until I am, I'm taking no chances." Tino grabbed Sparrow roughly. "We'll need to put him somewhere secure—he's been taught the tricks of the trade in escaping...."

Sparrow tried to bat Tino away. "Get your hands off me!"

"You mean the holding cell?" Warwick asked. "It's small—if we put him in it, there won't be room for anyone else who's captured later."

"Good point."

"Don't do this." Sparrow stopped struggling. "I'll prove to you that it wasn't me—I'll find whoever framed me!"

"Let him try," Rowan whispered, wide-eyed. Sparrow would not look at her. "Let him at least try...."

Tino shook his head. "I can't take that chance." He spun Sparrow round, pinning his arms behind his back, and jerked his head toward the bookcase. "The tunnels—you said it was a labyrinth down there. How dark is it?"

"Pitch black," Rowan answered, confused. "Why?"

"Open it again."

"But—"

"Do it! *Now!*"

Hating herself, Rowan quickly released the secret doorway.

"Help me search him," Tino commanded, holding Sparrow bodily to the wall. Warwick frisked his pockets.

"What am I looking for?"

"Matches, or a flashlight. He can't have any light. In fact, just remove everything he's got."

Sparrow began to fight again, crying out as Tino twisted his arm into a painful lock. "Don't! Please don't shut me in there!"

Warwick threw a slim book of matches on the floor. It was followed by some coins, string, and a penknife before he moved on to the next pocket.

Rowan watched, frozen. She helplessly watched as the surreal scene unfolded before her eyes.

"That's everything," Warwick said at last.

Tino bundled Sparrow into the stairwell, jostling to keep him under control.

"Stop struggling. I don't want to do this."

"Then don't!" Sparrow yelled. "I'm telling you, you've got the wrong person! I'd never hurt no one—least of all an old woman! What about Crooks? This is more his handiwork than mine—he was the one who used to rob the old folks' homes when you found him, wasn't he? If I remember right, I was the only one bothered by that, but you, all you saw was how you could use him. . . ."

Tino didn't react. "How long before the door closes, Red?"

"I don't know, maybe thirty seconds."

"Hope I can hold him for that long. . . ."

Grunts and scuffles came from the stairwell as Tino and Sparrow wrestled for control. Rowan watched, stricken, but there was only ever going to be one winner. A sharp jolt to Sparrow's arm put an end to every squirm.

The partition started to move.

"The door's closing." Warwick stepped forward. "You need to get out of there in the next few seconds."

More scuffles sounded, and Rowan shifted to get a view through the rapidly narrowing gap. Already the space beyond it was darkening.

"It wasn't me!" Sparrow twisted, in obvious pain, his eyes wide. "Tell them, Red! You know me! *You know I wouldn't do this!*"

"I'm sorry, Sparrow," Tino said through gritted teeth. He maneuvered Sparrow away from him, then sent him flying with one huge shove.

"No, the stairs!" Rowan cried, her hands flying to her mouth. Sickening sounds of bumps and scuffs reached her as Sparrow rolled down the hard stone staircase, then Tino squeezed through the closing gap.

"That was the idea," said Tino, unable to look at her. "It was the only thing I could think of."

"But he could be hurt. . . ." She ran to the gap and pressed her face against it. Groans came from somewhere below, then stopped as the doorway sealed itself.

"What are the chances of him finding the ball of string?" Tino asked.

"Without any light, slim to none." She continued to stare at the bookcase. "Tino, we can't do this."

"We just did."

"But I don't think it was him—I don't believe it."

"You don't want to believe it," Tino said softly. "And neither do I. But look at the evidence. We can't ignore it. Until we find something to say it wasn't Sparrow, that's the best place for him. If someone else did set him up, they'll give themselves away eventually—we need to keep our eyes open."

He moved toward the door. "For now, this stays between us. If someone is framing Sparrow, they'll know we're on the lookout if we tell them what's just happened."

"Wait." Rowan closed her eyes. "At least let me listen for a minute. As soon as I can hear him moving, I'll come out."

"We don't have time." Warwick's voice was gentle, but firm. "We've got work to do—we don't even know that he'll try to come back up the stairs straight away. He could go off into the tunnels. . . ."

"He could get lost," she whispered, allowing Warwick to herd her out of the room. Tino was already in the hallway and had been joined by Crooks. Evidently, he had overheard most of what had happened, and Tino did not look pleased.

"Not a word to anyone about this," he hissed to him. "Get back to whatever you were doing."

Crooks slunk off as Warwick locked the library door. "No one is to go into this room, understand?"

She nodded blankly.

"We'll need a new safe room," Tino muttered as he and Warwick went off in the direction of the kitchen. "For now, let's say the exit in the library has jammed."

"There's one upstairs," Warwick answered. "An old servants' room with a false fireplace. Door doesn't lock, but Crooks could fix that...."

Rowan stared at the library door. In a daze she went upstairs to her room, closing the door quietly, and then she went and sat on the bed. For a full minute she stared at the wall, seeing only Sparrow's eyes, wide and disbelieving.

"What have I done?" she whispered to herself. The tears came then, hot and plentiful, soaking her face in a flood. It was only as one ran all the way down her wrist that she suddenly became aware that her fingers were pressed against her cheek, touching the exact spot where Sparrow had kissed her yesterday. She did not even remember lifting her hand.

I might not get a second chance, Sparrow had said. Now it seemed he had been right.

She dropped her hand, wiping her face with her cuff, and got up to check herself in the mirror.

"Why are you crying?"

Rowan gasped and spun to face the door.

Fabian stared back in concern. "Are you all right?"

"I'm fine," she snapped. "I'm not crying. I've got dust in my eye. And will you please learn to knock?"

"Sorry." Without waiting for an invitation, Fabian shuffled across the room and sat down on the bed.

"What are you doing? I never told you to come in."

"Sorry," said Fabian again.

Rowan turned away from the mirror. "What's wrong with you?" she asked. "Your voice sounds strange."

"I found something in one of the rooms," said Fabian. He was staring into his lap. One of his hands was in a fist.

"Spit it out, then."

He flinched at her tone and got up. "Never mind."

"Fabian, wait. I'm sorry for snapping." She gestured to the bed and sat down on the stool, sniffing. "What did you find?"

Fabian's lips were pinched together. Slowly, he unfurled his hand and pushed it toward her.

"There's nothing in it."

"Look closer."

Rowan wiped at her eyes again. Then she saw it. A very long, very red hair, the exact same color as her own.

"It's Rose's," she said, frowning. "Why are you showing me this?"

"I found it in my dad's room." His voice was tight. "I was in there looking for red stuff, and I saw that his pillowcase was red. That's where I found this." He looked up at her, his blue eyes huge behind his glasses.

"My dad, and your mum . . ."

"No," she said. "They can't be . . . they *wouldn't*."

"Wouldn't they?" Fabian gave a hollow laugh. "Why not? They seem to have been getting along just fine. He gives her a ride home every night, and she's been staying later and later."

"But that's because of the animals," said Rowan. "And because of me. That's why she's always here. One hair doesn't mean anything, Fabian. You're jumping to conclusions. It was probably just caught up on his clothes."

"It wasn't the only one." Fabian wound the hair around his fingers, tighter and tighter until it snapped. "There were more. Do you still think they were just caught on his clothes?"

She swallowed, trying to process the thought, but unable to. Her head was already swimming with confusion.

"I don't know . . . I can't think about this now, Fabian. I'm sorry. . . ."

He stared at her in disbelief. "Don't you want to at least ask them?"

"No . . . yes. . . ." She sighed. "I'm not sure."

"Thanks for the support." He got up in disgust.

"Look, I'm not saying we shouldn't ask, but just not *yet*. This can wait—there's too much going on. If you leave it until this is over, then we'll confront them together."

"Promise?"

"Yes." She got up and went toward him. "I promise. But I still think there'll be an explanation. There's no way they'd be able to keep something like that a secret."

Fabian let the broken hair drop to the floor. "Fine. I'll keep quiet, for now. But do you want to know what I think? I think everyone in this house is full of secrets, and they don't give them up easily." He went to the door and flung it open. "Including you. I'll leave you to get that *dust* out of your eye."

"Fabian—"

A heavy thud sounded from above, startling them both.

"What was that noise?" Fabian asked, his rant momentarily forgotten.

"It came from over by the window," said Rowan. She moved away from the dressing table and closer to the bed. "I thought I heard something earlier, on the roof...I thought it was mice. Maybe it's a bird."

"It'd have to be the size of an emu to make a thunk that loud."

Scratches and scrabbling came from above. A piece of slate slipped past the window a second later. Fabian ran to the bed and jumped on it, his nose pressed against the glass. They both heard the slate smash on the path at the side of the house.

"Whoa," Fabian breathed, his breath misting the glass. He twisted his head, trying to get a glimpse of whatever was on the roof. Another tile slid past and shattered below. He reached for the catch on the window.

"Don't open it," she said sharply.

"I just want to see what's up there," he protested, his fingers working the catch.

"I said leave it!"

They both froze as a long tail dropped into view in front of the window. It was thin at the tip, growing wider as it went up, and it was the color and texture of an elephant's hide. It flicked from side to side in the manner of an agitated cat, then disappeared above again.

Fabian found his limbs and scrambled back off the bed.

"What the hell was that?"

They got their answer an instant later when it dropped into view, landing on the windowsill. Its thick claws scrabbled for a hold, and two leathery wings flapped to give it balance on the narrow ledge. It was about the size of a four- or five-year-old child, but there the similarity ended. The domed head was bald, and the lips drew back in an ugly snarl as it gazed into the room. A metal ring was clamped around its neck, with one broken link dangling from it.

Rowan recognized it immediately. "It was a spy," she whispered. "For the Hedgewitch... Someone's freed it." She shoved Fabian toward the door, never taking her eyes off the window. "Move, now!" she whispered urgently.

The creature hissed, its yellow eyes fixed on her,

but made no attempt to get in. They staggered out into the hallway, slamming the bedroom door.

Rowan ran for the stairs, Fabian at her heels.

"Where are we going?"

"To tell Warwick. If that thing's here, then I'm guessing Eldritch isn't far behind it."

24

Tanya was salting the windowsills in the dining room when chaos broke out. Feet thundered down the hallway, and she saw Fabian and Rowan racing for the kitchen, shouting Warwick's name. She left the sack of salt and hurried around the table.

Going through the hallway, she was aware of people upstairs. Voices, including those of her grandmother and Rose, drifted down to her, and in a closed room nearby she thought she heard Morag and Suki. However, it seemed that everyone else on the ground floor had either witnessed or heard Fabian and Rowan's panic and was gathering to find out the cause of it.

The kitchen was a swarming hive. Merchant and Crooks leaned over the sink to look through the window into the garden. To the side of them, Rowan and Fabian were in the doorway. Outside, Warwick,

Victor, and Tino were beneath the horse chestnut tree, looking to the skies and shielding their eyes from the sunlight. At the rear of the garden stood Samson, also looking up.

Tanya wedged herself between Rowan and Fabian. "What's going on?"

Fabian turned, pasty-faced. "There's something on the roof."

"Where did it go?" she heard Warwick say.

"There." Tino pointed, his eyes both golden in the sun. "Behind those chimneys."

"See if we can get it closer," Victor said in a low voice. His hand gripped one of his daggers, and there were several more lined up in his belt. "Just a few more meters and I could take it out, no problem."

"Not yet," said Tino. "No kills, remember? Not unless we have to. It hasn't attacked."

"Yet," said Victor.

"It's moving again," said Warwick. "Over by that window—it's looking in."

Tiles fell and smashed at the side of the house.

Victor's hand tightened around his dagger. "Not exactly subtle, is it?"

"I don't think it means to be," said Warwick. "It's not attacking, but it's watching us all right. It *wants* us to know it's there."

Samson's head turned suddenly. "Look!"

Warwick and Tino stepped back to view where he was pointing. Victor stayed where he was, his knife at the ready.

Warwick's eyes fixed on something. He swore. "Another one. Up there. See it?"

Tino lowered his hand. "I see it." He looked to Samson, making a small signal. "Let's try something—a little experiment."

Warwick looked around in alarm. All eyes were on Samson as he lifted the latch to the gate and took a few steps out of the garden.

No sooner had the gate swung closed than a terrible, hissing screech sounded from above. Tanya saw the creature's shadow gliding across her grandmother's garden toward Samson. Its cries pierced her ears and filled her with dread. Then it came into view, a gray, ugly thing, not dissimilar from the gargoyles on the front gates. It swooped toward Samson, talons scraping and grabbing, narrowly missing his face as he ducked out of the way and vaulted the gate back into the garden.

The creature turned in the air, its snakelike tail curving in a wide arc as it twisted and changed direction.

"It's coming back," said Warwick. "Samson, move! Come back to the house, quickly!" He climbed up the steps to the door, shepherding them all further back into the kitchen. "Tino, Victor—get in here!"

Tino stepped into the house, taking Crooks's place at the window, but Victor remained outside, his eyes on his brother. Samson had started to run, but though he was only a short way from the house, his heavy build meant that speed wasn't on his side. It was clear he could not outrun the flying creature.

"Keep moving!" Victor yelled. He dropped into a crouch, the blade poised. "I'm covering you!"

Samson continued to run, hazarding quick looks over his shoulder at the approaching creature. It was almost upon him.

"Stop looking back!" Victor cried. "It's slowing you down!"

By now everyone knew that Samson was not going to make it to the door unscathed. Less than three meters from his target, the creature caught up with him. He bellowed as it sank its talons into his shoulder.

At the same time, Victor unleashed his dagger. It spun unwaveringly through the air, missing Samson's face by a handspan, and sliced the top corner of one leathery wing clean away. With a howl the creature released him and surged into the air, showering the garden with droplets of blood. The dagger continued on its way, finally ending its journey a short distance away in one of the wooden fence posts.

Victor pulled his brother into the kitchen. The shoulder of Samson's tunic hung in shreds, already steeped in blood.

He craned his neck to view the damage. "It's just scratches. Could have been a lot worse. Anyone know what those demons are?" He accepted a tea towel soaked in water from Victor and held it to his shoulder, wincing.

"Yes," said Merchant unexpectedly. "They're called garvern. I saw one once a few years back—Peg helped me to identify it through her books. They're a rare fey breed—a mixture of gargoyles and wyvern—both vicious creatures in their own right. The hybrid of the two is even more deadly. They're highly territorial and make excellent hunters—usually working in packs. More could be coming."

"Great," said Warwick. "And now we've got one on the roof that's bound to be cranky. Just what we need. What were you thinking of, goading it like that?" he asked Tino.

"Testing it," Tino replied calmly. "Now we know why they're really here—to keep us where we are. For now, at least."

"So if anyone attempts to leave the grounds of the house, they'll be attacked?" said Warwick, glancing at Tanya. "Is that what you're saying?"

"It's what I'm guessing, after witnessing that."

"What about if we're protected—wearing red, or turning clothes inside out?"

"Then they can't touch you," said Merchant. "But they can still do other things—their size means they can cause accidents by attacking vehicles—even jumping in front of them to cause a distraction."

Warwick rubbed his hands over his face. "Looks like you got what you wanted, after all," he told Tanya. "You're not going anywhere."

She felt her insides flip. Warwick looked to Tino. "I thought we'd have more time." He shut the back door and locked it. "From now on we should remain inside the house until whatever's coming comes. Those of you with jobs, continue with what you're doing, and make it quick. Those who have finished, see Tino or me for what to do next. Be prepared to move fast now—they could strike at any time. When they do, head for the safe room on the second floor, or remain in position if you're fighting." He glanced at Tanya with a warning look in his eyes. "In case you're in any doubt at all, you'll be in the safe room. I'll go and tell Florence."

"Do you think Gredin and Raven will come?"

"I don't doubt it," said Warwick grimly. "I'm just concerned with them getting in, if we can't even get out."

The pantry held enough salt only to make safe the windows of the ground floor. Tanya's hands were dry and stinging from it. Throughout the house, fewer words were spoken; the only conversation was relevant to the tasks at hand. In the kitchen, Brunswick deftly stitched together the red garments that had been gathered, and gradually, those windows free from salt barriers were swathed in red fabric.

Flames sprung up in every working grate, laid by the brownie of the tea caddy and lit by the hearthfay, to prevent the chimneys being breached. With the windows closed and at the height of summer, the heat in the individual rooms soared to unbearable heights.

The garvern could be heard scratching overhead

on the second floor. Frequently, a contorted gray face or tail appeared in a window that wasn't yet protected, causing another flurry of panic. Merchant had been right—more had come.

❦

Rowan moved around the house, a stick of chalk in her hand. She checked each room one by one, closing the door and marking it with a cross to show it was protected.

She passed Crooks, who was fixing the lock to the safe room. Fabian crouched in a door on the opposite side of the hallway.

"What are you doing?" she asked him.

"All the red cloth's been used. For the rest of the rooms with no protection I'm rigging up trip wires. They could warn us if something enters, provided it's not flying."

"Good plan." She left him, continuing to cross off the rest of the doors, then went downstairs to mark the doors there, and then finally, the ground floor.

When she reached the library, she lingered outside. She pressed her ear to the door, straining for any sound of Sparrow from behind the hidden partition, but she heard nothing. The sickened feeling she had been carrying with her ever since deepened. Thoughts of Sparrow, injured and defenseless if the house should be breached, played in her mind. If anything happened to him, it would be her fault. She tried the door, but of course, no one had been in since Warwick had locked it, taking the key with him.

She continued through the house, her mind working furiously. She had to at least know that Sparrow was all right, that he hadn't been seriously hurt when Tino had pushed him. She marked the doors, methodically and savagely, grimacing at the intense heat of the fires.

She pushed open the door to a disused parlor room. Inside, Morag was at the table. Papers were spread across it before her. Suki sat with her eyes closed at the center of a large circle crudely drawn with chalk on the tiled floor. She opened her eyes as Rowan entered.

"Sorry," said Rowan. "I didn't know you were still in here. I'll come back—"

"We were just about to come out," said Suki, getting up. "Morag's done it—she's lifted the hex on me." She held her hands to her head, swaying a little. "I'm already sensing things—scenes are coming through again. I have to find Tino." She left the room and staggered off in the direction of the kitchen.

Morag rose from the table, deep in thought. One of her hands fluttered at her neck, and with the other, she ran a bony finger over one of the pieces of paper and tapped at it. "I was sure..." she began, then tutted. "Never mind. I'm old and forgetful now."

"Is something bothering you?" Rowan asked, moving to her side.

"This hex," Morag said. "It's a particularly nasty one—I've only seen it crop up once or twice in my lifetime. Both times I was able to lift it with a purifying spell." She gestured to the chalk circle.

"Suki says it worked," Rowan reminded her gently. "You did it."

"Yes," said Morag. "But in both cases before this, the reaction to the hex being lifted was quite different, if my memory serves."

Rowan frowned. "How do you mean?"

"Well, for one thing, the afflicted person would be very ill after having such a hex removed," said Morag. "I didn't tell the girl this beforehand—I needed her to be calm and relaxed for it to work. One of the side effects of the hex working its way out of the system is cramps, violent cramps. Even sickness, in some cases. And often, the healer lifting the hex experiences these symptoms too, to a milder extent."

"But Suki isn't ill," said Rowan. "She just seemed a bit dizzy."

"Yes," said Morag. "And I'm feeling no different. Which means that either I haven't lifted it properly, despite what she says, or that I wrongly identified the hex."

Rowan stared at the piece of paper under Morag's hand. A circular diagram had been sketched on to it, with odd little squiggles and symbols. "Did Suki draw this?"

"Yes."

"It doesn't look right." Rowan picked up the

piece of paper and examined it more closely. "I saw what was underneath her caravan, and it wasn't this."

Morag's eyes narrowed, and she looked toward the door. Rowan caught the hint. She went over and checked the hallway before closing it.

"Do you think you can remember what you saw?" Morag said gravely.

"A little." Rowan grabbed a nearby pencil and a blank sheet of paper. "She's got parts of it right, like the photograph of herself in the center, but the arrangement was different." She drew out a circle and added the square at the center. "That's the photograph. There was something covering her face— mud...no, candle wax." She closed her eyes, trying to remember. "I can't picture any more. But other people saw it too." She laid the pencil down. "I don't understand it—how could Suki have got it so wrong? Surely out of everyone, she'd have remembered it correctly. Unless..."

"Unless she deliberately misled me," Morag finished. Her gnarled hand gripped the paper. "I need to find out what this is, but to identify it I must have more detail."

Rowan held out her hand for the paper, folded it, and tucked it in her back pocket. "I'll get it. Don't tell anyone what you've just told me—we can't have this getting back to Suki until we know what we're dealing with." Her thoughts were a jumble as she left the room. She passed the kitchen, noting that Tino,

Samson, Crooks, Victor, and Merchant were in there. Unfortunately, so was Suki. That left only one other person who had seen the carved circle—and he was shut in the stone tunnel below the library.

Two people had keys to the door: Warwick and Florence. Rowan's only option was to steal one of them.

She bolted up the stairs. Tanya was now helping Fabian rig doors with trip wire. They were being solemnly overlooked by Oberon, who had been let out of whichever room he'd been shut in earlier.

"I need your help," she told them. "I have to get a skeleton key. Can you create some kind of distraction?"

Fabian got up. "Whose key?"

"Whoever we find first—I need it quickly."

Fabian jerked his head to the safe room. "I just saw Warwick go in there."

Rowan set off. "That'll do."

They stopped outside the door.

"What do you want us to do to distract him?" Tanya asked.

Rowan put her hand on the doorknob. "Whatever comes to mind." She pushed the door open and went into the room.

The first thing she saw was that Warwick was not alone in the room. Rose was with him. They stepped apart swiftly, but not before Rowan saw that they were holding hands. From Fabian's gasp, it was clear he had seen it too.

"So it's true then?" he demanded. "Something *is* going on between you two?"

Rowan closed her eyes. This was not what she had planned. Nevertheless, the look of horror on Warwick's face showed her one thing—all his attention was on Fabian now.

Rose looked past them to Tanya, holding back in the doorway behind them.

"You told them? Why?"

Now it was Rowan's turn to be shocked.

"I never said anything," Tanya gasped.

"What?" Fabian rounded on her. "You knew? *You knew about this?"*

"Believe me, I didn't want to know," Tanya protested.

"She found out by accident. We asked her not to say anything," Warwick said hoarsely. "It's not Tanya's fault. We should have told you both—but it never seemed to be the right time. *Now's* not the right time...."

"You got that right," Fabian shot back.

"Do you really begrudge us being together?" Rose asked. Her face looked thinner, and it was pale against her masses of red hair.

"No," Rowan managed at last. She wanted to scream with anger, and frustration, and confusion. "No...I don't begrudge it. It doesn't feel wrong, exactly. Just odd." She stared at Rose. "Ever since you've been here, things have been complicated. Why did you have to complicate them more?"

"I don't see what's so complicated." Rose's voice was soft. "I'm here because I love you." She glanced at Warwick. "And I...I love him. It's quite simple, really."

"I remember when we were in the fairy realm," Rowan said, looking at Warwick. "You said you didn't think you'd ever be happy again, not without Evelyn. You blamed yourself for her death, even though it wasn't really your fault. If this will make you happy, then I'm glad."

Too late she noticed Fabian tense beside her.

"What do you mean by that? Why should he blame himself for my mother's death? It was an accident!"

Warwick's mouth opened and closed, but no words came out.

"It was an accident," Fabian repeated through gritted teeth. *"Wasn't it?"*

"Tell him, Warwick," Rowan said sadly. "It's time he knew the truth."

"It wasn't an accident." Warwick moved toward Fabian, his arms outstretched, but Fabian backed away. "It was revenge, against me, for meddling in the fairy world. They wanted to hurt me—so they... they took your mother."

"No!" said Fabian. "You told me she'd been sleepwalking! That's how she ended up falling into the brook! That's how she drowned—"

"She was enchanted," Warwick cut in. "She didn't have a chance. I've wanted to tell you the truth for a long time."

"But it was easier to lie," Fabian spat. "And

Florence must have known, and"—he shot a venomous look at Rose—"I'm guessing *she* did."

An injured look crept into Rose's eyes. She pushed past Rowan and Tanya and walked out of the room, leaving Fabian to his tirade.

"Even Rowan knew before I did. Be honest— were you ever going to tell me?"

"Of course!"

Fabian laughed without mirth. "I don't think any of you in this room know how to tell the truth. You've all lied to me—every single one of you." He cast his eyes around, and Rowan saw that hers was not the only face burning with shame.

Without another word, Fabian left, his footsteps thudding across the hall to his bedroom. Warwick rushed after him. "Fabian!"

"Go away!" Fabian roared, slamming his door.

"I'm sorry I didn't tell you about Warwick and Rose," Tanya said. She knelt by Oberon and buried her face in his fur. "I didn't know how to...and I thought they should be the ones to do it. I didn't think it'd come out like this."

"It doesn't matter." Rowan shook her head. "None of it matters anymore." She smiled bitterly. "I wanted a distraction—and I got one. And a lot more than I bargained for."

She nodded to the door, which had started to swing closed after Warwick's exit. "Turns out I didn't even need it."

His keys dangled from the lock.

25

The keys rattled traitorously in Rowan's hand as she searched for the right one to the library. Twice she moved away at the sound of approaching voices, but no one had yet seen her trying to access the room. Sweat poured from her forehead, not helped by the roaring fires all around the house. Her nausea magnified with each wave of heat.

Finally she found it. After letting herself into the room and locking the door behind her, she removed the key from the ring and left it in the lock. She stuffed the remaining ones in her pocket and crept to the bookcase, knocking softly on the wood.

"Sparrow?" she whispered.

There was no answer. She tapped harder. "Sparrow? Are you there?"

Something shuffled on the other side. "Where

else would I be?" His voice was groggy, but sarcastic.

She leaned her head against the wood. "Sparrow, I'm sorry."

There was a silence. Then, "Who else is there with you?"

"No one. I'm alone—they don't know I'm in here."

"Have you found something that proves it wasn't me who attacked Morag?"

"No." She bit her lip. "But I trust you." As she spoke, a realization hit her. "Wait—you *couldn't* have attacked Morag...because it happened when we were at Dawn's. I was with you all day!"

Sparrow was quiet. "Shame you didn't remember that earlier. Are you letting me out?"

"I don't think I can—not yet."

"Then why did you bother coming in here?"

"Because I wanted to check you're all right. Are you?"

"You mean after Tino chucked me down the stairs?" His bitterness permeated the wall. "Yeah. A few scrapes and bruises. I've had worse."

She closed her eyes, picturing his chipped tooth. "Listen. I need to show you something."

"*Show* me something? Wouldn't that involve you opening this door?"

"Yes. Will you promise not to run?"

He laughed. "Give me one good reason why not."

She opened her eyes and took a deep breath. "Because if you do you'll be caught and it'll only make you look more guilty."

"I'll take my chances."

"Even if you got out, you wouldn't get far. The house is being watched."

"Not good enough—I'd still run."

"Fine. Because I'm asking you not to."

"Fair enough."

Rowan blinked. "Are you serious?"

"I'm locked in a damp, stinking tunnel. I'm not exactly in the mood to joke."

Before she could change her mind her fingers found the mechanism. She stood aside as the narrow passageway was slowly revealed. Sparrow huddled at the top of the stairs, shivering. He squinted as the light from the room flooded in, blinking at her miserably, then moved into the warm library.

"Get by the fire," said Rowan. She wanted to cry at the sight of him, she was so ashamed. She waited a couple of minutes to let him warm himself before pulling the piece of paper from her pocket. She unfolded it and passed it to him.

"What's this?" he asked through chattering teeth.

"I'm trying to help Morag with a diagram of the hex under Suki's caravan. This is what I've remembered so far—I was wondering if you could remember any more."

Sparrow took it from her. His hand was shaking,

and his fingernails were caked with dirt. "Yeah, I can remember bits of it, but wouldn't you be better off asking Suki?"

"That's what I thought," said Rowan. "She's been with Morag all day, trying to identify the hex. But I saw what she drew, and it's nothing like what was under the caravan. Sparrow, I think she lied—I think she's hiding something. If we can remember what those symbols were then maybe we can figure out what she's up to."

"You think she's involved in what's been happening?"

"Why else would she deliberately mislead someone who was trying to help her? Morag recognized the hex she drew and confirmed it was a nasty one— but that hex was never cast."

Sparrow studied the paper. "Got a pen?"

She reached over and grabbed one from the desk, and Sparrow began to sketch. "Burned-out matches, I remember those. Candles. And the symbols . . . they were sort of curly, like this. . . ."

"There was something holding her picture down," Rowan remembered, the sketch jogging her memory. "A pebble. That's it. That's everything—I think you've done it."

Sparrow stared at the paper, then folded it and handed it back.

"I just thought of something else," he said. "When the dog started growling before, it wasn't only at me. Suki was there too—both times. Even if it was my top he could smell, what's to say he wasn't reacting to her scent as well?"

A tremor of fear went through Rowan. "You think Suki's the one?"

Sparrow shrugged. "She was quick enough to come out with a story about being afraid of dogs. I've never known Suki to admit to being scared of anything before, have you? And if she lied about that piece of paper, who knows what else she's lied about?" He leaned toward her. "Think about it for a second. She's been with the Coven for less than a year. Now half of us are gone, with virtually no signs of a struggle anywhere. They trusted whoever got to them—that's what got them killed."

"But why? Why would she do this?"

"I don't know," said Sparrow. "All I know is that we're trapped in this house with her, and you say the outside is being watched—"

"She can't be working alone," Rowan said, horrified. "We've got to tell Tino and the others!"

"No," said Sparrow fiercely. He stabbed at the diagram. "Until we know what that is, we don't have proof of anything—she'll just wriggle out of it by saying she remembered it wrong. At the moment, they all still think it's me, and while we're in this house, with her on the inside—and whoever she's working with on the outside—we're sitting ducks."

"They've rounded us up like sheep," Rowan said as the realization hit her.

"But we've got a chance to catch them off guard,"

Sparrow whispered. "Don't you see? If you give me what I need to find my way out, the tunnel leads far away enough from the house for me to see what's happening, but not be seen. I'd have the advantage."

"You're right." Rowan got up and headed back to the bookcase, opening the secret passageway.

Reluctantly, Sparrow stepped back inside, his skin graying in the gloom.

"Will you help me, Red?"

She nodded. "I'll be back as soon as I can. I'm going to get this to Morag, and then get us some flashlights and my fox-skin coat."

"Us?"

"I'm coming with you." Impulsively, she leaned into the tunnel and put her arms around him. His hair no longer smelled of shampoo. He smelled like Sparrow, her Sparrow. "It's the least I can do."

Something scuffled at the bottom of the stairwell.

"Go on," he said gruffly, nudging her away. "Before the door closes us both in the dark."

She slid back out of the tunnel and into the warm library. "I won't be long."

The partition started to close.

"Hurry back," he whispered through the gap. "I can hear something down there—have I ever told you I hate rats?"

The tunnel entrance sealed itself, cutting him off.

Rowan let herself out of the library, her hands shaking as she fumbled to lock the door. The hallway was clear. She darted through it, her eyes peeled for the old gypsy woman. Eventually she found her in the kitchen, talking to Tino and Suki. Warwick was there, subdued after the confrontation. He stood at the table distributing the green liquid from the vat into some of the smaller bottles, then handed one to Morag and another to Rose. He pocketed another one, and then handed Rowan a fourth.

"Will you give this to Fabian? He won't open his door to me."

She took it, glancing at Suki out of the corner of her eye. "I doubt he'll open it to me either." She went to the sink and rummaged in the cupboard below it.

"What are you after?" Warwick asked.

"A flashlight. I thought it'd be useful in the safe room, just in case," she lied.

He nodded and turned back to what he was doing. Eventually she found a flashlight, and after changing the batteries, she headed for the stairs. She was halfway there when a window smashed somewhere on the first floor.

She ran to the top, reaching the landing at the same instant as Tanya came out of her room, the compass and scissors in her hand, her eyes wild.

They both saw the garvern at the same time. It clung to the windowsill in the hall that overlooked the back garden. Fragments of glass glittered on the floor underneath the window, and the creature hissed at them, swiping through the window with its fist, but unable to cross the salt barrier.

"It's starting," Rowan whispered. "They're going

363

to try and get in." She dug the keys out of her pocket and thrust them, and the bottle Warwick had given her, at Tanya. "Give this to Fabian, and put the keys back where we found them. In a few minutes come down to the library and take the key out of the door. Hide it." She tucked the piece of paper into Tanya's pocket. "Once you've done that, get this to Morag and *do not* let anyone else see, especially Suki."

"Rowan, you're scaring me. What's this all about—where are you going?"

"You have to trust me. Whatever Morag tells you, take her to Tino and make her tell him." She pulled Tanya into her room and collected her bag from under the bed. She stuffed the flashlight in it and checked that her knife and the coat were there. "Suki lied about the hex. Whatever you do, don't trust her. Sparrow and I are using the tunnel to get out. Having us all in one place may make it easier to defend ourselves, but it makes us easier to attack too. If Sparrow and I can get out we might be able to surprise them and get the upper hand somehow."

Another window smashed from further away.

"To the safe room, now!" Warwick yelled.

Rowan slung her backpack over her shoulder. "I've got to go."

"Wait." Tanya pushed the scissors at her. "If you're going outside, take these."

"No. You keep them."

"But it's dangerous out there—"

"It's dangerous in here too." She pulled Tanya

out of her room and gave her a gentle push. "Stay safe."

The grandfather clock began to chime as she hurtled down the stairs. Crooks passed her on the way up, a knife clenched in his hand.

"Come with me," he shouted. "You're meant to be in the safe room."

"Be there in a minute," she called, not looking back. "There's just something I need to do...."

Shouts came from the kitchen. Warwick and the Coven members were taking up their positions, calling instructions to one another. Her heart thumping, she jammed the key into the library door and unlocked it, and then closed it, leaving the key for Tanya.

She kept glancing at the unlocked door as she waited for the tunnel entrance to open. It seemed to be moving in slow motion.

"Come on, come *on*," she told it desperately.

Finally it was open wide enough for her to slide through into the stone passageway. Sparrow turned his face away from the sudden brightness of the library.

"I've got a flashlight." She fumbled in the backpack and pulled it out.

"Here," said Sparrow. "I'll take it."

She peered around the edge of the wall partition. "Should we wait until it closes again?"

"What for?"

"To make sure we're not being followed."

He shook his head and clicked on the flashlight.

"Let's just get going. It'll be closed within a minute anyway."

"Wait." She darted back into the library and plucked the book of matches from the pile of Sparrow's belongings, still on the carpet from before. Kneeling in the cramped space, she wedged the matches discreetly into the bottom of the door jamb. "In case we need to come back again—it should stop the catch from closing completely, but won't be obvious from inside the library."

Sparrow started down the narrow staircase, the flashlight flickering ahead. Rowan went after him, placing her feet cautiously. The steps were slightly slippery, damp with a film of moisture and green mold.

"I'd forgotten how bad it stinks down here," she said. Her voice bounced off the walls. The temperature plummeted as they went deeper underground, and she shivered.

"Put on the fox-skin if you're cold."

"No." She slid a little as they reached the bottom of the stairwell. "My senses are magnified when I wear it—the smell will be even more unbearable than it is now."

Sparrow played the flashlight over the stone walls. Like the floor, they were largely covered in green mold. Four tunnels lay ahead, each twisting away from the next.

She pointed. "There's the string leading out."

He headed toward the first tunnel swiftly.

"Slow down," she said, holding on to his sleeve.

"I can't see too well with the flashlight in front of you."

"Sorry." He slowed a fraction as they neared the tunnel, allowing her to catch up. "I just want to get out of here. I can't stand confined spaces like this."

She pointed at the pebble to which the string was attached.

"Do you think we should take that with us?"

"What for?"

"In case someone follows."

"But then how will we get back if we need to?"

"Good point." As they neared the center of the cavern, a waft of air washed over her, and with it, a sudden flash of fear. She shook herself and carried on, but Sparrow paused, watching her.

"What's the matter?"

"I just... I don't know."

"Come on," said Sparrow. "Let's keep moving."

They continued on through the tunnel, the flashlight trained on the damp, dirty trail of string. On and on it led them, through the dank, winding darkness. The air became crisper and cleaner when they came into a little open cavern, passing the iron bedstead and tiny table and chair where Rowan had been staying with the changeling when Tanya had first discovered her. From there the tunnel narrowed and grew musty once more, pressing in on them.

"Not too far now, surely?" Sparrow asked.

"I don't think so. I'm not sure how long we've been down here—it feels like hours."

Onward they trawled, twisting through the underground labyrinth.

"I can see steps," said Sparrow a while later. "They're leading up."

"That's it," Rowan breathed in relief. "That's the way out, through the fake grave."

They climbed the steps, careful not to lose their footing, and paused beneath the stone slab.

"I'll need you to help me shift it," Sparrow said, positioning himself at the top end of the steps. He put the flashlight on the ground with its beam pointing up and placed his left hand above his head against the slab. His other hand was deep in his pocket.

"What's the matter with your hand?" she asked.

"Nothing."

"You hurt it, didn't you?" she guessed. "When Tino pushed you."

"Yeah."

"Why didn't you say?"

"I didn't want you to worry."

She steadied herself and put her hands in place. "On the count of three, lift and slide to the right. Ready? One, two, three!"

The slab slid across with a grating noise of stone on stone that set Rowan's teeth on edge. Afternoon light and fresh air carrying the scent of grass and the woods rushed into the tunnel. "Just a bit more...." she panted. "There." She clambered up a few more steps and then hauled herself out into the graveyard, reaching down to grab Sparrow's hand. He rolled out onto the grass, a film of sweat glistening on his face. His skin looked waxy and pale. He switched off the flashlight and pocketed it, then grabbed her hand.

"Come on."

"Where are we going?"

"Let's move across to the woods—we can see the house better from there."

Rowan glanced toward the manor. It looked like a dollhouse in the distance. "We can see it from here."

"But we're on open land," said Sparrow. "We'd be better concealed in the woods—the garvern might catch a glimpse of us."

She allowed him to pull her onward and out of the churchyard, taking quick, fearful glances over her shoulder. Gray clouds roiled above, blotting out the sun. From where they were, she could not make out any figures or movement from the house. They were too far away now.

"Slow down," she gasped, stumbling as he tugged her toward the brook, but he did not seem to hear. They reached the stepping stones. Water rushed past her feet as she navigated the way across, and she cast another wary look behind her, half expecting to see a swooping garvern heading for them—

And suddenly she stopped, stock-still, balancing on one of the stones halfway across. The standstill jerked Sparrow to a halt, and he spun round to face her.

"Why are you stopping? Keep going, quickly."

"How did you know about the garvern?" she asked, her voice tight.

"What? You told me. Now come on—"

"No, I didn't." She stared at him, her heart racing. "I said the house was being *watched*. I never mentioned the word 'garvern.'"

The grip on her hand tightened and began to pull, harder.

"Ouch! You're hurting me! *Sparrow!*"

His fingers had turned white from grasping her so hard.

It was then that she caught sight of his fingernails, pale and clean. She surged back in shock, sliding off the stepping stone—but still he held on. Freezing water soaked her ankles. Then she was down on her knees, spiteful pebbles on the riverbed scraping her as she was dragged through the water and onto the other side of the bank.

A dry sob forced its way up her throat as she thrashed and flailed through mud and grass, her arm screaming with the brunt of her weight. By the time she had twisted herself around she already knew what—or rather, *who*—she was going to see.

Eldritch grinned back at her with a chipped front tooth. Even as she watched, it grew, becoming whole again.

Rowan began to scream.

26

Tanya banged on Fabian's door, ignoring Crooks's calls to head for the safe room.

"Fabian? It's me. Open up."

She heard raised voices on the floor below and the sounds of people scattering, changing position. Oberon whined at her side. She thumped the door again. "Fabian, I know you don't want to speak to any of us at the moment, but you have to. Open the door—I've got eye drops. You'll need them."

The door opened a crack and Fabian glared out.

"I've already got some," he said coldly. "Swiped them off the kitchen table earlier." He reached out and took the bottle out of her hands. "Still, won't hurt to have extra." He pushed the bottle into an inside pocket of his jacket and came out onto the landing. Oberon stuck his nose into Fabian's hand, but found his greeting ignored.

"Why have you got your jacket on?" she asked. She reached for his arm but he shrugged away from her.

"I'm not staying here, waiting to be attacked."

"Then where are you going?"

"I'm leaving. I'm going to find out who killed my mother, and I'm going to get them."

He ran for the stairs, but Tanya would not be shaken off. She followed him, her words jolting with each step down. The grandfather clock chimed in her ears. "If you go out there, *you'll* be the one getting killed. The house is surrounded. Just calm down and speak to Warwick—"

"Warwick's had eight years to talk to me, to tell me the truth," Fabian spat. "He chose not to."

"What are you going to do?" Tanya hissed. "You're crazy if you think anyone will just let you walk out of the house—"

"They won't see me. I'll use the tunnel. It comes out far away enough to give me a head start."

Florence's voice drew them to a halt as they reached the middle of the stairs, and Tanya's knees buckled as Oberon collided with her legs.

"Tanya! And Fabian—what are you two *doing*? Get up here this instant! And where's Rowan?"

"We're just going to get her and bring her upstairs," Tanya babbled, turning. Her grandmother was leaning over the banister. "We're coming straight back."

"Well, hurry!" Florence flinched as another window shattered. She spun around furiously as a garvern reached through an unprotected window, its claws shredding the curtains. Tanya started back up the stairs, afraid for her grandmother, but before she could take two steps Florence had grabbed a nearby water spray on the sill and fired it into the garvern's snarling face. "This is my house!" she shrieked, her finger working the nozzle with every word. "And you have overstayed your welcome!"

The garvern screamed, its skin bubbling and blistering as the salt water came into contact with it, but it still managed to cling on, hissing in fury. Footsteps charged across the landing. It was Rose, her hair streaming behind her like a red flag and a broom in her hands. She whacked the bristle end into the creature's face, and it toppled with a scream away from the window.

Fabian edged away from the stairs and went in the direction of the library. Tanya ran after him, no longer concerned for her grandmother. It was clear Florence could look after herself.

The key was in the door, as Rowan had left it. Fabian got there first, turning the doorknob and pushing his way into the library.

"Fabian, just hang on a minute," she began. She retrieved the key and pushed the library door, but before it was quite closed, the sounds of a skirmish came from the hallway.

Quickly she repositioned herself at the door

opening, peering through the crack. Another garvern had shattered a window, downstairs this time, although a layer of salt on the ledge stopped it from entering. A vase balanced on the sill had smashed on the tiled floor below it. As she watched, Victor came racing from the direction of the kitchen, knives drawn, yelling for backup.

A knife whizzed past the library door and embedded itself in the garvern's shoulder. A spray of blood hit the wall, and the creature's howl filled the passage. Victor flew toward it, sending a second knife curving through the air.

Light footsteps hurried after him. Tanya saw Suki running down the hall, checking behind her.

"It's all right," Victor told her as she neared his side. "It's dead."

"What's going on?" Fabian whispered from behind her.

"Nothing. It's under control," Tanya told him. She was about to close the door when an unexpected movement made her freeze and grip the doorframe.

Suki had lunged for Victor's sword, drawing it from its sheath at his side. Victor barely had time to react before Suki expertly plunged the sword into the center of his chest.

"No—" Tanya grasped at Fabian as Victor sank to his knees, his hands floundering uselessly at his own blade, staring down at it, and then at Suki, in disbelief.

With a satisfied smile, Suki retracted the blade

and stood over him, her eyes darting toward the kitchen. Victor's mouth opened and closed like that of a puppet, bubbling with blood. His limbs twitched uselessly at his sides, then stopped moving altogether.

Quietly, Suki lowered the bloody sword to the floor and let it rest beside him. Then her shoulders stiffened, and her head tilted to one side. Slowly, deliberately, she turned to face the library.

"Get back!" Tanya hissed, pushing a terrified Fabian away from the door. "She knows... she's *coming*!" She jabbed the key, slick with sweat, into the lock and turned it, then raced toward the bookcase, fumbling with the indents that worked the mechanism for the secret door. For the first time, it would not open.

"It must be jammed!" she said, frantic.

The handle to the library door turned. The door rattled.

"Quickly," Fabian moaned, his blue eyes glassy with shock. Tanya tried again, pressing her fingers into the indents, but still nothing happened.

The key flew out of the lock as something was inserted on the other side. Fabian pressed himself into the bookcase as Tanya grappled with the wooden panel yet again. The lock clicked, and the library door swung open.

Suki entered the room and closed the door quietly behind her, a hair pin in one hand and one of Victor's knives in the other.

"DAD!" Fabian yelled. "DAD—"

Suki crossed the room, the blade flashing in her hand. "Shut up and don't be stupid. I'm not afraid to use this, as you well know."

Fabian hushed immediately, his eyes squeezed shut.

Tanya's gaze fell upon a tattered red book on a nearby shelf. She seized it, scrabbling through the pages.

Suki's eyes danced with amusement. "*One Hundred and One Perfect Puff Pastry Recipes*? Is that supposed to save you?"

"It's not what it seems." Tanya found what she was looking for within its pages: a small green leaf, a black feather, and a long brown whisker. "I'm calling upon my guardian, and my grandmother's."

"Go ahead," said Suki, shrugging. "Even if they make it in time, they'll have a tough job getting into the house."

Tanya moved to the fireplace, fumbling the items with a wary eye on Suki. She pulled three strands of hair from her head and then threw everything into the flames with the words: "By the powers that be, I call thee to me."

Suki watched in silence, then took a step toward them. Oberon went rigid, his hackles rising.

Suki's green eyes rested on the dog. She raised the knife.

"I didn't want you two involved in this," she said, almost apologetically. "But now you are, and so you have to be dealt with."

"Please don't do this...don't kill us," Fabian stammered.

"Oh, I don't think that's necessary just yet," Suki said.

"Why are you doing this?" Tanya asked, her hand on Oberon's collar. He was panting and gasping, and it was taking all her strength to keep him under control. "Why are you attacking the Coven?"

"No questions." Suki jerked her head to the bookcase. "Into the tunnel. Now."

Tanya edged back to the bookcase, shaking her head in confusion. With trembling hands, she pressed her fingers into the indents in the carved wood, praying it would work this time.

"Hurry," Fabian pleaded.

Suki waved the knife, agitated. "Work the mechanism and get in there. I know you know how to."

"I don't get it," Tanya said, jabbing the panel again in frustration. "It's stuck."

"Stop messing around and open it. If you're not out of here in the next ten seconds, you won't like the alternative."

"I can't!" Tanya eyed the knife in Suki's hand, panicking. She knocked a row of books from the shelf built into the panel and grabbed on to it, pulling. Slowly, the secret door opened.

She stumbled into the musty tunnel after Fabian. Oberon's claws scraped on the stone as Tanya pulled him in with them. A low growl rumbled in his throat.

Suki glanced over her shoulder at the library

door, then stood blocking their exit from the tunnel. Her eyes skimmed Tanya's pocket, where the diagram of the hex was folded.

"In case you're wondering," Suki said softly, "I knew what was in your pocket anyway. I would have come after you even if you hadn't witnessed me killing Victor."

"What's she talking about?" said Fabian. "What's in your pocket?"

"It's a sketch of a spell for psychic protection, to prevent your gypsy friend from having any more little insights about me. Shame you won't be showing it to anyone."

"So it was *you*?" Tanya breathed. "*You* were the one who attacked Morag?"

Suki shrugged. "Guilty."

The light in the tunnel faded as the partition began to close. Oberon was snapping and snarling now, and it took both of them to hold him back. Through the rapidly decreasing gap, Tanya saw Suki turn and head for the library door. Then they were in darkness as the tunnel closed completely. There was a click from the other side, in the library.

"She's locked the library door," Tanya whispered, finally releasing her hold on Oberon's collar. "We can't get back through. We're trapped in here."

"No, we're not." Fabian's elbow dug into her as he rummaged for something. A small flashlight clicked on. "Like I said, I was planning on coming this way anyway. That's why I brought this."

He started down the steps. Tanya stayed close to him, her hands clamped on the slimy walls on either side of her. Her breathing became shallow as she tried not to take in the dank stench of the tunnel. Fabian's light wavered ahead, making her feel unsteady.

"What were you doing with the sketch?" Fabian asked.

"Rowan drew it after Suki lied to Morag about the hex. I was supposed to get it to Tino somehow to prove Suki's guilt—but now we've just seen it with our own eyes."

"So if Suki wasn't hexed, she never lost her powers."

"Exactly."

"So where is Rowan now?"

"She escaped, with Sparrow, to try and find a way of attacking from outside. They came this way—we can't be far behind them."

They reached the bottom of the stairwell, shivering in the damp gloom.

"Want my jacket?" Fabian asked.

Tanya shook her head. "I'll be all right. Let's just move quickly to keep warm." She stayed close to Fabian as he played the flashlight over the dripping green walls, then over the floor in search of the pebble knotted with string.

"There." Tanya pointed as she saw it just outside the nearest of the four tunnels leading away from the house. She gripped Fabian's sleeve and pulled him into the narrow tunnel. "Let's get out of here—if we hurry we could catch up to Rowan and Sparrow. We've got to stop Suki before she kills again."

❧❦

Eldritch twisted Rowan's wrist painfully, causing her to yell out again. No matter how she wrenched and pulled, his grip was like iron and she could not free herself.

"Strong, aren't I?" he said with a grin that was now his own. "I suppose I have you to thank for that. When you only have one hand, you have to make sure it's up to scratch."

"Where's Sparrow? What have you done with him?" she cried.

Eldritch laughed, yanking her onward. "I'm afraid little Sparrow has had his wings clipped. You won't find him so chirpy anymore." He wrinkled his nose in disgust. "*Sparrow.* 'Pigeon' would have been more appropriate."

Dread rose up in her at these words. Rowan dug her heels into the soft grass, resisting, but Eldritch pulled her on relentlessly, even when she went down. She let herself go limp, a deadweight, but it made little difference. The woods loomed closer.

"How long...how long have you been using him as a glamour?" She fought to keep her voice under control. Had it been Sparrow in her room yesterday? Or had it been Eldritch all along? Whose lips had brushed her cheek?

"Oh, not long," Eldritch said cheerfully. "I was hoping for it to last a little longer—to the woods at least—but the running water proved a problem." Color worked its way into his waxen cheeks as he walked. His long, oily black hair fell over his face. "It was your smelly little friend who you threw into the tunnels earlier today, and your smelly little friend who you plotted to escape with, and your smelly little friend who was going to help you overpower Suki. I heard it all. I was there. *Listening.*" His dark eyes were scornful. "*Have I ever told you I hate rats?*" he mimicked, then chuckled. "It's not the first time I've been called a rat. I doubt it'll be the last."

"If you've hurt him," she growled. "If you've so much as touched him, I'll—"

"You'll do nothing!" Eldritch crowed. He spun around and tutted. "It's no good getting yourself into a state over little Sparrow when, really, you handed him to me on a plate."

"Go to hell!" Rowan snarled, blinded by tears. "Tell me what you did to him!" She fumbled with her bag, trying to reach inside for her knife and cursing herself for not strapping it to her thigh. Eldritch twisted her wrist again, forcing her to the ground. His boot came down on her, pinning her hand in place. She heard him unzip the bag, then saw it flung away, out of her reach. He kicked her over to face him. He was holding the fox-skin coat.

"Put it on." He threw it at her. "Now."

Rowan started to scramble away, but his boot

found its way into her side, winding her, and she collapsed on the ground, gasping for air.

He leaned over her, his black eyes full of hate. "I'll only tell you once more."

"Why..." She coughed. "Why do you want me to...put it on...?"

"You'll find out. I've got a nice little surprise lined up for you."

"You can't harm me," she bluffed. "Remember the Hedgewitch, and Snatcher? They tried to hurt me, and look what happened to them!"

"They tried to use magic against you," Eldritch growled. "But I know better than that, don't I, *Rowan*? Why do you suppose I've waited this long? Do you think I'd have let you get away before if I could have used magic on you? Give me some credit. I'm not planning anything magical. Just something far more straightforward."

She struggled into a sitting position, clutching at her ribs. "Where's Sparrow?" she pleaded. "Please... you haven't hurt him?"

He ignored her, motioning to the coat. "Put. It. On." He smirked. "Then maybe I'll tell you."

She forced her way into the coat, her eyes darting around. The fox-skin could aid her in an escape if she managed to get free in the woods, but the knowledge that Eldritch wanted her to put it on terrified her. She fastened the clasp and felt herself shrinking and her senses sharpen. Before she knew what was happening, Eldritch produced a length of cord from his pocket and looped it tightly around her neck.

"There," he said, then threw back his head and laughed. "You're almost like my pet now!" He started to walk again, tugging her toward Hangman's Wood. Rowan was powerless to resist—a quick yank from Eldritch's end bruised her windpipe and made her eyes bulge.

"Move," he commanded.

"I did what you asked," she rasped, her throat dry and aching. "Now tell me what you did with him!"

"What do you *think* I did with him?" Eldritch sneered. "Fed him a few crumbs? I killed him, you stupid girl!"

"No!" she sobbed. "Please—you're lying!"

He grinned and tugged the cord again spitefully, robbing her of air. "All right. I admit it—I elaborated slightly. He's not dead...yet. But he soon will be. He waved his stumpy arm in the air theatrically. "I could have done it. Could have finished him off easily, but that wasn't part of the plan. I had to save him for Suki, so she can pierce his little heart straight through...stop it beating for good. But let's just say he won't be coming to your rescue this time. You can count on that."

"NO!" she screamed. "You haven't hurt him, *please!*" She twisted and jerked at the end of the rope, rage lending her strength. She darted for Eldritch's ankles and sank her teeth into them, but they missed the flesh and found only the leather of his boots beneath his trousers, and by the time she lunged in a second attempt he had raised the rope and lifted her into the air, choking the last of the breath from her. She dangled, helpless and in agony, unable to scream, speak, or breathe. Her vision flickered from lack of oxygen. Eldritch grinned back at her as she struggled to remain conscious.

"Don't worry, little fox," he whispered. "I didn't bring you out here all this way just to strangle you. I could have done that in the tunnel. No, I've got something better in mind."

Rowan's claws scrabbled helplessly at the rope. Black and white shapes danced at the edge of her vision. Any moment now she knew she would pass out.

"I thought about it for a long time," Eldritch continued. "Dreamed of it, even." They were on the border of the woods now, the trees swaying and creaking overhead. In the air above them, a black shape swooped. A bird of some kind.

"That's it, nearly there." Eldritch ran his stump over her head, between her fox ears. His voice was a soft croon, as though he were stroking a beloved pet. "Just go to sleep."

Rowan could hold on to consciousness no longer. It slipped away, leaving everything empty and black.

27

Tanya and Fabian emerged from the tunnel into the gray gloom of the churchyard. Overhead, the sky was a brooding swirl of dark clouds, and as they searched the land for any sign of Rowan, fat droplets of water began to shower on them.

"They must have come this way," said Tanya, squinting against the rain. "The entrance to the tunnel was still open."

"I don't see them anywhere," Fabian said. His thick glasses were spattered with raindrops, and he wiped them away, only for more to take their place. "What do we do? We've lost them. We'll have to go back to the house—but what if we're seen by the garvern, and attacked?"

"If we get close enough maybe the others will see us and help," said Tanya, desperately. "But we've got to get back and warn them. Suki is completely insane." The rain came down heavier now, in thick sheets. Though it was still only the afternoon, the sky was almost dark as dusk.

Keeping low, they made their way over to the little stone wall skirting the churchyard and scanned the land between the house and the forest. Oberon pressed closer to Tanya, water running off his brown fur and dripping onto her.

"Something's moving." Fabian pointed. "There—at the edge of the woods!"

Tanya peered over the wall and caught a glimpse of a dark figure on the border of the forest. Something small and rust-colored was suspended from its hand. It took her a moment to process what she was seeing.

"Someone's carrying a fox," she said. "It's got to be her—it's Rowan! But that's not Sparrow with her...." She felt a stab of fear.

"Then who is it?" Fabian whispered.

The figure vanished into the woods, but Tanya kept her eyes glued to the spot. "Come on," she whispered. "We've got to follow and see where's she's being taken."

"She wasn't moving," Fabian said, his eyes glazed in shock. "Didn't you see? It's already too late."

"We don't know that!" she said fiercely. "She could be drugged or knocked out or something! We can't just give up now—we've got to *try*!" She pulled him toward the stream. "Quickly—let's get across the brook before we lose them."

They raced to the water's edge, skidding on the wet grass, until finally, they reached the stepping stones.

"Don't bother with them." Fabian gritted his teeth as the rain lashed down harder. "It's too dangerous—we'll slip." He plunged into the stream, ankle-deep, and started to wade across.

Tanya jumped in after him, gasping at the icy water. It soaked into her jeans, sucking at her legs, and she felt pebbles on the riverbed shift under her feet. Oberon was across in three bounds, and with a good shake seemed none the worse for it. They ran for the woods, heading to the spot where Rowan had disappeared from sight. The rain eased off a little as they stepped beneath the trees, but by now they were both saturated and shivering.

"Do you see anything?" Tanya whispered.

Fabian shook his head. "We've lost them. I don't know how we can expect to find them again—it's just too huge an area to cover."

"Let's try going a little way in." Tanya led the way. "I'm not giving up, and neither are you. We might hear something."

The ground underfoot was moist, taking the crackle out of their footsteps as they moved. A sudden, desperate idea occurred to her. Tanya looked up, searching for tree fays among the branches, and saw something scuttling within a nest.

"Can you help us?" she begged. "We're looking for someone who just came this way."

"What are you doing?" Fabian hissed.

"Rowan's half-fey," she reminded him. "There's a chance that they might—" She dodged out of the way as a shower of droppings rained down on them from the nest above.

"Clearly not." Fabian pulled her away, his mouth twisted in disgust.

Tanya gulped back tears, her eyes smarting. With a glare at the tree fay, she allowed Fabian to tug her away.

Within the depths of the woods a scream pierced the silence, chilling Tanya to the core. Oberon stood stock-still, scenting the air. Then he was off, bounding through the forest.

"That was her," Fabian gasped, as they sprinted after Oberon. "It was Rowan—she's alive!"

❖

The scream escaped Rowan's mouth before she even registered what had happened to her. All she knew was that, as she gained consciousness once more, she was in excruciating pain. It was the pain that had awoken her.

The first thing she saw when her eyes opened were the bars. She was in some kind of prison. As she shifted position to better understand her surroundings, the pain seared once more, and she cried out again, twisting around.

Her back right leg was trapped within the jaws of

a cruel steel trap. A hunter's trap. Its metal teeth had snapped shut, crushing her paw. Every movement, every muscle spasm, sent a shudder of agony through her and made blood ooze from the wound. Underneath this main source of pain she felt more—tiny pinpricks all the way down the front of her body. She wriggled, noticing glinting strands of thread in neat rows down her coat. With mounting horror she knew that she had been sewn into it, preventing her from taking the coat off.

As her mind sharpened, she saw the sky through the trees above. She wasn't in a prison after all. The bars were, in fact, silver railings, and they were horribly familiar. Only this time, she was viewing them from the inside, rather than the outside. Turning her head, she saw Eldritch staring down at her. Beyond him a gaping chasm yawned in the ground, a tree growing at its side almost toppling in, most of its roots exposed. He had brought her to the edge of one of the catacombs.

Eldritch knelt to pick up the chain attached to the end of the trap. The other end was looped around the tree securely, preventing her from running— even if she had been able to withstand the pain. He grimaced, glancing down at his gloved hand, and even through the haze of agony Rowan saw that his nearness to the iron was causing him discomfort.

"It still burns," he told her. "Always will. But after the time in the cellar, I can endure it better. Especially when the outcome is worth it. And this will be." He dragged her closer to him by the chain, forcing more screams from her throat. Waves of pain rolled over her, and she wished she would pass out again. Kneeling, he grabbed her head and wrapped something tightly around it.

"Eldritch, no!" she screamed, but he forced her jaws closed with a muzzle that reduced her cries to muffled whimpers. Once it was fastened he stood up and hauled her closer to the denehole.

"So now you have it," he told her triumphantly, his hair hanging over his face as he stared down at her. "I told you I'd find you, Rowan Fox." He circled the hole in the ground slowly, peering into the depths. "I know this is the point where the villain usually gives a long and convoluted speech of how he's been wronged, but I don't think there's any need for that, do you? We both know that had you not left me to die, then you wouldn't be here at all. But here you are." He paused, gloating. "Trapped in iron, in a place where no one can hear you and no one will find you. It all fits beautifully—and not only in a poetic justice kind of way. No, it fits with Suki's plans too. Which is fine by me—I owe her a lot, you see. I owe her my life, in fact. If she hadn't come by for her coat—the coat you stole—and heard me in the cellar, I'd still be there. Rotted away to nothing.

"By now I expect you've figured out that each of the thirteen secrets is meeting their end in a significant way, and you're no exception. Because you're going to vanish, Rowan Fox, and no one will ever know what's become of you, except me." He finished circling the catacomb and loomed over her. "And as you know better than most, it's the *not* knowing that's the worst thing, isn't it?"

Rowan looked up at him, her eyes clouded with fear and pain. *This is it,* she thought. *This is how I'm going to die.* And a moment later, when Eldritch kicked her over the edge of the hole, leaving her dangling upside down from the trap, the tendons in her leg screaming, the agony made her wish she *were* dead.

Her front paws scrabbled for a hold at the sides of the hole, scraping at the earth. The catacomb stretched below her, twice as wide as she was tall and black as ink as it plummeted down. She wondered if the fall would kill her instantly or whether, once the chain was released from the tree, it would snare on some jutting root further down, leaving her to hang in misery and starve to death. She prayed for the former.

❧❦

Oberon stopped just short of the clearing with the first catacomb. Tanya reached out, a warning hand on his collar, but remained hidden behind a large oak tree. From her position, she saw Eldritch and Rowan within the railings. His cruel words carried to them and, as he kicked Rowan into the depths of the catacomb, she bit down on her hand to prevent herself from screaming.

"H-he's going to let her drop!" Fabian stuttered

his words in fear. "How are we going to get her out of there?"

"There's no time," Tanya answered. "And there's no one else to help us. We've got to act, quickly."

"Unless..."

"Unless what?"

"Before we left the library—you called the fairies. If they come—"

"It was a bluff—I was just trying to buy us time."

"But you threw the feather and the leaf into the fire...."

"Yes, but I was missing something," she told him. "Don't you remember? Last year when we called upon Raven and Gredin, there was something else we threw into the flames."

Fabian looked blank.

"Four-leaf clovers."

The hope in Fabian's eyes faded.

"So unless they turn up of their own accord, we're on our own."

Tanya spotted a gap in the railings where one of the posts was missing. "The only way we're going to save Rowan is by getting through there and tackling Eldritch. I think I can squeeze through the gap, just."

"I can't let you do that—"

"It's our only chance. I need you to catch him off guard. We're both protected—he'll have to physically attack us to harm us. So just don't let him catch you." She edged out from behind the tree. Eldritch leaned over the catacomb, his back to them. Then he started to walk to the tree—the only thing that prevented Rowan from tumbling into the cavern below.

"Go!" Tanya mouthed. "Now, go!"

Fabian shot out from behind the tree and crashed through the clearing, approaching the railings from the opposite direction.

"Hey!" he yelled. "Let her go!"

Eldritch leaped back from the edge of the cavern. A low growl escaped him.

Fabian turned back to face the way he had come, and bellowed into the depths of the forest to an imaginary companion. "She's here! I've found her, come quick!"

Eldritch's head snapped from side to side, craning into the woods.

Tanya crept toward the gap in the railings, the sound of her blood pulsing in her ears. Gripping the sides, she slipped through it and screwed up every ounce of her strength and anger, using it to charge at Eldritch. Her feet skidded over loose earth and sent pebbles scattering, alerting him to her presence.

He turned the moment she made contact with him, his mouth agape in surprise. Her outstretched arms hit him square in chest, and he tumbled backwards, teetering on the edge of the catacomb. His arms flailed in the air, and it was all Tanya could do to stop the momentum of her run from taking her over the edge too. She lost her balance and fell, her feet skidding across the ground until she felt the nothingness of the hole beneath. With a yell she flung her arm out, grabbing the first thing she could find—the chain tethered to the tree. She clung on, heaving herself away from the catacomb and glancing over her shoulder in terror.

Somehow Eldritch had managed to regain his balance. With a mad grin he stepped toward her... then grunted as a large stone came out of nowhere, striking him on the temple. He swayed dangerously. Blood spurted in a line down his face, and with a defeated howl he toppled into the catacomb.

Tanya crawled, sobbing, to the edge of the dene-hole, her face streaked with tears and dirt. She was aware of Fabian dancing around the perimeter of the railings, yelling at her to pull Rowan out, and she was aware that Oberon was at her side, having squeezed through the hole after her. Peering over the edge, she saw Rowan, muzzled and dangling by one bloody paw. There was no way to get her out other than to pull on the chain attached to the steel trap. Gritting her teeth, she started to haul, trying to block out the muffled whimpers from Rowan as each tug yanked at her tendons. Her mind raced with possible ideas to lessen Rowan's obvious distress, and an idea came to her from something she had once read.

She scrambled closer to the tree and wound her legs around the exposed roots, hooking her feet into place. Secure, she leaned headfirst into the cata-comb, one hand still straining to grasp the chain and the other reaching for her friend. Her legs quickly started to burn under the weight. With another short pull on the chain her fingers brushed the fox's tail. She wrapped her hand around the tail and heaved, finally mustering the last of her strength to throw Rowan, and the trap, clear.

She sagged with relief, allowing a moment to gather a last burst of strength to heave herself out of the hole. Aboveground, she could hear Rowan breathing in trembling gasps.

Eldritch's stump came out of nowhere, skimming her hand from below. Tanya screamed, yanking her hand out of the way and pulling herself backward. Once she was free, she stood up and staggered past Rowan to the opposite side of the catacomb, where the angle provided a more telling view.

Beneath a slight overhang of damp earth, Eldritch clung to a root with his one good hand. The other swung about uselessly, trying—and failing—to find something to hook onto. He twisted his head to look over his shoulder at her. Already she could see that he was weak. He wouldn't last much longer.

"Please," he begged, his eyes wide with terror. "Don't let me fall. Don't let me die."

"Leave him!" Fabian yelled, trying without success to squeeze through the gap in the railings. "He's a murderer!"

"I know," Tanya whispered—but the sight haunted her. She had not thought through her plan, and instead had acted on impulse in the moment of rage when she had intended for Eldritch to fall into the hole. But now, with him hanging on to his life by a thread, she wondered if she would be able to live with herself if he fell. Unable to hold back, she drew closer to him. His face was beaded with sweat and covered in blood from the stone Fabian had thrown.

A sudden breeze whipped up around her, dotting her with errant rain droplets from above and showering the clearing with leaves. They swirled and swooped, as though with a life of their own, to form a figure at the center of the maelstrom. Only when the figure spoke did she recognize it.

"Get away from there. And don't allow any pity in your heart for him."

"Gredin?" Tanya whispered as the leaves flew wildly about her, stinging her eyes and her skin. "You're really here? Even after all the things I said—"

"It doesn't matter what was said. I have a duty to you."

Her guardian stepped closer to the catacomb, his yellow stare fixed and unforgiving. The flurry of leaves followed him, whirling frenziedly, and from within the catacomb she heard Eldritch coughing and choking as they engulfed him.

Gredin raised his hands, and with them, the leaves flew into the air. She saw Eldritch twisting and clawing, saw his fingers slowly unfurl from the root. He vanished at the same moment Gredin flung his arms down, and the sea of leaves poured forth into the catacomb.

Tanya ran to Rowan's side and fumbled with the muzzle, pulling it from her face. Her hair flew around her head in a dark cloud, tangling with the leaves, and she saw Fabian pressed against the railings, shouting through them with his own bushy hair whipped up around him. For the first time she noticed a large black bird circling the catacomb with the whirlwind of leaves. It was Raven.

Gently, she released the lever on the trap and eased the crushed paw from it, grimacing as Rowan cursed and yelled. She tugged the trap free from the tree, gathered up the chain, and flung it into the swirling pit of leaves after Eldritch.

Rowan was trying to tell her something, but with the howl of the wind Tanya could not hear. She leaned closer to the fox's jaws.

"... Can't take it off... I'm sewn into it."

With horror she finally saw the spidertwine stitches, neatly tacked down the front of the coat. "The scissors..."

She pulled them from her pocket and began cutting the stitches one by one. Soon the last stitch was severed, but Rowan made no move to take it off.

"I need to keep it on," she yelled. "I won't fit through the gap otherwise—plus I can run three-legged as a fox."

Already Gredin was pulling at them, drawing them away to the gap in the railings. With a jolt, Tanya felt the earth shift beneath her. A cloud of dust flew up from the catacomb.

"The denehole!" she yelled. "It's caving in—we've got to get away from it!" She shoved Rowan and Oberon through the space to the other side and clambered through after them. Gredin vanished in a swirl of leaves, then materialized on the other side of the railings, where Raven joined him.

Tanya looked back and saw the tree by the side of the denehole—the one she had used to wind her legs around—vanish into the cavern as the ground around it collapsed. A section of the railing had fallen forward.

"Out of the woods!" Gredin roared.

They raced ahead, with Gredin in the lead and Oberon and Rowan bounding along side by side, her injured paw held aloft. Above them, Raven circled in the sky, navigating the way out. Swirls of dirt and dust from the shifting earth chased them, close at their heels.

They reached the edge of the forest, gasping and trembling. The rain had slowed to a drizzle now, and they viewed the manor through a gray haze.

"Everyone's in there," Tanya said softly. "We've got to help them. Victor's already dead—Suki could have killed again by now."

"But we'll be attacked before we even make it to the house," said Fabian. "The garvern are guarding the grounds—they'll see us coming from the roof!"

"Not if we use the tunnel," said Rowan. "I left something wedged into the doorway so it wouldn't latch properly. We can get back in and stop Suki." Her face twisted into a mask of hate. "She'll be expecting Eldritch to return after finishing me off. Instead, she'll get us."

"With reinforcements," Gredin finished.

28

The musky scent of the tunnel mingled with the tang of Rowan's blood. She loped along, second in line behind Gredin, who led the way.

"Sparrow?" she yelled. Her voice rasped. She was already exhausted and still trembling from fear and shock. There was no reply to her call. She shouted Sparrow's name again, only to be met by silence. "He must be down here somewhere," she mumbled tearfully, taking great sniffs of air, trying to catch his scent.

"He could be anywhere," Tanya said gently. "If Eldritch attacked him he could have run off into the tunnels, or even got out through the grave—"

"No." Rowan cut across her. "He's here somewhere, I know it. The way Eldritch spoke...he was confident, sure that Sparrow was going nowhere."

The tunnel opened out into the main cavern where the other tunnels looped away from the house. The pebble tied with string sat in the center. As Rowan neared it, she remembered the terror that had swept over her on her way out of the tunnel and halted. Only now did she understand it. Her human senses had picked up on the faintest strains of a smell. Now her fox senses screamed an alarm. The smell was blood.

"What is it?" Tanya asked.

"He's near!" She circled the stone frantically. "Sparrow's near!" She pawed the stone over. Something dark and faintly wet glistened on its underside.

"Over here." Fabian's flashlight was aimed at the ground in front of the second tunnel. Another dark smear vanished into the blackness. "Is it...?"

"Blood," Tanya croaked. "It's leading into the tunnel."

Rowan squeezed her eyes shut. Suddenly there was not enough air. Her eyes flew open again as Gredin led the way into the passage, guided by Fabian's flashlight. Its beam fell upon great chunks of fallen stone and earth.

"It's one of the tunnels that collapsed," Fabian said. "Be careful." His voice bounced off the walls, too loudly.

Gredin stopped. "There's someone in here."

At the foot of the rubble a dark shape slumped, unmoving.

"Sparrow!" Rowan cried, pushing past Gredin

to arrive at the body's side. Sparrow lay facedown, his dirty blond hair matted with blood on one side. She threw off the fox-skin coat and placed her hands on him. He was a deadweight—motionless.

"He's been hit. Someone help me!"

Fabian rushed to kneel beside her, and together they rolled Sparrow's prone body so that he lay on his back. Rowan brushed a strand of hair away from his face. Her fingertips came away sticky. Her eyes blurred with tears, and she leaned over him, laying her fingers against the skin of his neck. It was clammy and cool, but underneath she thought she felt something—the faintest beat of life.

"He's alive," she sobbed, shaking him gently. "Sparrow, please wake up. Please be all right!" She pressed her face against his chest, hot tears leaking from her eyes and soaking into the fabric of his shirt. His heart thudded dully, slowly, pulsing against her cheek. Then a groan escaped his lips.

"Red? Is that…you?"

"Yes! I'm here." She lifted her head and threw her arms around him. He was now shivering, as well as groaning. His lips drew back over his teeth in a grimace. "I'm cold, Red. I'm so c-cold. My head—"

"Shh," she told him, holding his hand and smoothing his hair. "I know. But you're going to be all right now." She pressed her lips against his brow, her tears running onto his face.

"Here," said Fabian, pulling off his jacket. "Let me put this around him."

Rowan stood back, biting her lip against the pain as she put weight on her injured foot, and allowed Fabian and Gredin to tend to Sparrow. Together they lifted him to his feet, supporting him as he swayed. His face was ghastly white, his lips blue with cold.

"Get inside the house." Raven circled their heads. "Quickly, now. He needs to be warm."

"And I need to stop Suki," Rowan growled, wiping the last of her tears away. She limped out of the way as Gredin and Fabian edged past her, Sparrow between them, to the foot of the steps.

Gredin led the way up the narrow staircase. The stone tunnel was flooded with light and warm air as he pushed the secret doorway open, motioning for caution as they came through one by one. Rowan kicked the book of matches out of the base of the doorframe, then moved aside for Tanya and Oberon, and finally Raven, who had shed her bird form to become a woman. The doorway to the tunnel closed, leaving them standing in the stifling room. The fire still danced in the grate as it was tended to by the hearthfay. She squeaked as they came nearer, and vanished from the room.

"Put him by the fire," Rowan said anxiously. Fabian and Gredin eased Sparrow into the armchair by the hearthside. She tucked Fabian's jacket, inside out, around Sparrow's shoulders, then threw the fox-skin coat around her own and fastened the catch. She shrank back into a fox and turned away from the fire. "Let's finish this."

"Most of the windows are camouflaged or protected with salt," Tanya whispered to Gredin. "You won't be able to pass them."

"How do we get through the door?" asked Fabian, but Gredin had already moved to it. With a flick of his fingers they heard a low click as the door unlocked, and then he reached out and quietly opened it.

Rowan stood by Tanya, fury overriding the throbbing of her injured paw. She saw Fabian grab a sturdy wooden candlestick from the desk and noticed that Tanya held the magical scissors aloft. They were ready.

They stepped into the cool, dark hallway—and met with an awful sight.

Victor's lifeless body lay below the window, his sword to one side of him, covered in blood. Samson clung to his body, racked with silent sobs. He did not look up as they approached, but lay there, utterly defeated. A short way from them, the dead garvern was sprawled, one of Victor's knives jutting from its corpse. Another one, injured but alive, was in a cage of iron under the watchful eyes of Brunswick and the tea caddy brownie, who sat nearby. For the first time the brownie was without his walking stick, but then Rowan spied it. It was embedded in the imprisoned garvern's neck.

Looking over the scene was Tino, his swarthy face contorted with horror. A long cut sliced the side of his face from the edge of his eye to the corner of his mouth. He looked up sharply, raising his knife as they approached and eyeing Gredin and Raven with suspicion.

"They're with us," Rowan said. "Tino, I can explain everything, but you've got to listen to me—"

"Rowan?" Rose's voice echoed from above. "Is that you?"

All hell broke loose upstairs as a scramble of footsteps fled across the landing. Florence's face appeared, haggard and drawn, as she called out for Tanya and Fabian.

"They're safe," Gredin yelled. "Stay where you are!"

Warwick thundered down the stairs to join them at the same time as Suki skidded into the hallway, blanching as she took in the new arrivals.

"Bet you weren't expecting to see us again, were you?" Rowan spat.

Suki glanced at Tino wildly. "I just saw Crooks. He left through the back, covered in blood—he must have hidden after he attacked Victor and then escaped!"

"*Liar!*" Rowan shrieked, springing at Suki, but her injured back paw jarred as she leapt, throwing her off balance. She hit the girl clumsily, snapping and snarling, aiming for her throat, but Suki was fast. She caught Rowan in a headlock, lifting her off the ground and shaking her until her teeth rattled. A second later, a sharp blade was pressed to her throat.

"One move from anyone and I'll kill her," Suki hissed. "Lower that gun."

Warwick had raised his rifle the instant Suki's knife had appeared. "I mean it."

Reluctantly, Warwick lowered the weapon.

Tino's face drained of color. "*Suki?* What are you *doing*?"

"She lied about everything!" Fabian yelled. "She was working with Eldritch all this time—she planned to let him in through the tunnel to help her finish you all off!"

"The tunnel?" Tino's face fell. "But Sparrow's down there—"

"He's in the library," said Tanya. "Eldritch knocked him unconscious and left him for Suki to kill."

Tino roared in rage and flung himself at Suki, but Warwick grabbed him.

"Back off!" Suki yelled. She lowered her lips to Rowan's ear. "You should be dead by now. Why aren't you?"

"Because Eldritch is." Rowan squirmed in Suki's grasp. "Your little plan backfired—he ended up at the bottom of one of the catacombs, where he planned to leave me!"

"I can't say he wasn't useful," Suki sneered. "Although I'd have preferred it if he'd just finished Sparrow off. Desperate times, and all that."

Tears of rage sprang to Rowan's eyes once more. "You evil—"

"Shut up!" Suki shook her, and she felt the sharp sting of the blade as it pierced through her fur.

"Let her go, Suki," Tino said, his mouth slack. "Just let her go—you don't want this. Why would you do this? We're your friends—we *trusted* you."

"*Don't tell me what I want!*" Suki screamed, waving the knife in the air. "I'm sick of you controlling me!" Her normally pale face flooded scarlet with rage.

"*Controlling you?*" Tino's face screwed up in disbelief. "I gave you a chance! I gave you the choice! And this is how you repay me, you ungrateful little traitor!"

"You ruined my life." Suki spoke through gritted teeth, every syllable dripping with hatred.

"*I saved you!*" Tino cried. "When the fairies took you, I brought you back—"

"Yes, you brought me back! But to what? Did you ever ask yourself that? Did you stop to consider my surroundings when you found me? No—you just did your little do-gooder act and stuck your nose in where it wasn't wanted. I never wanted to go back to my parents! I hated them—HATED THEM!"

Tino took a step back in shock, but Suki's tirade had only just begun.

"For the first time in my life I was happy, wanted. I'd never known that before. Every day I'd been told I was stupid and useless. My mother never wanted me and she made it clear." She laughed bitterly. "She thought more of the dogs than she did of me. I used to sleep in the shoe cupboard with them...cuddling up to them was the only bit of affection I ever got.

Until one of them had puppies. Then I was bitten. Rejected, even by them."

"But they were so glad to have you back," Tino stuttered. "We watched you, made sure the fairies never came back for you—"

"And why were they glad? Well, firstly, it got them off the hook with the authorities—no changeling was left in my place and by all accounts I'd just vanished. But secondly, they were glad of my return because of what I'd brought back with me." Suki tapped her temple. "The sight. Oh, yes, Tino. You got *that* wrong as well. I wasn't taken because I was gifted. I was taken because I was unwanted. *Because I wouldn't be missed.* I was *given* the sight—I never had it before then. The second sight too—I couldn't even see *fairies* before then! As soon as I returned it was evident that I was different."

"That's why you had no guardian," Tino said, understanding at last. "You weren't born with the second sight."

Suki ignored him. "At first, it earned me a few more slaps and the odd night in the cellar. But then they noticed that what I was saying came true. They saw how it could be used—my mother set up a fortune-telling scam. While customers waited in the kitchen I sat by them, quietly getting flashes of their lives to feed back to her before she took them to the room for their readings. With a few true facts that I picked up, she was free to add on any old nonsense of her own and they swallowed it all. Suddenly, I was useful to her...her and my lazy, good-for-nothing stepfather. But still that couldn't make her love me. And being useful wasn't enough." Her eyes narrowed. "Sometimes I refused to tell them things, or gave them the wrong information on purpose. They called me a freak. One evening we argued...and something snapped in my head. I knew I couldn't take it anymore. I wondered...if they were gone, would the other mother—the mother from the fairy realm—come back for me?" She smiled. "So I said I was sorry, like a good girl. Made them a bedtime drink laced with a sleeping draught to knock them out."

"No," Tino murmured. "No, you didn't...you can't have..."

"My mother was the hardest," Suki said dreamily. "Even after everything, I still loved her. *He* was much easier."

"There was no fairy..." Tino whispered, horrified. "You did it. You killed your parents."

"And then you came along, offering your sympathy and a position with the Coven," Suki said sarcastically. "Like a fairy godfather, weren't you, Tino? How could I refuse? How could I possibly turn down the chance to ruin more lives? Only I saw the chance I was being given. Unlike any of you, I knew I'd be able to make the right choices, despite the 'no exceptions' rule. If a child was better off where it was, then I could leave it.

"I was happy enough with that for a while, until one day when I'd just completed a switch in the fairy realm. I'd done it as a favor to Merchant—he'd hit some trouble and needed to lie low for a while. Anyway, I came across a little cottage. It looked familiar, and in my mind's eye, I saw why. I knocked. When the door opened, I recognized the woman instantly— she looked exactly the same as she had when she'd taken me all those years ago. She invited me in to sit among the animal pelts and the bones....I didn't remember those...."

"The Hedgewitch's cottage," Rowan gasped, but was silenced by another jab of the knife.

"She'd been an outcast too, she told me. That's why she was there, alone. That's why she'd stolen me, for a child of her own. But even that was taken from her."

"You'd have ended up more crazy than you are now if you'd stayed with her!" Rowan braced herself for another shaking, but it didn't come.

"That's where you're wrong." Suki sounded sad. "Perhaps, if I'd stayed with her, we'd both have been saved. That's when I first knew I wanted revenge. I had the chance to stop you all, for good. She promised to make the fox-skin coat for me and to have it ready for the next time I went back. It would make my work a lot easier and it was better than any glamour Tino was capable of." Her voice hardened. "Only the next time I went back, she was dead, wasn't she, Red? And not only had you killed her, but you'd taken my coat!"

"I didn't mean to kill her." Rowan fumbled with

the catch on the coat. If she could undo it while Suki was talking, maybe there was a chance she could escape. "I didn't even know what I'd done until I found out the truth about my name!"

Suki sighed, tightening her hold on Rowan's neck. "I'm only sorry I didn't get to display more of my handiwork before the game was up. I had so much more planned." She glanced at Tino, a cruel smile curving her lips. "A special mask for you."

Tino's mouth dropped open. "What kind of mask?"

"An iron one that would ensure you spent the rest of your life disfigured. You have so many masks that I thought you might want to put them to good use. And for Merchant, a cauldron large enough to boil his bones in—I was especially looking forward to *that*." She stared toward Samson scornfully. He had not moved from his brother's body. "He was the dullest. I knew he'd be beaten as soon as Victor was dead." She smiled. "I could've killed him, I'm sure. But I knew that for Samson, death wasn't the worst thing. And I must say, there's something...satisfying about breaking a strong man's will. Still, I can get creative with Red, although really she was promised to Eldritch. And when all's said and done, nine out of twelve isn't a bad effort."

"You're delusional if you think you're leaving here with Rowan," Warwick told her.

Suki tilted her head. "And how do you propose to

stop me? If any of you take a single step in my direction, I'll gut her like a fish."

"I'd rather die than let you escape after what you've done!" Rowan yelled. She wriggled, catching her claw on the clasp a second time, but failing to free it. Suki did not notice. "Just do it, Tino! Someone go for her, now!"

But no one would take the risk, for Suki was both protected and armed. She began edging toward the front door.

"Wait!" a voice called out, quiet and desperate. Suki paused.

Rose stood on the stairs, her frizzy red hair billowing past her shoulders.

"I'll be your mother." She took another step toward them.

"Stay back." Suki moved the knife to Rowan's throat again. "I'm warning you...I'll cut her."

"I'll be your mother," Rose repeated. "That's all you want really, isn't it? To be loved? So do I." She held out her arms and took another step.

"Rose, what are you saying?" Rowan whispered.

"Rowan doesn't want me," Rose continued. "It doesn't matter what I do. Things will never be right between us. See, I wanted a daughter too, but it's too late."

"No, it's not!" Rowan cried. "It's not too late! I *do* love you...."

"Let her go," Rose begged, her arms outstretched.

"Let her live, and I'll be your mother...we can go somewhere new, where no one knows us...."

And for a moment, it almost seemed that it would work. Suki's grasp on Rowan loosened very slightly, and she lowered the knife. Then Rose's gaze flitted to Rowan, and in that one look it was clear for all to see that there was only one daughter she could ever love.

"Nice try. You almost had me." Suki raised the knife, her eyes glittering with unshed tears—but in that moment's distraction, Rowan finally freed the clasp on the fox-skin coat. The transformation was instant. Suki gasped and toppled forward, caught unaware as Rowan's weight pulled her off balance.

Rowan hit the floor, rolling out of the way a split second before Suki's knife came flashing down, screeching across the quarry stone floor. With a growl she advanced at Rowan for a second time. Warwick raised the gun and took aim but Suki was now almost upon Rowan.

"I can't get a clean shot!" he shouted.

Rowan glanced about, desperate for something to defend herself with but seeing nothing.

"Here!" Tanya yelled, throwing the scissors at her.

Rowan caught them and drew them out of the small silver sheath, tossing it to the floor. She brandished the scissors, trying to ignore the stabbing sensation in her injured foot.

Suki backed away, then she fled to a nearby window, sweeping the salt away with her arms in one smooth motion. She smashed the glass with her elbow and vaulted on to the ledge. She was almost through it when her leg caught on a shard of broken glass. She screamed and fell back. Seeing his chance, Warwick threw the rifle to Merchant and dived on her, wrestling her to the ground and slamming her hand repeatedly against the tiles. Suki swore and scratched like a wildcat, flailing and tearing at his face with her other hand until Rowan grabbed it and held it to the floor with her knees. Still Suki thrashed until with one final blow from Warwick, she let out an almighty yell and the knife clattered to the floor.

"Oh...." Warwick flinched. "I think I broke her wrist...."

"It's over, Suki," Tino told her grimly. "You're beaten." He looked to Merchant. "Bring the spidertwine—we'll have to bind her."

Suki's rigid body suddenly went limp as the fight left her. Instead she turned her head to the side, the thin slash of blond hair falling over her face as she wept bitter tears.

"What are you going to do with her?" Rowan whispered, relinquishing the arm she held down as Merchant returned with the skein of spidertwine.

"Take her to the courts," said Tino, turning away in disgust. "They can deal with her. Just get her out of my sight."

Suki continued to sob softly as her wrists and ankles were laced with spidertwine.

"Where's Crooks?" someone said suddenly. "She said 'nine out of twelve'—search the house!"

Rowan stood up, dazed. Rose was nearby, watching her. Her fingers twitched at her sides, and then she turned away—but Rowan reached out and touched her shoulder and threw herself into her mother's arms.

"I meant it," she whispered into Rose's hair, so no one else could hear. Her eyes were damp. "I do love you...it's just..."

"I know," Rose whispered back, stroking her head. "You don't have to say anything. I know."

A screech from the broken window drove them apart. Two garvern clambered through it, their way clear now that Suki had swept away the salt. Their splintered talons clattered over the wooden sill, then they were in the air, hissing and swooping.

"Everyone take cover!" Warwick bellowed, but before he had even finished the sentence one of them was upon him. He lashed out with his knife, and the creature flew across the hall in a spray of blood. Then the second one attacked.

"*Dad!*" Fabian shouted, rushing to his defense, but Merchant seized him and pulled him back. Instead Tino hastened to Warwick's aid, grabbing the bloodied sword that had slaughtered Victor and charging in with a battle cry. The injured garvern hit the ground, unmoving, but the second one had now wrapped itself around Warwick's face and was raking great gashes in his coat. He stabbed at it blindly and swayed about, preventing Tino from taking aim.

Raven transformed in a flurry of feathers. By

now, Tanya, Rowan, and Fabian were on the stairs, urged forward by Gredin, Rose, and Merchant, and as Raven glided past them Tanya felt the soft touch of a wing skim her cheek.

Then Raven was upon the garvern, cawing, pecking, gouging. The creature screamed, and Rowan looked on in horror as blood flowed from one of its eyes. It batted its hands about, plucking Raven from the air as it launched itself away from Warwick. As the garvern flew past her, Rowan heard something crackle.

"*Raven!*" Florence cried.

"Stay back!" Tino fired Victor's sword through the air. It arced in a clean sweep, burying itself in the garvern's belly. With a screech the creature fell to the floor, writhing in a widening pool of red, with Raven still clenched in its hands. By the time Warwick had reached it, his knife raised, its life had drained away.

"Raven," he moaned, easing the clenched hand open and taking her gently into his own.

"No...." Florence ran down the stairs to his side, her hair loose and trailing down her back. Her face was wet with tears as she cradled Warwick's hands in her own. "No, not Raven...."

The smallest trickle of blood escaped Raven's beak with her last feeble caw. Her crushed body twitched. One wing lifted, then fell. Then she grew still.

Epilogue

We buried Raven the morning after, under the horse chestnut tree in the back garden. My grandmother stood at the front, holding the Mizhog in her arms. Even after everything that had happened, she was pristine, perfect, except for that one little strand of hair that escaped the knot at the back of her neck. She managed to hold herself together until Gredin stopped speaking, but then her face crumpled and she rushed inside. No one saw her again until the evening.

    We kept to our rooms that day, Rowan, Fabian, and me, while they moved the dead out of the house. Warwick disposed of the dead garvern in the woods, while the captive living one and Victor's body would be returned to the fairy realm—along with Suki, for the courts to deal with. For although she was human, her crimes against the fairies and their people were altogether easier to explain to them than to the police. Tino saw to it that any risk of her exposing the Coven vanished with her memories. The last anyone heard, she was due to be sentenced on Halloween— the day the courts change over.

We found Crooks after searching the house, expecting the body count to rise by one more, but it seems that Suki had something more drawn-out lined up for him. He was cramped in the priest hole with a bump on his head and a look in his eyes that none of the Coven had seen before. Finally, the boy who thought he could escape from anywhere had been proved wrong. He left with the remaining members of the Coven—apart from Sparrow— the same day.

Sparrow stayed in Tickey End. With some help from Warwick, he found a job and a place to live. Though it's never been said, everyone knows he stayed for Rowan.

None of the Coven members have contacted her since. Not yet, anyway. But despite everything, she says Tino will never stop. The roots, and the need to honor those who died, go too deep for that.

It'll take some time, but he'll rebuild the Coven. And it'll be stronger for its past mistakes. This I know myself— Tino put it in a letter that arrived for me a few weeks later, along with the offer that if I want it, there's a place for me with them. I almost destroyed it on the spot, but something—I don't know what—stopped me. Instead I hid it and never spoke of it to anyone. I still haven't.

I haven't seen Gredin since that day, either. Next to my grandmother, he was hit hardest by Raven's death. Before he left, we spoke about what my grandmother told me about how he came to be my guardian, and we came to an agreement. The agreement is this: He will only come when I call upon him for help. Because in spite of everything I said to him, and all the threats and punish-

ments, I was never so glad to see anyone as I was when he turned up in Hangman's Wood that day.

You would think the manor would feel different after what occurred there. And it does. Of course it does. It's part of the history of it now; along with Elizabeth, and Amos, and my grandmother and Morwenna, not to mention Rowan and Fabian, and me. A place can't see that much and not be changed by it. But it's different from how you might expect. The air is clearer somehow, like there's been a big storm and it's chased the last of the cobwebs away.

Fabian says it's to do with the secrets. Not just the thirteen secrets, but everything that came out that summer. About his mother, and Warwick and Rose. It's all out in the open. Me? I still have my secrets, like everyone. Things I want kept out of the way, like a certain letter, and an old compass and a pair of scissors given to me by the gypsy woman believed to be mad—or a witch—by most people. They're all still here, under the floorboard. These days my secrets are mostly small, written on these pages, and hidden within a red cover. Just in case.

Thanks to:

All my family and friends for putting up with my
hibernation when writing, talking through plotlines,
and letting me know when I'd killed one character
too many (yes, you were right, Mum).

Huge thanks to Darren for making the website so
brilliant, and for all the computer wizardry in general.

Darley, Madeleine, and everyone at the Darley
Anderson Agency for looking after me, and Julie,
Pam, Lisa, and everybody at Little, Brown and
Company for making this a better book.

Finally, and perhaps most importantly, to the
readers who have let Tanya, Fabian, and Rowan into
your lives: thank you so much for your messages
and support!